THE PROPHETIC MAYAN QUEEN

K'INUUW MAT OF PALENQUE

THE PROPHETIC MAYAN QUEEN

K'INUUW MAT OF PALENQUE

BORN 655? CE – MARRIED 673 CE – DIED 722? CE

LEONIDE MARTIN

Mists of Palenque Series Book 4

Made for Wonder PUBLISHING

Made for Success
P.O. Box 1775
Issaquah, WA 98027

The Prophetic Mayan Queen: K'inuuw Mat of Palenque

Designed by Valerie Heathman

Library of Congress Cataloging-in-Publication data

Martin, Leonide
     The Prophetic Mayan Queen: K'inuuw Mat of Palenque
     Mists of Palenque: Series Book 4

     p. cm.

ISBN: 978-1-64146-365-2
LCCN: 2018961980

To contact the publisher,
please email service@MadeforSuccess.net or call +1 (425) 657-0300.
Made for Wonder is an imprint of Made for Success Publishing.
Printed in the United States of America

CONTENTS

List of Characters and Places 7

Maya Regions in Middle Classic Period (500 – 800 CE) 14

Lakam Ha (Palenque) Central and Eastern Areas
Newer Sections of City (650 – 800 CE) 15

K'inuuw Mat—I   Baktun 9 Katun 11 Tun 12 – Baktun 9
Katun 11 Tun 13 (664 – 665 CE) 17

K'inuuw Mat—II   Baktun 9 Katun 11 Tun 13 – Baktun 9
Katun 12 Tun 0 (665 – 673 CE) 53

K'inuuw Mat—III   Baktun 9 Katun 12 Tun 0 – Baktun 9
Katun 12 Tun 0 (673 CE) 78

K'inuuw Mat—IV   Baktun 9 Katun 12 Tun 0 – Baktun 9
Katun 12 Tun 1 (673 – 674 CE) 111

K'inuuw Mat—V   Baktun 9 Katun 12 Tun 1 – Baktun 9
Katun 12 Tun 5 (674 – 677 CE) 146

K'inuuw Mat—VI   Baktun 9 Katun 12 Tun 5 – Baktun 9
Katun 12 Tun 6 (677 – 678 CE) 184

K'inuuw Mat—VII   Baktun 9 Katun 12 Tun 7 – Baktun 9
Katun 13 Tun 10 (679 – 702 CE) 227

K'inuuw Mat—VIII Baktun 9 Katun 13 Tun 16 – Baktun 9
Katun 14 Tun 10 (708 – 722 CE) 285

Afterword 305

Field Journal   Tumbala, Chiapas, México 314

Dynasty of Lakam Ha (Palenque) 354

Alliances Among Maya Cities... *355*

Long Count Maya Calendar *356*

The Tzolk'in and Haab Calendars *358*

About the Author *361*

Author Notes... *363*

Notes on Orthography (Pronunciation) *366*

Acknowledgements *369*

Other Works By Author *373*

List of Characters and Places

K'inuuw Mat—Characters

Royal Family of Lakam Ha
K'inuuw Mat* – wife of Tiwol Chan Mat
Tiwol Chan Mat* – fourth son of Pakal, husband of K'inuuw Mat
K'inich Janaab Pakal I*- ruler of Lakam Ha (615 – 683 CE)
K'inich Kan Bahlam II* – first son of Pakal, ruler of Lakam Ha
   (684 – 702 CE)
K'inich Kan Joy Chitam II* – third son of Pakal, ruler of Lakam Ha
   (702 – 721 CE)
K'inich Ahkal Mo' Nab III* – son of K'inuuw Mat and Tiwol Chan Mat,
   ruler of Lakam Ha (721 – 740 CE)
Yax Chel – first daughter of K'inuuw Mat and Tiwol Chan Mat
Siyah Chan – second daughter of K'inuuw Mat and Tiwol Chan Mat
Sak'uay – third daughter of K'inuuw Mat and Tiwol Chan Mat
Talol – wife of Kan Bahlam, sister of Chak Chan
Te' Kuy – wife of Kan Joy Chitam II, from Chuuah family
Chab' Nikte – daughter of Kan Joy Chitam and Te' Kuy
Mayuy – son of Kan Joy Chitam and Te' Kuy
Chik – husband of Sak'uay

Sons of K'inich Ahkal Mo' Nab and Men Nich (ruled after story ends)
Upakal K'inich*- first son, ruler of Lakam Ha (742 – 750 CE)
K'inich Kan Bahlam III* – second son, ruler of Lakam Ha (750 – 764 CE)
K'inich K'uk Bahlam II* – third son, ruler of Lakam Ha (764 – 799 CE)

Main Courtiers/Warriors of Lakam Ha
K'akmo – Nakom (Elder Warrior Chief) of Lakam Ha
Yax Chan*- architect of Lakam Ha
Aj Sul* – Nakom (Younger Warrior Chief), Ah K'uhun, Ah Yahau K'ak to
   Pakal, member Chuuah family

---

* — historical person

Chak Chan* – brother-in-law of Kan Bahlam, astronomer, scientist, Ah K'uhun

Mut* – assistant to Kan Bahlam, painter, stone carver, historian, Ah K'uhun

Yuhk Makab'te* – assistant to Kan Bahlam, Sahal, administrator

Ab'uk – young two spirit courtier, lover of Kan Bahlam II

Chak Zotz* – Yahau K'ak, Sahal, becomes Nakom after Aj Sul

Priests/Priestesses
Ib'ach – High Priest of Lakam Ha
Yaxhal – High Priestess of Lakam Ha
Yatik – Ix Chel Priestess of Cuzamil, sister of Chelte'
K'ak Sihom – Ix Chel High Priestess and Ruler of Cuzamil
Ab'uk Cen – Ix Chel Oracle of Cuzamil
Olal – acolyte at Cuzamil
Chilkay – Ix Chel priestess-healer of Lakam Ha
B'akel – Chief Ix Chel priestess of Lakam Ha

Attendants/Tutors
K'anal – scribe of Lakam Ha
Muk Kab – Royal Steward to Pakal (elder)
Akan – Royal Steward to Pakal (younger)
Tohom – personal attendant to Pakal
Kuy – noble attendant to K'inuuw Mat, came from Uxte'kuh
Tukun – noble attendant to K'inuuw Mat at Lakam Ha
Muyal – young noble woman, wife of Yax Chan

Uxte'kuh Characters
Ox B'iyan – father of K'inuuw Mat
Chelte' – mother of K'inuuw Mat
Sak T'ul – older sister of K'inuuw Mat
Chumib – older brother of K'inuuw Mat
Kuy – attendant to Sak T'ul, accompanies K'inuuw Mat to Lakam Ha

Kan Characters
Yuknoom Ch'een II* "The Great" – ruler of Kan (636 – 686 CE)
Yuknoom Yich'aak K'ak* – ruler of Kan (686 – 695 CE)

---

* — historical person

Popo' Characters

Yuknoom Bahlam* – ruler of Popo' (668 – 688 CE)

K'inich B'aaknal Chaak* – ruler Popo' (688 – 717 CE)

K'inich K'ak Bahlam* – ruler Popo' (717 – 723 CE)

Characters from other cities

Nuun Ujol Chaak* – ruler of Mutul (648 – 679 CE), half-brother Balaj Chan K'awiil

Balaj Chan K'awiil* – ruler of Imix-ha (648 – 692 CE), half-brother Nuun Ujol Chaak

Hasau Chan K'awiil* – son of Nuun Ujol Chaak, ruler of Mutul (682 – 734 CE)

Hawk Skull* – ruler of Amalah, "third crowning" by Kan Bahlam in 690

Ancestors

Yohl Ik'nal* – grandmother of Pakal, first woman ruler of Lakam Ha (583 – 604 CE)

Kan Bahlam I* – father of Yohl Ik'nal, ruler of Lakam Ha (572 – 583 CE)

Aj Ne Ohl Mat* – brother of Yohl Ik'nal, ruler of Lakam Ha (605 – 612 CE)

Tz'aakb'u Ahau* – wife of Janaab Pakal, called Lalak

Sak K'uk* – ruler of Lakam Ha (612 – 615 CE), mother of Janaab Pakal

U K'ix Kan – quasi-human created by Triad Deities, founder of Bahlam lineage

Elie – foreign woman with blue eyes and yellow hair, spirit domain friend of Yohl Ik'nal

Cities and Polities

Ancestral Places

Matawiil – mythohistoric B'aakal origin lands at Six Sky Place

Toktan – ancestral city of K'uk Bahlam, founder of Lakam Ha dynasty, "Place of Reeds"

Petén – lowlands area in north Guatemala, densely populated with Maya sites

Teotihuacan – powerful empire in central Mexica area (north of Mexico City)

---

* — historical person

B'aakal Polity and Allies

B'aakal – "Kingdom of the Bone," regional polity governed by Bahlam (Jaguar) Dynasty

Lakam Ha – (Palenque) "Big Waters," major city of B'aakal polity, May Ku

Anaay Te – (Anayte) small polity city

B'aak – (Tortuguero) birthplace of Lalak, ally of Lakam Ha

Mutul – (Tikal) great city of southern region, ally of Lakam Ha, enemy of Kan

Nab'nahotot – (Comalcalco) city on coast of Great North Sea (Gulf of Mexico)

Nututun – City on Chakamax River, near Lakam Ha

Oxwitik – (Copan) southern city allied with Lakam Ha by marriage (in Honduras)

Popo' – (Tonina) former Lakam Ha ally, changed allegiance to Kan

Sak Nikte' – (La Corona, Site Q) ally city courted by Kan

Sak Tz'i – (White Dog) ally of Lakam Ha

Uxte'kuh – city raided by B'aak, linked later to Lakam Ha by royal marriage

Wa-Mut – (Wa-Bird, Santa Elena) later allied with Kan

Yokib – (Piedras Negras) former ally, switched alliance to Kan

Ka'an Polity and Allies

Ka'an – "Kingdom of the Snake," regional polity governed by Kan

Kan – refers to residence city of Kan (Snake) Dynasty

Dzibanche – home city of Kan dynasty (circa 400 – 600 CE)

Imix-ha – (Dos Pilas) southern city, ally of Tan-nal and Kan

Pa'chan – (Yaxchilan) Kan ally located on banks of K'umaxha River

Pakab – (Pia) joined Usihwitz in raid on Lakam Ha

Pipá – (Pomona) contested city on northeast plains near K'umaxha River

Uxte'tun – (Kalakmul) early home city of Kan, reclaimed from Zotz (Bat) Dynasty

Usihwitz – (Bonampak) switched alliance from Lakam Ha, allied with Kan

Waka' – (El Peru) ally of Kan, enemy of Mutul

Amalah – (Moral-Reforma) subsidiary city of Lakam Ha, overtaken by Kan

Coastal, Trading and Yukatek Cities

Yukatek region – northern Maya region in Yucatan Peninsula

Altun Ha – trading city near eastern coast (in Belize)

Chel Nah – main city on Cuzamil

Chayha – trading village on north tip of Cuzamil

Cuzamil – (Cozumel) sacred island of Ix Chel priestesses

Paalmul – mainland port village for Cuzamil voyages

Tulum – coastal city on high cliff above Great East Sea

Seas, Rivers, and Mountains

Chakamax – river flowing into K'umaxha, southeast of Lakam Ha
Chik'in-nab – Great West Sea (Pacific Ocean)
K'ak-nab – Great East Sea (Gulf of Honduras, Caribbean Sea)
K'uk Lakam Witz – Fiery Water Mountain, sacred mountain of Lakam Ha
K'umaxha – Sacred Monkey River (Usumacinta River), largest river in region,
    crosses plains north of Lakam Ha, empties into Gulf of Mexico
Michol – river on plains northwest of Lakam Ha, flows below city plateau
Nab'nah – Great North Sea (Gulf of Mexico)
Wukhalal – lagoon of seven colors (Bacalar Lagoon)

Small rivers flowing across Lakam Ha ridges
Ach' – Ach' River
Balunte – Balunte River
Bisik – Picota River
Ixha – Motiepa River
Kisiin – Diablo River
Otolum – Otulum River
Sutzha – Murcielagos River
Tun Pitz – Piedras Bolas

Maya Deities

Ahau K'in/K'in Ahau – Lord Sun/Sun Lord
Ahau Kinh – Lord Time
Ahauob (Lords) of the First Sky:
    B'olon Chan Yoch'ok'in (Sky That Enters the Sun) – 9 Sky Place
    Waklahun Ch'ok'in (Emergent Young Sun) – 16 Sky Place
    B'olon Tz'ak Ahau (Conjuring Lord) – 9 Sky Place
Bacabs – Lords of the Four Directions, Hold up the Sky
Chaak – God of Rain, Storms, Thunder
Hun Ahau – (One Lord) – First born of Triad, Celestial Realm
Hunahpu – first Hero Twin, also called Hun Ahau
Hun Hunahpu – Maize God, First Father, resurrected by Hero Twins,
    ancestor of Mayas
Itzam Kab Ayin – Earth Crocodile-Snake Wizard-Centipede

Itzamna/Itzamnaaj – Primary Sky God, Sky Bar Deity, Magician of Water-Sacred Itz, Inventor of Writing and Calendars, First Shaman, Master Teacher-Builder

Ix Chel – Earth Mother Goddess, healer, weaver of life, fertility and abundance, Lady Rainbow

Ix Ma Uh – Young Moon Goddess

Mah Kinah Ahau (Underworld Sun Lord) – Second born of Triad, Underworld Realm, Jaguar Sun, Underworld Sun-Moon, Waterlily Jaguar

Muwaan Mat (Duck Hawk, Cormorant) – Primordial Mother Goddess, mother of B'aakal Triad, named ruler of Lakam Ha 612 – 615 CE

Unen K'awill (Infant Powerful One) – Third born of Triad, Earthly Realm, Baby Jaguar, patron of royal bloodlines, lightning in forehead, often has one snake-foot

Wakah Chan Te' – Jeweled Sky Tree, connects the three dimensions (roots-Underworld, trunk-Middleworld, branches-Upperworld)

Witz Monster – Cave openings to Underworld depicted as fanged monster mask

Wuqub' Kaquix – Seven Macaw, false deity of polestar, defeated by Hero Twins

Xibalba – Underworld, realm of the Lords of Death

Yax Bahlam – (Xbalanque), second Hero Twin

Yum K'ax – Young Maize God, foliated god of growing corn, resurrected Hun Hunahpu

Titles

Ah – honorable way to address men

Ahau – Lord

Ah K'in – Solar Priest, plural Ah K'inob

Ah K'uhun – warrior-priest, learned member of royal court, worshipper

Ah pitzlal – he of the ballgame; ballplayer

Ba-ch'ok – heir designate

Batab – town governor, local leader from noble lineage

Chilam – spokesperson, prophet

Halach Uinik – True Human

Ix – honorable way to address women

Ixik – Lady

Ix K'in – Solar Priestess, plural Ix K'inob

Juntan – precious one, "beloved of" parents or deities

Kalomte – K'uhul Ahau ruling several cities, used often at Mutul and Oxwitik

K'uhul Ahau – Divine/Holy Lord
K'uhul Ixik – Divine/Holy Lady
K'uhul Ixik Me' – Holy Lady Mother
May Ku – seat of the *may* cycle (260 tuns, 256 solar years), dominant city of region
Nakom – Warrior Chief
Sahal – ruler of subsidiary city
Yahau – His Lord (high subordinate noble)
Yahau K'ak – His Lord of Fire (high ceremonial-military noble)
Yum – Master

Names of Planets (Wandering Stars) and Celestial Bodies

Ayin Ek – Saturn
Am' – Orion (3 "hearthstone" stars: Rigel-Tunsel, Alnitak-Mehem Ek, Saiph-Hun Rakam)
Budz Ek – comet
Chak Ek – Mars
Ix Uc – Lady Moon
K'awiil Ek – Jupiter
K'in Ahau – Sun Lord
Noh Ek – Venus
Tzab Kan – Pleiades
Xaman Ek – North Polar Star
Xux Ek – Mercury

Maya Regions in Middle Classic Period (500 – 800 CE)

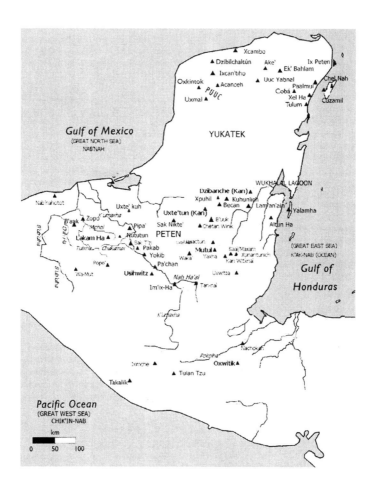

Names of cities, rivers, and seas are the ones used in this book. Most are know Classic Period names; some have been created for the story. Many other cities existed but are omitted for simplicity.

(Present-day Yucatan Peninsula Chiapas, and Tabasco, Mexico; Belize, Guatemala, and Honduras.)

Lakam Ha (Palenque) Central and Eastern Areas, Newer Sections of City (650 – 800 CE)

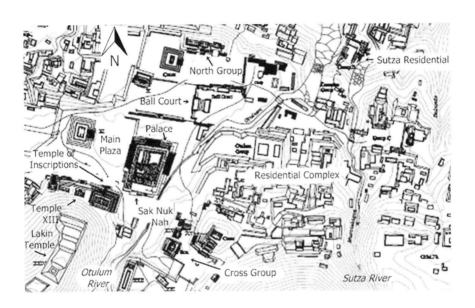

The most important buildings in the story are darker, with labels according to current archeological conventions. Most of these were done by Janaab Pakal and his son, Kan Bahlam II.

Based upon maps from The Palenque Mapping Project, Edwin Barnhart, 1999.

A FAMSI-sponsored project. Used with permission of Edwin Barnhart.

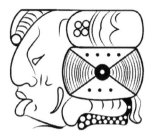

K'inuuw Mat—I

Baktun 9 Katun 11 Tun 12 – Baktun 9 Katun 11 Tun 13 (664 – 665 CE)

1

The prow of the sea canoe sliced through choppy waves, sending foamy spray along its length. As the beach receded, the sea turned from turquoise to deep blue, dotted by small whitecaps. On the far eastern horizon, a dark expanse of land formed an island, a low mound surrounded by glittering waters. Overhead the cries of sea birds merged with the rhythmic slap of oars against the waves. Eight muscular men pulled at the oars, four on each side. The sea canoe was the length of six men and the width of two, and carried twenty-five women and girls. Wind whipped their dark hair that was tied in topknots or wound in long braids. All wore white garments, the ceremonial color of pilgrimage. Most of the passengers crouched inside the hull, grasping ropes to stay put as the canoe tossed over turbulent waves. The passage from the mainland to the island was treacherous, swept by unpredictable currents that could cast a canoe far from its destination.

The sun peeped out between billowing white clouds. It had moved halfway across the sky since the sea canoe launched forth to make its way among deceptive currents. From time to time, four additional men traded places to relieve paddlers, rotating after a short period of rest. To complete the journey during daylight, they had to paddle relentlessly, struggling against wind and currents. Women offered them water from long-necked gourds, but no food was taken during the journey. Some passengers dozed fitfully and a few retched over the canoe sides, seasick from the constant pitching and dipping. One passenger, however, stood braced against the prow as far forward as she was allowed. Face tilted to receive salty spray, hands clinging to ropes and feet widely apart for balance; she swayed with the canoe's motion. Strands of dark hair had pulled loose and whipped in the wind. Soundless songs escaped from her lips, simple chants to the Goddess she had learned from earliest childhood. She felt as though she was coming home.

K'inuuw Mat had waited all her life for this journey to Cuzamil. Now she had reached twelve solar years; about to blossom into womanhood. Small pink breast buds rubbed against her simple white shift, called a *huipil* by her people. A few hairs sprouted under armpits and over her pubis. Her mother said she would soon be graced with the first moon blood, a sacred gift from the Goddess that gave women the power to create life. Her mother Chelte' was taking her to the island for the puberty pilgrimage. It would be especially powerful to have her initial moon blood on the Goddess' special island. With the flow of this sacred *itz*, liquid of life and precious fluid of the deities, she would dedicate herself to serving Ix Chel.

A large wave burst against the prow and drenched her, but she only laughed, shaking water out of her hair. The forward paddlers exchanged smiles, nodding in appreciation of her adventuresome spirit. K'inuuw Mat blinked as salty water stung her eyes, keeping her focus on the gradually enlarging mound of land where she could begin to distinguish treetops.

The sea journey to the island of Cuzamil, abode of the Great Mother Goddess Ix Chel, required most of a day. Only a very few men, members of a hereditary lineage dedicated to serving the Goddess, could navigate the secret currents. Any who tried paddling canoes to Cuzamil without knowing these currents were repeatedly swept back to the mainland, or propelled into the deep seas where huge waves could crush them. The Cuzamil paddler lineage lived on the mainland by a small bay that provided shelter for their canoes, in a village called Paalmul. The paddlers' wives provided housing and meals, offered freely to honor the women and girls who came on pilgrimage to the island of Ix Chel. In the coastal Maya lands bordering the Great East Sea, the K'ak-nab, women had a long tradition of making pilgrimage to the Goddess' island at least twice during their lives: at the time when their moon cycles started and again when these ceased. Many women also sought the Ix Chel priestesses' healing skills, especially for problems with childbearing and infertility. For a child to be born on Cuzamil was considered a special blessing.

K'inuuw Mat remembered many things her mother told her about Cuzamil. It was the larger of two islands off the coast of the Yukatek peninsula, both dedicated to Ix Chel. Cuzamil was the main pilgrimage site, with a sizeable village and several temples. Some temples sat on pyramids of modest height; others took different shapes or were inside caves. One shrine had a long wall of seven high stone towers in the central ceremonial district. Every year, flocks of swallows called *cuzam* returned to nest in these towers, giving the island its name Cuzamil, Place of Swallows (Swifts). The city had complexes where the priestesses offered their healing work, residences for villagers and visitors, workshops and marketplaces, and a royal complex where the ruling family lived.

Cuzamil was ruled by a female lineage; the ruler also served as High Priestess of Ix Chel. Before K'inuuw Mat's mother was born, the ruler decreed that only women could live permanently on the island. Children of both sexes could stay there with their mothers, but once the boys reached puberty, they were sent back to their family's city for male training. On the northern tip of the island, a trading village called Chayha had long existed. It engaged in lucrative trade in salt, honey and marine products, holding a monopoly on sea mollusks whose shells were ground into powder for intense purple or blue dyes. These were highly prized for dyeing fabric worn by elites throughout the Maya world. No permanent stone structures were allowed in the village, and its wood and thatch-roofed palapas needed frequent replacement. It was separated from the rest of the island by a mangrove swamp with dense, tangled roots and swampy regions, making travel over land from the village impossible. Men could reside in Chayha on a temporary basis. None were permitted to make it their permanent home; they needed to leave periodically to ply their trade routes along the coast.

The royal family resided in Chel Nah, Place of Large Rainbows, and largest city on Cuzamil. They arranged marriages for their daughters to nobles on the mainland, often with the stipulation that the first daughter born of this union would be returned to the island to serve the Goddess. Rulership was not strictly hereditary; the Ix Chel priestesses held council to determine who would next ascend to the throne.

When K'inuuw Mat asked her mother why men were excluded, she was told that prophecies warned the priestesses of perilous times to come when men would attempt to dominate the Maya world, even trying to take over Ix Chel's domain. These men would strive to place a male ruler upon the throne. While many men were sincerely devoted to the Goddess and served her faithfully, those who would attempt the takeover had selfish motives. They coveted the lucrative trade of Cuzamil Island, and intended to appropriate its wealth. To forestall this from happening, the island was turned into a sanctuary for only women and children so it could continue to fulfill its sacred mission.

Cuzamil had served as a sanctuary for women since distant times. It welcomed those women whom society rejected and despised: abandoned childless women, orphaned girls, women who preferred the love of other women, cripples and the deformed, and those whose soul journeyed in other dimensions. On the island, childless women were given the responsibility of raising orphans, a compassionate practice that benefitted all. Selling orphaned children into slavery was a common Maya practice, so the island was their hope for a meaningful life. Childless women, often rejected by husbands and families, would suffer in poverty and servitude without this sanctuary.

Women came to the island on pilgrimage to honor Ix Chel and her priestesses, and to make requests of the Goddess. They asked for a happy marriage, prosperous life, fertility and health for themselves and their daughters. They might remain there to study midwifery and women's care, the weaving of sacred patterns, and the mysteries of the Goddess. They could learn divination by water scrying and crystal gazing, astronomy and calendar lore. Those who showed aptitude would be trained in the demanding art of prophecy. A famous oracle lived on the island; her prophecies were sought by many women throughout the Maya world.

Everything about Cuzamil was enthralling to K'inuuw Mat. For generations her maternal lineage had been devoted to the Goddess Ix Chel. Her mother was born in Altun Ha, a city near the coast south of the Wukhalal Lagoon, the renowned waters of seven colors. The girl could picture its many-shaded waters clearly from her mother's descriptions, transitioning from deep blue to turquoise, then gradually fading to shades of green and ending in milky white at the shore. Now the sea below the canoe was dark blue, but in the distance it became lighter, what she imagined the turquoise of the lagoon might be.

K'inuuw Mat anticipated her first moon blood eagerly. She would follow her family's tradition by saving a few bark paper strips holding this rare substance, placed in a hollow gourd with a tight cap. She would use it for an important future request. When she wanted something very much, she would burn the strips in a censer with sacred copal resin, saying invocations to the Goddess. There was no offering more precious to Ix Chel than blood from a maiden's first menses. To collect this offering on the island of the Goddess made it immensely potent. The Goddess could not refuse a request so empowered.

Another family tradition had her insides in a dance of delight. Whenever possible, at least one woman per generation was dedicated to serving the Goddess. It was a special honor to be selected, for it meant you would become a Priestess of Ix Chel and live on Cuzamil. She could not imagine a better life! Spending her days doing rituals, taking part in seasonal ceremonies, learning the skill for which she was best suited, and applying that skill to serve the needs of others. Priestesses supervised acolytes, carefully assessing each girl's unique gifts, then giving the Charge of the Goddess: You will be a healer, you a midwife, an artist or stoneworker, or a dancer and song-maker. Yet others would become weavers or musicians or herbalists, teachers or preparers of food. Of all the charges a girl might be given, the one that she most desired was that of a seer.

Had her mother not hinted of such abilities? Since earliest childhood, K'inuuw Mat recalled being able to sense things that others could not. She always seemed to know where the first ripe plums hung in the orchards, and under which bush the delectable wild grapes were concealed. Even before the *Uo* frogs began their rain song, she could smell the Goddess' sky *itz* preparing to refresh the dry earth. Her friends refused to play hide and seek games with her, because she always knew their hiding places. She had even foreseen her grandmother's death, an ability that pained and frightened her. To be given the charge of a seer caused her some trepidation; she knew it involved both joy and sadness. But an urge beyond all reason pushed upward in her young mind. She felt the beckoning to open her awareness to messages from the cosmos, the sky and earth deities, even the Lords of the Underworld.

What form that calling might take, she did not know. She had heard about women who were visionaries, who made prophecies, who could foresee things in the future, and even who became oracles for a particular God or Goddess. Coming to Cuzamil would give her understanding of these things. She was eager to learn, to meet women who served as seers, and to explore her own aptitude. In particular, she was excited to meet her mother's sister Yatik, an Ix Chel priestess, who was skilled in the art of scrying with both water and crystal. Her mother told many stories about Yatik's uncanny abilities to read what the stars reflected in gazing pools, and what mysteries were revealed in the veins and inclusions of crystals.

Most of all, she was thrilled to be able to watch the famous Oracle of Cuzamil in action. The Oracle was a priestess selected by her peers, and approved by the High Priestess, to actually receive into her own body the Goddess Ix Chel. Through using a secret recipe of mind-altering substances, the Oracle would vacate her body and offer it as a vessel for the Goddess. It required great strength and extensive training to survive the rigors of this process, and rumor said that some priestesses died of its effects. During the time that the Oracle was the Goddess' vessel, people could ask any question and receive a true answer. They came from near and far, the wives and daughters of rulers and commoners, seeking knowledge to guide their lives. Their gifts to the Oracle were another source of Cuzamil's wealth.

The canoe slammed against an undertow current rushing around the island's northwest edge, tipping sideways in the cross-currents. The paddlers made quick adjustments to set the canoe upright and continue their course around the point, but not before wails from the exhausted passengers pierced through the wind. K'inuuw Mat braced herself and managed to remain on her feet, gaining more nods of respect from the men. She glanced toward her mother, who was cradling her older sister's head against a shoulder, arms securely around the distraught girl. Sak T'ul looked awful; her contorted face a sickly yellow, eyes squeezed shut. She huddled against her mother's chest, knees pulled up into fetal position. Her entire being was a statement of misery.

It is good that she was not chosen to serve Ix Chel, K'inuuw Mat thought to herself. *She has no stamina. And besides, she is betrothed to the son of our Nakom—Warrior Chief. The life of a noble wife will suit her better; she will marry upon our return from Cuzamil.*

K'inuuw Mat was almost certain that she would be the one chosen for the Goddess' service during this pilgrimage. It was her utmost yearning, and she knew that her mother had discussed it with her father.

I am a worthy offering to Ix Chel, she asserted. *I am strong and smart. I will do whatever the Goddess requires of me. No reward is greater than living on her island.*

A sudden pang pierced her heart. Living on the island and serving the Goddess meant that she would never see her home again, her father and brother, cousins and friends in Uxte'kuh. Their modest-sized city sat in the middle of the broad plains that stretched north from the K'umaxha River to the Great North Sea, the Nab'nah. It was a pleasant place with gentle hills, waving grasses and clusters of forests. The fertile soil provided crops and several creeks fed clear waters to their fields and basins. As second daughter of the ruler, her life there was one of ease and abundance. Was she ready to leave the security of her comforting home?

A flood of conflicting emotions surged through her, breaking her concentration and causing her to fall to her knees when the canoe hit the next big wave. Sharp pain from bruised knees cleared her mind, and she arose resolutely to fix her gaze upon the approaching island. Whatever the Goddess chose for her, then that would be her dedicated path in life. She did not have to decide now. The Goddess would guide her way.

The paddlers followed the island's contour around the point, passing along beaches lined with palm trees. Leaving the rough currents of the channel, they pointed the prow toward a white crescent of sandy beach that cradled a calm lagoon. It was the harbor of sanctuary, a safe landing place for pilgrims arriving to honor the Goddess. When the canoe stopped tossing, sighs of relief were heard from many passengers. Sak T'ul raised her head from her mother's chest, opened teary eyes and gasped a few words.

"Are we there? Is the canoe ride over?"

"Yes, my heart," whispered Chelte' into her daughter's ear. "Only a few more moments."

K'inuuw Mat kept her gaze fixed on the beach, now able to discern several palapas shaded by trees and three long sea canoes pulled up on the beach. Several women came from the palapas to meet them as the forward paddlers jumped into the water to pull the canoe onto the beach. They helped the passengers climb out of the canoe and gather their belongings. As older women stretched cramping legs and mothers held tight to daughter's hands, K'inuuw Mat leapt ahead and ran up the beach, her toes digging into the warm sand. She turned at the tree line to watch her mother and sister, who were moving slowly and casting long shadows as the sun dipped toward the western horizon. She had never been on an island before, and the sensation of being surrounded by a vast expanse of water was exhilarating.

Ix Chel priestesses in blue and white robes greeted the pilgrims, offering gourds of water and honey maize cakes. They guided the travelers to an area where they could relieve themselves after their long sea passage, and explained that the walk to Chel Nah was short and easy. They would travel on a wide white road, a sakbe, built of stones covered with smooth plaster that stood well above ground level. The men who served as paddlers would remain in the beach palapas overnight, and then in the morning convey departing pilgrims on the return trip from the island. The priestesses provided the paddlers with food, drink, and bathing supplies.

In the gathering dusk, the weary pilgrims set foot on the sakbe for the last phase of their journey to the Place of Large Rainbows, city of the Goddess Ix Chel—Lady Rainbow. Twitters and squawks of birds settling onto night perches mixed with the loud humming of insects and the shrill screeches of monkeys in the jungle canopy. Palms, shrubs, and low trees lined the sakbe, many with red and yellow flowers. The smell of rich humus mingled with fragrances of allspice berries and sweet nectar exuded by thousands of tiny white Chakah flowers. Stingless bees collected this nectar to make a high-quality, pale honey for which Cuzamil was famous.

Chelte' called K'inuuw Mat to her side, reaching to squeeze her daughter's hand, and smiling despite her fatigue. In the twilight, she could still see the sparkle in the younger girl's eyes. Sak T'ul trudged behind, head lowered and feet dragging.

"We are here at last. Can you feel the Goddess' presence?" Chelte' asked.

"Yes, Mother. She is everywhere. My heart is singing. This place feels so familiar, as though we are in our true home."

2

"Sister! Greetings in the name of the Goddess. It has been too long since we beheld each other. Your daughters are two budding flowers. Come, enter in peace and love." Yatik spread her arms to embrace Chelte' and the two girls.

After embracing her aunt, whose resemblance to her mother was striking, K'inuuw Mat glanced around the palapa. Two small torches set in sconces on the doorway frame spread soft, wavering light around the interior. Shaped as a large oval, the dwelling had a hard-packed dirt floor and walls constructed of thin poles filled in with plaster. The roof was made of dried palm fronds tied to a wooden frame that left an open strip all around the top of the walls. How different this simple dwelling was than the stone-and-stucco home of her family in Uxte'kuh. She wondered if rain blew in through the opening below the roof. Several sleeping pallets were spread against the far wall, and sitting mats surrounded a central altar holding a clay image of Ix Chel, several offering bundles, flowers, and a small censer. Hanging from the walls were various household implements, including a broom, woven baskets, and strands of rope holding garments and mantles.

"You will all stay with me during your visit," said Yatik. "The other priestesses who live with me are staying elsewhere, so we can have private time for visiting."

"Of this we are deeply appreciative, Sister," replied Chelte'. "Indeed, it has been many years since I last came to Cuzamil."

"Was it not shortly after the birth of your youngest?"

"So it was. I made pilgrimage to offer gratitude to Ix Chel for giving me three healthy children and a life of abundance. Blessed be the Goddess. And here is my younger daughter, K'inuuw Mat, now almost a young woman. We planned this trip so her first moon flow will happen on the Island of the Goddess."

"Excellent!"

K'inuuw Mat blushed and bowed respectfully, clasping her left shoulder with her right hand. Sak T'ul looked annoyed and pulled at her mother's skirt; she felt slighted because as first daughter, she should have been introduced first.

"Here is my older daughter, Sak T'ul," Chelte' hastened to add. "She has reached sixteen solar years, and is betrothed to one of our city's leading nobles. Their marriage will take place after we return."

Sak T'ul made the bow of respect to her aunt, and then they settled onto mats as Yatik called for the evening meal. Next to the large palapas of the priestesses were smaller ones, made in the same style, in which their attendants lived. Cooking palapas were set near the periphery of the complex, with walls left unsealed so smoke and heat could dissipate. Each priestess had attendants, women of common status who committed their lives to Ix Chel. Two women in simple white and blue huipils brought wicker trays filled with an assortment of savory items: gourd bowls with a steaming stew made of peccary, squash, tomatoes, and beans; ceramic plates containing fresh papaya, mamey, mangos, and plums; and flat maize bread used to scoop up the stew. For seasoning, red chiles gave spiciness, golden annatto added astringency, and an assortment of herbs such as basil, oregano, epazote, and coriander contributed depth and subtlety. After setting the trays on the floor between the pilgrims, the two women returned with cups of kob'al, a drink made of ground maize mixed with water and fruit juice.

K'inuuw Mat realized that she was starving as soon the succulent aromas reached her nose. Her sister reached greedily for a bowl of stew, but their mother grasped her arm.

"Let us give thanks to the Goddess first," Chelte' whispered.

Yatik was already reciting the food blessing with closed eyes. K'inuuw Mat felt glad that she had not reached for food along with her sister. Eyes closed, she joined the chant which she had learned from her mother.

"Ix Chel, Mother of All Creation,
Giver of life and sustenance,
For those of your creatures whose flesh feeds our flesh,
For those of your plants whose leaves and fruits nourish us,
We offer our gratitude; we honor their ch'ulel, their soul-essence.
All comes from you, all returns to you.
Thus it is. Highest praise to you, Great Goddess."

Satiated by the delicious meal, the two girls were tucked into sleeping pallets by their mother, who then rejoined her sister for further talk. Soon Sak T'ul fell asleep, her regular breathing blending with chirps and hums of night insects. Although K'inuuw Mat's stomach was full, her mind was still alert. Lying with her back to the women, she pretended to be asleep while she listened to the conversation.

"When is the next speaking of the Oracle?" asked Chelte'.

"On the full moon at fall equinox," replied Yatik. "Ab'uk Cen is growing old; she does not speak as often as before. Now she speaks only at the four major sun positions, the equinoxes and solstices. Some grumble because her services are not more available. Women often must wait several moons to seek the Oracle's answers, and this causes complaints."

"This is not fitting. Followers of Ix Chel should realize that what happens is in the Goddess' timing, not their own. They must learn the virtue of patience."

"Would that all the Goddess' followers were as wise as you, dear Sister. Wives of rulers and daughters of ahauob think the world revolves around their desires."

"All are equal in the eyes of Ix Chel! They deserve no better treatment simply because their blood is elite."

"This we know, those of us who are truly devoted to the Goddess and what she teaches. Commoner and noble, slave and servant, man and woman, human and animal, all have the same innate worth to the Creator and Destroyer of All. But, very few are able to live by these principles. This is the great flaw of humanity: that we fail to remember the divine *itz* of all existence, and come to believe we are better than others. Even here, in the very heart of the Goddess' domain, this forgetting happens."

"That is sad to hear," murmured Chelte'.

"Ah, so it is. Let us speak of your pilgrimage. Do you seek an audience with the Oracle?"

"Yes, I wish to hear her pronouncement about the path of my daughter, K'inuuw Mat. It has been considered by her father and me, that she might be dedicated to serving the Goddess."

K'inuuw Mat's eyes widened and she caught her breath. She desperately wanted to know what the decision would be.

"My own thoughts had traveled to this consideration," said Yatik. "It would be a fine continuation of our family tradition. Does she show aptitude for such service?"

"She appears to have the potential for being a seer," Chelte' replied, and described some of her daughter's uncanny abilities to foresee events and discern things others could not. "Would you teach her scrying, and further test these abilities? I am certain she would be thrilled to study with you."

Yatik nodded in agreement. She was one of the leading priestesses of scrying, and was pleased to be asked.

"This I will undertake immediately," she said. "Since you must wait another two moon cycles until the Oracle speaks, there will be time to evaluate your daughter's talents. Although there are many ways of being a seer, scrying is a most useful tool for those who become adepts."

Tears moistened K'inuuw Mat's eyes. Her heart beat a glorious little pattern of happiness; its greatest hope was about to be fulfilled. That is, if the Oracle pronounced this as her destiny. Her ears perked again as her mother asked more about the Oracle.

"What will happen when Ab'uk Cen can no longer fulfill the Oracle's duties?"

"We will enter the difficult process of selecting a successor to the Oracle," Yatik said while making the hand sign for trouble. "I have been part of this once before, when I had just arrived as an acolyte. It was a rude initiation into the unseemly politics of power among women. My ideals became somewhat frayed, to express myself politely. You recall how much we revered all the Ix Chel priestesses when we were growing up in Altun Ha? We could not imagine anything but sincere dedication and the highest morals among them. In that cloud of blissful anticipation, I expected my life on Cuzamil to be filled with only serenity and comradeship, as we all found happiness serving the Goddess. So soon was I disillusioned, my youthful ideals shattered. Selecting the new Oracle was an ugly process."

"Tell me about it, dear Sister. Much am I saddened over your suffering. Why did you not mention this before?"

"Ah, for many reasons . . . such things are usually best kept to oneself. But, since my niece might be dedicated to the Goddess, I am guided now to tell you. There are competing lineages upon Cuzamil, women from elite families who cannot put away the quest for power. Perhaps it is bred into the fiber of their being. These women seek prominent positions within our simple society; they reach for status through becoming the ruler, or the Oracle, or the Head Priestess of one guild or another. Since all noble priestesses have a voice in these selections, and even the views of commoners and artisans are heeded by the High Council, much is done to influence them. Everything from making arguments in support of a candidate, to bribes of goods or favors, to outright threats have been used. Giving reasons why one woman would make a better Oracle than another is understandable; but threats and bribes violate the Goddess' own teachings."

"Just so! She instructs her followers to be ethical in all things, and to consider the greater good when taking actions. It sounds very similar to what happens when royal succession is challenged in our cities. I can understand your disappointment."

"Perhaps the worst thing is the evil words spoken against each other during these contests for power. This pains my heart above all. Festering wounds in the soul can persist that sustain long-lasting enmities. These divisions mar the unity that I imagined on this island. At the least, women have not taken to using physical force to further their ambitions." Yatik gave a wry smile and shook her head. "If certain men attain their goals to dominate Cuzamil, this tactic may yet come to us."

"Let us pray to the Goddess that such a time never comes to pass."

Both women raised their hands in the supplication gesture and whispered a fervent prayer. K'inuuw Mat was bewildered; she could not imagine that women who had dedicated their lives to the Goddess would do such selfish and destructive things. Could her aunt be wrong? Perhaps she misunderstood the other women's intentions. There did seem an edge of bitterness in Yatik's voice.

"Do not misunderstand me, Sister," Yatik murmured after their prayer was finished. "I love my life here, I am ever close to the Goddess, and many among us live in harmony and sisterhood. These conflicted times come and go. In the opportunity to overcome enmities, the Goddess gives us a path for growth."

K'inuuw Mat was startled; had her aunt read her thoughts? She must remember that many priestesses had intuitive abilities. She would not be so different here. Her mother whispered something that she could not hear, and then silence prevailed for what seemed a long time. Eyelids heavy, the girl began to drift toward sleep. She roused enough to catch a few more phrases when the women's conversation continued.

"When Ahau K'in, the Lord Sun, raises his face in the dawn, the newly arrived pilgrims will undergo purification," said Yatik. "After this ceremony, you will be received and welcomed by the ruler of Chel Nah, she who is also our High Priestess, K'ak Sihom. Her leadership has brought us a long period of harmony. She has earned my great respect; you will find her impressive."

"So have I heard," Chelte' replied. "Much do I anticipate meeting her, and presenting my daughters for her blessings."

As the women discussed aspects of the ceremony and reception, their voices blended into the humming and chirping nighttime choir and eased K'inuuw Mat into sleep.

In the grey pre-dawn light, a line of pilgrims followed Ix Chel priestesses along a sakbe leading into the center of Chel Nah. They walked in silence, white mantles wrapped closely around their naked bodies, hair loose and streaming down. At a juncture of the plastered roadways, the lead priestess veered to the right and continued to a plaza facing a small flat-roofed building, its stucco façade painted sky-toned Maya blue with black lines in flowing designs. They entered through a single doorway into a rectangular chamber, where images of Ix Chel were painted on the walls. As an Earth and Moon Goddess, she represented the three phases of a woman's life: maiden, mother, and grandmother.

As the maiden, Ix Chel was portrayed as a young woman kneeling before a backstrap loom, weaving in the traditional Maya fashion. Bare to the waist, she wore a colorful woven skirt with a twisted waistband that hung between her thighs. In her right hand, she held a smooth, tapered stick used to create the warp and woof on the loom, which was tied to a sacred ceiba tree. She wore a coiled snake headdress to signify her powers of healing and intuitive knowledge, her skills at medicine and midwifery, and her ability to control earthly forces. The glyph for *sak*, Mayan word for white, appeared in her headdress to indicate her presence in visible phases of the waxing moon. A blue-green jade necklace and earspools associated her with waters, where rainbows often appeared. From this came her title, Lady Rainbow.

As the mother, Ix Chel appeared seated inside a crescent moon, holding a rabbit. She wore a short, latticed bead skirt, her headdress full of maize foliation to signify her merger with the Young Maize God—Yum K'ax. Both the rabbit and maize imagery announced her powers of fertility, and associated her with sexual desire, motherhood, earth, crops, abundance, and fecundity. The symbol for sacred breath hung below her nose, signifying that she had the power to breathe life into creation. As her left arm cradled the rabbit, her right arm extended out, with the hand making the bestowing gesture. In this potent form, the Goddess exuded sexuality and reproductive prowess. She was the mother of all Maya people, and took many lovers to create the various Maya groups. She controlled all aspects of reproduction, determined the face and gender of children, women's moon cycles, pregnancy, and childbirth. As mother, Ix Chel did not wear the coiled snake headdress of healer, because she was too busy as wife and mother to attend to healing needs. The headdress did contain weaving symbols, indicating domestic responsibilities and her powers to weave the fabric of people's lives. With qualities of both moon and earth Goddesses, her title was Ixik Kab—Lady Earth.

As grandmother, Ix Chel was depicted with both benevolent and destructive aspects. The larger image on the wall showed an old woman wearing the coiled snake headdress, bare to the waist with a long, woven skirt that had patterns along the waist and lower fringed border. A twisted waistband hung in front, nearly to her feet. She wore a jade necklace, earspools, and wristbands, and poured water from a womb-shaped clay pot onto the earth. These symbolized her dispensing blessings and healing onto the world, preparing soils for planting, restoring waters of lakes and streams, and managing menstrual bleeding and childbearing fluids. She again attended to healing needs and dispensed intuitive wisdom, functioning as the aged healer, diviner, and midwife, who also eased people through the dying process and absorbed their bodies into her great body, the Earth.

A smaller image below the benevolent grandmother depicted her destructive aspects. Here she had a monstrous appearance with sharp claws and a long skirt covered with crossed bones. Jaguar spotted eyes and clawed hands and feet conveyed the power of the jungle's most dangerous predator, the taker of lives. The coiled snake headdress, jade jewelry, and water motifs in her skirt continued her shamanic and life force associations, now with an ominous portent. From the upturned clay pot, she poured huge amounts of water, sending forth storms, floods, and hurricanes. A large sky serpent hovered above her head, disgorging more deluge from its mouth. In Maya mythology, the creator deities destroyed their second attempt at human creation, the mud people, by an immense deluge that flooded the lands and dissolved the people.

The grandmother was also a moon goddess, called Ix Chak Chel— Lady Red Rainbow. The Mayan word *chak* could mean either red or great, associating her with the full moon before heavy rains that had a red glow.

Goddess of the waning moon, she was connected with frightening solar eclipses, because these were more frequent when the new moon appeared.

Small altars were stationed below each of the three images of Ix Chel. Priestesses gave the pilgrims granules of copal to drop into burning censers on each alter, while reciting prayers to each aspect of the Giver and Taker of Life. K'inuuw Mat offered her copal granules reverently, transfixed by the vivid images of the Goddess. She crossed both arms over her chest and bowed deeply, giving the salute of highest respect in front of each image, while murmuring prayers she had memorized in early childhood. The slowly moving line prevented her from staying as long as she wanted with each Goddess aspect. Moving from the last images of the grandmother, the line passed through a side doorway that opened on a small alcove shrouded by trees and vines. A few steps brought them across the alcove and into a cave entrance.

The smells of wet stones and bat guano filled K'inuuw Mat's nose as she stepped carefully along the damp stone passageway, gradually descending into the cave. Its ceiling was high enough to walk upright, and the walls stood an arm's length away on each side. Only the sounds of water dripping and bare feet splashing reached her ears. She glanced ahead at her sister's back, craning her neck to make sure her mother was still in front. Reassured, she attuned her senses to the mysterious cave energies and focused on placing her feet carefully.

Caves and all watery places were sacred to the Goddess. Pilgrimage circuits on the island were centered on caves and sunken water holes, called *t'zonot*. The Yukatek lands, of which Cuzamil Island was an offshoot, had no ground level rivers. Set upon a limestone plateau, the Yukatek had a web of underground rivers traversing all through its regions. Openings occurred when the ground over a portion of the rivers eroded and collapsed, forming the *t'zonot* or water hole. Some *t'zonotob* were close to the surface, while others could be extremely deep. They were an important source of water in this dry tropical landscape. On Cuzamil, shrines were built at the entrances to caves and water holes, and the white causeways that connected them defined the paths followed during pilgrimages. Rites at these shrines drew upon the energies of water, earth, the moon, and the rising sun, since the island was located at the far eastern limit of the Maya lands. The focus of the rituals included fertility, healing, renewal, women's mysteries, and the wellbeing of humans and the cosmos.

The group of pilgrims reached a t'zonot at the bottom of the cave. A tiny opening in the ceiling far above allowed a thin shaft of light to penetrate the gloom. Since the sun was still low in the east, only a dim glow entered the cavern. Clusters of roots hung from the ceiling, reaching toward the water below. Long fingers of stone protruded where constant dripping formed calcifications over many years. The priestesses guided the pilgrims to stand at the water's edge and drop their mantles. Using small hand-held censers, the priestesses waved feather fans to blow fragrant copal smoke around the heads, bodies, and feet of the pilgrims. Copal was the resinous blood of a sacred tree, used by the Mayas since time immemorial for purification. Its dried sap formed granules, highly prized and ceremonially harvested for ritual use. As they cleansed the pilgrims, the priestesses chanted in low monotones.

"Holy Goddess, Our Mother and Protector, receive into your waters these women and girls.

They have come to your sacred island to pay homage, to make offerings, to seek your wisdom.

Make them pure; remove all impediments, so they may be worthy to come before you.

This we ask, Beloved Mother, because we know you love us."

With gestures, the priestesses indicated that the pilgrims should enter the water. K'inuuw Mat stepped in quickly, anticipating the cold and blowing out through her mouth to prevent shuddering. She had learned this technique from her mother; it eased her body into harmony with the chilly waters. In a few steps, she was submerged to her neck. The water was sweet, clear and cool. Its stillness contrasted with the rushing streams and swirling rivers of her home on the plains. She turned to watch her mother, who was encouraging her sister to advance further into the pool. Sak T'ul was being cowardly as usual, arms wrapped tightly around her shoulders and shivering mightily.

What a timid mouse! K'inuuw Mat thought. Tossing her head, she submerged completely and swam a few strokes. The cool water cleansed her skin, hair, and soul. She reveled in the Goddess' life-giving, sacred fluid. *Accept me, Holy Mother. I was meant for this. Purify and strengthen me. I am yours.*

After the sunlight made a bright beam that reflected on the pool's surface, the pilgrims were called out of the water and wrapped in their mantles. Skin tingling and hair dripping, they followed the priestesses out of the cave, and returned to their dwellings to prepare for the ruler's reception.

Later that morning, the steady beat of drums summoned the pilgrims. Wearing newly made white shifts without adornment, their hair braided and tied with rainbow-colored ribbons they walked on bare feet over the smooth plaster sakbeob leading past the flat-roofed temple with Ix Chel murals, and entered the city center. The causeway continued under an archway, wide enough for four women to walk through, its white surface painted with an arcing rainbow. Beyond the archway was the central temple complex, a large plaza paved with stone and stucco, bordered by modest-height pyramids. Three tiers of stairs led up the north and south pyramids; the eastern one was tallest and had five tiers. On top of this pyramid was a square palapa-type structure, four thick poles at each corner supporting a thatched roof, with open sides. In the center was the throne of the Cuzamil ruler.

The throne was made of stone carved in the shape of a large marine bufo toad. Fat, bulging legs supported the throne; the frog's flattened face formed the front with huge poison glands swelling behind prominent round eyes, bumpy skin, and a curved, smiling mouth. A panel below the frog face was decorated with water swirls, fish and lilies. Ceramic incense burners shaped as mythical creatures with animal and human features stood knee-high lining the stairway. Clouds of pungent copal smoke poured through their mouths, eyes, and ears. A line of priestesses in blue and white robes stretched along the base of the pyramid, their headdresses waving in a rainbow blend of assorted bird feathers. The plaza was filled with many women and children, who gathered to behold their ruler greeting the new group of pilgrims now passing across the plaza.

Repeated blasts from large conch shells sounded from the four directions, announcing the appearance of the ruler. Musicians blew high trills on clay whistles, clacked wooden sticks and shook gourd rattles as the Ruler of Cuzamil, Ix Chel High Priestess K'ak Sihom stepped onto the plaza, entering around the northeastern edge of the tall pyramid. She presented an impressive figure, richly adorned with jade and pearl jewelry, wearing a fine blue and white woven huipil and shoulder cape covered with glittering shells. On her head was an impossibly tall headdress of multicolored feathers, with rare blue quetzal tail feathers soaring above. Voices from the crowd rose in salutation. Drums and rattles kept rhythm as the ruler's stately figure walked along the pyramid and then climbed the stairs, followed by her main officials. At the top, she turned and raised both arms in the blessing gesture to the crowd below. Again, their voices soared in acknowledgement.

Turning slowly, K'ak Sihom sat upon the throne and signaled her steward to bring the pilgrims forth. As the small group climbed upward, priestesses below sang lilting songs of the Goddess' love for all her children. Their pure, sweet tones brought tears to K'inuuw Mat's eyes, and she surreptitiously wiped them with hair ribbons. This was a moment she had long anticipated: her first meeting with the revered Cuzamil ruler.

Each pilgrim was introduced to the ruler by the steward, who asked their name and city. In contrast to court protocol in other Maya cities, no gifts for the ruler were expected. The tradition on Cuzamil was for visitors to bring gifts and offerings only to Ix Chel, and place these at various shrines according to their particular quest. K'ak Sihom greeted each pilgrim warmly, taking hold of both hands while inquiring about the purpose of this visit. She exchanged a few words of information or encouragement, and wished the pilgrim well in fulfilling her quest.

Mothers kept young children at their sides when they approached the ruler; girls who had already begun their moon cycles could approach on their own as emerging women. When Yatik had discussed this with Chelte' and the girls, Sak T'ul immediately demurred, saying she preferred to stay beside her mother. K'inuuw Mat was not surprised. If *she* were having moon cycles, she would certainly have enough courage to approach the ruler alone.

Now standing before the elegant form of K'ak Sihom, whose penetrating eyes seemed to bore into one's soul, K'inuuw Mat felt awe-struck by the immense magnetism that the ruler emanated. Instinctively, she grasped both her shoulders and made the bow of highest respect. As she looked up from her bow, the ruler's eyes met hers. A spark passed between them that the girl felt stabbing deep inside her bowels, making her knees weak. A quiver of fear passed up her spine. What did this High Priestess already know about her? And why did it frighten her?

A slight curl moved the corner of K'ak Sihom's chiseled lips. Her eyes became hooded and she shifted them to look at Chelte' and Sak T'ul, smiling broadly and inquiring about their purpose for visiting the island. K'inuuw Mat kept her eyes downcast and listened as her mother explained.

"For myself, I come to give thanks again to the Goddess, who has given me healthy children and an abundant life. For my older daughter Sak T'ul, we seek the Goddess' blessings on her marriage, to bring her fertility and happiness. For my younger daughter, we request that the Goddess give us guidance for her path in life. K'inuuw Mat is drawn to serve Ix Chel, in accord with my family tradition, although we live in far western lands that do not follow the Goddess."

"You are wife of the Uxte'kuh ruler, is that correct?" asked K'ak Sihom.

"Yes, Holy Lady," replied Chelte'.

"As daughter of a ruler, there might be reasons for making a marriage alliance for K'inuuw Mat that serves her city," observed K'ak Sihom. "Has this been discussed in your family? Does your husband concur with her serving the Goddess?"

"This we have discussed. My husband remains open to both possibilities. I believe that what happens during our pilgrimage, what guidance we receive, will be of utmost importance in this decision."

"Indeed, so shall it be. Do you stay long enough to hear the Oracle speak?"

"Yes, we intend to remain for some time, waiting for K'inuuw Mat to begin her moon flow. The Oracle speaks next when Ahau K'in reaches the midpoint of his travels southward, I have been told. That is not far off."

"You are correctly informed. It is good that you bring your question to the Oracle. You are to be commended for seeking Ix Chel's guidance in this matter. The ways of the deities are often beyond our human capacity for understanding. What may seem obvious to us as the proper choice may not be so, in divine vision. Receive my blessings upon all aspects this quest, for yourself and your daughters. May the Goddess grant what you request."

Chelte' bowed and thanked the ruler, turning to walk away. K'inuuw Mat remained motionless, her feet unable to move; they felt heavy as huge stones. Glancing back with a puzzled look, Chelte' grasped her daughter's hand and pulled gently. K'inuuw Mat stumbled as her numb feet failed to step evenly. Both her mother and sister grasped her arms to keep her upright. Through a haze, she heard her name called, and looked back.

"K'inuuw Mat!" The imperious voice of the ruler pierced the girl's ears. "Listen well to the words of the Oracle."

Startled, Chelte' looked up toward the ruler, but K'ak Sihom was already greeting the next pilgrim. Sensing her daughter's disorientation, she kept an arm around her as they descended the stairs, and wondered what had transpired to cause such upset in the usually confident girl.

3

K'inuuw Mat and Yatik knelt in front of a wide, low-brimmed clay bowl filled with water. On the other side, Olal, an acolyte who was studying scrying with Yatik, sat cross-legged with eyes closed in deep concentration. The surface of the clear water was completely smooth, protected by the nearby buildings surrounding the small patio of Yatik's workshop. The priestess held a small gourd full of flat oval-shaped rocks, offering them to K'inuuw Mat.

"Select one of these scrying stones," Yatik said softly. "These stones have been activated through prescribed rituals. It is best to use experienced stones in the beginning. Once you become familiar with this technique, you must find your own collection."

The girl placed a hand above the stones, palm open to sense which stone would call to her. A tingling sensation in her fingertips led toward a reddish-brown streaked stone, and she picked it up from the rest. Following instructions Yatik had recently given, she blew several breaths over the stone and recited the scrying chant.

"From the depths, from the dark,
In the mystery of the unseen,
On the surface of these waters,
Show me that which I ask.
In the name of the Goddess,
She, the Knower of All."

Eyes closed, K'inuuw Mat breathed again on the stone and said her own prayer inwardly: *Ix Chel, guide my vision, open my inner sight. All is done in your service.*

Extending her arm over the bowl, she gently slipped the stone into the water and watched as it settled to the bottom. Rings of ripples spread quickly across the water's surface, rebounded from the rim and crossed each other, creating a tiny jumble that soon dissipated. When the surface was again smooth, K'inuuw Mat stared fixedly at it, clearing her mind of all thoughts. She watched and waited for an image to appear. Her task was to read in the scrying water the image of the animal that the acolyte Olal held in mind.

At first the water only reflected clouds passing above and a corner of one building. Trying not to blink, K'inuuw Mat kept staring and intensified her focus.

Animal of the jungle, animal of the fields, animal of the plains, whoever you are, come to me now, she called mentally.

Slowly, tantalizing shapes began forming on the water's surface. She could not make out a distinct feature that might reveal which animal was starting to appear. Breathing in deeply, she closed both eyes and intensified her intention. On the exhalation, she expanded her awareness and opened herself to receive.

Both eyelids flew up and she fixed her gaze upon the water. There, almost as clearly as if she was seeing it on a jungle path, was the face of a gray fox. Its dark nose quivered, sniffing for a scent; its sharp eyes with pale brows stared at her below large cupped ears. The image remained for a brief time on the surface, and then dissolved.

"A gray fox!" she exclaimed.

Olal, the acolyte holding the animal image in mind smiled and clapped her hands together.

"It is so!" she said. "You have seen truly."

Yatik squeezed her new student's arm and nodded.

"You have done well, to be successful on your first attempt at scrying. Your mother is right; you must have the seer's gift. Let us do another practice."

As the morning went by, K'inuuw Mat made repeated attempts at scrying the image of an animal, bird, or marine creature which Olal held in mind, and was mostly successful. Yatik ended the session when time for the midday meal approached, adding that the next level of scrying would involve plants. This was more difficult, because plant images had fewer distinctions than those of animals. After that, they would proceed to identifying locations, such as cities or rivers, and implements with symbolic meanings. Once a good command of the art was attained working with an acolyte who held the image in mind, they would move to the next skill level. This required working alone, posing a question and scrying for an image that would give the answer.

K'inuuw Mat and Olal walked together to the acolyte dining palapa. Olal was two years older and had the square face and short body of Yukatek Mayas, making her just taller than her companion from the highlands. The southern highland Mayas had long, narrow faces and slender bodies, their skin tones lighter brown and noses sharper than those of the northern plateau. Although their dialects were different, most ahauob learned several during childhood, and all Mayas of the period shared a common courtly language used by scribes and carved on monuments.

"It appears that Yatik is pleased with your first scrying session," said Olal. "Plan you to train as a priestess of scrying?"

"I am not certain," replied K'inuuw Mat. "My hope is to learn the seer arts, and through this find the path the Goddess has chosen for me."

"Will you be dedicated to her service?"

"This is my most fervent wish, although it seems that the Oracle must confirm it."

"Let us make offerings that it be so. I can take you to a special place where I feel Ix Chel's presence strongly. It is a hidden cove on the eastern shore of the island. There you will find many flat stones to collect your own for scrying. You might also find a sastun. Or, more accurately, a sastun might find you, if you are meant to have one."

"What is a sastun?"

"It is a crystal or clear stone, about the size of your hand, which is used for divining," said Olal. "Most healers have their sastun, and use it to scan the body and emanations of those seeking healings. I am surprised that you do not know of it."

"I have not been much interested in the healing path. Perhaps the healers of my home regions do not use such stones."

"All priestesses of Ix Chel must know some healing arts, even if this is not our primary path. You never know when such skills will be needed. Certainly, you will receive training in herbs and remedies while you are here. The path of the midwife is more specialized; one must feel the call to follow it. The training is rigorous. Personally, I am not drawn to this, but I have found much fascination in herbal studies. It will be fun to test you with plant images; there are many that I can call to mind."

"You will try to trick me!"

"Not so, only to stretch your talents. You will do well, do not worry. Let us hasten or the best food will be gone."

The two girls took longer strides as they turned into the patio of the dining palapa.

Several days later, Olal took K'inuuw Mat to the hidden cove. They followed a causeway from the center of Chel Nah that went some distance eastward, ending at a large plaza facing a rectangular shrine set upon a round substructure. Olal explained that this shrine was the place of sunrise rituals. Two columns stood at each end of the round building, marking the farthest point of the rising sun during winter and summer solstices. The round substructure was a *pib nah*, a sweat bath used for purification before the solstice ceremonies. These were major events on Cuzamil, filled with potent itz and attended by everyone.

Lush jungle foliage and vine-draped trees crowded in at the edges of the plaza. Olal headed to a place that looked no different from everywhere else to K'inuuw Mat's eye. Waving her companion to follow, Olal slipped into an obscure opening between waving palmettos and wild papaya bushes. Quickly K'inuuw Mat stepped down from the plaza before the bushes closed over the entrance, and found she was on a dimly lit, narrow path shrouded by dense, moist jungle. Stillness descended, an expectant hush, as the girls' footsteps squished softly. They were startled when a pack of spider monkeys began chattering angrily at the disturbance. Squawks of green parrots and honks of toucans filtered through the trees.

"Watch for snakes," whispered Olal.

K'inuuw Mat treaded gingerly and kept her arms close at her sides, as she had learned to do when traveling jungle paths. Her feet had little protection in their woven strap sandals, and she looked apprehensively at every dark stick on the ground or green branch hanging across the path.

"If we sing chants to the Goddess, she will keep us safe," she whispered to Olal.

"That is a good thought," Olal replied.

Their voices joined in soft chanting, each taking turns leading. They were certain that the Goddess must have heard them, for soon they arrived safely at the cove. It was a magical place. Tumbled masses of black volcanic rock formed a cup-shaped basin with a small beach at its base. The pale golden sand sparkled with thousands of tiny shells, from pure white to rosy red. Gentle waves lapped the shore; the light turquoise of shallow cove waters gradually deepening to blue as they merged into the ocean. The crash of waves against rocky outcroppings sounded in the distance.

"Oh, how beautiful!" breathed K'inuuw Mat.

"Ummm, every time here is special," Olal murmured.

They removed their sandals and walked on warm sand, toes curling into its softness. Back and forth from one side to the other, they danced and cavorted on the small beach, arms swinging freely and feet kicking up sand. After several passes, they collapsed breathlessly and rolled, laughing and throwing sand on each other. Thoroughly sand-covered, they pulled off their huipils and splashed into the cove, walking out until it deepened and forced them to swim. Colorful fish with white and coral stripes, iridescent blues and tawny gold spots dodged around their legs. A few small sea turtles hastily paddled out to open waters.

"Over here!" called Olal. "Here are many flat stones."

K'inuuw Mat swam to join her companion, who crouched near the beach pointing behind a cluster of lava rocks. Spread around the edges, she saw rocks of many shapes and colors. Kneeling, she carefully passed her palm over the rocks, waiting for a signal. Whispering a prayer for Ix Chel's guidance, she began selecting those stones that signaled her palm with a subtle sense of warmth or a tingle. After selecting seven flat stones, she set them aside and went for her pouch beside the discarded huipil. Still naked, she placed the stones in the pouch and strung it over her neck, returning to the water. She swam with the stones, feeling their weight pulling against her neck. Returning to shore, she took each stone out and reverently washed it in the gentle waves. She examined each, imprinting its color and design on her mind. She would practice with each rock to learn its particular conjuring patterns, and then use each accordingly in her scrying.

The girls combed the beach searching for interesting shells. K'inuuw Mat wanted to find gifts for her mother and Ix Chel. She discovered an elegant conch tip, cut by waves and sand abrasion into a perfect flat spiral, its glowing pink hues shading into pearlescent edges. This would make a magnificent pendant for her mother's neck. For Ix Chel, she found three perfectly shaped scallop shells. After cleaning these gifts and putting them into her pouch, she guiltily remembered her sister. She should find a present for Sak T'ul, for her wedding. A little more searching led to a sea star of purest white, its round rim the size of her palm. The perfect star that formed the shell's interior held the promise of Sky God blessings. Her sister would appreciate this as a wedding pendant.

Before leaving, both girls replaced their huipils and joined in prayers of gratitude to Ix Chel. K'inuuw Mat thanked Olal profusely, embracing her warmly. Olal returned thanks for the opportunity to be of service to a follower of the Goddess. Filled with happiness and refreshed by the sacred waters of the sea, they returned buoyantly, albeit carefully, along the path to the city.

4

"Mother, my breasts are very sore," said K'inuuw Mat. "Ah, it is a sign that your moon flow will begin soon," Chelte' replied, giving her daughter a hug. "We must get everything ready."

They had been on the island nearly long enough to watch the moon complete two cycles. Lady Uc was starting to diminish in size, the edge fading from her glorious silvery globe. The next time she became full would be near the fall equinox, and the Oracle would speak.

Chelte' rummaged in bags she had brought with her, pulling out three small pouches. She took them to her daughter's sleeping pallet, where the girl sat cross-legged. Opening the first pouch, she withdrew a small yellow gourd decorated with conjuring symbols. It had a tight-fitting lid, which she twisted off to show the strips of bark paper inside.

"The earliest drops of first moon blood hold the greatest *itz*, although the entire flow is full of power," Chelte' said. "As soon as the blood appears, soak all the strips. This may take some time, because first flow is often slight and erratic. When the strips are dry, put them in the bowl and keep it on your home altar. Be most selective in using this sacred offering, burning the strips ceremonially while making your heart's deepest requests."

"And the Goddess cannot refuse these requests!" exclaimed K'inuuw Mat.

"Exactly so," her mother replied. "That is why you must be careful of what you ask."

From the next pouch Chelte' removed wadded cotton along with a loincloth to hold it in place. She showed her daughter how to secure the wadded portion in position to catch the blood, held up with a band around the waist. There were several cotton wads and an extra loincloth in the pouch. She remarked that the fine green moss found on trunks and branches of mahogany and oak trees made a nice substitute for cotton, and was often used when women were traveling. All of the cotton wads from the first moon flow were placed in a special bowl full of water kept for that purpose. The blood-tinged water was poured onto the city's maize fields as a blessing to keep the soil fertile.

The third pouch held offerings for Ix Chel. Chelte' had placed jade and obsidian beads from home inside, along with the finest quality cacao beans from K'inuuw Mat's father. The girl was to add her own gifts as her moon time approached. She eagerly brought out the pouch of shells she had gathered at the hidden cove, and removed the three lovely sea scallops, their interiors glowing in rose-hued mother of pearl. Each was perfectly shaped without the slightest defect, and they were graduated in size. She explained that from smallest to largest, they represented the three phases of a woman's life. Chelte' nodded approval and gave assurances that Ix Chel would be pleased.

Each day K'inuuw Mat watched for drops of blood, aware of intermittent belly cramps. Her emotional sensitivity increased, and she became teary-eyed easily. After her trainings, now focused on herbal healing, she spent time alone at the jungle's edge singing songs to nature and its wonders. After a particularly sweet song, during which butterflies danced around her head, she stood up from the stone on which she had been sitting, and felt wetness between her thighs. Dabbing a finger to check, she saw red-streaked mucus on the fingertip.

It had happened! Her first moon flow had begun.

But, she was a distance from her palapa, without the gourd of bark paper strips. Glancing around, she saw a green mango leaf that was just the right size and shape. Picking the leaf, she tore a strip from the hem of her huipil and wrapped it to hold the leaf in place. The leaf felt scratchy and she walked straddle-legged, feeling a little foolish. It was vitally important to catch the first flow, however, so she slowly waddled back to her dwelling. Once there, she carefully removed the mango leaf and soaked up the small pool of blood with a bark strip from her gourd. She placed another strip to catch more blood, and lay to rest on her pallet, hoping to ease the cramps.

When the others returned to the palapa and she informed them, excited congratulations and comments about the menarche ceremonies flew around. A first moon flow ceremony was held during each new moon at Chel Nah, which served as a rite of passage into womanhood. All the girls beginning their flow since the previous new moon would take part, receiving public acknowledgement and being ritually ushered into their new status as vessels of the Goddess. They were now young women, who were able to bring forth new life in their wombs. The Ruler and High Priestess, K'ak Sihom, would officiate at this transformation ritual. It denoted that the participants were now transformed from one phase of life to another; from the state of child to that of maiden. Transformation rituals were held by the Mayas for each important life phase. The final rite was a transition ritual, performed after death to demarcate moving from life in the Middleworld to spirit in the Underworld.

Before the public ceremony, Chelte' and Yatik held one just for their family. The women led the two girls close to the forest's edge, where a young ceiba tree stood. The ceiba tree was sacred to the Mayas; it was the Wakah Chan Te', the Jeweled Sky Tree that connected the three dimensions. Its large roots reached into the Underworld, its trunk stood straight and strong in the Middleworld, and its branches soared into the Upperworld. The trunk of the young ceiba was covered with thick thorns, which protected it from assault. When the tree matured, it became immense with a trunk as thick as half a man's height, and branches disappearing into the forest canopy. Then it no longer needed thorns. Root buttresses emerging from the trunk base could be higher than a man. Among the tallest trees in the forest, the ceiba's branches were laden with mossy clusters and lovely orchids. In early spring it dropped its narrow green leaves and replaced them with bouquets of whitish pink flowers, whose blossoms opened after the Sun Lord slipped from sight into the Underworld. At night, bats drank flower nectar and ate pollen, and in the morning many songbirds, hummingbirds, and brown jays flocked to the branches along with bees, wasps, and beetles.

In addition to giving nourishment to many creatures with its flowers, the ceiba provided a luxurious item to humans from its fruit. After attaining the age of seven to ten years, the ceiba produced fruit, as many as four thousand slender oval-shaped fruits the length of a hand. The fruits appeared in clusters on branches that only grew at the top of the tree. The husks were gray and rough, but when they opened the inside was lined with a bed of lustrous, silky white fibers. Soft and slippery, the fibers were used to stuff bedding and pillows. They cushioned the heads and bodies of the people, soothing them into relaxation and sleep. The fruit of the ceiba was another gift of the deities who looked after the Mayas. The ancient Mayan word for ceiba was *yáaxché,* meaning "first tree."

The family knelt at the base of the young ceiba; the tree was already the height of three men, its trunk well-covered with pointed thorns. They bowed with their arms across their chests. Yatik led a prayer to honor the ceiba tree, and then Chelte' instructed K'inuuw Mat to remove her loincloth and squat over the ground close to the trunk of the tree. The girl was to remain squatting until several drops of moon blood fell onto the ground. Chelte' made the pronouncement that now the divine woman's essence flowed onto the ground. The ch'ulel of K'inuuw Mat, her soul energies, became one with the ceiba tree, the earth, and the Great Mother Goddess. Then Chelte' joined the others, singing the traditional song to welcome a girl into maidenhood.

"In her company, the drops of blood and her,
The blood of the lineage, of the creation, and the night are untied.
Her strength is tied up in the company of her,
The drops of blood and her, the blood of the lineage."

"Bin Inca ix hun pucub kik ix hun,
Pucub olom u colba chab u coolba akab tit.
Kax u kinam icnal ix hun pucub,
Kik ix hun pucub olom."

Taking a carved bone staff, Yatik worked the ground until it had absorbed the drops of K'inuuw Mat's blood. Replacing her loincloth, K'inuuw Mat stood and repeated the song, her voice lilting as she sang the time-honored words that proclaimed the ritual power of women's menstrual blood. The term *kik* meant menstrual blood, and the term *olom* signified both lineage and coagulated blood. Used together, they united the powerful symbols of blood and lineage, the power to bring forth life and to continue family lineages.

The others hugged her when she finished singing, showering her face with kisses and stroking her hair.

"By giving your first moon blood, you are now merged with the Goddess, the Earth, and the sacred ceiba tree. May Ix Chel protect you and bless your womb, the sacred vessel of life. All honor to Ix Chel, our mother and our guide." Yatik raised her hands in the blessing sign as she pronounced the words that denoted becoming a maiden.

At the first sliver of the new moon, the public menarche ceremony took place. It began just before sunrise, when the thin crescent hung over the eastern horizon. Everything signified newness, fresh beginnings, and the dawning of a new life phase. Thirteen girls participated; a significant number that symbolized a circle and the endless spirit domain. For the Mayas, thirteen represented the major articulations of the human body, the wandering stars of the solar system, the cycles of the moon, the number coefficients of the days, and subdivisions of the day. This number was the basis for the sacred Tzolk'in calendar, with its 13 x 20 = 260 computations, which integrated into most of their other calendars.

Yatik considered it most auspicious that thirteen girls would undergo transformation into maidenhood rituals. K'inuuw Mat gathered with the other girls, all wearing fine white huipils, with rainbow-colored ribbons streaming from headdresses of white shells and feathers. They stood in a line in front of the large temple in the main square, waiting for the High Priestess to appear. Shivering in the pre-dawn chill, K'inuuw Mat worried about facing K'ak Sihom again. Her last encounter had left her shaken, and she feared another such episode. As the voices of priestesses trilled the sunrise chant, the regal figure of K'ak Sihom appeared at the top of the temple stairs, and she slowly descended to the line of girls below.

The High Priestess walked slowly along the line, taking a bundle of herbs from an assistant and dipping it into sea water, then sprinkling each girl. Another priestess came behind, wafting copal incense around the girls' heads, bodies, and feet. The priestess chorus chanted the traditional coming to maidenhood song. K'inuuw Mat tensed her body against flinching as the cold drops of water struck her, and glanced up at K'ak Sihom. The ruler did not meet her eyes, however, gazing above her head with a distant look, appearing to be in a trance. Walking behind the line of girls, she repeated the sprinkling of their backs, followed by the incense cleansing. Once this was completed, the ruler returned to the stairway and walked halfway up. There she turned and lifted her arms, giving the hand sign for blessing with palms open to the girls below. She made a short speech of welcome to the status of maiden, congratulated them upon becoming vessels for the lives given by Ix Chel, and invoked fertility to their wombs.

The plaza was filled with observers who came to bear witness to this change of status. After the ruler finished speaking, the observers raised their voices in acknowledgement, while tossing flowers upon the new maidens who proceeded across the plaza onto the sakbe leading to the small flat-roofed Ix Chel shrine. Once inside the sky-toned building with flowing black designs, the maidens placed their offerings on the altar of Ix Chel portrayed as the maiden. When K'inuuw Mat's turn came, she knelt and reverently placed her scallop shells, jade and obsidian jewels, and cacao beans before the young

Goddess. She murmured her thanks and prayed fervently that the Goddess accept her offerings, and take her into service on the island.

5

K'inuuw Mat could barely contain her excitement as the time of the full moon arrived. This was the full moon of the fall equinox, and the Oracle would speak. She would accompany her mother and sister to a session with the Oracle, at which her mother would ask about her daughters' futures. A quiver of trepidation arose; would the Oracle confirm a life of serving the Goddess? She wanted to find out as much as she could about the Oracle. For this, she queried her aunt.

"Tell me about the esteemed Ab'uk Cen," she entreated. "How does she prepare to serve as Oracle for the Goddess? What things does she say, and how does she speak?"

"Your interest in the Oracle is commendable. She lives a most secluded life," Yatik explained. "When a priestess is chosen for this vast responsibility, she knows that her life is forever changed. She lives alone, attended by specialized priestesses who prepare her food, maintain her quarters, and communicate with the outside world. Everything the Oracle needs is provided. But, she revokes family connections and personal desires. Her complete focus is upon staying in a high spiritual state, and following prescribed regimens for making prophecies as the Oracle."

"How does she appear when she makes prophecies?"

"Inside the Oracle's temple, which adjoins her residence, is a large wooden statue of Ix Chel. It is hollow inside, and large enough to hold a person. The Oracle sits inside the statue and speaks through its open mouth. You cannot see the Oracle, for she is not her priestess self; she has become the Goddess. Therefore, we are to look only upon the image of the Goddess, not upon a human face. There are other priestesses in the chamber, who remain in the shadows, and tend the incense burners and snakes. Only the supplicant asking a question of the Oracle can enter the chamber, so her quest is kept private. Of course, when it is a mother with her daughters, as in your situation, all three of you enter together."

"There are snakes free in the chamber?"

Yatik laughed and replied, "Yes, these are special snakes. They have been tamed and trained; they convey subtle perceptions to the Oracle. Snakes are among the animal uayob, the familiars of Ix Chel along with felines, butterflies, hummingbirds, and rabbits. The snakes have extra sensitivities beyond those of humans, and they impart information to the Oracle that may be unknown even to the supplicant. Although the Oracle's snakes are poisonous, they will not harm you. Usually, they remain inside the statue."

K'inuuw Mat hoped that the snakes would do this during her visit. She had heard about the Oracle taking substances to alter her consciousness, and was curious.

"What does the Oracle do to prepare herself to become the Goddess?"

"Ah, this is a complicated process, but I will tell you, since your goal is to become a priestess of Ix Chel," Yatik said. "It is complicated and dangerous. The preparation must be undertaken very precisely. The substances that the Oracle uses are highly toxic, and must be exactly prepared or they can kill her. The life of the Oracle is in the hands of her medicinal priestesses who mix these ingredients. These women also give over their lives, remaining inside the Oracle's chambers except when they must collect more herbs and substances. They tend a garden within an interior courtyard, where plants and toads are kept. It is a solitary life, and they are carefully chosen.

"When the time for making prophecy comes, the Oracle undertakes ritual preparations. First, the body of Ab'uk Cen must be rigorously purified in a special *pib nah*. This steam bath is located inside her chambers, and it is scrubbed with water infused with crushed sour orange flowers. This imparts a fresh citrus odor that repels malevolent forces. Censers of clay with faces of protector deities stand beside the door, burning dried herbs that include basil, cedar, Pay-che and vervain to clear away evil magic and spirits. The Oracle fasts for two days before, and is cleansed with copal smoke before she enters the pib nah. She removes her robe and enters naked, lying upon a stone bench while attendants pour sour orange flower water over the heated rocks. The flower-filled steam gives another level of body purification through sweat, and protection from of evil spirits.

"Once this process is completed, the Oracle is taken to a small room hidden deep inside her chambers. Only her most trusted attendants know the location of this room. It is the place where substances are administered that will separate the Oracle's awareness from her body."

Yatik paused, gauging whether to reveal more. K'inuuw Mat appeared totally absorbed in the description, her eyes wide with eagerness. *Perhaps such knowledge would serve her well in her path*, the aunt thought.

"Three priestesses do the final preparation," Yatik continued. "They are the ones who prepare the ingredients for each stage. First, the eldest priestess, who represents the grandmother, gives the Oracle a small clay pipe to smoke. It holds rare blue-leafed tobacco grown only on Cuzamil, dried and crushed while secret chants are sung to enhance its potency. The Oracle takes four puffs while facing each of the four corners of the world upheld by the four Pahuatuns, inhaling deeply. The tobacco smoke causes her to begin distancing from her body, feeling a floating sensation.

"Next, the middle-age priestess, who represents the mother, massages the Oracle's body with a mixture of crushed morning glory seeds and cohune palm oil, rendered over a fire of cedar wood and copal. Both cedar and copal are cleansing agents; morning glory seeds change one's consciousness and open the path to disembodiment. Palm oil gives off smoky, dark aromas of fertile earth. Every part of the body is massaged, including all the openings of the head and bottom. As this mixture takes effect, the Oracle floats in semi-consciousness, and needs assistance walking. At this point, before the final stage, she is dressed in flowing white robes embroidered with Ix Chel's sacred colors: blue, red, purple.

"The last stage is an enema administered by the youngest priestess, representing the maiden. She uses a long-neck gourd with a small tip, cut and smoothed at the end. The enema solution contains a mixture of poison from the glands on the bufo toad's neck, fermented juice from maguey, and a concentrated solution made with Datura flowers. The milky substance from glands of older toads is hard to control, so it must be obtained while the toad is young, but mature. Then, it must be measured very carefully. The juice extracted from thick maguey stalks is combined with honey and fermented until a powerful alcoholic brew is produced. Datura, which is known as *tah k'u*, "with god," invokes the capacity for envisioning. Many use it to seek the vision serpent. All three substances are toxic, and together their power is immense.

"So you see this is an exacting formula. If not made correctly, the Oracle can die. Even when carefully made, with the Oracle's weight and age taken into consideration, the enema mixture causes sickness for several days after use. It does have cumulative effects, weakening the Oracle over time. Ab'uk Cen has served as Oracle for more years than most, I am told. She is growing weaker, however, and must step down soon."

"Might this be her last prophesying?" asked K'inuuw Mat, genuinely concerned.

"It is possible. You are fortunate to benefit from her long experience. You may trust the prophecy she gives for you."

"What happens once the Oracle is given the enema?"

"This becomes the final severance of the Oracle's human presence. There are frightening physical changes, in which she sees flashing lights and grotesque creatures, feels intense pressure within her body, and her heart races. She becomes nauseated; sometimes she will vomit several times. Her limbs shake and tremble; soon she has seizures which throw her out of her body. Once her body becomes still, it is an empty and purified vessel for the Goddess. This stillness signals the attendants that she is ready. They carry her into the wooden statue, place her in a wooden frame with seat and back to support her body, and tie her wrists, waist, and ankles to prevent slipping off. They release the two snakes from baskets inside the statue, light the censers to diffuse copal smoke through the statue's eyes and mouth, and then stand behind until needed. A different priestess acts as the Oracle's steward to summon supplicants for an audience.

"There. That is more than I have ever told any acolyte before."

"How can the Oracle speak, when she has taken so many substances?"

"She speaks through the power of the Goddess. It is beyond human capacities. You will see soon for yourself."

A stream of pilgrims began filling the plaza early in the morning. At the north edge was the entrance to the sakbe leading to the Oracle's shrine. A solitary arch framed the sakbe; tall censers emitting copal smoke stood near each pillar. Ix Chel priestesses waited beside the arch with large baskets to receive pilgrim's offerings, an expression of gratitude for this opportunity to question the Oracle. Each day that the Oracle did prophecy, the priestesses allowed 100 pilgrims to pass under the arch and continue on the sakbe that led straight north, ending with a second arch that opened onto the Oracle's plaza. There the pilgrims waited until called into the Oracle's shrine. It was traditional for the Oracle to continue daily sessions until all pilgrims were received. Given Ab'uk Cen's fragile health, however, this year it was uncertain how many days she could continue.

An air of tension mingled with anticipation as pilgrims jostled each other trying to get through the arch. The sky reflected uncertainty; brisk winds blew from the north and storm clouds gathered on the horizon. Palm fronds and tall branches tossed and hissed in the wind that whipped the pilgrim's hair, headdresses, and huipils. Wealthy noble women regretted their fancy feathers that threatened to fly off their headbands, and their layered jewelry that clinked and jangled excessively. Children milling around the plaza earned shells and beans by rescuing escaped feathers.

Chelte' and her daughters had dressed simply and kept heads bare, except for braiding rainbow-colored ribbons in their hair. She believed her family's wealth was better expressed in gifts to the Oracle, which were recorded by the priestesses. An early start and light snack at home allowed them to arrive among the first in the plaza, and they stood near the head of the line. Conches blew to announce the beginning session, and soon Chelte' and the girls handed their gift bundles of cacao, jade, and weaving to the priestesses. Crossing through the arch, they were cleansed with copal smoke and basil-infused water by other priestesses, and then walked the sakbe in silence.

K'inuuw Mat kept her eyes downcast and concentrated on repeating mental prayers to Ix Chel. She desperately wanted the Oracle to prophesy her dedication to serving the Goddess. Chelte' watched the horizon and puzzled about the ominous appearing clouds and wind. Storms were not uncommon in the islands, and this was the stormy season. A flicker of uneasiness made her whisper a quick prayer that all would go well with their Oracle prophecies. Sak T'ul used her mother's body to shield her from the wind and cast fearful glances up the sakbe. She was not looking forward to meeting the Oracle.

At the second arch, another cadre of priestesses held smoking censers emitting copal and cedar smoke, the final purification. Entering the small plaza, Chelte' and the girls sat in order of arrival on lines of mats where pilgrims waited to be summoned. The Oracle's shrine was situated on the north border of the plaza, set on a base rising four stone tiers to a tall temple made of wood with thatched roof. The temple walls were enclosed, constructed of large tree trunks joined solidly, smoothed and painted in sea and snake motifs. A wooden door was guarded by two priestesses, who opened it just enough to allow the summoned pilgrim to enter and exit. Incense smoke wafted through the opening between the thatched roof and upper walls. A chorus of priestesses seated on the stairs kept up monotone chanting accompanied by soft rattles and drumbeats.

When her mother was signaled to come forward, K'inuuw Mat's heart skipped a beat. She jumped to her feet and followed behind the lagging Sak T'ul, hardly able to keep from pushing her sister. The large door swung silently open, and the triad entered a dimly lit chamber filled with smoke. Immediately the towering wooden statue of Ix Chel commanded attention. The standing figure soared to the height of three people, feet firmly planted apart and arms held in the "creation or break sign" gesture that signified emergence or renewal events. With elbows bent 90 degrees held close to the waist, the left land flexed upward with fingers aligned to the sky, and the right hand flexed downward with fingers aligned to the earth. It was an immensely significant hand sign, used for all creation or birth events— whether of universes, planets, people, or creatures. It represented daybreak, breaking through to new levels, breaking away from constraints.

The Goddess commands us to rebirth into new identities, thought K'inuuw Mat, transfixed by the arresting image.

A priestess stood at either side of the statue. The pungent, woody scent of copal was strong and smoke burned eyes and nostrils. Other aromas combined in an intoxicating mixture of sweet flowers and acrid minerals. Sak T'ul appeared to be almost swooning and clung to her mother's arm. K'inuuw Mat breathed the fumes fearlessly and felt her awareness beginning to change. She looked carefully around the chamber to commit details to memory, but found nothing else inside except the statue and priestesses. The inner walls were unadorned, and the stone floor was bare.

"Speak, pilgrim. Ask what you will of the Ix Chel Oracle," intoned one priestess.

Chelte' bowed with crossed arms, and the girls followed suit.

"Esteemed and honored Oracle, this one before you is Chelte' of Altun Ha, wife of the Uxte'kuh ruler." Chelte' said reverently. "For myself, I have no questions. My purpose is to give thanks to Ix Chel for her blessings, for an abundant and comfortable life, and for my three children. Please accept my undying gratitude and unceasing devotion."

New curls of smoke emanated from the statue's mouth and nose, and an eerie voice replied, seeming to come from nowhere and everywhere.

"Pleased am I to accept your gratitude, Chelte' of Altun Ha. Your family is well known to me, true servants of my work. May you abide in my future blessings. So it is."

Chelte' bowed, pushed Sak T'ul in front of the statue, and spoke again: "For my eldest daughter, Sak T'ul, I seek your prophecy for her upcoming marriage, her fertility and happiness in our city. She is shy and requested that I ask for her."

After another release of smoke, the Oracle's voice wafted through the thick air.

"The fate of this one hovers on jungle vines,
wherein the balance of wisdom and audacity are tested.
Aptly balanced, she lives a life of ease, abundance, and blessed fertility.
But failed, her life is short. Destiny lies not in her hands.
Those close to her take care. Great happiness can be hers."

Sak T'ul was crying, her body shaking as the Oracle ended the prophecy. Chelte' wrapped both arms around her daughter to keep her from crumpling to the floor. In her mind, Chelte' repeated the Oracle's words to memorize them for future analysis. She nodded to K'inuuw Mat to pose her question.

Although shaken, K'inuuw Mat mustered her courage and stepped in front of the statue. Gazing upward at the implacable face, crowned with a coiled serpent headdress and wearing huge earspools, the girl breathed deeply and felt the edges of her awareness dissolving. Quickly she posed her question, afraid she might lose consciousness soon.

"Oh, great and glorious Goddess, standing before you is the new maiden K'inuuw Mat of Uxte'kuh, second daughter of Chelte', one who comes to your sacred island for first moon rites. My deepest desire is to remain here and dedicate my life to your service. May I receive your prophecy for the purpose and direction of my life."

It appeared to K'inuuw Mat that an unusual amount of new smoke poured out of the statue's mouth and nose. As the spirals drifted down, they circled around her body almost making her cough. She felt something cold and smooth against her leg, and then a squeezing sensation caused her to gasp. Looking down, she saw a long black snake slithering up her right leg. Its wedge-shaped head alerted her that this was a poisonous viper, and a bolt of terror shot through her. The snake halted its ascent, drew its head upward and fixated beady eyes upon her face, forked tongue rapidly quivering.

She glanced wide-eyed at the nearest priestess, but the woman simply stared into space, appearing not to notice. The statue was half-hidden by smoke and her mother not visible behind her. Remembering her aunt's description of the Oracle's snakes, she withdrew her awareness and dropped into her center, willing a state of calmness. Mentally she communicated to the snake: *You are welcome here, servant of Ix Chel. You come in peace and I receive you in gratitude.*

The snake waved its head several times, flicked its tongue and slowly slithered down from her leg. She watched it disappear through a hole in the base of the statue. The Oracle's voice startled her.

"A seer you are and well command your fears.

The gift of prophecy resides within you; use it in service of others.

Deep is your tie to Ix Chel, but not to be realized here.

A destiny beyond your own awaits. A people's legacy depends on you.

In the high court of royalty shall your life unfold.

Rulers shall seek your wisdom; leaders your guidance.

Through you shall dynasties abide."

K'inuuw Mat stood in stunned silence. The Oracle's prophecy was emblazoned in her mind, but she refused to accept it. Surely this was not correct! How could her destiny be other than serving the Goddess on Cuzamil?

She managed a slight bow when prompted by Chelte', who led her daughters, both in tears, out of the Oracle's shrine.

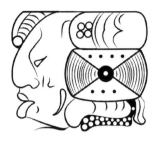

K'inuuw Mat—II

Baktun 9 Katun 11 Tun 13 – Baktun 9 Katun 12 Tun 0 (665 – 673 CE)

1

"How fares our daughter K'inuuw Mat? Clearly, she was disappointed when she could not remain on Cuzamil to serve the Goddess." Ox B'iyan was observant, not just as a father, but as a ruler. The ability to read emotions was an important asset in governing.

"She still is not herself," replied Chelte' with a sigh. "I do not believe she has fully accepted the Oracle's prophecy. She spends much time alone and seems moody. Her teachers mark how she has lost interest in studies that engaged her before. But, she reveals nothing to me."

The ruler and his wife reclined on soft woven mats set on the plaster floor of their residence, leaning against plush pillows. Servants brought platters of fruit and ceramic cups full of warm maize mixed with bitter cacao, spicy from ground chiles. The ruler's residential compound was a collection of chambers and hallways surrounding several patios, constructed of limestone blocks bound by mortar, and covered with plaster. The rooms were narrow, their square stone roofs supported by corbelled arches not strong enough to carry a wide roof. Many walls were painted with flower, sky, or water motifs while the ruler's reception and throne room had impressive murals of dancing gods and ancestors.

Uxte'kuh was a moderate-sized city located on wide plains of gently rolling hills. The region was crossed by several rivers, with collections of dense forest in-between. It was within the polity of B'aakal, a region encompassing the foothills and lower reaches of K'uk Lakam Witz, a vast mountain range that climbed to cloud-covered heights as it stretched south. The B'aakal polity followed the mighty K'umaxha River where it crossed the wide plains, and continued southward toward the river's source until bumping up against neighbor polities, some friendly and some hostile. To the east lay the arch-enemy polity of Ka'an. To the west, the polity touched a large sea, the Chik'in-nab. There were some fifteen cities within B'aakal polity, though the count varied according to shifting alliances and foreign usurpation.

Sipping from the cup of spicy cacao beverage, Ox B'iyan appeared lost in thought. He was a well-muscled man, trained in warrior arts, his appearance typical of Maya nobles: a long slender face, full lips, prominent nose and straight forehead leading to an elongated skull. Such skulls were well-suited to wearing elaborate, tall headdresses full of regal symbolism. Among the highest families these skulls were a genetic trait; the next echelons of nobles used headboards during infancy to mimic this shape.

"She always does best when she has something to accomplish, some goal or challenge," he said, nearly startling his wife after the long silence.

"That is so," Chelte' agreed. "But, I have not been able to think of any."

"Involve her in preparing for her sister's marriage. Is there some task you can give her, something difficult? It must seem natural, not contrived. She is perceptive for one so young."

"This will require some thought. The plans are well underway since the Calendar Priests advise that the ceremony take place before the coming rainy season. They are now calculating the most propitious calendar combination."

"I am confident you will find the right challenge for K'inuuw Mat. Although the Oracle's prophecy took away her dream of serving Ix Chel, I for one am pleased. She has excellent bloodlines and will be an attractive match for important royalty in another city. Such alliances are gems in a ruler's hands. The Oracle predicted exactly that, is it not so? The prophecy was for K'inuuw Mat to live at a high court, among royalty."

Chelte' glanced at her husband over the lid of the cup, hooding her eyes so he would not see her annoyance. Men, especially ruling men, were ever prowling for ways to increase their power. He loved his daughter, she knew, but was not above using her for political purposes.

"The Oracle did say this, and more," she replied, "that rulers would seek her wisdom and guidance, and a dynasty would abide through her."

"Powerful words," murmured Ox B'iyan. "Something important will come of this."

Chelte' congratulated herself on coming up with a challenging task for K'inuuw Mat in only a few days. She knew the girl loved to foray into the forests, walking along jungle trails and finding medicinal plants. At Cuzamil, her studies had included herbal medicine and sacred use of plants. This combination provided just the incentive to pull the girl out of her dejection. The task was to locate a blue-colored flower that possessed the qualities of clearing away obstacles. Chelte' vaguely remembered hearing about such a flower from Cuzamil priestesses. Blue was the featured color in the marriage costume for Sak T'ul. A large basket of these flowers would be collected and dried. Some would be ground into a ceremonial powder to be burned whenever Sak T'ul was facing a difficulty, so the obstacle could be removed. Others would be woven into the marriage headdress to symbolically remove obstacles to a happy and fruitful marriage.

The Oracle's strange prediction for Sak T'ul continued to trouble Chelte', but she decided to emphasize the positive part about a life of happiness, abundance, and fertility. Her older daughter was easily frightened, and it was best to ignore the ominous part of the prophecy. Surely the family and servants could keep her from harm. In a mood of confidence, she set out to find her younger daughter.

K'inuuw Mat spent as much time as she could in the secluded inner patio adjoining her chamber. The walls on three sides of the patio had no opening; her chamber gave the only access through a small veranda with arched support columns. Inside the patio were several large pots with shrubs and low trees. Smaller pots were used for growing medicinal herbs, which she lovingly tended as they grew, drying the leaves or flowers for her pouches. Usually, she carried a few pouches with her, in case some urgent need for healing remedies arose. Even in her state of despair, she took care of her herbs. They were her most immediate connection with Cuzamil.

The trip home from the island had been dismal. She felt as if her heart was being torn from her chest, filled as it was with anguish. After initial tears, her eyes remained dry due to sheer determination to avoid appearing weak. Despite her aunt's praise of the elderly Oracle's powers, she suspected that years of taking mind-altering substances and the physical strain of vacating the body to make it a vessel for the Goddess had reduced the Oracle's abilities to prophesy truly. The toll this took on the Oracle was apparent to all, as the days of prophesying had been cut short. Many pilgrims either left without their questions answered or had to remain on the island until the next session.

That must be what happened, she thought. It was inconceivable that Ix Chel had rejected her as an acolyte. Surely the destiny she had envisioned since early childhood, a life dedicated to the Goddess on Cuzamil, could not have been in error. The error must lie with the Oracle. Bolstered by such thoughts, she invented one scheme after another for returning to the island. She would coax her father to let her return, she would pretend illness that could only be cured by Cuzamil priestesses, or she would run away in the night with a trusted guide. Every plan seemed flawed, however, and her mind kept going in circles. She felt frustrated, and at this point, more angry than sad.

Her attendant's footsteps broke her mutinous reverie, and she looked up from the pot of herbs she was weeding.

"Your Lady Mother has come to visit," said the attendant.

K'inuuw Mat rose and brushed dirt from her knees, moving from the hot sun to join her mother on the shaded veranda. They settled on floor mats as the attendant brought cups of cool kob'al, maize gruel mixed with fruit juice. After exchanging pleasantries, Chelte' posed the task to her daughter.

"There is a request I have for you, to help me with the preparations for Sak T'ul's marriage. I have been thinking of ways to ensure her a future of happiness. She is timid, as you know, and does not take initiative as you do. When she encounters difficulties, she will need something to bolster her, a simple method that she only needs to remember to use. I am thinking of plant medicine, a preparation that would carry the qualities of removing obstacles. A vague memory of such a plant teases the edges of my mind, but I cannot remember. It seems I learned of it many years ago, on one of my early visits to Cuzamil. All I can recall is that this plant had a blue flower. You know much of medicinal plants, have you encountered this one?"

K'inuuw Mat searched her memory, but nothing came at once to mind.

"No, I regret to say, I do not recall such a plant. It has a blue flower and its qualities help one overcome difficulties? Perhaps if I spend time thinking, it will come to me," she said.

"Or, you might consult the elderly herbalist who lives in the commoner village at the river's edge," Chelte' suggested. "I have heard that her herbal lore surpasses even that of our city's Ix Chel healers."

"Hmmm. As a villager living near the forest, she would be familiar with plants in the area," K'inuuw Mat remarked. "This is a good idea, Mother. Do you know her name?"

"No, but I will send a servant to obtain it, and set up a visit for you."

"Very good, thank you." K'inuuw Mat pondered the plant's identity. "A blue flower. That is not a common color for medicinal plants; these tend to have red, yellow, or orange flowers. Oh, and many have white flowers, let me think . . . but blue, no, I cannot recall a single one."

"So you will take on this task for me?"

When K'inuuw Mat nodded, still lost in thought, Chelte' smiled to herself. Already the girl's active mind was off on a quest that promised to remove her sadness.

Information gathered from the elderly herbalist proved helpful in K'inuuw Mat's quest. The old villager remembered learning of an orchid with a blue flower that grew high in trees in the deep jungle. It was among the rarest of orchids, not easily found and difficult to harvest. When studying herbal healing with her venerated teacher, now long passed to the spirit world, she once obtained the blue orchids and made a powerful remedy for surmounting difficulties. The precious powder from dried and ground flowers was in great demand, and while it lasted the herbalist made a good living. Once the powder was gone, she had returned to the isolated grove where the orchids grew but could find no more. The plants had simply disappeared, and she never found another source.

K'inuuw Mat was excited to learn that the blue orchid with obstacle-removing qualities did exist. She found it was daunting, however, that none had been seen in the area for many years. She asked the city's Ix Chel healers if they knew about the plant, but none did. Another means of locating the orchids was needed, and for the first time since leaving Cuzamil, she felt drawn to use her abilities as a seer. She would do a scrying to find the orchids.

In the far corner of her patio, K'inuuw Mat set up a scrying station. She had her attendant bring a low, wide-rimmed bowl and fill it with water. After rituals for purification and dedication of the corner, the bowl was set in place with a thick floor mat in front for kneeling. She brought out her pouch holding the special scrying stones that she had collected at the hidden cove with Olal. Placing them on the mat, she meditated on each stone and felt its energies with her palm. The white stone with turquoise streaks sent the strongest emanations, so she selected it and blew breath and blessings across its smooth surface. She formulated the request for the orchid's location in her mind and held it firmly there while doing the scrying chant.

"From the depths, from the dark,
In the mystery of the unseen,
On the surface of these waters,
Show me that which I ask.
In the name of the Goddess,
She, the Knower of All."

Reverently she tossed the stone into the bowl, watching the ripples form and reform until the surface was once again still. She allowed her lids to droop to partially obscure vision, a technique she had perfected to hasten perception of the image. The clear surface became cloudy and seemed to tremble, although there was no breeze. From the edges a dark forest began forming, trees tall and festooned with lianas, dense with undergrowth. In the crevasse where upper boughs joined the truck, a collection of blue orchids sprouted. Quickly the image shifted to a bird's eye view of treetops, and then the trees receded until the topography of the land was revealed. Two small rivers converged, ran together a short distance and separated to form a small island before rejoining. She could tell the direction was west because the setting sun seemed to settle into the river. The image shifted again, and she was dizzied by a rapid descent into a dense grove of trees contained on the small island. Again she saw the blue orchids in their upper limbs.

The bowl of water went blank, its smooth surface reflecting the sky. She murmured a prayer of gratitude to Ix Chel and bowed deeply, arms across chest. Her next task would be finding hunters who could identify the unique river configuration and lead her to the island.

2

"Aiyee! Thorns are caught in my hair! Help, come help me!"
K'inuuw Mat and the nearest attendant leapt over low-lying brush, rushing toward Sak T'ul, whose hair was entangled in thorny vines dangling from branches over the narrow path.

"Stop moving!" yelled K'inuuw Mat. "Keep still; we are coming."

Reaching her sister, K'inuuw Mat grasped her upper arms to prevent more flailing. The attendant, a young woman from the ruler's household, carefully untangled the vines. Tears were streaming down Sak T'ul's cheeks, making a track through the dust and sweat.

"I should never have come!" she moaned. "Why did I allow you to persuade me? The jungle is dangerous; I try to avoid it. This is foolish. Oh, I wish I had stayed home!"

As her sister was freed of the grasping vines, K'inuuw Mat patted her shoulder and murmured reassurances.

"Everything will be fine. This is a great adventure; you would not want to miss discovering the rare blue orchids for your marriage. How often do we get to venture into the jungles? This may be your last chance before your responsibilities to husband and children tie you to the household."

"I prefer to stay in my household! At least we could have taken the palanquins. So much walking is hurting my feet. The thorns are tearing my huipil; it is ruined."

"Do not be unreasonable. The palanquins could not pass through these narrow jungle paths. See, we are almost there."

"I do not see anything but all these thorny vines and trees and bushes! Oh, I wish I had not come with you!"

K'inuuw Mat sighed, shaking her head at her sister's timidity. She had offered an invitation that painted a glowing picture, a fascinating trek to make a rare discovery. Perhaps it had been a mistake to convince Sak T'ul to come, against her resistance. The first part of the journey went well. They rode in canoes down the river and watched iguanas swim away as they approached, climbing branches on the riverbank. Higher in the trees spider monkeys chattered in annoyance, and brilliant red-headed scarlet macaws turned beady eyes in disapproval while brown jays cawed and flew away in packs. Several flocks of green parrots flapped across the river, their screeches tapering off as they sailed into the distance.

Their father had recommended hunters who remembered the convergence of two rivers that formed an island. He arranged for canoe and two paddlers, along with a guide who could clear the path with a long obsidian knife. Their mother insisted that Kuy, a female attendant from the household, accompany them, and added an agile servant boy to climb the trees. The attendant carried two woven wicker baskets for collecting the flowers. Since the trip would take the better part of a day, Chelte' had another basket filled with food, including dried maize cakes mixed with berries and turkey fat, and strips of dried wild boar meat. There would be water from the rivers, scooped with cupped avocado or yáaxché leaves.

The path on the river island was wilder than K'inuuw Mat had anticipated, though she had no experience with this part of the jungle. Trails in the forests surrounding her city were wide and well-maintained. She often walked alone on those trails, collecting herbs and enjoying the sounds of myriad creatures. But on this path the guide was a distance ahead, slashing away branches and vines to make a narrow passage, rough underfoot with roots and undergrowth. The boy and one paddler brought up the rear; the other paddler stayed to keep the canoe secure.

"When will we get there?" wailed Sak T'ul. "I am fainting from heat; my legs will not carry me anymore. Oh, sister, this is not a good idea, let us turn back." She waved an arm toward the rear, brushing against drooping branches.

"Sak T'ul, keep your arms and hands close by your side," admonished K'inuuw Mat. "And step only on the clearer areas of the path. Remember there are snakes in the jungle."

"Aiyee, snakes, this is terrible! I want to go home!" Sak T'ul plopped to the ground, sobbing.

Kuy and K'inuuw Mat quickly lifted her back to standing, Kuy wrapping arms around her distraught mistress.

"Please be calm, Sak T'ul," said K'inuuw Mat. "And do not sit on the ground, it is not safe. Here, rest a moment and I will seek to learn how much farther until we reach the orchid trees."

She called loudly to halt the guide, as the boy and paddler caught up and waited. Closing her eyes, she focused intensely and silently recited the prayer of seers. She had not attempted envisioning this way before, and fervently hoped it would work. Sweat dripped off her nose, but she held focus, using force of will to summon an image. Insects buzzed noisily, branches rustled, and birds chirped; the jungle was humming with life. Tantalizing but blurry images swam behind her closed lids. Soft whimpers from her sister heightened her resolve.

Ix Chel, show me the trees! Knower of all, bring me the information I seek!

She had not demanded so brashly before, but this was becoming a very difficult situation. Waiting, she was vaguely aware of the others shifting position and swatting insects. Calling again and again, she breathed deeply to take the surroundings inside her and forced the images to become clear. In a sudden flash, she saw the tall ebony trees with blue orchids in their upper branches. Like a tree squirrel, her awareness ran down the trunk and onto the faint path, wriggling around brush stalks and roots, moving closer until she arrived at the feet of the guide. But she was coming at an angle to the direction they were taking. The trees were only a short distance ahead, but off to the left. Releasing her breath in a tiny explosion, she lifted both hands in the gesture of gratitude to the Goddess.

"We must veer to the left," she told the guide, pointing at a slight angle from where he stood. "The trees are nearby, but in we must go that way."

"I see no path, Lady K'inuuw Mat," the guide said.

"Look closely, move forward a little. It must be there," she replied, trying to keep her voice even. While he searched, she turned to Sak T'ul.

"We are almost there. Bear up just a little longer, and you will see the most amazing flowers. Then the boy will gather them, and we all will have something to eat."

Sak T'ul sniffled and wiped her eyes, leaving more streaks on her cheeks, and nodded.

"Here it is!" the guide exclaimed. "Very easy to miss, this is a trail not recently used."

He hacked an opening with his knife and led the group slowly over an even more tangled path. They pushed aside encroaching branches, careful to avoid thorns, until the path opened to a small clearing at the base of towering ebony trees. There, almost hidden by foliage, were several clusters of blue orchids in the crooks of upper branches. Even in the dim light, their vivid cerulean color struck the eye. The orchids appeared to glow with captured sunlight in their petals. Tiny tongues of pale lavender graced the petals where they joined the throat.

"Oh! How beautiful!" whispered Sak T'ul. "I have never seen such exquisite flowers."

K'inuuw Mat breathed a sigh of relief. She placed an arm around her sister's shoulders and gave a squeeze, motioning the boy to climb. He fastened baskets over his shoulder with twine and scrambled up the nearest ebony tree, using lianas as a ladder. The group below chuckled, for he appeared much like a monkey with his thin, spindly limbs. He reached the orchids quickly, picking them and placing them reverently in the baskets. This he repeated, on adjoining trees, until the two baskets were full.

Thanking the boy and guide, K'inuuw Mat had Kuy open the food basket and distribute welcome nourishment to all. Sak T'ul insisted on sitting to eat, claiming that she was too exhausted to stand. Kuy checked the area carefully and sat beside her mistress. Before long, everyone was sitting and chewing happily.

The guide glanced at the sky, his experienced eye gauging time even through the thick jungle canopy. He motioned to the path, indicating it was time to return. The boy and paddler lifted the baskets of flowers, and the group followed the guide onto the faint path.

K'inuuw Mat felt a surge of satisfaction. She had accomplished the mission, even with her sister's complaining and the difficult trails. Her seer abilities had pointed out the way, with Ix Chel's help. Imagining her mother's delight with the flowers, she lifted her head and hummed a tuneless chant.

"Aiyee! Oh—oh! A snake—oh! It bit me, help . . . ahhhh!"

Sak T'ul collapsed, falling against prickly brush before Kuy could reach her. K'inuuw Mat turned, and in two huge strides, she knelt beside her sister.

"Where?" she cried.

"My foot, here, this one . . ."

Kuy pulled Sak T'ul back onto the cleared area, as K'inuuw Mat grabbed the extended right foot. Turning it, she saw two small punctures just above the ankle oozing a slight trickle of blood. The sound of dry rattling brought her glance to the brush, where she saw a small rattlesnake just off the path. It was coiled to strike again, and she flinched as her left arm offered a close target. Before the snake launched its strike, a wooden staff plunged down upon it, lifted the twisting creature and flung it into the brush. The guide stood above the two young women.

"It is a small rattlesnake," he said. "Very dangerous."

K'inuuw Mat knew that small snakes ejected more venom than larger, older ones that could judge the size of their prey. More experienced snakes did not waste venom on huge creatures they could not consume. But this snake's bite was potentially lethal.

"Find leaves of **makulan**, the snake plant," she commanded the guide. "And bring **zubin,** a piece of bark equal to the length of Sak T'ul's arm, and some root. Hurry!"

She reached under her huipil for the pouch of medicinal herbs that she always carried tied around her waist when in the jungle. Taking out a jadeite knife wrapped in cloth, she made two small cuts over the puncture marks. Kuy tore a strip from the hem of her huipil and helped tie a tourniquet below the knee as K'inuuw Mat murmured "Not too tight, pass a finger under."

Kuy supported Sak T'ul against her chest, while K'inuuw Mat gently applied pressure to encourage blood flow from the cuts. She took a small packet of snakebite powder, a special concoction of ground herbs, and sprinkled some on the wounds. She had learned how to treat snakebite on Cuzamil from one of the leading healers. The snakebite powder would begin the process of neutralizing the venom. The skin around the bite was already swelling and becoming discolored, a nasty purple-blue. Sak T'ul was crying and sweating heavily, but her skin felt cool. Her rapid breathing and dilated pupils indicated she was going into shock.

"Sak T'ul, you must calm yourself. Try to breathe slowly, stop crying and don't move. I have medicines to treat the bite, do not be afraid," said K'inuuw Mat, with more confidence than she felt. Would the guide never return with the plants?

Cracking brush signaled his return, and he handed her some long, stiff snake plant leaves along with a strip of zubin bark and a chunk of root. Taking the bark first, she forced one end into her sister's mouth and ordered her to chew and swallow the juice. This would delay reaction to the toxins. With the edge of her huipil, she cleaned the zubin root and mashed it against a stone to start releasing juice. While doing this, she instructed the guide to pound the snake plant leaves into a poultice and place this over the wound. She removed the bark strip from her sister's mount, replacing it with zubin root and urging her to chew and swallow its juices. Zubin root was a strong sedative; it would reduce anxiety and slow the heartbeat, delaying venom flow through the body.

Kuy had to keep encouraging Sak T'ul to chew, as the young woman was drifting toward unconsciousness. K'inuuw Mat pounded the remaining zubin bark into a poultice and applied it over the snake plant on the bite. The bark slowed reaction to the venom, while the snake plant relaxed muscles and decreased the risk of seizures. Once both poultices were in place, she wrapped cloth torn from her huipil in a bandage around the ankle.

"We must return as quickly as possible," she said to the guide. "This will help, but she needs the Ix Chel healers. She should move as little as possible. Can you carry her?"

The guide signaled to the paddler, responding that they would alternate carrying. K'inuuw Mat nodded and took the basket of flowers from the paddler while the boy carried the other basket. Solemnly the group returned to the canoe, walking as fast as roots and shrubs allowed. Once in the canoe, K'inuuw Mat removed the poultices and reapplied new zubin bark and snake plant fibers. Sak T'ul was unconscious, the wound more swollen and discolored, and K'inuuw Mat kept up a fervent stream of prayers as the sun descended. It was twilight when they reached the city. One of the paddlers had run ahead, and they were met by Ix Chel healers, who brought Sak T'ul to their temple for treatment.

The atmosphere in the ruler's household was tense in the days following Sak T'ul's snakebite. Although her parents did not criticize K'inuuw Mat and expressed gratitude for her emergency care, she sensed their underlying disapproval. She had, after all, persuaded her sister to come on the venture. She should have known that such temerity and fear would draw some untoward event. What good was her ability as a seer, if she could not foresee this catastrophe? In this mood of questioning, she doubted even the guidance of Ix Chel.

In the Ix Chel temple, the healer priestesses kept watch over Sak T'ul and continued treatment for several days before it was pronounced that she would recover. The first night was most difficult as the young woman became delirious and thrashed about while suffering vomiting and diarrhea. Herbal treatments eventually brought these under control, and she returned to consciousness the next day. She remained weak and lethargic, sleeping most of the next few days. There was much concern about tissue damage at the bite area, so the healers used methods to draw out the venom with astringent pastes of coriander leaves, root and seeds repeated four to five times daily. They watched for signs of internal bleeding, such as blood oozing from body orifices, and decreased respiration or heartbeat that could signal toxic failure of body organs. Herbal teas were administered to clear toxins and strengthen tissues. Nourishing broths were fed frequently.

The wound area eventually healed, leaving small scars but without serious tissue loss. It would take longer, however, for Sak T'ul to recover her strength. The marriage was delayed and a new date sought by calendar priests.

K'inuuw Mat could not stop feeling responsible. She kept to her chambers once again, confused and disheartened. Her yearning to return to Cuzamil became unbearable; it was only in memories of her stay there that she found any pleasure. She even started to neglect her herbal garden in the patio.

One evening she sat despondently on a floor mat on the patio veranda. She watched stars slowly appearing through wispy clouds and wondered about the souls of ancestors who had ascended to the sky as these twinkling lights. Perhaps it was time for her to join them. Tears welled as she thought about leaving life before she had truly lived it. As she slipped into an abyss of self-pity, her skin began to tingle with an electrifying presence. The hair on her arms stood on end, and a shiver ran up her spine. She jerked upright and looked around, wide-eyed. No one was in the patio or veranda. The presence pressed heavily against her body, and her head felt as if it would explode. Her vision blurred and her ears were buffeted by thunderous crashes. She reflexively tried to cover them with her hands, but found she could not move.

"HOW—DARE—YOU—QUESTION—ME?"

The words pounded her brain, body and ears. She wanted to fall prostrate but remained paralyzed. Materializing before her widely-opened eyes, the immense form of Ix Chel in her destructive mode—Chak

Chel—hovered in the twilight. The Goddess appeared as a crone wearing a coiled serpent headdress that signified her command of healing, intuition, and spiritual powers. Her downturned mouth opened ominously, and her hands and feet had sharp jaguar claws. She wore a skirt decorated with crossed bones, symbols of death. Her hooked nose protruded and her narrowed eyes peered from brows with jaguar spots. She held an overflowing water jar and rippling streams of storm water danced above her shoulders. An angry red moon hung above, its glow warning of heavy rains. Chak Chel was the Grandmother Earth Goddess, presiding over rain, moon, medicine, destruction, and death. Her bestial characteristics and death symbols proclaimed her as world destroyer.

"K'inuuw Mat, you received my prophecy for your destiny through the Oracle of Cuzamil. Yet you continue to question me! You doubt my Oracle, you doubt my guidance. You pine and wallow in sadness because you are not destined for a life in Cuzamil. You think those upon the island are my only servants? How foolish of you to presume to limit my domain! I am the Great Mother, I am the giver of life and the bringer of death, and I preside over everything in between. I weave my people's destiny on the loom of the heavens, and what is woven there must come to pass. Your desires are nothing in this immense pattern through which worlds turn.

"DO—YOU—UNDERSTAND—ME?"

Teeth chattering and body shaking, K'inuuw Mat managed to nod her head.

The Goddess tipped the water jar she held, and a deluge came pouring down, threatening to sweep over and drown K'inuuw Mat. She braced for the assault, but the water passed through her as if she were transparent. She felt strangely cleansed and peaceful as it receded away.

"You see that my Oracle's prophecy for your sister came to pass. You did not cause it; you were only its instrument. This was her destiny and could not be escaped. I commend you for using your healing skills to save her life; for that early care is indeed what kept her alive. Be at peace with this.

"Remember, K'inuuw Mat. Your destiny is to serve me in an important royal court. A dynasty will be carried in your womb; a people will be continued through your legacy. This is a far greater destiny than being a seer in Cuzamil. Remember, and never doubt again."

The form of the Goddess shimmered and dissolved until only a myriad of twinkling stars pulsated in the indigo arc above, and profound silence filled the patio.

3

On the day of her marriage, Sak T'ul looked radiant. Her cocoa skin glowed with the vigor of youth and the blush of excitement. A cascade of dried blue orchids trailed beside fluffy white feathers from her headdress, their ethereal color undiminished. The blue-and-white motif was repeated in her finely woven white huipil with blue sky bands at hem and neck. She wore cerulean jade jewelry with creamy streaks. The scars from her wounds were covered by high-back sandals with laces wrapping around the ankles, decorated with bands of tiny white shells that tinkled when she walked. She was a picture of health and loveliness.

K'inuuw Mat thanked Ix Chel daily for her sister's full recovery. Though the Goddess had resolved her sense of guilt, she still relished evidence that all was well. It was a splendid ceremony in the main plaza, with dancers and musicians, processions of nobles and priesthood, and a huge feast for all residents that went well into the night. The ruling family and elite nobles celebrated in the palace's main patio. K'inuuw Mat danced with her brother Chumib, beginning with the stately toe-heel step where partners faced each other and performed mirror image hand motions, palms nearly touching. As the evening wore on, with much consumption of fermented balche, an alcoholic drink made from bark of the balche tree, she became less contained and twirled around in joyful abandonment. Her brother laughed and performed high-stepping feats and acrobatic leaps, his short skirt and loincloth fanning straight out. Other young nobles joined in until the patio throbbed with feet pounding the stucco floor, bodies twisting and bobbing, and voices lifted in song and laughter.

After the wedding, ten moon cycles passed and life followed its normal pace at Uxte'kuh. Sak T'ul and her husband followed instructions of the Ix Chel priestesses, and she conceived near the date recommended by the Ah K'inob. Chelte' was pleased about her older daughter's pregnancy, and also relieved at her younger daughter's good humor. K'inuuw Mat applied herself to studies, tended her herbs, and joined the Ix Chel priestesses for rituals and healings. She never mentioned wanting to return to Cuzamil. Ox B'iyan was occupied searching for a suitable match for his son, the heir to the throne. He wondered about what alliance might come forth for his younger daughter, repeatedly pondering the Oracle's prophecy.

As the spring equinox approached, the height of the dry season when travel was most common, a messenger arrived. Received by ruler Ox B'iyan in his throne reception chamber, the messenger's communication carried immense portent for the royal family. Chumib was sent to bring the news to his sister.

"At last, the Cuzamil Oracle's prophecy for you is coming to fruition," Chumib announced, joining his sister on floor mats in her small reception chamber. "Today a messenger came from Lakam Ha. He gave us advance notice that a delegation is arriving, headed by none other than a son of the illustrious K'inich Janaab Pakal, with several leading courtiers. They wish to discuss an alliance with us by marriage—the younger daughter of our city's ruler to the youngest son of theirs."

"Oh! Lakam Ha, the dominant city of our polity!" K'inuuw Mat's heart leapt and she sat bolt upright. There could be no higher royal marriage for her. She marveled at the accuracy of the Oracle's statement. "Is he with the delegation?"

"I am not certain," said Chumib. "Pakal has three sons, as I recall a fourth died as a youth. The elder two are already married."

"Oh, I hope the youngest son has come with them! Then I can meet my future husband."

"It is more likely that Pakal sent an older son to negotiate. Soon we will know; they arrive in less than four days."

The royal household was in a buzz as the days flew past. Rooms were readied for the esteemed visiting lords, hunters sent to bring deer and tapir for roasting, corn ground into mountains of maize flour for making flat cakes and gruel, immense quantities of balche bark set into hollowed tree trunks to ferment with honey, and a multitude of servants sent into gardens and orchards to pick fruit and vegetables. Chelte' had the finest clothing and jewelry put out for the royal family, and ordered the thickest floor mats assembled for the feasts. It was a momentous occasion, and she wanted her family and city presented in the best possible light.

In finest regal attire, with soaring feathered headdresses, fine woven clothing and copiously adorned with heavy jade and shell jewelry, the royal family received the Lakam Ha delegation in the throne room. Nearly every resident of Uxte'kuh crowded the main plaza for a glimpse of the visitors, as the warriors kept open a walkway to the throne room stairs. The royal steward announced the visitors as they entered.

"Kan Joy Chitam, Ahau of Lakam Ha, son of K'inich Janaab Pakal, K'uhul B'aakal Ahau."

A tall, slender man approaching thirty solar years, Kan Joy Chitam had unmistakable regal bearing. He was modestly but richly adorned, wearing the most precious forest green jade earspools and an exquisitely carved Sun God pectoral. His face was long and thin, with prominent straight nose sweeping toward the forehead and merging with an elongated skull. His countenance was the perfect example of highland Maya nobility. Crossing right arm over his chest to clasp the left shoulder, he bowed respectfully to Ox B'iyan.

The next visitor was announced.

"Aj Sul, Ah K'uhun of Lakam Ha, Ah Yahau K'ak to K'inich Janaab Pakal."

Bearing the Yahau K'ak—Lord of Fire title, Aj Sul was a ranking advisor to Pakal. He held one of the highest ceremonial and military titles, with a haughty presence that testified to his authority. His appearance was typical highland Maya, with slender face and body and the refined features of elite nobility. His adornments were only slightly less rich than Pakal's son. He offered the standard bow and stood beside Kan Joy Chitam.

"Yuhk Makab'te, Ahau of Lakam Ha, Administrator, Sahal."

The youthful noble had elegant bearing and a sophisticated manner, having attained a high position for one so young. His appearance and dress resembled that of Aj Sul, with a more arched nose and dip in the bridge. Intelligent eyes and softly sculpted, full lips gave him a pleasant look.

"K'akmo, Nakom of Lakam Ha."

Pakal's Warrior Chief was heavily built and the oldest member of the delegation. He exuded an aura of fierceness and bore scars of a seasoned warrior. His bare shoulders and arms were heavily muscled, his face square with prominent brow ridges and a less elongated skull. Bulging thigh muscles were barely concealed by his short skirt as he stepped purposefully forward and bowed to the ruler.

Two other minor nobles who attended the main delegates were introduced. They carried bundles to present as gifts to the ruler. The remainder of the contingent consisted of six servants. They were greeted by Uxte'kuh families of similar status, who would serve as their hosts.

"Our honor is beyond measure, and we are graced by your visit, Esteemed Lords of Lakam Ha," said Ox B'iyan. "Please come forward and take your places on the mats." He indicated luxurious mats set in front of a slightly raised throne platform, leaning forward and making hand gestures of welcome. To his right, the ruling family gathered. They remained standing as the Lakam Ha lords took their seats.

"Is that him?" K'inuuw Mat whispered into Chumib's ear.

Her brother shook his head, making the negative hand sign.

"Kan Joy Chitam is Pakal's second son," he whispered back.

Chelte' shot a displeased look at her children, but their scarcely audible words were lost in clinking and rustling as the Lakam Ha lords sat.

"Much is it our pleasure to be so congenially welcomed to your fine city," replied Kan Joy Chitam. "We have brought gifts to express our appreciation for your hospitality." He signaled for the two minor nobles to bring their bundles forth.

Bowing deeply, each offered his bundle. The royal steward and an assistant received and ceremonially opened the cotton cloths. The steward announced the gifts to the court in a sonorous voice.

"This gift bundle contains a large quantity of cacao pods, the highland variety of excellent quality. The next gift bundle holds several finely worked jadeite and obsidian blades, from very small to beautifully balanced hand knives."

"May these gifts, small expressions of the esteem my father Pakal carries for the Noble Ruler of Uxte'kuh, be pleasing to you," said Kan Joy Chitam.

"Ah! Indeed these are most pleasing gifts, for they are rare and valuable, and for these may we express our deep appreciation," responded Ox B'iyan. "My heart is glad to see the honored son of the great K'inich Janaab Pakal and his leading ahauob. How fares your revered father? Gods grant him many more years of good health."

Maya royal courts followed long-established protocols, including flowery language and the bringing of gifts by visitors. How one spoke was as important as the content of the speech, for words themselves were infused with sacred *itz*, the essence of divinity that permeated all things with life force energy. In honoring this sacred essence, words were arranged and spoken to be beautiful to the ears of listeners, both mortal and divine. Classic Maya courtly exchanges formed a poetic language that was unique.

"So it is, Holy Lord, that my father continues to enjoy vigor and good health, blessed as he is by the Triad Gods. Truly he is *juntan* of the Gods, the precious one who is much beloved. This is clear for all to see when he performs katun ceremonies and embodies Hun Ahau, First Born of the Triad, Lord of the Celestial Realm. From his own blood sacrifice arises the Vision Serpent, and of his body rises the Wakah Chan Te', the Jeweled Sky Tree that gives connections among the three realms. Through this he keeps covenant with the Gods and ensures prosperity, abundance, and peace to our people. Let us honor the name of our great ruler: K'inich Janaab Pakal, K'uhul B'aakal Ahau—Holy Lord of B'aakal."

The seated ahauob stood and raised hands, palms outward, in the gesture of blessing. Ox B'iyan and his family followed suit, and all intoned Pakal's name and title. When they sat again, the ruler inquired about Pakal's latest building programs in Lakam Ha, and discussion ensued.

"Our beloved ruler's chief architect, Yax Chan, has developed innovative construction techniques for the newer part of Lakam Ha, the palace and structures around the main plaza," said Yuhk Makab'te. In his administrative role, he was responsible for organizing the workforce and overseeing their performance and payment. "Using a trapezoidal support with high-strength wooden beams, he was able to extend the arches and build wider chambers with higher ceilings. The arches themselves stand higher than before; it gives an airy and spacious feeling. To create grace and harmony for the exterior of buildings, he designed slanting roof edges that are parallel to the slope of the pyramid or building's sides. This lovely symmetry impresses the eye with lightness and elevation. Roofcombs centered on the top of temples and most other buildings are more elegant than older constructions. Two thin, parallel honeycombed walls are built, braced against each other with thin beams for stability. The large filigreed openings in the honeycomb allow free flow of breeze, producing a lovely sound."

"My father enlarged the new palace not long ago," added Kan Joy Chitam. "The East Court is completely enclosed with mirror image, parallel chambers and stairs leading down into the court on all sides. The main outer stairway facing north extends the entire length of the new chamber, going directly into the East Court. It is now the principal entrance into the public areas of the palace. Our finest carvers created lavishly decorated façades that relate the city's victories. I believe no grander and more impressive palace entrance exists."

"It is my fondest desire to view these architectural marvels at Lakam Ha," said Ox B'iyan. "Surely the Triad Gods are greatly pleased by these works by their *juntan*."

"This too is our desire, and perhaps our coming will give cause for your visit," said Kan Joy Chitam.

K'inuuw Mat had listened with acute interest to the discussion of architecture. She could imagine the soaring, elegant buildings and wanted to learn more about how they were built. Now her attention jumped to another level. Kan Joy Chitam was about to address their purpose in coming to her city.

"Long has Uxte'kuh been an ally of Lakam Ha," he said. "Over many tuns we have assisted one another in trade and military affairs. Now comes time for an even closer association between our cities. The Holy B'aakal Lord, K'inich Janaab Pakal, has sent me to speak with you about a marriage between his youngest son, Tiwol Chan Mat, and your younger daughter, K'inuuw Mat."

Murmurs arose among the courtiers who filled the edges of the throne chamber. Rumors had, of course, been circulating about this very thing, but nothing was certain until the words were spoken. Chelte' beamed and K'inuuw Mat flushed, lowering her eyes. Chumib, sitting beside her, squeezed her arm and her sister Sak T'ul, well advanced in pregnancy, sighed.

Ox B'iyan nodded gravely, taking time to savor the moment and conceal his satisfaction.

"It is so; this is an enormous honor for our family. It is a momentous occasion that brings us gladness. We are delighted to enter negotiations over this marriage alliance," the ruler said with dignified solemnity.

Kan Joy Chitam crossed an arm over his chest, grasped his left shoulder and bowed while seated.

"Let it be so; we shall commence with negotiations as you direct," he said. The marriage gifting from the Lakam Ha ruler, following Maya traditions, would be elaborate and costly. The bride's father would naturally bargain for as much as he could get.

"As Nakom, I desire to emphasize the military advantages of this alliance," said K'akmo. "Lakam Ha has the most powerful forces and largest resources of all cities in our polity. Such assets will serve well in any case of threat to your city."

"Indeed so, perhaps an off-setting of the misadventures of Bahlam Ahau," said Ox B'iyan wryly. He intended to use the unapproved raids made by Pakal's brother-in-law, though many years ago, as a bargaining point.

"As you say, a closer alliance with Lakam Ha could forestall such opportunism in the future," muttered K'akmo.

"This is something we all shall anticipate in good trust," Kan Joy Chitam added quickly. He did not want the discussion to proceed in this direction. "Honored Ruler, might you introduce your daughter K'inuuw Mat to our delegation?"

"With great pleasure," replied Ox B'iyan, turning toward his family and signaling. Chelte' rose at once and helped K'inuuw Mat to stand, taking her elbow and ushering her before the visiting ahauob.

"Most esteemed Ahau Kan Joy Chitam, and most respected Lords of Lakam Ha, here I present my younger daughter, K'inuuw Mat," said Chelte'.

K'inuuw Mat bowed, crossing both arms over her chest in the bow of highest regard. At her mother's gentle push on the shoulder, she sank to her knees before Kan Joy Chitam and looked directly at him. His dark almond eyes seemed amused and not unkind, and the hint of a smile curved his lips. Her heart beat faster; he was indeed a handsome man. She hoped Pakal's youngest son was also as handsome.

"Much is it my pleasure to behold you, K'inuuw Mat," he said softly. "You appear to be a young woman of grace and charm. I understand your family has long been dedicated to Ix Chel, and you made the pilgrimage to Cuzamil not many tuns ago."

"Yes, Honored Lord," she replied, "and thank you for your kind words. My pilgrimage was seven tuns ago, although it seems only yesterday. In the tradition of my mother's family, women are devoted to Ix Chel, and serve her as best they can."

"Did you not want to serve the Goddess on Cuzamil?"

K'inuuw Mat concealed her surprise, keeping eyes and face neutral as she wondered how he knew so much about her.

"Indeed, we all would be blessed by such service, but mine was to be another path," she said smoothly.

"Ah. Is this what the Oracle told you?"

"Even as you say, My Lord. You are most well-informed."

"It is the business of rulers to be well-informed," he retorted.

She smiled sweetly, saying: "Then perhaps I can learn such skills from you."

Kan Joy Chitam laughed, nodding his head while his feathered headdress swayed.

"Perhaps you can, and many other useful things," he replied. "Your daughter has a wit, Lady Chelte'. Her countenance bears the true stamp of ancient bloodlines to our ancestors. My father will be pleased." He directed the last remark to Ox B'iyan, who nodded gravely.

"Let us settle you and your companions in your chambers in our modest palace," Chelte' said. "Later we will gather for a feast in your honor, and then you men may sally forth on your negotiations. I welcome you again to our city."

4

Kuy held up a round obsidian mirror, its black surface perfectly smooth and shiny. The back was decorated with a delicate multicolored mosaic of flowers and vines made of small pieces of cut stone. Less than a finger's thickness, it was the most exquisite mirror she had ever seen. Mirrors usually were made of iron pyrite or mica; these less reflective surfaces clouded the image. She angled the mirror up and down, peering around the edge to check the reflection. When the light was just right, the mirror's surface held an almost flawless reproduction.

"It is amazing! My reflection is so clear!" exclaimed K'inuuw Mat.

"It is clearer than any other mirror," agreed Kuy. "Where did it come from?"

"Kan Joy Chitam told me they traded for it, and it came from a far distant region to the south, a place of high volcanic mountains. He said the obsidian in that region is the finest quality, and their method of polishing the surface excels in making it reflective." She had received the mirror as an advance marriage gift from the Lakam Ha ruler.

"Now you see, Lady, how beautiful you are," said Kuy. After Sak T'ul married and moved to her husband's residence, his family provided her with attendants and Kuy remained in the ruler's household. Kuy came from a respected noble family, and serving as attendant to a member of the royal family was a prestigious position. She intended to accompany K'inuuw Mat to Lakam Ha, eager for new experiences in the region's major city.

"Am I?" murmured K'inuuw Mat. "Think you that I am beautiful?"

She studied her features in the shining reflection. The deep tones of obsidian made her skin appear darker, but the image was strikingly clear. Her neck was long with crisp chin angle, her lips full and nicely curved, her cheekbones set high in a slender face. She liked the tilt of her almond eyes and noticed long curving lashes that enhanced their depth. The nose was somewhat large for the face, she thought, but it was straight to the forehead as elites so desired. Turning her head, she glimpsed the elongated skull, emphasized by hair swept up to the crown in twists that formed a turban. Her earlobes drooped from wearing heavy earspools.

"Indeed, Lady K'inuuw, you are most lovely. I am certain the Lakam Ha delegation will so inform their ruler."

"Hmmm. Kuy, the ears need some jewelry, they appear forsaken."

Kuy handed the mirror to her mistress and went to the basket of jewelry. K'inuuw Mat turned the elegant mirror over and admired the mosaic on the back. Returning to the reflective surface, she held it flat and realized its' amazing clarity would serve well for scrying. Kuy returned and put into place white helmet shell earplugs and a double stranded necklace of smaller white helmet shells. Both women admired the contrast of dark skin and white jewelry.

"Ah, that is better," said K'inuuw Mat.

"A study in contrasting beauty," added Kuy.

"I wonder if the youngest son, Tiwol Chan Mat, is as handsome as his brother Kan Joy Chitam. There is, if I remember correctly, only three years' difference in their ages."

"So it is said among the servants from Lakam Ha," replied Kuy. "They both resemble their illustrious father."

"No doubt you will find an equally handsome man to marry in Lakam Ha," teased K'inuuw Mat.

"Goddess willing, may it be so!"

"It will be a great adventure for us," K'inuuw Mat said. "I find that I am eager for the journey to Lakam Ha. Waiting for the return delegation seems so long! I wish we could have returned with them now. How many moons will it take, think you?"

"Only two or three, Lady. They must bring a palanquin for your proper travel. Making such noble ladies trek through the jungle on foot would be unsuitable."

They exchanged looks and laughed, recalling the trip to collect blue orchids and its mishap.

"Yes, we must have no more snake bites before marriages," said K'inuuw Mat.

Time passed more quickly than she had anticipated, due to the numerous preparations her mother insisted upon. New clothing must be designed and woven, proper gifts selected for members of the Lakam Ha royal family, jewelry cleaned, sandals made, hair adornments and headdresses gathered, and many small details managed. K'inuuw Mat went through her personal items saved from childhood, making decisions about what to take. She certainly would bring the small yellow gourd decorated with conjuring symbols that held the strips of bark paper with her first moon blood. This precious itz, sacred to Ix Chel, was to use for attaining her heart's deepest desire. She knew to be selective in using these sacred offerings. When she burned the strips ceremonially, the Goddess would surely fulfill her request.

A bark paper book given by her father was another treasured possession; it was with this codex that she learned to read hieroglyphs. Studying the intricate, complex designs that held many layers of communication never ceased to delight her. Learning to read the Maya glyphs was an ever-unfolding process. She planned also to bring her scrying bowl and the special stones gathered at the hidden cove in Cuzamil. Bringing her collection of medicinal herbs was also necessary; some dried and kept in pouches, and several live plants growing in ceramic pots.

As she went to get the scrying bowl from its corner of her inner patio, dedicated as an Ix Chel altar, a thought occurred to her. She could do a scrying to see the face of her future husband. The idea delighted her, and she felt surges of excitement. She would make it a special occasion that she would keep secret. With her studies of calendar lore, she knew enough to select a fortuitous date for seeking important information. She would cast auguries for the perfect junction of the Haab and Tzolk'in calendars.

The Mayas used numerous calendars; tracking significant movements of the sun, moon, and wandering stars. They followed a continuous count of days from the start of the last creation, denoted when the final Baktun 13 rolled over into a new Baktun 0. This was the time when the real people—*Halach Uinik*—came into being. After failing in the first three attempts with the animals, mud people, and wood people, the Creator Gods sought assistance of the Primordial Ancestors and formed people from maize, blood, and water. In the B'aakal polity of her city, creation of the people of the bone (b'aak) was brought about through the union of the Primordial Mother Goddess Muwaan Mat and First Father—Hun Hunahpu. Their three sons formed the B'aakal Triad Gods, special patrons of the polity and founders of the Lakam Ha ruling dynasty.

Actually, she reflected, all the elite nobles of their polity came from this original bloodline, including her family. The purity of bloodlines back to the founders was a determinant of status, as well as eligibility to become a ruler. She was found suitable for a union with the highest elite, the ruling family of Lakam Ha. It was gratifying, and she felt a sense of destiny and duty.

She sat with a calendar codex open before her, and several red beans mixed with blue and white glass beads for casting. The patterns formed when she shook these in her hand and threw them on the mat would indicate dates. She would examine the codex and study the meanings of the dates, to discover which was best for her quest. Breathing upon them to invoke guidance of spirits, she flung them and scrutinized their configuration.

The first casting was for the Haab calendar date. The Haab was the solar calendar, used for following the seasons and guiding agricultural activities. The Haab consisted of 18 uinals composed of 20 kins or days. The 18 uinals, each with a name, formed the solar year that was counted as 360 days: $18 \times 20 = 360$. The mathematics of this system resonated through vast cycles and synchronized with many other calendars through its multiples. Maya astronomers knew that the full solar year had 365 days plus an additional quarter day. They compensated for this by adding an extra short 5-day uinal called Uayeb, and adding one day to the count every four years. The Haab was used to track solstices, equinoxes, and eclipses of sun and moon. Each uinal had a patron deity and characteristics.

She made a second casting for the Tzolk'in calendar date. This was the sacred ceremonial calendar, used by her people since time immemorial. It was composed of 13 numbers, each with a name and special qualities, and each having a patron God. The value 13 signified spirit and movement; it was the sacred number of the endless circle. These 13 numbers paired with the 20 days each having a name and deity. The mathematics of the Tzolk'in formed the mystical number 260, the period of human gestation and also resonant within many astronomical cycles: 13 x 20 = 260. In operation together, the Tzolk'in and Haab created a 52-year cycle called the Tunben K'ak—New Fire. It was a major celebration of renewal, in which all old fires were extinguished at dusk, except one sacred flame kept glowing through the night by priests, and used the next morning to relight all the city's fires.

There was magical numerology in the meshing of calendars. The Haab, Tzolk'in, and Tunben K'ak were all evenly divisible into the same large multiples. Such patterns were believed ordained by the Gods, giving numbers their living, holy qualities. The numbers actually were their patron deities, as real and present in daily life as others of the Maya pantheon.

K'inuuw Mat studied the patterns created by the beans and stones and sought further elaboration in the calendar codex. She had set intention for dates in the next several days, for she could not bear waiting to see the face of her future husband. The dates revealed by her augury were only two days away: 5 Pop for the Haab; 1 Ik' for the Tzolk'in.

The Haab date 5 Pop was packed with power. The number five carried qualities of empowerment and integration, bringing the potential for conflict or creativity. *Ho* was the Maya word for 5; a number of inquiry, comparison, and questioning and a word implying part of the whole. The entire realm of possibility existed within the whole. What one chose would unleash forces for harmony and completeness, or set up ingredients for discord and contention. Pop was the uinal of the leader or ruler, carrying qualities of initiative and dominance. The combination resonated of authority and potency.

The Tzolk'in date 1 Ik' spoke of creativity and change. The number one signified beginnings and unity; the Maya word **Hun** meant first and often was part of men's names. The day name Ik' meant wind, also common in names. As wind blew into cities and structures and shifted things, the qualities of Ik' pushed toward transformations. This pairing of newness, creativity, union, and change bespoke immense alterations in what was in place. There would be transfiguration in those affected by these patterns.

With such profound auguries, K'inuuw Mat waited impatiently for the day of portent to arrive. Since the two numbers were small, she knew it was best to do the scrying early in the day, which was divided into 13 segments from sunrise to sunset, and another 13 during the night. As the sun was sending bright rays over the walls of her patio, she set up with fresh water in the bowl and flower gifts to Ix Chel. Kneeling on a mat, she whispered the seer's invocation and made her request.

"Beloved Goddess Ix Chel, knower of all, seer of everything, grant me this request in your clear waters of life. Show me the face of the son of Pakal, he with whom I am to continue their illustrious dynasty. This one, K'inuuw Mat, your devoted servant, does ask in all love and humility. Your will guides me in all things."

She breathed over the stones, the most beautiful and perfect of her collection, and with full intent she dropped them into the bowl of water. Soft splashes sent a few cool droplets onto her arm, and she watched the ripples form, change, and resolve. The surface returned to stillness, reflecting clouds moving overhead. Her vision softened as eyelids drooped and she moved into a meditative state. Cloud patterns changed, swirled and danced in tantalizing patterns. A face began to form, wavering and distorting. She kept her eyelids half-closed and waited for it to take shape. Keeping her breathing steady and deep, she maintained concentration despite her quickened heartbeat. She did not want to become too eager and alter the verity of her vision. The face became clearly defined and seemed to glare at her out of the bowl.

It was a striking and strong face. The man looking back at her from the bowl had coarse features, with a huge arched nose and thick prominent lips. The upper lip curved sensuously while the lower lip protruded out, hanging slightly open. The face was a long oval with flattened cheekbones and a heavy, aggressive chin. Large, tilted almond eyes stared fiercely at her, with brooding hidden in their depths. He had the elite straight nose bridge, sloping forehead and elongated cranium. His neck was thick and heavily muscled, with the swell of powerful shoulders just visible. This was a face of intensity and forcefulness mixed with voluptuousness. Not a handsome face but a compelling one.

K'inuuw Mat gave a tiny gasp, her mind spinning. This man did not much resemble Kan Joy Chitam. Was her vision in error? Or, were the reports of Pakal's youngest son less than accurate? Perhaps the delegates wanted to provide the most pleasing impression for this match. Before the image dissolved, she looked intensely to imprint it upon her memory. Yes, she could see the family resemblance to Kan Joy Chitam, the same eyes and shape of face, the unmistakable regal bearing. Her intuition sensed the truth of the scrying image. She would trust in Ix Chel.

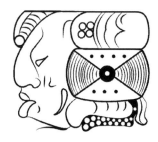

K'inuuw Mat—III

Baktun 9 Katun 12 Tun 0 – Baktun 9 Katun 12 Tun 0 (673 CE)

1

Kan Bahlam stood on the edge of long stairways that extended the width of three adjoined buildings. His gaze swept over the magnificent city that stretched across the broad plaza below, gleaming white in the brilliant tropical sun.

This is mine, he thought. *I am Ba-ch'ok, heir of the Bahlam dynasty. It is all rightfully mine . . . if only that tenacious old ruler would die.*

His father, K'inich Janaab Pakal, was now in his seventieth year and still going strong. The old man had been the ruler of Lakam Ha for fifty-eight years. It was enough. Now was the time for fresh leadership, changes in direction, creating something entirely new.

Looking over his shoulder, Kan Bahlam peered across the escarpment dropping precipitously just behind the three-building complex. The steep cliffs lifted his city high above vast plains below, covered with well-tended fields of maize, squash, and rows of beans that were dotted with bright red pepper bushes. Irrigation canals cut a neat cross-hatch pattern between crops and orchards of fruit and nut trees. The haze of mid-morning softened the flatness of the distant horizon.

The three parallel structures were set upon a raised platform that extended to the escarpment edge. A profusion of trees and jungle foliage covered the mountainside and hid the cascading river he could faintly hear. One of his family residences was tucked into an alcove beside the river. This complex on which he stood was his own; a school of astronomy, calendric studies, and sciences where the brightest minds of the city gathered to advance knowledge. The three buildings, low and rectangular, had multiple doors opening to chambers for study, reflection, and discussion. Here he and his contingent pursued new understandings of the mystical numerology hidden within Maya calendars.

He turned his tall, well-muscled frame back toward the immense main plaza of Lakam Ha, Place of Many Waters, major city of B'aakal polity, well beloved of the Triad Gods and home to his family, the Bahlam dynasty. Directly across the plaza to the west was another set of three buildings, modest-height pyramid temples that served as mortuary monuments. The largest one at the south end held the burial crypt and sarcophagus of his mother, Tz'aakb'u Ahau, called Lalak. The smaller two were memorials to his ancestors reaching back into distant time to the dynasty founder, K'uk Bahlam I. Several stylized skulls decorated the front panels of the northernmost temple, referred to as Temple of the Skulls. A massive pyramid temple stood alone at the north end of the plaza, used by Ah K'inob, the solar priests, for their ceremonies and auguries.

Covering the entire southern portion of the plaza was the immense palace complex. It was set on a three-tiered platform with wide stairways on three sides. The palace was framed by rectangular buildings with symmetrical sets of doorways. Richly carved panels rose between each door, and a long facade spanned the walls, also decorated with carvings and painted vibrant colors of blue, yellow, and black. An airy roofcomb lifted its latticework frame along the roofs. At evenly spaced intervals, carved panels set in the roofcomb displayed striking figures of ancestors, deities, and mythological beings. Inside the rectangle formed by the outer buildings were several other rectangular chambers that served various purposes: Pakal's throne room and reception chamber, the Popol Nah for meetings of the council of nobles, administrative chambers, and the private residences of the royal family. All of the buildings on the plaza were covered in smooth stucco, painted a warm red-orange color, providing a pleasing contrast to the white plaza and green forests. Only one building was left unpainted; the Sak Nuk Nah—White

Skin House. This was the most sacred shrine in Lakam Ha, dedicated to the Triad Gods, where the ruler would raise the Wakah Chan Te', the shining Jeweled Sky Tree by invoking the Vision Serpent in ritual blood-letting, seeking visions and guidance from the deities.

Beyond the main plaza to the west and south towered the K'uk Lakam Witz, the fiery water mountain, hovering over the fertile plains that reached to the Great North Sea, called Nab'nah. Draining from mountain heights and bubbling from springs dotting the ridge upon which the city rested, waters formed eight small rivers that cut across the plateau. These rivers merged to form four major cascades where their courses toppled over the rim of the ridge, feeding into the Michol River below. The Michol River, the nearby Chakamax and Tulixha Rivers, and the mighty K'umaxha River were the main sources of transportation in the regions around Lakam Ha. They provided rapid access to most regional cities, and eventually brought travelers to the Nab'nah and the Chik'in-nab, the Great West Sea whose vast expanses had never been crossed.

Lakam Ha was multiply blessed with an over-abundant water supply, rich fertile plains for farming, and a surrounding jungle teeming with plant and animal life. To contain the exuberant waters that led to flooding during the rainy season, Pakal had his engineers and architects build an underground system of aqueducts and reservoirs. These amazing subterranean structures channeled storm water, and were engineered to become narrow under the palace residential area. Water pressure forced upward flow through small ceramic tubes into palace chambers for fresh drinking, cooking, bathing, and fountains. Another system brought water to remove wastes from toilets that were built into bath chambers. Short-span bridges allowed walking across the rivers and joined the numerous white roads, called *sakbeob* that linked sections of the city.

A modest mountain ridge separated the new and old sections. To the west was the older part, its earliest structures nearly mythological and now deeply buried under newer construction. Some believed that the original ancestral city built by dynasty founder K'uk Bahlam, called Toktan or Place of Reeds, lay deep in the earth beneath the old section. The new part of the city was built almost entirely by Pakal. It was his vision of perfection, a statement in stone and stucco of grace, harmony, and grandeur worthy of honoring the Triad Gods and his hallowed dynasty.

Kan Bahlam had his own intentions for the cityscape. He envisioned the most spectacular statement yet made in building complexes, one that would reflect the essential beliefs of his people's religious charter, and leave no doubt in anyone's mind that what they saw in stone and stucco was a profound reflection of the sacred cosmos above. He had spent many years refining plans for this complex, consulting with the astronomers and architects in his Academy of Astronomy and Sciences. Once he became ruler, he would build a Triad Complex that would resonate with constellations in the sky. It would be redolent with symbolism that told the cosmological history of his people. His Triad Complex would be the crowning glory of the most magnificent city of B'aakal.

Kan Bahlam sighed. He frowned at the sun, as if to blame K'in Ahau for the passing of time. He had recently attained his thirty-eighth solar year. Many Maya rulers acceded to the throne well before this age, but they did not have an impossibly antiquarian father. In just two more years, Pakal would become a three-katun ruler. Few rulers lived to reign for three of these 20-year calendar periods. He should feel proud, but instead he felt annoyed.

Three men approaching from the plaza below broke his ruminations. As they began the ascent up the stairs, he recognized his brother-in-law Chak Chan, his younger brother Tiwol Chan Mat, and his assistant Yuhk Makab'te who had just returned from Uxte'kuh.

"Greetings, brother, we hope all is well with you," said Chak Chan. The men clasped arms in gestures of familiarity.

"As well as may be," Kan Bahlam replied. "It is good to see you well returned from your travels," he added to Yuhk Makab'te. "What news?"

"Negotiations for the marriage alliance with Uxte'kuh were successful. The agreements are made, though the bride price was high by my estimate," said Yuhk Makab'te.

"The alliance is most important," said Chak Chan. "Our esteemed ruler Pakal desired greatly that it be accomplished."

"Ah, but did you not say the bride is lovely?" Tiwol Chan Mat smiled cheerfully.

"Quite lovely. The younger daughter of Ox B'iyan is truly beautiful. You will be a happy man."

"When will she and her retinue arrive?" asked Kan Bahlam.

"Within two moon cycles, so the marriage may take place when Lady Uc shows her bright round face, glowing with love's quickening heartbeat, in the night sky at summer solstice," offered Chak Chan, an astronomer in the Academy of Kan Bahlam.

"Ever the sky watcher, and now also a poet!" exclaimed Tiwol Chan Mat.

"The palanquin contingent is underway," added Yuhk Makab'te. "They make haste for your throbbing desires, Tiwol, knowing for how long these remain unfulfilled."

The men laughed. Nobles of their status had no lack of opportunity to satisfy their sexual drives. The primary source was the Lunar Priestesses, women who dedicated their lives to sexual education and training for noble men. This system kept the lusts of youth contained, protecting the chastity of young noble women while teaching sexual skills to their future husbands. Ix Chel priestesses provided the noble women training in sexual skills, use of contraceptives, and techniques for conception. Premarital and extramarital relations were frowned upon, and being sexually continent was prized as a method for building inner potency.

"So, my brother's future bride is truly beautiful, by your good word, Yuhk Makab'te?" said Kan Bahlam.

"Indeed, My Lord," said the assistant. "By my honor, a shining jewel."

"A jewel you will do well to keep your hands off," shot Tiwol Chan Mat. His older brother's reputation as a womanizer was well known in the city.

"You do me wrong, brother!" exclaimed Kan Bahlam. "Can I not admire beauty for its own sake, and from a distance?"

"Much is allowed at a distance," observed Chak Chan.

"See you keep to it, brother," added Tiwol Chan Mat. "Let not such things cloud our closeness."

"Never. There are other gems for the picking." Kan Bahlam grasped his brother's shoulders and gave him a hearty hug.

Yuhk Makab'te watched Pakal's oldest and youngest sons as they stood beside each other. They could not have looked more different, he reflected. Tiwol Chan Mat was a younger and not as tall image of his father, with the classic highland Maya's slender body and features. Kan Bahlam resembled his mother Lalak, now an honored ancestor. He was tall, large and solidly built as she had been. The coarseness of his features could never be called handsome, but his visage was striking and powerful. The huge arched nose soared above unimposing cheekbones making his face unbalanced. Passion was barely contained by his thick sensuous lips. When he was preoccupied, his lower lip tended to droop and hang open. His large, tilted almond eyes were perhaps his best feature, holding both intensity and brooding pools of darkness. From the straight nose bridge to the elongated cranium, the rest of his head was what one expected of the lineage. His strong chin and muscular neck worked well with his large shoulders and body.

Tiwol Chan Mat was elegant and graceful, classically handsome and genteel. His long fingers testified to his talent as a ceramics artist. Kan Bahlam was infused with energy, potency, and authority with undertones of danger and dominion. His was a commanding presence not easily opposed.

Such a powerful man; born to be ruler, thought Yuhk Makab'te. Yet his life had already been full of disappointments. Now married for nearly 20 years, he had produced no children and insider knowledge was that a jungle fever in his youth had made him sterile. It was a doubly sad situation since his wife Talol was the sister of Chak Chan, one of their inner circle. Although Kan Bahlam kept his prodigious intelligence occupied with work of the Academy and his future building plans, it was amply clear that he chafed at his constraints. Until he became ruler, he could not begin any construction that would imprint his mark on the city, or take actions that would shape its history. And, unfortunately for Kan Bahlam, although undoubtedly to the city's benefit, Pakal showed few signs of decline. Pakal the Great, ruler for nearly two generations, longest reign recorded among Petén region dynasties, bringer of unparallel prosperity and peace to Lakam Ha.

Muk Kab awaited Pakal's visit with both eagerness and sadness. The Royal Steward had served his ruler for longer than most men's lives, but he could no longer carry out his duties. He shifted uncomfortably on the pallet, annoyed at his limbs' inability to follow his commands. Advanced age and an illness that weakened his muscles had kept him immobile for many moons. Pakal was coming to officially relieve him of his royal court duties, although in reality his replacement, who he had recommended, was already fulfilling this role.

An attendant pulled aside the drape covering the chamber door, bowed and formally announced the visitors' arrival.

"Here enter the K'uhul B'aakal Ahau, K'inich Janaab Pakal and his honored attendant, Tohom."

The majestic presence of the tall man entering the room never failed to thrill Muk Kab, regardless of their many years together. Pakal stood straight, despite his venerated age, taller than most men and with unmistakable regal bearing. Age had shrunken his muscles but touched his slender face lightly, leaving the classic elite features pleasingly handsome. The smile that curved his sculptured lips also shone from deep-set, dark almond eyes; a spark of vitality that enlivened all around him.

"Do not try to arise, Muk Kab," Pakal said. "Your homage has been given more times than either of us can remember."

The Royal Steward nodded and bowed his head, automatically trying to clasp his shoulder with his right hand in the standard greeting of respect, but his weakened arm only trembled at his side.

"Greetings and welcome, Holy Lord," Mut Kab muttered. His speech was mildly affected by the debilitating illness. "And to you, Tohom, I give thanks for coming."

Several large pillows were set upon the floor mats, so the visitors could sit at the level of Mut Kab's pallet. The stone slab that served as a bed was attached to one side wall of the chamber and covered with a reed pallet on which several thick, soft woven mats served as bedding. A light blanket covered him, even though the day was warm. Pakal and Tohom sat upon the pillows and the attendant brought cups of kob'al.

"It is a sad business, this growing old and slipping into decline," said Pakal. "Here we sit, three old men, in the twilight of our lives. Even though the paddlers of the celestial canoe will usher us into our next lives as ancestors in the stars, there is much we will miss in this Middleworld."

"Just so, the terrible beauty of life here leaves me nostalgic," said Tohom. Pakal's personal attendant was a few years younger, but his body was beginning to stoop and his strength was diminished.

"Ah, esteemed Lords, when the body has failed as much as mine, one welcomes the paddlers as the purveyors of release," said Mut Kab. "I am ready for the journey to Xibalba, to confront and outwit the Lords of Death. The next great adventure, to which I know you will send me well prepared."

"Indeed we shall; already the tools and ritual materials for navigating the Underworld are being gathered," Pakal assured.

"To the business at hand," Mut Kab continued with a sigh.

"Much is it my regret, most honored Royal Steward, that with this pronouncement I relieve you of your duties to my Royal Court," said Pakal gravely. "No ruler could have asked for a better steward; no words can fully express how I appreciate your years of service. We have seen much together."

"Much, indeed. With your vision and foresight, Lakam Ha has risen to its height, into a time of splendor and abundance." Mut Kab seemed lost in memories for some time. Then he murmured: "It is much my regret that I could not perform this one last service to you, Holy Lord, and head the delegation to Uxte'kuh."

"Be not troubled, Mut Kab," Pakal replied. "All went well with Kan Joy Chitam in charge. It was good for my son to assume that responsibility. He was in need of a challenge, some important diversion of his talents. He exercised skill in the negotiations, and we have sealed the alliance with this marriage." Pakal appeared thoughtful, rubbing his chin and smiling to himself. "It is difficult for my sons, most especially the middle one. Kan Bahlam has rulership to anticipate, and Tiwol Chan Mat knows he will most likely never rule as third son. Kan Joy Chitam sits in a place of ambiguity; as second son he might come to the throne, but he might not. And, I am living so long they all might well wonder if they will survive to see rulership!"

"None will ever be a finer ruler, Holy Lord," said Tohom. "Your reign will ever be seen as the apex of Lakam Ha, the greatest time of B'aakal."

Pakal nodded graciously to his attendant, adding: "You may underestimate Kan Bahlam; I believe there is greatness in him."

The two other men gave grunts of agreement. Moments of silence passed as each was lost in his contemplations.

"How soon does the bride of Tiwol Chan Mat arrive?" asked Mut Kab.

"We expect the entourage here within a moon cycle," Pakal answered.

"There is much yet to do," said Tohom. "Many preparations are yet needed to receive the Honored Lady and make her chambers in the palace comfortable. And then there are marriage arrangements to plan."

"Would that Lady Lalak was still here with us," sighed Pakal. His beloved wife had joined the ancestors nearly a year ago, and he missed her every day.

"We have placed Lady Talol in charge of overseeing these preparations," Tohom reminded him. The wife of Kan Bahlam was a competent organizer, if somewhat sour in personality. Long years of barrenness had embittered the once pleasant women.

"Yes, although my preference was for Te' Kuy, but her new baby son keeps her occupied," Pakal replied. Kan Joy Chitam's wife had suffered several miscarriages over the years, bearing one girl who survived and was now four years old. This new child, a son, was the much-awaited heir to the dynasty. His mother would not leave his side, determined to ensure his health and safety by the strength of her presence.

"It is for the best, as Lady Talol has precedence. Overlooking her for this responsibility would be insulting," said Tohom.

"You are correct, Tohom. Your sense of protocol is impeccable," Pakal laughed.

"Use the talents of Akan, now your new Royal Steward," added Mut Kab. "He is quite ingenious and will plan a fitting reception for the royal bride. He has a sense of what brings comfort to women. A good man and a good choice."

"Thanks to you. For whatever years may remain to both of us, I will treasure your service to our city, Mut Kab," said Pakal. "All your needs will be provided, and I will visit often. May the Underworld Jaguar Sun, Mah Kinah Ahau, be your constant companion in the journey to come."

2

Talol's sharp eyes scanned the residence chamber of the royal bride. Nothing escaped her penetrating vision, and none were spared her caustic tongue if aught was found lacking. The rectangular chamber was set against the outside wall of the palace with an eastern view. Several T-shaped windows allowed the sun's early rays to etch golden patterns upon the opposite wall, giving the room a cheerful and bright atmosphere. The only other opening was the entrance doorway facing an inside corridor. Most palace rooms were darker. The chamber was sparsely furnished, in typical Maya style, with several thick floor mats, a large wicker basket for holding clothes, a low tripod ceramic plate for personal items, and a decorative vase standing waist high, to be filled with fresh flowers or dried reeds, according to the season. A large water basin was built into a stucco stand against a side wall. Attached to the palace plumbing system, the basin had a constant flow of clear water from the aqueduct below. A separate chamber for bathing and toileting was a short distance down the corridor.

The sleeping bench was built against the other side wall, elevated to knee height to discourage crawling insects. It was the mat and blanket on the sleeping bench that caught Talol's eye. She turned abruptly to face the servant hovering behind her.

"Is this the best you could find?" snapped Talol. She had once been an attractive woman, but years of suffering had etched frown lines on her forehead and given a hard set to her mouth. "Among all the bedding in this palace, this is what you thought suitable for a royal bride? See, the mat is coming unraveled at one corner, and the blanket has snags. Cannot we present a finer appearance for her sleeping chamber? For shame! As you value your position, and it is one envied by many women of your status, remedy this affront to the taste and wealth of our great city. Take these rags and go at once! Mark that you replace them with our finest quality, or you shall answer for it."

The trembling young woman quickly bowed and sprinted into the corridor on her mission. Talol fingered the woven drape that hung on a rod anchored in small holes at the upper borders of the doorway. It felt supple yet substantial, heavy enough to keep out drafts and muffle voices. The design of chevrons between stylized flowers was pleasing, and the subtle colors, primarily mossy green and tan with golden hued flowers, exuded the quiet of a forest glade. It was a well-crafted fabric and met Talol's standards. The floor mats were appropriately plush and similarly colored. She made a mental note to select floor pillows herself, to properly coordinate the color scheme.

She might even accompany her attendants when they went to collect flowers. In the early summer, the forest would be abundant with many varieties. Reviewing the choices, she mentally selected several that would create a harmonious bouquet. Humming to herself with satisfaction, she pushed aside the door drape and walked down the cool interior corridor, rounded a corner and arrived at her own palace chambers. All the members of the royal family had chambers in the expansive palace, as well as additional residences in other locales in the city. They would all be staying in the palace chambers for the arrival of the new bride, and remain there until after the wedding.

Settling onto a floor mat and leaning against large pillows, Talol signaled her attendant to bring her afternoon refreshments, kob'al made of fresh ground corn and tropical fruit juices. Her self-pleased mood stayed with her through the first several sips of the deliciously cool drink. But that agreeable state vanished as soon as she thought of her husband.

Where is he now, and what mischief is he up to? Unbidden, these thoughts clamored in her mind, as they did all too frequently. It was shameful enough that she remained childless for over a katun of marriage, but for him to so blatantly seek the bed of other women—and yes, at times other men—made her situation unbearable. She felt certain that the nobles cast pitying glances in her direction, and that the attendants gossiped behind her back. Even worse, the servants most likely made jest of the haughty royal lady who could not satisfy her husband's appetites. If she could only catch them at it, their lives would no longer be worth living!

Sipping again, it seemed the kob'al had suddenly soured. She was no longer capable of shedding tears; those had been exhausted many years ago. The hot flames of anger had burned down to smoldering resentment. She found no more purgative pleasure in fighting with her husband. Although she felt justified in blaming him for her barrenness and knew that most nobles were aware of his sterility caused by fever, it was little comfort. The nagging doubts crept upon her repeatedly; maybe she actually could not conceive. Of course, his many years of womanizing had produced no offspring, at least none that were claimed. But, her few sexual liaisons had been equally non-productive.

The cold fist of despair curled in her stomach again. She put her drink aside, unable to swallow.

Now this new royal bride is coming. She and Tiwol will have children. Kan Joy Chitam and Te' Kuy now have two, and the last a boy. We are lost.

If she could muster any compassion for her husband, it would be due to this: they both had failed to produce an heir to the dynasty. How that must eat away inside him, she could only imagine. He was ambitious, he was a born leader, he was a many-talented man who most considered a genius. It must be excruciating for him to realize that no child of his loins would accede to the throne of Lakam Ha. She might be sad for him; she might even comfort him if it were not for his sexual promiscuity.

"Arrragh!" The painful cry burst from Talol's throat. When her attendant popped into the chamber to see what she needed, she gave a hand signal to get something quickly.

"Bring me picul-aqahla," she commanded.

"At this time, My Lady?" The attendant's voice quavered as these words escaped from her lips reflexively. The fermented, mildly alcoholic drink was never taken until the evening meal.

"Cease your impertinence! Do you wish to continue serving me? Get me picul-aqahla!"

The startled attendant dashed out as Talol's shout echoed off the stucco walls. Quickly the attendant returned and placed a tall ceramic cup in her mistress' hands, bowed and departed in haste. Talol knew this would become instant gossip in the palace.

Now she has resorted to alcoholic drink in the afternoon, they would say. *Why not? Something must be my consolation.*

Tiwol Chan Mat tarried at his residence in the Sutzha River Complex. He was reluctant to move back into his palace chambers, for he felt much more comfortable here. The modest residential structure had an ideal location; seated at the edge of a small level meadow that bordered cascades, its patio was open on one side to give full view of the waterfall and pond. Several attached buildings formed an L-shape, doors opening onto the patio. These provided sleeping and bathing chambers, as well as rooms for dining and other activities. Only the reception chamber opened onto the main plaza of the Sutzha River Complex. Its back door gave access to a second small meeting room that faced the patio. The buildings were one storey and had the sloped roof eaves and delicate roofcombs typical of Lakam Ha's new style.

This residence had been given to Tiwol by his father, shortly after his mother's death. Pakal could not bear to stay here, for it evoked too many heart-wrenching memories. The meadow had been a magical clearing beside hidden jungle cascades where he and Lalak realized their love for one another and came to actually know each other after years of marriage. Here they had first joined in passionate and truly loving union. From this joining was born their first surviving child, Kan Bahlam. Later Pakal had the residence built, and they spent many happy hours in its convivial embrace. Here also Lalak passed her final days in the Middleworld, and they said farewell while pledging undying love. Pakal's heart contained an empty chasm afterwards; she had left too soon, and he could not endure their place of rapture.

It was a perfect place for Tiwol. Buffered from plaza and larger complex activity, it gave a sense of seclusion. The patio was surrounded by a tree canopy, and across the pond the bank rose abruptly to the tall escarpment that formed the base of Lakam Ha's main plaza ridge. Birds twittered in treetops, insects buzzed, and monkeys chattered; these jungle sounds blended with the splashing waterfall. Dragonflies and butterflies sipped in the calm eddy of the pond, and occasionally small cranes fished its depths. When the river left the pond, it coursed into rapid descent down the escarpment in a series of crashing falls and swirling currents. The cliff was too steep for building, and the main complex was set behind Tiwol's residence.

Tiwol used one of the chambers for his art work; he was a skilled clay sculptor. Nobles were encouraged to develop their talents in various forms of art, including ceramics, sculpting, painting hieroglyphs, writing poetry and verse, music, and for women, weaving. Society had an artisan class, and the line between them and nobles not infrequently became blurred. It was becoming more common for non-nobles to move into leadership positions, not just in the arts, but in politics as well. Tiwol's specialty was creating life-like replicas, moderate sized figurines that were in great demand. He had an uncanny talent for reproducing facial features and expressions accurately, and shaping fine details of adornment and dress. His figurines were especially valued as grave goods; they were interred as an expression of the lifestyle and work of the deceased. Tiwol had a steady hand for writing intricate Maya glyphs in the flowing cursive style of his city, and his color palate was sprightly with a unique signature. His painted pottery could be seen in most noble homes of Lakam Ha, and was sought by visitors from polities both near and far away.

He set aside his current work, a large platter for serving fruit at banquets that was commissioned by a wealthy trader of Tulum, a prosperous coastal city of the K'ak-nab, the Great East Sea. It should be finished before his marriage, but he doubted that was possible with his moving to the palace. Giving a sigh, he washed paint from his hands and reviewed his schedule again. Maybe he could sneak away, miss a royal dinner or two, avoid some reception or another, and return to paint. His art fed his soul and bolstered his self-regard. He smiled inwardly at being such a center of attention now;

surely that would irk Kan Bahlam. His arrogant older brother needed to be set down a bit from time to time.

Thinking of his marriage did quicken his pulse, for he had been without intimate female companionship for some time. It was by his own choice; he had tired of the Lunar Priestesses and was reluctant to seek an affair. These assignations always came with undesired consequences, by his observation. He shook his head at how many times Kan Bahlam had to pay off some irate husband or arrange a favorable marriage for some artisan's daughter. No, that was not the path for him, and he thanked the deities that his sex drive was not so intense that it pushed him into foolish liaisons.

Now feeling eager, Tiwol began gathering his things for moving into his palace quarters.

3

The royal palanquin swayed in rhythm with the bearers' footsteps, side to side in a hypnotizing succession. Kuy dozed against plump pillows, a tendril of hair swinging across her forehead in time with the palanquin's sway. K'inuuw Mat resisted the hypnotic effect, eager for the first sight of her new city. She knew it could not be far now; her guides told her they would arrive at the base of the mountain after two days walk across the plains. The second day was reaching late afternoon, she gauged by the angle of sunlight through the palanquin drapes. Leaning forward, she pushed a drape aside to look out. The entourage was proceeding along a wide sakbe that cut a straight path through orchards of avocado and mamey trees. She was impressed by how large the orchards and cultivated fields were; they stretched for the better part of a day's walk. They also blocked her view unless she leaned far out to peer around the palanquin's side.

She waited a few more moments, and then decided she would risk it. Her patience with the journey had been worn out; she had to see what was ahead. Balancing carefully on her knees, she held onto a pole with one hand and pushed the drape aside with the other. The drape swayed precariously and she nearly lost balance; quickly she wrapped the drape around her neck and caught the platform edge. It was rather awkward, but gave stability to crane her neck as far out as she could. The white road, coated with crushed limestone, ran straight and gave view through the row of tree foliage. In the distance, she could see a mountain rising precipitously to the sky. Never had she beheld such a high mountain. Its peak was shrouded in misty clouds, its sides forested densely, and sparkling sunlight was reflected off a cascading set of waterfalls. Although she could not see the river, she knew it was there from descriptions her guides provided.

Squinting, she tried to bring the mountainside into better focus. Was it her imagination, or did she see a reddish structure hovering on a cliff? She wondered how a city could be built upon such a high mountain. Her focus was so intent that she was startled to hear a man's voice beside the palanquin.

"We will soon be there; do you see our city upon the mountain?"

With flushed cheeks, K'inuuw Mat turned her head to meet the laughing eyes of Kan Joy Chitam. She nodded and smiled.

"I am eager to see Lakam Ha. Yes, I think I did see a building," she replied.

"We will be in the city by sunset. A runner was sent alerting the boatmen to be ready for taking us across the river," said Kan Joy Chitam. "Then follows a steep climb up the sakbe to the main city plaza. This is a new entrance into our city that my father had built nearly six tuns ago. It is wider and has fewer curves than either of the other two paths that ascend beside the north and east cascades. And, it is less steep, although you may find that hard to believe."

"Was it difficult to build a city upon these high mountain ridges? How did your workers achieve that feat?" K'inuuw Mat settled back in a cross-legged position, holding the drape aside more widely. She felt more secure but still held onto the pole. Kuy stirred and opened her eyes, but remained recumbent while listening. Kan Joy Chitam entertained them with descriptions of how Lakam Ha was constructed until they reached the river.

The Michol River was running low during the late part of the dry season. The canoe crossing was easy, and the women relieved to step down from the palanquin and walk. Although K'inuuw Mat wanted to keep walking up the steep sakbe, Kan Joy Chitam insisted it was not proper for a royal bride to arrive on foot, and she reluctantly climbed back into her now acutely tilted and decidedly unstable-feeling transport. If this was the less steep road into the city, she could only imagine how terrifyingly sheer the other two must be. Both women held onto forward poles to keep from sliding out the back drapes of the palanquin, while their bearers panted heavily with effort.

Upon climbing the final rise, the bearers put the palanquin down while attendants came to tie back the drapes. Kuy brought out small headdresses from her travel bag, a cloth to wipe her mistress' face of road dust, and tried to smooth their huipils. A contingent of greeters arrived, including fresh bearers, and with Kan Joy Chitam and his retinue in front, they made procession into the main plaza accompanied by drums, whistles, and conches.

Her view unobstructed, K'inuuw Mat marveled at the cityscape around her. The main plaza was huge and built upon three wide platforms. To her left was a long, narrow complex with a towering pyramid temple as its edge. To her right appeared a string of three pyramid temples of ascending height, their stairways leading up stepped pyramid sides to a single temple chamber on top crowned by exquisitely painted, airy roofcombs. She had never seen such beautiful structures and wondered why their shapes made such a pleasing impression. Behind these three structures rose level after level of platforms climbing a tall peak, with several small buildings halfway up and an immense complex of modest height pyramids on top. She counted six but felt sure there were more hidden from view.

Kuy tapped K'inuuw Mat's shoulder and pointed behind them. Twisting around, K'inuuw gasped as the setting sun cast golden highlights upon roofcombs and darkening shadows fell on stairways of complex after complex poised upon hilly terrain as far as she could see. Some were residential with trails of smoke curling upward from cooking fires. It appeared that every possible buildable surface was covered with city structures.

When the two women turned forward again, they were entranced by lengthening shadows across the broad white expanse of the main plaza. On the far end of the plaza arose the most magnificent building that they had ever seen. It could be nothing else but the royal palace, of which they had heard wondrous tales. The palace complex was essential a huge square with amazingly symmetrical, long rectangular buildings all around its edges. As they approached its northwest side, two twin buildings greeted them, each building with six equal sized doors divided by intricately decorated piers, and set upon a triple platform base with wide stairways leading up the middle third of the platform span. A narrow passageway ran between these buildings. The utter symmetry of these two buildings was breath-taking. The eaves and the roof mimicked each other in harmonious angle, and the roofcombs spanned the entire roof length. Although the figures decorating the piers, eaves, and roofcombs were too far away to be seen clearly, they leapt to life in rich coloration cast by the last sunrays: blue, green, yellow, white glowed as if by magic.

A number of people crossed the plaza following their own purposes, perhaps returning home for the evening meal or tending to some duty. There was no formal welcoming group, although many glanced curiously at the palanquin and its small retinue, preceded by several musicians. Passing a corner of the palace, the procession was engulfed in shadows cast by the mountains. Kan Joy Chitam waited until the palanquin caught up with him, then walked alongside talking to the women.

"We are passing by the part of the palace called the subterranean," he explained. "Below those two long platforms is a maze of tunnels connecting to small chambers. These are used to simulate the Underworld when we hold our rituals based on the history of our people's creation. One tunnel leads to the Sak Nuk Nah, our most sacred shrine. When the ruler climbs stairs from the tunnel into the shrine, he becomes First Father—Hun Hunahpu resurrected from the clutches of the Death Lords, reborn as the Young Maize God. It is most dramatic; you will have many opportunities to observe this compelling ritual."

Both women looked at the smooth surfaces of the platforms, reached by several narrow sets of stairways. Only a small chamber with three doorways at the far end of the top platform appeared to offer access to the tunnels below. If not pointed out, these would remain concealed from visitors. Their palanquin rounded the southernmost corner of the palace, and in the dusk they could see palm trees growing beside a river, its banks lined with plaster forming an aqueduct. A short-span bridge led across to another huge complex that sprawled over gentle hillsides. Smoke from cooking fires and fruit trees growing in patios signaled that it was a residential area. They arrived at a wide stairway leading up the three-platform base of the palace to another set of symmetrical rectangular buildings, very similar to those they first viewed. The bearers set the palanquin down.

"These stairs lead to the royal residences of the palace," said Kan Joy Chitam. "Your long journey is finally ended. Welcome to your new home at Lakam Ha."

Assistants quickly helped the women to step out of the palanquin. As they straightened their huipils and adjusted headdresses, a regal looking woman and her retinue descended the stairway. Four men carried torches against the gathering darkness. Kan Joy Chitam gestured toward the regal woman then turned to his charges.

"Esteemed ladies of Uxte'kuh, may I introduce my sister-in-law, the Great Lady Talol, wife of the Bahlam dynasty Ba-ch'ok, Kan Bahlam," he said, bowing to all.

Talol bowed, crossing right arm over her chest to grasp left shoulder. Her stern visage bore no sign of a smile, and her slender body moved stiffly. The two women returned a bow.

"Welcome and good end to your travels," she said. "Receive my greetings on behalf of our K'uhul B'aakal Ahau, K'inich Janaab Pakal. It is my great pleasure to act as your hostess as you settle into your chambers in the palace. Whatever you shall need or want, do not hesitate to inform me. Any questions you may have, know that I am here to provide answers. We, the royal family and the people of Lakam Ha, rejoice at the arrival of the honored bride of Tiwol Chan Mat, and her respected attendant, Kuy."

"Much do we appreciate your welcome, Lady Talol," replied K'inuuw Mat. "We are grateful for your generous help and shall avail ourselves of it often. We indeed find this to be a good end to our travels."

"Quite so. Undoubtedly you are fatigued from your days upon the road, so I will convey you straight to your chambers," said Talol. "Tonight is a time for rest, in consideration of your needs, so you will understand the lack of formal ceremony to welcome you. Tomorrow you shall be received by our ruler, Holy Lord Pakal. He is most eager to meet and become acquainted with his newest daughter-in-law. Shortly after that, you will be introduced to your betrothed and the royal family."

"All in perfect consideration of you, Lady K'inuuw Mat," added Kan Joy Chitam. "Ours is a large royal family and we do not want to overwhelm you, all at once."

K'inuuw Mat thought she detected a mischievous twinkle in his eyes to accompany the slightest wry smile turning up the corners of his mouth. She also caught Talol's frown shot at her brother-in-law before the lady's face became inscrutable once again.

"You have been the very essence of consideration, Lord Kan Joy Chitam," K'inuuw Mat replied. "I must give deepest thanks for your kindness throughout your visit to my city, and your attentiveness to our every need during the journey here. No better ambassador could be found for your great city and esteemed family."

Kan Joy Chitam bowed deeply, clasping his shoulder. His smile was even more wry.

"No doubt you are eager to reunite with your wife and babes," K'inuuw Mat continued. "Please do not tarry on our behalf. We are in excellent hands with Lady Talol."

"Then I shall bid you all goodnight," said Kan Joy Chitam. "Tomorrow we shall gather again to continue our friendship," he added to K'inuuw Mat.

"This way, Ladies K'inuuw Mat and Kuy," said Talol, gesturing up the stairway. "Attendants will bring your bags and bundles. You will find a light repast waiting in your chambers, with your own servants close by. May you find your first rest in our palace congenial and peaceful."

The shrill cries of parrots awoke K'inuuw Mat as brilliant morning sunbeams streamed through the T-shaped windows and bounced off the wall of her chamber. She sprang to her feet and peered out a window just wide enough to admit her face. Below she saw a stream of people passing on the walkway next to the aqueduct, all busy with their morning's tasks. Curling smoke drifted lazily from residential complexes across the river, wafting smells of roasting corn cakes and whetting her appetite.

She did not have long to wait for her morning meal, brought by servants accompanied by Kuy, whose quarters were nearby. Over warm corn cakes and fresh fruit, the two women remarked on the beauty of their new home. As they finished eating, a young noble woman entered the chamber and introduced herself as Tukun, assigned to be palace attendant to K'inuuw Mat. It was an honor to be chosen for this prestigious position, she explained, and she hoped to serve well for many years.

Tukun explained the palace routines and described locations of various places including the *Pib Nah*, the "oven house" or sweat bath that was very popular among residents. She would later guide them to the royal family dining area, a wide veranda facing a private inner patio, where all would gather the next afternoon for a welcoming feast. After the two ladies completed their morning bathing and toileting in the adjacent bath chamber, supplied with clear water through the palace aqueduct system, she would convey them to the informal reception chamber of the ruler, K'inich Janaab Pakal. He planned to welcome the Uxte'kuh ladies first by himself; something Tukun considered a special boon. She advised fine but less formal attire, since this meeting was not in the Royal Court throne room. That ceremonious event would take place several days in the future, when the bride would be introduced to the nobles of the city.

The women found the bath chamber amazing. It was spacious, with a sunken tub through which a continuous supply of water flowed. In the summer its coolness was welcome; in the colder season jugs of heated water were added. A bench at sitting height was built against one wall, with an opening for toileting that emptied into a separate water flow system used to remove wastes. Such conveniences were unknown in every city K'inuuw Mat had visited, and she praised Lakam Ha's modern technology. She was eager to visit the Pib Nah, since a steam bath was something that she had not experienced before. Tukun assured her they would find time for this soon.

Dressed in well-made and subtly embroidered huipils, wearing turban headdresses with beads instead of feathers, the two women followed Tukun through a long corridor. It was wider and taller than those of K'inuuw Mat's residence in Uxte'kuh, giving a spacious feeling. She was glad to have a guide, as the inner corridors of the palace formed a complex maze. The corridor opened onto an inside patio lined on two sides by a veranda, its ceiling supported by high arches and walls painted with graceful floral and watery motifs. At the far end of the veranda was a chamber with a wide doorway; standing beside it was Talol.

Talol bowed as they approached; her manner was formal and aloof.

"Greetings of the morning," she said. "I trust you slept well. We shall wait here a few moments until the K'uhul B'aakal Ahau K'inich Janaab Pakal enters his reception chamber."

K'inuuw Mat and Kuy returned the bow as Tukun hovered in the background.

"Our rest was excellent," replied K'inuuw Mat. "We have been marveling at the modern facilities of the palace. Tukun has been most helpful in showing us around and giving orientation." She nodded to her new attendant and smiled.

"As it should be. And, as you observe, our Holy Lord Pakal serves as a fount for creativity in many areas. Seldom has a city been so blessed with his quality of leadership. You are fortunate to be here." Talol stated this like undisputable fact that all should know, tilting her chin forward in a gesture of arrogance.

K'inuuw Mat raised her eyebrows slightly but kept her expression smooth. Kuy appeared intimidated, revealed by the small drop of her shoulders and downcast eyes. Silently K'inuuw Mat called upon Ix Chel for strength. She would not let this woman intimidate her.

The sound of footsteps within the chamber signaled Pakal's presence, and a commanding voice resounded: "You may bring our honored guests in, Talol."

She swept inside the chamber and bowed deeply, waving an arm toward the women following her.

"Here with me are the ladies of Uxte'kuh, may you be pleased to receive Lady K'inuuw Mat and her attendant, Kuy."

K'inuuw Mat knew the expected routine was to drop to the knees and bow to the floor, both arms crossed on the chest. The Holy Lord of a great city was considered to be divine, the very embodiment of the Gods. Pakal was reputed to be a powerful shaman-ruler, one who commanded forces of the Upperworld and Underworld, one who raised the Vision Serpent in bloodletting rituals and communed with the Triad Deities and ancestors. His apotheosis was completed while he still lived; so said the traders and emissaries of the region.

She could not resist a first glimpse at the hallowed ruler. Even as Kuy was already folded on her knees with forehead against the floor,

K'inuuw Mat lifted her eyes to view Pakal as she sunk gracefully, and most slowly, downward.

Pakal sat with his long body draped casually across the pillows covering the low raised platform. One knee was bent while the other leg dangled across it, a typical posture for rulers during informal audiences. He held the right hand facing his visitors, palm open in the gesture of blessing; the left hand resting on his thigh made the gesture of dispensing. From a distance, it was hard to tell his age, although K'inuuw Mat knew he had attained three and a half katuns; seventy solar years. His limbs and body were slender but still had defined musculature; he wore only a loincloth with decorated waistband and large pectoral collar of colored beads and shells. On his elongated cranium was an elegant headdress of white heron feathers accented by rare blue quetzal tail feathers that trailed down his back. He wore jade earplugs with white shells embedded, with matching wrist and ankle bands. His feet were bare, a common practice while inside one's quarters.

The outstanding effect was to create the image of relaxed elegance and natural power. Here was a man who had no need to prove himself or create a statement of dominance. His very nature was that of command and leadership.

K'inuuw Mat did not have time to study his face, for she had to continue her homage by settling onto her knees as had Kuy. Both remained in this deeply bowed position until Pakal told them to rise and take seats upon the floor mats next to his platform.

"Great is my pleasure to welcome you both to Lakam Ha," said Pakal. "Lady K'inuuw Mat, we are filled with happiness and greatly honored that you have consented to join in marriage with Tiwol Chan Mat. This is a union that much benefits both of our cities and dynasties. It is my fondest wish that it also bring satisfaction and joy to you and my son."

"My heart is singing at your kind welcome, Holy Lord Pakal," replied K'inuuw Mat. "For myself and my family, and for my city, may I return gratitude that this union has been agreed upon. It is my destiny to serve the Gods and my felicity to join your revered family, the Bahlam dynasty. I can only give highest praise to the welcome given to us, to the attention and solicitation of the Lady Talol and palace attendants. We have been made most comfortable, and we give deepest thanks."

Looking directly at Pakal's face from a closer point, she saw the clear resemblance to Kan Joy Chitam. She had been told that her betrothed, Tiwol Chan Mat, also looked like his father, but her vision had informed her otherwise. A flicker of confusion crossed her mind, but she could not dwell upon it as the conversation continued with Pakal asking about experiences on the journey, and the state of affairs in her home city and with her family. Kuy, sitting a little behind her mistress, became more relaxed although her face still registered awe at being in the great ruler's presence. She only murmured an occasional "yes that is so" or gave a nod in agreement.

"I have heard, Lady K'inuuw Mat, that you were trained as an acolyte of Ix Chel upon her island of Cuzamil," Pakal said, redirecting the conversation.

"Indeed, that is correct," K'inuuw Mat replied. "In my family, we have a tradition of dedicating one daughter to serve the Goddess. My sister did not have inclination, so it appeared I would be the one. When my mother took us to Cuzamil for my first moon ceremonies, I was able to study the Goddess' arts and showed aptitude as a seer. I also learned healing skills, although not completely trained as an Ix Chel healer."

"Why did you not remain on Cuzamil to serve Ix Chel?"

"The Oracle of Ix Chel gave prophecy for my destiny, and it was not to continue as an acolyte. It was to . . . in the words of the Oracle, my life would unfold in the high court of royalty. She also said that dynasties would abide through me, and . . . ah, that leaders would seek my wisdom." K'inuuw Mat blushed as she repeated the prophecy, hoping it did not sound too pretentious.

Pakal paused, appearing absorbed in some memory.

"Dynasties would abide through you . . . yes, that stirs memories within me, things I have not considered recently," said Pakal softly. He glanced at Talol, who held her body rigidly but kept her face impassive.

"That is quite a prophecy from the Oracle," he continued. "Were you disappointed, since you felt called to serve the Goddess?"

"In truth, I was saddened, and I resisted in my heart for some time," said K'inuuw Mat. She felt an odd affinity with Pakal, as though she could share her innermost secrets with him. "When I returned home with my mother and sister, I was withdrawn and tried to think of ways to escape back to Cuzamil. Then some things happened . . . the Goddess gave me signs that I could not ignore. She made it clear that I must accept the Oracle's prophecy. Now I am resolved to fulfill the destiny given me by the Goddess."

"Ah, your abilities as a seer, or perhaps a visionary, did continue," Pakal observed.

Their eyes met and held for what seemed a very long time. K'inuuw Mat felt that she was falling into depthless pools hidden in his black eyes, pools of mystical knowledge that drew her into comradeship. She merged into those depths, filled with a sense of security within magical realms. Their visionary souls connected beyond words or mental images.

"There is much that we have in common, Lady K'inuuw Mat," breathed Pakal, almost too softly to be heard. "We shall meet often again and speak of these things. Let me say with all sincerity, that I am happy the Oracle of Ix Chel set your destiny to arrive here, to join my family. And, I am certain that my son Tiwol will be even happier."

Pakal spoke more about his son, praising Tiwol's talents as a ceramics artist and describing some of the amazing figurines he crafted. He included his other sons, mentioning Kan Joy Chitam's developing diplomatic abilities, which K'inuuw Mat eagerly confirmed by telling about the negotiations conducted to seal the marriage alliance. When Pakal spoke about his oldest son, Kan Bahlam, she thought she detected something amiss. Pakal praised Kan Bahlam for his intelligence and leadership in forming a school of astronomy and mathematics, which was exploring intricacies of numerological relations among star clusters and moving stars. He mentioned his son's travels through the Maya world, far beyond their region, and the good will for intra-city trade and firming up of alliances that were accomplished. Kan Bahlam brought back information about the Goddess Ix Chel's island and her followers, which raised Pakal's interest and led to seeking an alliance with families of coastal cities. K'inuuw Mat hastened to relate her family background, with her mother coming from the coastal city Altun Ha. Pakal's knowing smile confirmed that this was part of his reason for seeking her lineage in marriage.

As the meeting was drawing to a close, Pakal asked how she liked the palace. This spurred K'inuuw Mat to ask about its unique structures.

"Your palace is surprisingly lovely for such an immense building," she said. "It seems light and airy, although it is massive. The outsides of buildings are so pleasing; there is some symmetry that I cannot explain. Rooms and corridors have such high ceilings and seem wider than those of my city; I wonder how this was accomplished without weakening the support for roofs. Oh, and your style of art and glyphic writing is graceful and flowing, more pleasing to the eye than any I have seen."

"So, you have the eye of a budding architect!" Pakal exclaimed. "The things you mention are just those that we have worked so hard to accomplish in our style of art and construction. I will tell you the story; it began many years ago when I was a young man determined to rebuild our damaged city to a new level of perfection."

He launched into an enthusiastic telling of how his friend and chief architect, Yax Chan, developed new styles of sloping mansards and eaves on parallel angles with roofs. More details were provided than her mind could absorb about creating a trapezoidal linear truss to allow building wider rooms and higher ceilings. The steady refinement of cursive writing for glyphs that skilled scribes developed led to stone carvers following suit, working the fine limestone abundant in their hillsides into panels and tablets, pillars and frescoes that followed this graceful style. The realistic portrayal of rulers and their families was a departure from the usual stiff formalized images that appeared on buildings and standing stone monuments of other cities.

K'inuuw Mat's head was reeling after Pakal's complicated explanations. Obviously, he loved this subject, and she resolved to learn more. She was gratified that he so appreciated her observations.

"Yes, yes we will discuss all these techniques more," Pakal assured her. "Few women show such interest. You must meet Yax Chan; he will be delighted that someone unfamiliar with our city noticed the very impressions he worked so hard to achieve! I will have my steward Akan set up a meeting for us all very soon."

Pakal rose from the platform and stepped down, offering a hand to K'inuuw Mat and drawing her up from the mat into a warm embrace. She was surprised and thrilled; such a show of affection from the great ruler was entirely unexpected. It felt wonderful to have his arms surrounding her, and she felt their kindred spirits even more strongly. Exchanging smiles, they parted and bowed to each other, while Kuy and Talol also bowed.

"My dearest K'inuuw Mat, for you are becoming most dear to me, I have greatly enjoyed our first meeting and look forward to many more," Pakal said warmly. "Lady Kuy, please feel that this is your home, and ask for whatever you need to be comfortable. Lady Talol, my thanks to you for bringing these two delightful young women to meet me. I am certain you will assure that they become increasingly at ease until they know beyond doubt they are in their home."

In the flush of joy over her first meeting with the Holy Lord, the Great Ruler Pakal, K'inuuw Mat did not notice the flash of anger in Talol's eyes or the deepening frown on her brow. Kuy did notice, however, and sensed the woman's barely concealed hostility. Kuy wondered what family secrets were simmering under that hostility, and how she could alert her mistress without disrupting her happiness.

4

"Lady K'inuuw! Here comes something very important! Your sweet young palace attendant, Tukun, has the ear of every gossip in this huge complex, and in return they fill her ear with their stories. She is a treasure trove of tidbits about the royal family!"

Kuy burst breathlessly into K'inuuw Mat's chamber and dropped onto a floor mat. It was their second morning in the palace, and Kuy had been scouting around ever since they finished the early meal.

"Sit beside me, My Lady," she said with an inviting gesture. "You must listen closely to this. It is of great significance."

With a sigh, K'inuuw Mat sat beside her excited attendant. She felt reluctant to tarnish the glow of joining this illustrious family, and still reveled in her meeting with Pakal. But, she was not so naive as to imagine any royal family was devoid of dark secrets.

"You now have my ear, tell me," she said.

"Oh, Dear Lady, I have no desire to diminish the great Bahlam family. Surely the Holy Lord Pakal is the finest ruler alive, and he showed you much affection yesterday. This does not concern him or your betrothed. It is about the Lady Talol." Kuy shook her head adamantly.

"Lady Talol . . . she has been most congenial to us," said K'inuuw Mat.

"Yes, on the surface, but did you not detect her scowl? Or her hostility after your discussion with Pakal?"

"She does appear to be endlessly frowning, and her manner does lack warmth. But hostility? No, I did not sense that."

"Ah, there is much to this story and I shall try to tell it quickly, before we are interrupted. I bring it to your attention because I believe there is some danger for you, though I do not know what."

"It is best to be prepared," K'inuuw Mat said with a touch of sadness. "Even if this gossip proves to be just meanness, and not truth."

Kuy jumped up to look through the door drape into the corridor. Assured that no one was eavesdropping, she returned to her mat and continued.

"Lady Talol, although married for over twelve years, has never conceived a child. It is known that her husband, Lord Kan Bahlam, had a severe illness as a youth, with a high fever for many days, and almost died. The healers warned that he might never be able to father children as a result. Now with the test of time, this does appear true."

"Then we should extend our sympathy to Lady Talol, and not gossip about her," rebuked K'inuuw Mat.

"Ah, but the Lady sought her own remedies. After many years of seeing her husband in and out of the sleeping mats of untold women, wives and daughters of both high and low status, she determined to seek lovers for herself. They say she had several, and consulted the Ix Chel priestesses about planning conceptions with some of them. This was to be kept secret, of course, but little can be concealed from astute palace gossips. And as all can observe, no child came of these liaisons, either."

"What of Kan Bahlam's escapades? Did none of these produce children?"

"No, not one. Oh, there was mention of one noble woman who did become pregnant after her unions with the Lord, and claimed that the baby was his, but he denied it. When the child was born, it had no resemblance to Kan Bahlam, and was the very image of the woman's husband. To this day, the gossips report that the Ba-ch'ok continues his lascivious ways, sometimes even with two-spirits." Kuy paused for dramatic effect. Two-spirits were those men or women who found attraction to others of their own gender. While they were accepted in society, viewed as a third gender group that blended qualities of the other two, it was unusual for rulers or heirs to engage in cross-gender sex.

"Oh," K'inuuw Mat whispered. "It seems the Lord Kan Bahlam's appetites are quite broad, if all this is true."

"It is true, My Lady. Tukun assures me that many in the palace have observed these things, and at times the Lord's own servants spread gossip."

"So, relations between Talol and her husband are strained," observed K'inuuw Mat. "She feels resentment over a situation she cannot control, and realizes many are talking of her behind her back. As are we, and I am not happy for it."

"They say Lady Talol is vengeful, with an obsidian-sharp tongue and unforgiving ways. A number of servants and palace attendants have lost their positions due to her. Most are afraid of her and try to keep out of her way. She has been cruel to her sister-in-law, Te' Kuy, wife of Kan Joy Chitam. That lady also has suffered in childbearing, having miscarried several pregnancies, for which Lady Talol showed little sympathy. Some whisper there is fear that the two surviving children might be poisoned, by someone full of anger and bitterness . . . you can guess."

"Kuy, you go too far!" K'inuuw Mat swung her gaze toward the door drape and looked worried. "I forbid you to repeat this ever again! This is treason against the dynasty; it could be cause for execution. Seal your lips and do not let a whisper of this gossip escape."

Kuy hung her head, and tears formed.

"I was only trying to forewarn you," she whispered between soft sobs. "Even if only a small portion of this is true, there is fuel for great passions. Lady Talol can be dangerous; please be careful of her."

K'inuuw Mat put an arm around her attendant, wiping away tears with one finger.

"Be still, be calm. I am not angry with you, and I do realize you only want my safety. Let us avoid further involvement in palace gossip, shall we? There is so much to learn, and we will certainly gain from other viewpoints."

"Yes, My Lady." Kuy sniffed and finished drying her eyes. "I will avoid gossiping myself, but I must keep an ear open to listen. We are in a much larger world now, and it is very complex. We must keep on the alert."

They hugged and helped each other rise. K'inuuw Mat walked to a window to gauge the angle of the sun. It had passed zenith and started its early descent toward the west.

"You should rest and gather your energies before you meet the entire Bahlam royal family this afternoon," advised Kuy. "I want you to be the most beautiful woman at the feast, and your face must be smooth, free of concern."

"Ever my little caretaker," laughed K'inuuw Mat. "Yes, I shall rest, and you can make me beautiful beyond my dreams."

"So it will be." Kuy took a step toward the door, then turned with a worried expression.

"My Lady?"

"Yes?"

"Please be careful of Lady Talol . . . and of her husband."

The palace was buzzing with the big event that afternoon, servants flying to and fro down corridors, attendants fussing with clothing and headdresses to make their lords and ladies magnificent. It was some time since the entire royal family had gathered in the palace. Cooking palapas emitted copious smoke and delicious odors as tapir, turkey, and deer stews bubbled on three-stone hearths. The rhythmic pat-pat-pat of busy hands slapping maize cakes into thin rounds echoed across the plaza. Cooking areas were set apart from residences, but close enough to permit rapid carrying of dishes to the dining chambers. Musicians practiced and dancers preened, servants spread thick mats in the dining patio and veranda, and men stirred the fermenting bark to make potent liquor, balche, which would flow freely that evening.

Akan, the Royal Steward, seemed everywhere to assure all preparations went well. The day was hot, and many servants waving palmetto fans were stationed around the sitting mats. The order of sitting was most important, arranged hierarchically according to status. Akan checked that the mats for the ruler, the Ba-ch'ok, and the second and third brothers were of the finest quality and most plush. Their families would join them on these mats, while a few select noble courtiers and attendants would occupy mats farther on the periphery. The mat for the ladies from Uxte'kuh was placed adjacent to that of the ruler, by his request.

For dramatic effect, the ruler ordered that everyone should be seated before Lady K'inuuw Mat and her attendant Lady Kuy entered the royal dining patio. That way, all eyes would be upon the bride as she made her first formal entrance into the domain of the Bahlam dynasty of Lakam Ha. Pakal wished to acknowledge K'inuuw Mat and give the most honored tribute for her joining the family. He felt certain, after their discussion the prior day, that she was fully capable of handling such ceremonious presentation. She was a young woman of great poise and self-assurance, not a shy and untutored girl as his wife had been when she arrived at Lakam Ha.

K'inuuw Mat was feeling anything but self-confident at the moment. Her stomach felt fluttery and her palms moist; her unruly mind tumbled with confused thoughts and vague uneasiness. She knew that Pakal would be warm and supportive, and that was the most important element. But, she could not help being jittery, even apprehensive, about meeting her future husband. Taking some deep breaths, she tried to focus her thoughts on why this was so. Perhaps it was due to the recent warnings given by Kuy, or the sense of confusion she had about the looks of her betrothed, or it might simply be a natural reaction to such a big event.

Kuy made final adjustments in her mistress' elegant huipil and charmingly understated headdress. Only a diadem of silver discs with interspersed pearls adorned her forehead, allowing the glistening coils of black hair to make a crown that emphasized her tilted almond eyes, high cheekbones, and narrow face. One strand of hair draped gracefully over her left shoulder, bound with a tie of seed pearls that dangled into its tip. Kuy had a true sense of glamour and insisted that minimal adornment would bring out a woman's natural beauty.

When Kuy held up a mica-coated ceramic mirror to demonstrate the effect, K'inuuw Mat had to agree. She felt reassured that indeed her appearance was beautiful. Surely she could draw upon her training and native intelligence to perform well for her introductions. *All will be well*, she repeated as a chant. Just before the summons, she closed her eyes for one final assessment. She wanted to recall the face that had appeared in her scrying bowl. The image came quickly to her experienced inner vision, and she re-examined every aspect of the man's face. It was a strong, compelling but not handsome face with heavy, large features. It did not closely resemble Pakal's face, or that of his son Kan Joy Chitam. She felt the wave of confusion sweep across her mind; why did everyone say that Tiwol Chan Mat looked like his father?

A call at the door signaled time to leave. She put aside her confusion and wrapped her mind inside the chant: *all will be well.*

"Here enters the esteemed royal Lady K'inuuw Mat of Uxte'kuh," intoned the steward Akan in a resonant bass voice. "With her is Lady Kuy, respected attendant from her city."

Wooden flutes and clay whistles tweeted a sprightly tune, joined by hollow branch clackers setting a stately rhythm. Akan stepped aside to allow the women to pass from the corridor onto the patio veranda. K'inuuw Mat lifted her chin and squared her shoulders, stepping forward with grace and confidence. Although her eyes held straight ahead, toward the mat on which Pakal sat, she took in the scene with peripheral vision.

Verandas framed the moderate-sized patio on all sides, and in the welcome shade these provided sat many people on mats. They were richly attired with fine clothing, jewelry, and headdresses of many styles. The closer they sat to Pakal, the more elegant was their appearance. She imagined that Kuy would have a fine time studying clothing and adornment styles. Her path was straight across the patio to approach Pakal and the royal family seated near him. She realized this march in the bright sunlight was to allow everyone to have a good look. In time to the clacker's beat, she set a deliberate pace and projected the ultimate in regal bearing that she could muster. Soft murmurs of appreciation confirmed that she was making a good impression.

As she drew near Pakal, she recognized Kan Joy Chitam. Sitting beside him was a slender woman holding an infant, with a girl of about four years at her feet. Across from this family group was Talol, sitting by herself on a mat. Next to Kan Joy Chitam's mat was another occupied by a single man, whose appearance was a slightly younger image of the ruler. His eager expression left little doubt in K'inuuw Mat's mind about who he was. This must be her betrothed. Confusion flooded her mind again, and she hesitated just as Pakal rose to his feet and approached.

"My dearest daughter to be, Lady K'inuuw Mat, it is my immense pleasure to receive you to this family gathering," Pakal said, stretching his arms toward her. She moved her arm to grasp her shoulder and bow, but he caught her and drew her into an embrace. The pure love that emanated from his being engulfed her, and for delicious moments she forgot all worries. He kissed her on both cheeks, then held her at arms' length.

"You are the very essence of loveliness," he said. "The rarest flower blooming high in forest canopy. We are most fortunate that you are joining our family. Now I shall introduce you to them."

He turned first to Talol, who rose stiffly and bowed.

"The Lady Talol you have met already," Pakal said. "She is so kindly assuming the duties of Royal Consort, in the absence of my beloved wife, Lalak. I am certain she is making your stay in our palace comfortable, only ask and she will assist your every need."

"Indeed, yes. May I express my deepest gratitude to Lady Talol for the outstanding hospitality in which my attendant Kuy and I have luxuriated," said K'inuuw Mat. Although her mind felt numb, she was performing courtly niceties automatically.

"Where, may I ask, is your husband, the Ba-ch'ok Kan Bahlam?" Pakal asked.

"Holy Lord, he is delayed," replied Talol, looking decidedly uncomfortable. "You will recall that he was away on a diplomatic mission to Anaay Te. His arrival is anticipated at any time."

"Ah, just so. Let us anticipate his arrival, then." Pakal kept his voice even, but a frown crossed his forehead. He gestured to the young man who rose from the mat next to Talol's, accompanied by two women and another older man.

"Here we find Talol's brother, Chak Chan, and his wife, with his honored parents." Pakal continued smoothly. He spoke all their names rapidly, and K'inuuw Mat made a mental note to ask about them later. "Chak Chan is a close associate of Kan Bahlam's in the advanced work they are pursuing at the Academy of Astronomy, in addition to being his brother-in-law. Since you have interest in the influences of the stars, having studied as an Ix Chel acolyte, I am certain you will find much to discuss with Chak Chan."

The astronomer bowed, followed by his family members, and expressed words of welcome and greeting that blended into a stream of lilting sound, words indistinct to K'inuuw Mat's ears. She smiled and bowed in return, murmuring some appropriate syllables of thanks.

Turning to the other side, he faced Kan Joy Chitam's family as they all rose to bow.

"Of our family, you know Kan Joy Chitam best, as he guided your journey," Pakal said. "Here is his wife, Te' Kuy, with their children, by whom we are multiply blessed. Our sweet little Chab' Nikte, honeybee flower, is a charming girl who delights the heart of her grandfather. And here is my long-awaited first grandson, Mayuy, who may someday replace me, though it is hazardous to try and outguess the deities."

Pakal stooped to pat the cheek of the girl, who squirmed playfully and smiled. He rose and stroked the fuzzy dark hair of the boy, a gesture full of tenderness. After bowing, Kan Joy Chitam embraced K'inuuw Mat and expressed his happiness to have her with them. Te' Kuy also gave welcome, assuring that she would send an invitation to visit soon. The parents of Te' Kuy were on a mat just behind, and were included in bows and introductions. By now K'inuuw Mat's mind felt wrapped in a thick cloud.

The young man on the adjoining mat was already standing, a smile lighting his face and eyes. Pakal guided K'inuuw Mat to stand facing him.

"It is my utmost pleasure to introduce you to your betrothed, my third son Tiwol Chan Mat," said Pakal. "Tiwol, you are indeed a fortunate man."

K'inuuw Mat and Tiwol exchanged bows. The cloud in her mind thinned as she gazed into his eyes, full of gentleness and hinting of passion. He was an even closer image of his father than Kan Joy Chitam, perhaps even more handsome. She felt her pulse quicken accompanied by a slight twinge of disappointment that her scrying had been inaccurate.

That must be the answer, she thought. *Something interfered with my scrying; I made an error.* The thought reassured her, and she took a deep breath of relief.

"My heart leaps at meeting you, Lady K'inuuw Mat," said Tiwol Chan Mat. "You are the fulfillment of my dearest wish, a bride of such beauty and regal presence. No more could I ask of the deities or my revered father. Receive my welcome; accept my affections."

"These I most happily do, Lord Tiwol Chan Mat," she replied. "Surely a fate greater than our own has guided me here. My most profound desire is to fulfill my duties and bring you happiness. It is my own joy to meet you, and my honor to become a member of your most respected royal family."

"Please join me with your future husband at my mat," said Pakal. "Other courtiers and attendants will come by to give their greetings, and soon afterwards we shall begin feasting to celebrate your arrival." He led them to the mat set beside his, the place of honor for the feast.

When she settled upon the mat, K'inuuw Mat realized her legs were trembling. She was glad to be sitting, and relieved that the introductions had gone smoothly. She glanced around, saw Kuy and motioned her to sit with them on the mat. A flow of smiling faces moved past, with Tiwol making introductions. He smiled between visitors and murmured that he did not expect her to remember them all; he would later inform her about their status and roles. She liked sitting next to him, as he had a comforting presence. He made Kuy also feel welcome and included.

Soon the sun dropped behind the tall western mountains, and servants brought out the first dishes of the feast while musicians played softly in the background. Platter followed platter of luscious tropical fruits: figs, papaya, mamey, nance, pitahaya, guava, plums, and wild grapes. With this was served both kob'al and picul-aqahla for those preferring a mild alcoholic drink. More platters with vegetables and maize cakes next appeared, an assortment of roasted squash and sweet potatoes, boiled and mashed yucca root, and simmered bright green chaya leaves. The next course consisted of savory stews that had been cooking all day, meats simmered with beans, squash, and tomatoes and seasoned with salt, chiles, epazote, coriander, oregano, and annato for its rich yellow color and astringent flavor. Hand-sized dried gourds cut in half served as bowls, and maize cakes were used to scoop up the stews and vegetables.

Balche, a strong alcoholic drink, was offered with the stew course. Preferred by men, this drink was potent. Neither Pakal nor Tiwol partook, although many around were imbibing and the conversation was becoming quite animated.

Kuy tapped K'inuuw Mat's elbow and leaned to whisper in her ear, at a moment when Tiwol was in a discussion with his father.

"Look quickly at Lady Talol," whispered Kuy. "She appears completely miserable, like an abandoned island. I wonder where her husband could be. She seems to console herself with picul-aqahla. If he delays much longer, she may resort to balche."

K'inuuw Mat glanced toward Talol, trying to minimize her head movement. Indeed, the unfortunate woman appeared distraught. Turning back to Kuy she whispered: "Be not unkind, this is a major embarrassment to her. Let us show compassion."

Kuy shrugged. K'inuuw Mat's attention was taken by Tiwol who invited her to dance. At Maya feasts, dancing was greatly enjoyed and considered an art form in itself. Musicians began playing more loudly, tunes with regular beats so dancers could easily follow the rhythms. The beginning dances were stately, but as dancers warmed up, more vigorous and acrobatic performances would occur. In the first dance, two lines formed, pairs of men and women facing each other. Keeping their upper bodies straight, the pairs did a toe-heel step on alternating feet while moving arms in small arcs, palms outward and almost touching the partner's. After several repetitions of the steps, each dancer spun around and moved one partner to the right. The end man danced down the line to join the woman by herself at the other end. In this way, the line kept re-assembling until back to the original pairs.

This was a well-known dance throughout the Maya regions. K'inuuw Mat joined Tiwol and danced with confidence; she had done this step many times before. Soon the patio was filled with dancers, feathers swaying, jewelry clanking, huipils and loincloths flaring as they twirled. With deepening shadows playing across the patio, servants placed torches in wall sconces. The flickering light glinted off adornments of stone, shells, and copper. Laughter and murmurs of conversation drifted through the patio, joining the drums, flutes, and whistles of musicians.

After several rounds of dancing, Tiwol took K'inuuw Mat's hand and they returned to their mat. Her fingers entwined with his; she liked the warmth of his grasp. She felt happy and content, thinking that the Goddess' intentions were surely coming to pass. Tiwol turned to talk with two young men who stood by the mat. Still standing, K'inuuw Mat looked across the patio to watch the more vigorous dancing that had started. She patted one foot in rhythm to the music, until suddenly she caught view of the man who had just entered from the far veranda.

Her heart did a flip-flop and began pounding, while her stomach clenched into a tight knot. Eyes wide in disbelief, she stared at the tall man slowly weaving his way between dancers. Torchlight caught his face and brought his features into sharp focus—the face she had seen in her scrying bowl.

No-nooo! Her mind screamed silently. This could not be happening. The exact face, every feature she had so carefully memorized, of the man who would be her husband. Just when she accepted that her scrying was inaccurate, he appeared precisely as she had been shown. A wave of nausea swept over her and she clutched her stomach, dropping her gaze and collapsing onto the mat. Kuy looked with puzzlement and gave the hand sign for "what is happening." K'inuuw Mat could only shake her head and wait for her stomach to settle a bit. She tried to collect herself before anyone else noticed.

She did not have long, as the tall man arrived at the mat of Talol and the two exchanged heated words. Her ears could not detect any distinct words. It seemed as if a roaring waterfall was inside her head. She saw Pakal walk over to the man, and their conversation also appeared strained. Tiwol stooped down, offering a hand to help her rise.

"My wayward brother Kan Bahlam has arrived," he said with a sardonic smile.

Automatically, she took his hand and rose unsteadily to her feet. She hoped Tiwol did not think she had consumed too much alcohol. In fact, she had not taken a sip, preferring to drink only fruit juices. He steadied her with a grasp on her elbow and steered her to face the new arrival. She could not yet lift her gaze toward him.

"Greetings, Kan Bahlam," said Tiwol. "May I present to you my betrothed, the esteemed Lady K'inuuw Mat of Uxte'kuh? We are gratified that you managed to arrive at her reception feast before it ended. K'inuuw Mat, please meet my brother, the Lakam Ha Ba-ch'ok, Kan Bahlam."

She bowed to avoid looking at him. But, while she was still bowing, she felt a hand upon her upper arm and heard words as through a fog.

"It is my greatest pleasure and highest honor to meet you, Lady K'inuuw Mat. Please accept my profound apologies for arriving late; I was unavoidably delayed in my return from Anaay Te. Had I possessed the wings of an eagle, I should have soared above rivers, mountains, and jungles to arrive sooner, that my eyes might be graced with your divinely lovely presence."

She did not know which sensation disturbed her the most: the burning of his hand on her skin, the rich baritone timbre of his voice, the masculine smell of his heated body. With extreme effort, she straightened and lifted her eyes to meet his, and was immediately pierced with another overwhelming sensation. From the depths of his black eyes came a bolt of lightning that coursed through her body and shot into her toes. Her insides were quivering and her knees felt weak. It was all she could do to choke out a few words.

"The-the pleasure is mine . . . to-to meet you . . . Lord Kan Bahlam."

His hand continued burning into her flesh and his eyes boring into her soul. Her body felt drawn by a powerful magnetic force toward his, as if at any moment she would fall into his arms. This very image created a sensation of her body pressing into his that was intoxicating. She felt herself swaying and her mind screamed warnings again. Magnetic waves of energy thrummed between their bodies, and he seemed unable to remove his hand from her arm.

Pakal appeared from the side and placed an arm around her shoulders, drawing her away from Kan Bahlam and breaking his hold on her. She was too confused and overcome by intense sensations to assess what impression this encounter might have made on those around. Dimly she was aware that Pakal and Tiwol led her back to their mat, where she sat as Kuy fanned her with a small palmetto leaf and gave her juice to drink. The rest of the evening was a blur. She thought she managed to respond appropriately to conversation and appear reasonably present. Her mind felt numb, and she resisted any thoughts. She needed a good night's sleep before she tried to understand what had happened.

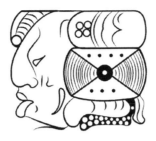

K'inuuw Mat—IV

Baktun 9 Katun 12 Tun 0 – Baktun 9 Katun 12 Tun 1 (673 – 674 CE)

1

The city of Lakam Ha was buzzing with activity on the eve of the summer solstice, preparing for the marriage ceremony and feasting that followed. Visitors from polity cities were arriving and needed accommodations, decorations for the ceremony must be set up, food was being gathered and prepared, balche fermented, clothing and adornments readied. Akan, the Royal Steward, oversaw most of the arrangements with a cadre of assistants. K'anal, the main scribe, organized his bark paper books, wooden stylus collection and feather tip brushes, lined up pots of pigments, and assigned duties to under-scribes. Such royal events must be properly recorded, to join the vast library of codices containing the dynastic history and scientific knowledge of generations, back to the founding of the city. Most of the library of codices resided in special chambers in the temple of the High Priest, Ib'ach, who, along with the High Priestess Yaxhal, would perform the ceremony.

The ceremony was to take place in the main plaza, at the base of the wide palace stairway facing northwest. Nobles would have places on the stairways and at the bases of bordering pyramids. Commoners would stand at the plaza edge in hopes of catching glimpses of the celebration. The plaza could hold several thousand people, and would be packed. To secure space for the ceremony, a thick rope marked off a square close to the palace stairway. This square represented the cosmos, which to the Mayas was quadripartite. Its four parts had multiple layers of meaning, from the infinite to the minuscule. Earth mirrored the quadripartite cosmos, having four cardinal directions and four deities called Pahuatuns who held up the firmament to separate earth from sky. Each of the four directions had a Bacab—Lord of Winds, and a Chaak—Lord of Waters. Marking lines between these deities formed an equal-sided cross, a symbol of immense holiness and reverence.

Decorations for the marriage ceremony took into account complex symbolism for the four directions. Flowers of appropriate colors were placed along the rope at each quarter: Red was for the east, Lak'in, where the sun rises; the color of new light, the domain of the god Chak Xib Chaak. Yellow was for the south, Nohol, the source of warmth and growth; the color of summertime, domain of the god Kan Xib Chaak. Black was for the west, Chik'in, color of the watery underworld; place of renewal and transformation, domain of the god Ek Xib Chaak. White was for the north, Xaman, the color of cold winds and polar stars, place of mystery and magic; domain of the god Sak Xib Chaak. Together with different colored flowers, elements representing the four directions were placed at the appropriate side: fire for the east, wind chimes for the south, water for the west, and soil for the north. These would be offered to the deities during the ceremony.

In the center of the roped off area stood a large wooden image of the Wakah Chan Te', the Jeweled Sky Tree with its nine roots for the Underworld, thick trunk for the Middleworld, and thirteen branches for the Upperworld. This sacred tree spanned the three dimensions of Maya existence and provided a path for moving back and forth between them. The ability to travel between dimensions was attained through years of shamanic study. Only rulers, elite nobles, and select priests and priestesses possessed this skill. The ruler was expected to journey and encounter Gods and ancestors using the Wakah Chan Te', most often in the form of a rising Vision Serpent. Drawing blood from one's body, a form of self-sacrifice was the usual method for invoking the Vision Serpent. As the blood-soaked bark paper strips burned, the undulating column of smoke turned into the serpent and allowed ascent up the Wakah Chan Te'. The sacred mandate of the ruler was to intervene for his people, to call forth the blessings of the deities, to bring prosperity, peace, and abundance. Rulers also made spiritual journeys to seek information and guidance, and to receive predictions for the coming katun.

A raised wooden platform was placed next to the Wakah Chan Te', on which the marriage ritual would take place. Woven mats covering the platform made a four-part square, each section the color of the direction it faced, with dangling tassels hanging off edges.

Akan, Ib'ach, and Yaxhal met at the platform, ascended the steps and gazed across the plaza. They made certain all items needed for the ceremony were in place. Warriors were stationed at the four corners of the rope square to prevent anyone from entering. The High Priest and Priestess had ritually cleansed the space, and it was important to maintain this sanctity until the ceremony tomorrow. All appeared to be in order, they agreed. The plaza and the city were prepared for this momentous event; the marriage of the youngest son of their K'uhul B'aakal Ahau, the Holy B'aakal Lord and Embodiment of the Triad Gods, K'inich Janaab Pakal.

The bride, however, was feeling anything but ready. The short time between her arrival and the ceremony had flown past, and her state of confusion interfered with her ability to concentrate on preparations. Kuy and her palace attendant Tukun worked tirelessly on her garments and adornments, the High Priestess Yaxhal came several times to describe the ceremony and give instructions, and the Ix Chel priestess Chilkay, assigned to keeping her healthy and ensure successful conception, visited frequently.

Usually, royals and elite nobles waited before conceiving, providing time for the relationship to solidify and the couple to settle into a routine. A long-standing tradition of herbal knowledge was used to control or augment fertility among elite Mayas. Conceptions were planned to assure particular characteristics for the child. An understanding of stellar configurations guided this art, for the pattern of forces among the stars was reflected in earthly events, shaping the qualities, abilities, consciousness, and destiny of those born under their influences. Maya astronomy, the domain of calendar priests and priestesses, used potent rituals to invoke cosmic influences and to focus these forces upon people and places.

The herbal skills of Ix Chel priestesses combined with the esoteric knowledge of calendar priests to manage the processes of conception and birth. The Maya knew pregnancy usually lasts 260 days, a sacred number expressed in the Tzolk'in calendar of 13 numbers by 20 days = 260. The date of birth was determined by when the child was conceived. Thus, timing of conception was critically important. Conception was the key to assure that the child would be born on the calendar date that held the desired characteristics. The time of a woman's fertility was determined by detailed knowledge of menstrual cycles and physical signs of ovulation, including watching changes in characteristics of vaginal secretions. Divination techniques and herbs to enhance fertility were also part of these arts. Herbs could also be used to prevent conception, when this was desired, and other herbs could be used to terminate an early pregnancy.

K'inuuw Mat had been surprised to learn from the Ix Chel priestess that Pakal desired an immediate conception. While no explanation was offered, she could surmise that he was concerned about succession. His two older sons had failed to produce male heirs for years, and Kan Bahlam still had no children. Pakal most likely did not want to rely on only one grandson. This added another duty that she thought might be delayed a few years. It also fed her sense of not being prepared.

What troubled her the most, however, was her experience of meeting Kan Bahlam. Getting a good night's sleep had not given her clear insight into the situation. She reviewed the process she followed in scrying for the face of her husband. No matter how many times she went over it, she could not detect a mistake in her technique. The scrying was certainly accurate in depicting the man's face; it just was not the face of her future husband. Why did Kan Bahlam's face appear? For this, she could not find an answer. She longed to discuss her concerns with another woman trained as a seer, but knew of none in Lakam Ha. She imagined that among the Ix Chel priestesses of the city were some with visionary powers. But she was reluctant to ask Chilkay because she feared to reveal the link with Kan Bahlam.

The reaction of her body, its overwhelming feelings toward him, caused her intense distress. She had never experienced such emotions or such primal physical responses, and these frightened her. There must be some way to suppress them and prevent their recurrence. She felt so unschooled in sexual passions, why had she not studied them more?

Thinking of Tiwol Chan Mat evoked pleasant sensations and an honest physical attraction. She felt happy that he was to be her husband. Instinctively she knew he would be kind and tender, and no doubt an excellent father. But, the feelings Kan Bahlam evoked were altogether different: immense passion, magnetic attraction, and a huge sense of danger.

A wave of relief passed over K'inuuw Mat when she learned that her parents and brother had arrived in Lakam Ha to attend the marriage ceremony. She was uncertain if they would be able to come due to her sister's pregnancy. All was going well at home, however, and they undertook the journey, arriving just in time. She sent word to her mother that she urgently needed to meet, even though the family would not all be together until after the ceremony.

In the mid-afternoon of the day before the ceremony, Chelte' was ushered by Tukun into her daughter's chamber in the royal palace. Kuy was present, consulting about jewelry, and joined her mistress in rushing to embrace Chelte'. After many tearful hugs and kisses, Kuy sensed that this needed to become a private meeting and left, ushering Tukun out with her. Glancing at K'inuuw Mat, her eyes flashed an acknowledgement, and she made a subtle hand sign for taking care of things. She realized this meeting between mother and daughter should not be overheard.

After reassuring her mother that everything was going well and that she had been graciously welcomed by the royal family, K'inuuw Mat drew Chelte' to the farthest corner of the chamber. Settling on mats, she signaled to speak quietly and they drew close to each other.

"Mother, something happened that has left me confused and worried," said K'inuuw Mat in a soft voice. Her mother nodded to go on, and she related her scrying experience and the meetings with both Tiwol Chan Mat and Kan Bahlam.

"I am so confused, Mother. Where did I go wrong? What am I to make of my responses?"

"First, as to the scrying, I can see no fault in your approach, although you are more knowledgeable of those techniques than am I," said Chelte'. "The most important elements were in place. You entered the sacred awareness, and your heart was pure in its request. You put your trust in Ix Chel to bring you the vision. What that vision actually is depends upon the Goddess. Through her vast consciousness in the Upperworld, she allows communications to take place, images to be projected. She serves as a conduit between those super-conscious forces that serve the deities, and the vision seekers in this Middleworld. The deities sent this image to your scrying bowl for reasons of their own, far beyond our understanding. There is a message in this, but it is not clear to me."

"But Kan Bahlam is not to be my husband! There is no mistake that I am marrying Tiwol, and Kan Bahlam is already married. I cannot see what message the deities could be sending me."

"There is some connection with Kan Bahlam, but it must not be yours to know at present. The energies of these brothers are surely interconnected in the spiritual domain, perhaps there was a cross-over and this affected the scrying image. You tell me that Kan Bahlam has a most powerful presence."

"Ah, yes, that is my other concern. The sheer force of magnetic pull between us was overwhelming. It is not that I am attracted to him in the way I feel for Tiwol. It almost has the power of an evil curse. I am frightened."

Tears began forming in K'inuuw Mat's eyes. Her mother wrapped arms around her and murmured comforting words. When she felt her daughter was calmer, she continued the discussion.

"You must use protections against this magnetic force," she said. "I have learned a few spells that the healers use with women in such predicaments. Listen closely; memorize these words and the melody, for they are infused with the Goddess' magic. Keep repeating them in your mind whenever you feel these sensations, either when in his presence or alone."

Chelte' repeated the simple chant several times, and then signaled K'inuuw Mat to join in. Their soft voices rose and fell in the solemn melody until K'inuuw Mat nodded and smiled.

"It is committed to memory, and already I feel lighter," she breathed gratefully. "Yes, this will surely help me to get my reactions under control."

"You must avoid him as much as possible," Chelte' advised. "His intentions may not be for the good of all. There are many rumors about him."

"Of this, I am fully aware, Mother. I will avoid him."

They hugged in silence for long moments.

"Truly I am sad that such distress clouds your marriage eve," Chelte' said. "Set your mind upon your betrothed and the warm feelings you hold for him. Keep that focus, use the chant, and all will be well."

"Mother, thank you. I am so blessed to be your daughter."

"Ix Chel be thanked, for she is our source of wisdom and guidance. Never loosen your tie to the Goddess, and she will support you through all your challenges. She sets our destiny, and yours is here in the royal family. Be comforted and stand strong."

Four trumpeters stood on the highest platform of the Priests' Pyramid Temple at the north end of the main plaza. They rested their trumpets, longer than a man's height, on the platform edge, one facing each cardinal direction. Bass blares from the trumpets resonated throughout Lakam Ha, echoing across courtyards and through alleys, announcing the start of the marriage ceremony. Four trumpet blasts were sounded in each direction. People began streaming from residences toward the main plaza, as the bright sun approached zenith on the longest day of the year. Soon the plaza was packed, people pushing to be as close to the roped off square as possible and nobles assuming positions on pyramid stairways. Musicians played flutes, drums, and whistles; chanting priests and priestesses lined the inside of the rope. At each cardinal point at the corners of the rope square, priests blew large conches with red-tinged shells making wailing blares while priestesses used small white conches to create shrill trebles.

As the conch chorus ended, the ruler and his family appeared at the top of the palace stairway. A roar of welcome erupted from the crowd, for the royals made a splendid appearance with their swaying feather headdresses, glistening metallic and gemstone jewelry, and luxuriant clothing. After Pakal gave the blessing sign to the people, his family descended the stairway and stood to one side. Next appeared the family of K'inuuw Mat wearing their ceremonial finery; they were also greeted by roars and cheers. Regally the bride led the way down the stairway, greeted by cheers and whistles of the gathered people.

The High Priest and Priestess walked ceremonially from the stairs of the raised platform to the two groups of royals. Ib'ach faced Pakal and Tiwol Chan Mat; Yaxhal faced K'inuuw Mat and her father, Ox B'iyan. Each asked the parents to give permission for this marriage, and to release their children to a life together as a new family. After permission was granted, they led the couple in a procession around the roped off square, as more roars from the crowd nearly drowned out the music, ending with the ascent up the stairs to the platform. The couple stood next to the Wakah Chan Te' as the High Priest and Priestess chanted invocations to the Triad Deities for blessings upon this union. Attendants brought censers with copal for purification of the couple. Waves of pungent copal smoke poured from the censers, wrapping around the couple and spreading across the plaza. Simply breathing these heady fumes transported most Mayas into sacred space and altered consciousness.

K'inuuw Mat felt her normal awareness shifting. She loved the smell of copal and released her consciousness to its expansive effects. Standing close to Tiwol, she looked into his eyes and felt a wave of warmth spreading through her body. He smiled, and her heart leapt in gladness. She had chanted her mother's spell almost constantly since rising that morning, and its magic had erased her feelings for Kan Bahlam. Although she had glimpsed him standing with the Lakam Ha royal family, only a twinge of tension passed her mind.

The High Priest and Priestess went to the east side of the platform and gestured the couple to begin the ritual. Soft chanting accompanied by a slow drumbeat brought the crowd to breathless anticipation, as sunlight shimmered off the jeweled and flowered headdresses of the royal couple. Together they held an incense cup with glowing coals into which the High Priestess dropped more copal. A swirl of copal smoke rose like a sinuous serpent as the couple lifted the cup and murmured a prayer to the Lord of the East. Tiwol's fingers wrapped around those of K'inuuw Mat, and she followed his movement as he guided the cup to form the Maya cross in the air: moving from east to west, and then north to south, finishing with circles, the first counter-clockwise and the next clockwise. Turning to the west, they crossed the platform and took a cup of water offered by the High Priest, praying to the Lord of the West, and performing the ritual cross and circle movements. Next, they went to the north and accepted a cup of soil from the High Priestess, praying to the Lord of the North, and repeating the movements. For the final direction, they received wind chimes from the High Priest, praying to the Lord of the South, who was no doubt delighted as the chimes jingled during the ritual movements.

The couple returned to the center and stood in front of the Wakah Chan Te'. The symbolic offerings they gave each other came from ancient roots of Maya agricultural tradition. Tiwol presented cacao pods and corn cobs in a basket, representing the raw materials for making food and drink. K'inuuw Mat offered prepared maize cakes and a cup of cacao drink on a small tray, the food fashioned from his raw materials. She had taken part in making these, touching the ingredients with her hands, as the tradition required. They exchanged the offerings and Tiwol took a bite of a maize cake, and then a sip of cacao. He raised the maize cake to her lips for her to nibble, and gave her a sip of cacao. The sweetness of honey in both maize cake and cacao signified the pleasures of married life, the raw materials his commitment to provide for her, and the prepared foods her dedication to caring for him. Once he had eaten food prepared by her hand, the marriage bond was sealed between them. This simple ritual was enough to seal a marriage between commoners, but among elites, an ornate ceremony was expected.

The High Priestess intoned the conventional words to acknowledge their marriage.

"Tiwol Chan Mat, you have eaten food prepared by the hand of K'inuuw Mat. By this act, your marriage is sealed. Now I shall bind your hands that all may see that your lives are bound together in everything: in joy and sorrow, in scarcity and abundance. The man is the provider of the seed; the woman is the preparer of sustenance, the bearer and nurturer. Together may you bring forth progeny, happiness, and abundance through the beneficence of the Gods."

She wrapped his right wrist and her left wrist together with a strand of red agate beads. Once their wrists were bound, she lifted their arms so the crowd could see. Thousands of throats gave roars of approval and well-wishes. She next led the couple around the edges of the platform with their arms uplifted, displaying their bound wrists in all directions, to the crowd's continued cheers and whistles.

Returning to the center, the couple faced the High Priest who carried a large white cloak trimmed with a geometric border of sky and earth symbols colored red and black. Swinging the cloak out in a dramatic flair, he let it settle around the couple's shoulders until all but their heads were completely enclosed.

"May the sacred flow of love and the honoring of all life surround you and enclose you, may you always be at peace and secure," intoned the High Priest. "As this cloak is a protection against the wind and cold, may you always guard your marriage against the dulling forces of daily living, from the negative forces of bitterness and resentment, from the destructive forces of gossip and evil-sayers. Keep your hearts open to the truth in each other. Listen well and speak with care. Remember your highest loyalty is to each other, even as you are loyal to B'aakal, our K'uhul Ahau, and the Triad Gods. Receive now my invocation that the deities protect your spirits so the love grows within you as one."

Tiwol slipped his free arm around K'inuuw Mat under the cloak and pulled her against him. She relaxed her body into his embrace and breathed her own prayer to Ix Chel that everything said in their marriage ceremony would hold true.

The High Priest and Priestess merged their voices into a long litany of chants, calling the names of all Maya deities to recognize this sacred bond and provide the couple with guidance and protection through their life together. Accompanied by devout music, a chorus of other priests around the rope square echoed each deity's name. The sun beat down intensely, and the couple began sweating under the cloak; she was thankful for his embrace to keep her steady on her feet. Finally, the chants ended, the cloak and wrist cords were removed, and the couple returned to their family groups. Still in ceremonial mode, they ascended the stairway into the palace followed by their families, accompanied by deep-voiced turtle carapace drums beating a stately cadence.

As the sun descended, sending long shadows across the main plaza, the ritual decorations were removed and the space de-sanctified in preparation for the feast. That evening the commoners would over-indulge in rich food and alcoholic drinks provided by the ruler, dance and cavort to music and drums, and celebrate their good fortune to live in the great city Lakam Ha. The ahauob attended separate feasts served inside the palace courtyards, while the royal family, select elite nobles and priesthood, and new relatives from Uxte'kuh dined in the ruler's patio. The newlyweds joined the ruler's feast for a short time, then were allowed to leave so they could be together. Tiwol planned to bring his bride to the private residence he so loved in the Sutzha River Complex, beside the cascades.

K'inuuw Mat felt the flush of excitement and exertion in the hot sun coloring her cheeks. She hoped this made her appear radiant rather than sunburned, despite the facial creams that Kuy applied to ward off sunrays. Standing beside Tiwol Chan Mat, she smiled and exchanged pleasantries with a seemingly endless line of well-wishers. After that, she sat and chatted happily with her family, touched by her father's obvious pleasure in being at the center of attention. Her mother was gracious as usual and sent continuing supportive smiles. Her brother Chumib kept himself busy meeting nobles and engaging the royal sons in animated conversations. She knew he was forming connections for future purposes, something any heir to a dynasty would do in these circumstances. She saw Chumib talking to Kan Bahlam, but quickly turned her eyes aside. She did not want her attention to be drawn to the ruler's older son.

Tiwol leaned toward her and grasped her hand, motioning with his other hand toward a regally attired man approaching them.

"Here approaches an important ally, the ruler of Mutul and Imix-Ha, Nuun Ujol Chaak," he said. "Only a tun ago he and my father conducted a victorious campaign to oust the usurper to the throne, his own half-brother Balaj Chan K'awiil. Now, this traitor resides in Dzibanche, home of the Kan dynasty. You are aware that Kan is the mortal enemy of Lakam Ha?"

"So I have learned," replied K'inuuw Mat. She arose as Tiwol assisted her, bowing to the visiting ruler during introductions. He expressed his deepest regards and well wishes for their union in flowery court language. Tiwol inquired about conditions in the subsidiary city Imix-Ha, where the half-brother had resided; a discussion ensued between the men about instability during power transitions. Nuun Ujol Chaak mentioned that he put his son, Hasau Chan K'awiil, in charge of the larger city Mutul, home of their dynasty, during this transition.

"It is my intention," said Nuun Ujol Chaak, "to soon restore Mutul to its former glory and political prominence. Once Imix-Ha is more stable, I plan to return there and commence a new building program. Many monuments and pyramids were damaged during the long siege by Kan, and we have been unable to devote resources to restoration due to their continued threat. Now that Balaj is banished, licking his wounds at Dzibanche, this threat is diminished."

"May your efforts be successful, and your building program proceed apace," said Tiwol. "There is nothing as eloquent as impressive new structures to declare a city's prosperity and security."

"Just so, as your honored father has so aptly demonstrated in your magnificent new cityscape. He is an inspiration to us all, the very epitome of fine leadership."

The men talked a short while more, and then Tiwol accompanied the visiting ruler as he returned to his mat, as a show of honoring his presence. K'inuuw Mat was about to sit down again when a powerful presence drew up beside her. Without looking, she knew it was Kan Bahlam. She hesitated, keeping her eyes downcast and scrambling in her mind to recall the chant for protection.

"Sister! Let me embrace you to give my personal welcome into our family," exuded Kan Bahlam.

Before she could resist, he swept her into his arms and planted a hot kiss on her cheek, very close to her mouth. As he pressed her body into his, arms tight around her waist and shoulders, she felt a searing jolt course through her. A powerful surge of sexual energy pulsated between them, causing her knees to weaken and thighs to tremble. He held her close for longer than was proper, his cheek against her crown. She felt his heart pounding on her breasts. Struggling to break the embrace, she pushed her hands against his chest.

"Oh . . . ah, Kan Bahlam . . . t-thank you . . ." she gasped. "Y-you give a . . . most warm welcome."

She pushed again, more strongly this time. Slowly he loosened his grasp, hands sliding along her back farther down than they should. She twisted and broke away, staring at him with wide eyes, her breath coming rapidly.

"You deserve only the warmest of welcomes," he murmured, heavy lids half concealing his eyes. His thick, sensuous lips were parted but not smiling. She could see the blood vessels pulsating in his temples. The air between their bodies fairly crackled with electric charge.

"You, ah . . . you enjoyed the marriage ceremony?" she said, feeling her words were inane but unable to think of anything else to say. What was that chant? Why could she not recall it?

"Indeed, I did enjoy the ceremony, and you looked exceptionally lovely," he replied.

"It became most hot toward the end, under the cloak." She had no idea why she said that.

A wicked smile curled Kan Bahlam's lips and his lids lifted. With eyes boring into hers, he leaned a little closer and whispered: "My wish is that I was under that cloak with you."

She gasped and looked away, refusing to be lured into his gaze. Trying to see beyond his broad shoulders, she searched for Tiwol but could not find him in the crowd.

"I . . . am feeling weak," she murmured. "I must sit, please forgive me, and thank you for your welcome."

She dropped onto the mat and lowered her head, hoping he would go away. His feet remained planted in front, and she focused on the fine workmanship of his woven sandals inlaid with copper discs and beads. As through a fog, her mind remarked on how large his feet were and how muscled his calves. Then these objects of her contemplation disappeared. She took several deep breaths and searched her memory again for the chant. It came to her, and she sang its soothing melody under her breath. Gradually she felt the disturbing sensations ebbing from her body, and her heartbeat slowed. By the time Tiwol returned, she appeared normal.

He offered her a cup of picul-aqahla, and she gratefully drank the alcoholic beverage. When servants brought dishes around, she had little appetite but picked at them to maintain appearances. She wondered if anyone had watched her interchange with Kan Bahlam, hoping it would not appear as intense as she experienced it. Once she caught her mother's eyes, and the concern reflected there told her that Chelte' had observed and understood. If only she could meet again with her mother before her family departed, but she doubted there would be time.

She waited, continuing to chant silently until she believed a suitable time period had passed. All she wanted was to leave the feast and be alone with Tiwol.

"Might we depart soon?" she whispered into his ear.

"Ah, yes. We have put in a sufficient appearance at our marriage feast." Tiwol gave her a wide smile, his eyes twinkling. "It is also my great desire to depart. I shall summon the palanquin."

Once the order was given, he helped her rise and guided her to offer parting remarks to Pakal and the royal family, as well as her family from Uxte'kuh. Mercifully, Kan Bahlam was nowhere in sight during their leave-taking. Her mother kissed and hugged her, promising to seek a visit before they departed. All guests stood and the musicians played a fanfare as the newlyweds crossed the patio and left through the veranda. Descending the eastern palace stairway, they climbed into the festively adorned palanquin and were carried to the edge of the plaza, along the steep path beside the river cascades, and let off outside Tiwol's private residence.

Servants had prepared baths and clean robes for them inside the residence. Grateful to wash away the day's sweat and cool their bodies in clear water, the couple bathed separately and donned loose robes, rejoining each other on mats in the sleeping chamber. Discretely placing cool atole and fresh fruit beside the mats, the servants departed.

"Come, my beloved," murmured Tiwol as he placed an arm around her shoulders.

The magic spell of the chant had cast its protection around K'inuuw Mat. Her body felt cleansed and her mind calm, her heart pure and open to her husband. She slid into his embrace and they kissed, long and passionate. In his warm and loving arms, she surrendered herself completely into ecstatic union. No thoughts of a troubling presence sullied their marriage night.

2

Pakal sat cross-legged on a raised platform, his slender torso supported by several plump pillows. The platform mat was woven in crosshatch patterns, and the olive and tan colors resembled the reeds that they symbolized. To sit on the reed mat indicated leadership and had become an icon of Maya rulers, who often wore short skirts with woven reed patterns when acting in official capacities. Pakal was attired in a simple white loincloth with a blue and green waistband and wore a large pectoral collar of multicolored beads and shells. His earspools were of matching design and his headdress a white conical cap with a single white lily arching above his forehead. Three white-and-tan fabric streamers hung toward the back over a ponytail of hair, still dark although mingled with silver strands. White wrist cuffs jangled their copper discs when he moved his arms, and his feet were bare.

This informal attire was customary when the ruler met in the Popol Nah, the Council House where many ahauob were gathered. Sitting benches lined the walls of the rectangular building that had four arched openings along its two long sides. The practice of shared governance had prevailed at Lakam Ha for several generations of rulers, and during Pakal's reign, the importance of non-elite nobles had grown. Several of his closest advisors were of this group, genealogically unrelated to the ruler but participating in key decisions. Three men in particular collaborated with Pakal in planning construction, designing adornments such as figures and glyphs on panels, and devise political and military strategies.

Chak Zotz had risen in governance to the rank of Sahal, ruler of a subsidiary city, appointed when Pakal's forces had ousted the antagonistic ruler of Amalah. Unfortunately, that city had been re-captured by Kan forces a katun in the past, and Chak Zotz escaped to Lakam Ha. He continued to play a leading role in military matters, attaining the title of Yahau K'ak, His Lord of Fire. He moved to the status of Nakom—Warrior Chief of Lakam Ha, when his elderly predecessor K'akmo died.

Yuhk Makab'te was also a Sahal, having sat in temporary rulership of the polity city Anaay Te until a local ruler could be selected and trained. He had developed administrative skills that made him a valuable assistant, selected by Kan Bahlam to oversee operations of the Academy of Astronomy and Sciences. Pakal also respected his abilities and consulted with him frequently.

Mut held the title Ah K'uhun, He of the Sacred Book, a priest with special esoteric training denoted as a "worshipper." Mut was skilled as an artist-scribe, versed in astronomy and astrology. He combined these talents to produce exceptional drawings that expressed the profound interrelations of stellar and earthly events. Pakal had a special project in mind for Mut: the designs to be carved upon his sarcophagus and painted on the walls of his burial crypt. Kan Bahlam had recruited Mut to join the artists and scientists at the Academy.

Two elite nobles were also in the royal family inner circle. Yax Chan was Pakal's chief architect and good friend; together they conceptualized the magnificent Lakam Ha cityscape that now flourished under the tropical sun. Chak Chan was Kan Bahlam's brother-in-law, also holding the title Ah K'uhun, and deeply involved in the work of the Academy.

All of these men, and fifteen more nobles of the city, including Pakal's three sons, were assembled in the Popol Nah. They were making assessment of the political situation within the B'aakal polity.

"The situation in Anaay Te appears to be stable," reported Kan Bahlam. "The young ruler has gained respect and appears to be discharging his duties competently. From many official and casual conversations during my last visit, I could glean no rumbles of discontent."

"How susceptible might they be to overtures from Kan?" asked Pakal.

"Of this, visits from emissaries of Kan, I could find no evidence," replied Kan Bahlam. "Anaay Te seems untroubled by the tendrils of the snake dynasty of Kan, at least at this point."

"Popo' offers concern in this regard," said Chak Zotz. "My informants there relate that several traders from the eastern coast visited, bringing gifts sent by Kan ruler Yuknoom Ch'een as a gesture of friendship. The young Popo' ruler Yuknoom Bahlam, you recall he has only been in office for five years, seemed pleased with the gifts. He sent back his gratitude to Kan and expressed interest in continued trade relations."

"This does not necessarily point to problems," observed Mut. "Most cities desire reliable trade relations with coastal regions since their marine goods and salt are so valued."

"Indeed, this is so," said Pakal. "But why not trade directly with coastal cities, such as Altun Ha and Tulum? It is suspicious that this trade delegation was sent from Kan."

"Precisely my thought, Holy Lord," replied Chak Zotz. "This delegation may serve to create a foundation of interaction with Kan, one that will be used to build a Ka'an polity alliance and woo the city away from B'aakal. It would not surprise me if some supposed traders were actually Kan nobles in disguise."

"Did you obtain information about their discussions with Yuknoom Bahlam?" Pakal asked.

"To my regret, my informants could not find ways to seek this information without revealing their true purposes," said Chak Zotz. "That would negate their usefulness to us."

Pakal nodded. Having undercover informants in polity cities was critical to political strategies.

"We must keep a close watch on Popo' and the attitude of its ruler," Pakal remarked. "This city has not been as generous in tribute to Lakam Ha as we deserve. I sense a cooling in our relations with them, despite the fact that the ruler's father was essentially raised in our court by my revered grandmother, Yohl Ik'nal."

"This will I discuss in detail with my informants, upon our next meeting," said Chak Sutz. "It is sad to observe how forgetful a ruler can be of his history and traditions."

Several other cities were reported as firmly allied with Lakam Ha, bountiful in tribute and quick in sending delegations to important polity events. B'aak, the birthplace of Pakal's deceased wife, was securely bound by blood ties. With the recent marriage of Tiwol and K'inuuw Mat, her city Uxte'kuh was similarly bound. Nab'nahotot, a city on the coast of the Great North Sea, was remote enough to avoid polity intrigues, and rich enough from trade to avoid seeking other alliances. Nututun and Sak Tz'i were nearby on the Chakamax River, close under the wing of Lakam Ha. The two large allies to the south had been consistent over many katuns: Oxwitik had stable dynastic progressions while Mutul had suffered severe disruptions due to a long-standing series of battles with Kan, resulting in a lengthy hiatus in new constructions. Several smaller cities posed no concern, but the list of questionable allies was growing alarmingly.

Yokib, a sizeable city on the banks of the mighty K'umaxha River, had switched alliance to Kan during the reign of Pakal's mother, Sak K'uk. Another city called Wa-Mut, even closer to Lakam Ha on this river, followed suit. Significant river cities farther south, Pa'chan and Usihwitz, had been Kan allies for katuns. Now with the north river city Pipá in the Kan camp, Lakam Ha had enemies on both sides. This posed significant threats to river travel along the major artery of the region.

It was critical to maintain ties with other polity cities that were considered questionable. In addition to Popo', the city of Sak Nikte' was known to have contacts with Kan. The men in the Council House reviewed recent information about these two cities and agreed on increased surveillance. Sending a royal emissary with both gifts and veiled threats was proposed, and Pakal agreed to dispatch one son to each city in the near future.

Kan Joy Chitam drew the Council's attention to Imix-Ha, the much-contested city on the K'umaxha River where Pakal had reinstated the Mutul ruler, Nuun Ujol Chaak, just one year ago. Imix-Ha was an offshoot of that great city, founded by the ruler's half-brother Balaj Chan K'awiil in a quest to establish his own rulership. Balaj claimed to be the rightful heir to Mutul and recruited Kan's forces to place him on the throne. Kan was always happy to engage in more warfare with Mutul, but the conflicts had not ended in the snake dynasty's favor. Lakam Ha prevailed and sent Balaj scurrying into exile at Dzibanche, the Kan stronghold.

"I am troubled by the situation at Imix-Ha," said Kan Joy Chitam. "It was unfortunate that Balaj Chan K'awiil escaped. He will never rest until he reasserts his power in this city, and as all are aware, he lusts after the Mutul throne. Kan will support him in these goals, ever seeking to weaken or destroy their hereditary enemy. While here for my brother's marriage, Nuun Ujol Chaak expressed these very sentiments himself. He sought reassurance that Lakam Ha would come to his defense once again, should Kan attack."

"This reassurance you gave to him, I presume?" asked Pakal.

"Just so. It would help this cause to have more knowledge of Kan's plans, so we can prepare in advance. This, I realize, will be difficult. We have not found effective avenues to infiltrate Dzibanche and establish intelligence networks."

"Let us put more effort into it," said Pakal. "Chak Zotz, meet with your best informants and devise some method to get into the city of Kan. Whatever resources you need shall be provided; this takes high priority." He turned to his son. "Since you have discussed this with Nuun Ujol Chaak, keep in regular contact with him."

"I will plan to visit Imix-Ha soon," said Kan Joy Chitam.

"Kan Bahlam, you are designated to visit Popo'." Pakal turned his head to locate his third son, Tiwol Chan Mat, who had remained silent through the discussion. "Tiwol, you shall be my delegate to Sak Nikte'; speak with your older brothers and Chak Zotz about details of your visit there. They have experience and much knowledge of diplomacy, which you will find serves you well."

Tiwol Chan Mat had no interest in diplomacy and little in politics. His was an artistic nature, and he preferred the company of his pots and paints. But, he had no choice except to bow and signal acquiescence to his father's orders.

Tiwol led K'inuuw Mat across the main plaza after they climbed the sakbe from the cascades residence, approaching the palace from the northeast. This side of the palace had the widest stairway, spanning from corner to corner in a dizzying ascent to the upper platform. A long structure with multiple equidistant doorways greeted the visitor, each doorway panel carved in low relief with mythological creatures, deities, and ancestors. The same vibrant colors and elegant roofcomb found on the other exterior buildings of the palace delighted the senses. Entering through the central corbelled arch, the couple passed into the East Court, the largest palace courtyard, used for official receptions and important state ceremonies. Stairways descended into the courtyard from all four surrounding buildings, but only the stairs from the main entrance spanned the entire distance. The other stairways covered one-third of their building's length and were decorated with carved panels.

K'inuuw Mat was impressed with the grandeur and sense of power this palace entrance conveyed. She could see why it was used to receive visiting rulers and ahauob, for it made an indisputable statement that Lakam Ha was the center of power in the region. Tiwol had undertaken to educate his wife on the history and politics of her new city, and his family's dynastic background. This trip to the East Court was part of the process.

"My father intends this East Court to make an impact upon political delegations," Tiwol said. "You have already seen how splendid the entrance stairway and building are; now you will understand the symbolism within this courtyard. Here to the right is the Royal Court of Lakam Ha with the ruler's official double-headed jaguar throne. This throne has a male and female jaguar head, one on each end, with a sky band forming the base of the seat and a Witz Monster mask below. Just as the jaguar is the most powerful animal in the jungle, and using a play on words, it serves as the emblem of our jaguar-Bahlam family. This throne communicates that whoever sits upon it commands the male and female energies of life, and has mastery over elements of the sky, earth, and underworld. Usually, a jaguar pelt is draped over the seat to emphasize the lineage."

"It is truly an impressive building," said K'inuuw Mat, peering through the doorways to locate the throne. "I shall anticipate seeing your father seated upon the throne when the Royal Court is in session."

"Royal Court sessions are most glorious and majestic," said Tiwol. "I believe one is scheduled for the next tun ending, several moons away."

He gestured across the court at a smaller building with four doorways and several interior chambers.

"This is the administrative center with chambers for various officials, those dealing with tribute recording and storage, writing city records in codices, tallying crop output and difficulties, managing disputes among city residents, and other such items. On the side opposite the Royal Court is the Popol Nah, where the ahauob meet in council with the ruler. This tradition of a council of ahauob was started by one of our ancestors, but its origin goes so far back that I cannot recall when. There was recently a session of the Popol Nah, the one when I was assigned the diplomatic mission to Sak Nikte' which I mentioned."

She turned to examine each building as he described it, tangibly sensing the symmetry of the nearly parallel structures. That they were slightly offset, making the courtyard wider on one end, added somehow to the attractiveness. Her eyes scanned the angles of rooflines and eaves, noticing how these again kept nearly parallel relationships that added grace and completeness. Despite the massive size of the buildings and their ornate decorations, they conveyed a sense of airiness, an uplifting lightness, that she felt was created by the roof angles and filigreed roofcombs.

They stepped down the stairway and walked across the white plaster plaza. Patterns of shadow and light played on its surface when clouds passed overhead. Tiwol stopped facing the Royal Court building at the base of the stairs. He pointed to six piers carved in bas-relief and other carved figures on both sides of the stairs and along the wall base. The figures appeared to be captives from their submissive and bound postures; their finery removed, ropes around wrists or necks, and pieces of cloth inserted into earlobe openings. Glyphs carved on their thighs or above their heads denoted their names, cities, and status.

"These carvings record the most painful part of Lakam Ha's history," said Tiwol. "We suffered a terrible attack from Kan, aided by Usihwitz that destroyed many monuments and pyramids. The worst damage to our city was the desecration of our sacred shrine, the Sak Nuk Nah. Through evil shamanic curses, Kan was able to collapse the portal this shrine held. The religious charter of our city was shattered, and our rulers could no longer ascend the Wakah Chan Te' to commune with Gods and ancestors. Perhaps you have already heard of this; it put us into chaos for many years. My grandmother Sak K'uk undertook a dangerous journey into the Underworld, trying to find a way to the Triad Gods, our benefactors. She was successful and gained the help of Muwaan Mat, the Progenitor Goddess and mother of the Triad. They essentially co-reigned, my grandmother the earthly ruler while the Goddess performed rituals the Triad Gods required in the Upperworld. She kept Lakam Ha stable and held the throne until my father acceded. You know he was seated at age twelve? He freely admits that she remained co-regent with him for many years, until he reached manhood."

"I have heard fragments of these events," said K'inuuw Mat. "But I never understood the entire situation. You must tell me more details. It is a fascinating story."

"Indeed it is. My father's sacred mission, which took most of his life to accomplish, was to resurrect the portal and restore our city's religious charter. Many years of ritual and deep spiritual communion were needed. He built the new Sak Nuk Nah, which you have seen, as the first structure of this palace." Tiwol smiled mischievously and slipped an arm around her waist. "How my father erected and revived the Wakah Chan Te' is the most wondrous story of all. He needed to awaken the primal life force of creation from deep within the earth, the Underworld, and channel it through the Middleworld to the Upperworld. For that he could not use his male powers alone; he had to combine these with female procreative abilities. And so, he and my mother assumed the forms of First Father—Maize God, and Primordial Mother—Serpent of Life in an awesome ritual. It was set for a solar eclipse, harnessing astrological energies of the highest magnitude. It was dangerous for them to open themselves as channels for such explosive energies, but they knew it must be done. Have you heard of this?"

She smiled up at his eager face and pressed closer to him, and he bent to brush a kiss across her lips.

"Of this wondrous story I have heard very little," she murmured, lips still against his. "Tell me more."

After taking a full kiss, he whispered into her ear. "They used sexual alchemy, in which both were well-trained, to conceive a new Wakah Chan Te' and to birth it upon the throne in the Sak Nuk Nah. This extraordinary event was witnessed by select priests and nobles. From that moment, the sacred portal was restored. Now it has been strengthened by years of use, and our ability to provide proper offerings to the Triad Gods is stabilized. From the ruler's communications with these deities, our city receives guidance and protection."

"Ah, that is a most amazing story," breathed K'inuuw Mat.

The sound of footsteps along one of the corridors broke their embrace, although Tiwol kept hold of his wife's hand. He waved to some official entering the administration building with the other hand, then continued his lesson.

"Here, let us observe the figures carved by the stairs," he said. They were lifelike, in contorted positions, and their faces clearly showed their fear and humiliation. "These are several lords of opposing cities, those in Kan's network of alliances, who suffered for this heinous attack. They are from Wa-Mut, Pipá, and Usihwitz. After being displayed in parades and publically humiliated, they were executed for their treachery. This shows how deeply my father was wounded by the devastating Kan attack. Normally the art and sculpture he commissions depicts our rulers, ancestors, and deities, conveying the history and accomplishments of our city. Lakam Ha rulers have never assumed aggressive postures on public monuments, as is common among other cities. Of note, we have not erected any standing stone monuments on public plazas to commemorate victories or record accessions. Our monuments are more personal and often private."

He waved across the East Court, indicating the stairway of the Popol Nah, and then led K'inuuw Mat to stand in front. Flanking the stairs was another set of panels with carved figures, four on the left and five on the right. These were also portrayed as captives in submissive poses.

"My father was just eight years old when Kan and Usihwitz attacked three katuns ago," said Tiwol, his face contemplative. "Can you imagine what he must have gone through? To see your entire world fall apart, your most sacred shrine destroyed, your city leaderless? It is rumored that he vowed to take revenge upon Kan, and I believe this courtyard framed by captives who were executed is the fulfillment of that vow. These lords are from Imix-Ha and other vassal cities of Kan. Only in this courtyard, the place of official reception and demonstration of Lakam Ha's prowess, will you find carvings of captives. This is my father's statement: the axing, the chopping down of Lakam Ha, has been avenged."

K'inuuw Mat stood thoughtfully beside her husband, trying to imagine the impact such events would have on a child. She was not much older when her mother took her to Cuzamil, and her experience there with the Ix Chel oracle was emblazoned upon her memory. Pakal's experiences would have been much more traumatic. It was an admirable testimony to his strength of character that he had overcome such emotional damage to become the great ruler that he was now.

While Tiwol was away on his diplomatic mission to Sak Nikte', K'inuuw Mat realized that she was pregnant. She first suspected it when her moon cycle was delayed, and then noticed subtle changes in her body along with morning queasiness. She waited until the next expected moon flow failed to appear, and then informed the Ix Chel priestess-healer, Chilkay. Delighted that conception occurred so quickly, Chilkay confirmed the pregnancy after examination. K'inuuw Mat asked that the priestess delay telling Pakal and the royal family until after Tiwol's return, so he could hear the news first. Since Tiwol's return was expected within a few days, Chilkay agreed.

K'inuuw Mat reflected on how often the Goddess Ix Chel had been in her dreams of late. Although details of these dreams escaped her, the overall theme seemed to be the Goddess' work on Cuzamil. At times she sensed Ix Chel's presence strongly, feeling that if she suddenly turned she would see the radiant form hovering over her left shoulder. These experiences, along with the last conversation she had with her mother, led her to believe that this newly conceived child was connected to the Goddess.

Chelte' had arranged a visit before she returned to Uxte'kuh two days after her daughter's marriage. They spent a morning together in the sun-dappled patio of the cascades residence, enjoying the sound of waterfalls and the misty spray that cooled the summer air. After remarking on the lavish marriage ceremony and feasts, the impressive palace complex, the congeniality of the royal family, and the serene beauty of her daughter's new residence, Chelte' brought up the subject of Ix Chel.

"It is my hope that you keep strong your dedication to Ix Chel," Chelte' said. "There will be many distractions in your new situation, and less support for practicing the Goddess' ways. Even now I sometimes find it hard to understand her ways; we all thought your life would be devoted to her service on Cuzamil. It seems this tradition of our family will skip a generation."

"So it appears, but never fear that my devotion to the Goddess will wane," said K'inuuw Mat. "Already I have located a hidden nook beside the waterfall for my altar and will set it up soon. My days would be incomplete without a place for communion with her."

"Excellent! Your husband Tiwol Chan Mat seems a gentle and reasonable man; he will probably be accepting of your spiritual traditions."

"Of this, I have no doubt. He is a wonderful man, and our love deepens daily."

"Much am I thankful to hear this. I know one of the most important purposes of royal marriages is to produce dynastic heirs, and that Pakal expects grandsons from this union."

"Yes, I have been instructed by my priestess-healer in techniques for conceiving sons, which she urges us to accomplish immediately." K'inuuw Mat laughed. "It appears our intimate relations are of great interest to many."

"Your life is unavoidably public," sighed Chelte', "far more under scrutiny than mine has been. That is one price for marrying into the polity's governing family. And, this emphasizes the necessity for keeping your actions above reproach."

The eyes of mother and daughter met in unspoken acknowledgement.

"How have you fared with the chant I taught you?" Chelte' asked.

"It is serving me well," replied K'inuuw Mat. "The effects are profound and immediate. It encloses me in a shield of protection and brings inner tranquility. I cannot thank you enough for providing me with this tool."

"Good, and use it daily. There are forces here that would disrupt your happiness, if allowed to run their course."

K'inuuw Mat nodded, glancing around to see if any servants were listening, but none were in sight.

"I realize that your first child is expected to be a son," said Chelte'. "Perhaps the next could be a daughter? My fondest dream is that a daughter of yours, my granddaughter, would take up the family tradition and become an acolyte of Ix Chel. Surely the Bahlam family would respect this long-standing tradition; they do understand obligations to ancestors and deities. What think you? I realize it is early in your relationship with the royal family to know for certain."

"In my meetings with Pakal, I have found him most kind and respectful. My sense is that he would understand and support this. I believe that Tiwol would be similarly accepting, once we have produced a son."

"Ah, this comforts my heart. It would be a great disappointment to me, should the venerable pattern of our women to serve Ix Chel be broken by my descendants."

As K'inuuw Mat reviewed this conversation, walking beside the pond and watching frogs hop from the bank when she approached, she had the sensation that Ix Chel was within her body. It was more than that; the Goddess was inside her womb.

This child is a girl! An immediate knowing flooded her awareness. She stopped short and caught her breath, partly in surprise but with a touch of delight. The child was a girl, and one already claimed by Ix Chel.

Conflicting thoughts tumbled through her mind. Tiwol and Pakal would be disappointed that this first child was not a boy. She was loath to fail their expectations and wondered how to explain what happened with the conception. She and Tiwol had initially followed the priestess' instructions faithfully, using the prescribed timing and position to conceive a male. After several days, however, they became lax and simply followed their pleasure. In theory, the conception should already have occurred and the incipient male child formed in her womb.

But the Goddess had intervened. As a result of the mysterious Upperworld powers under Ix Chel's command, the meticulous procedures developed by the priestesses were circumvented, and the outcome followed the purposes of the Goddess. While K'inuuw Mat could understand this completely, and even celebrate the divine hand shaping earthly lives, would her husband and father-in-law be so accepting?

She needed time to reflect, to seek guidance on the best approach. It was not necessary to share this information immediately, even if they would believe it. That her inner knowing was accurate, however, she had no doubt.

3

Clouds gathering over the mountains predicted afternoon rain. Their billowing white caps and soggy grey bellies promised a heavy downpour. Fresh wind swept across the main plaza, offering welcome coolness on the muggy, hot day. Groups of men squatting or seated on mats occupied numerous chambers of the Academy of Astronomy and Sciences. Some wrote in bark paper books, while others made calculations with the Maya dot-and-bar numerical system using newly plastered walls inside chambers. When doing calendar calculations, it was usual to write with paints and brushes upon chamber walls. The numbers often became long strings of a dot for one and bar for five, with multiples of twenty gained with each ascending row. Using walls gave more space for writing and permitted several scholars to take part in the calculations at hand. Sometimes numbers were drawn as heads with faces. Time, to the Maya, consisted of living entities, beings with unique identities and personalities, having intentions of their own.

Time was ruled by the Lords of Time, who carried the burden of the time period using a tumpline across their foreheads. When the time period they carried was completed, they would put down their burden and step aside. The Lord of the next time period would then be seated, denoting the first day of his reign. When the Mayas wrote calendar numbers, they used zero for the day of seating. Thus a 20-day uinal (month) was counted from 0 to 19, and an 18-uinal tun (year) was counted from 0 to 17. With their base-20 system, computations rapidly reached huge numbers: 20 tuns made a katun of 7200 days; 20 katuns made a baktun of 144,000 days; 20 baktuns created a number so large that few could imagine it, almost 8,000 solar years. Using a face glyph for the Lords of Time when they became immense provided a code immediately recognizable by educated Mayas. This simplified calendar studies.

When a set of calendar calculations was finished, it could be recorded in codices if desired. Then the wall was re-plastered for the next project. The chambers were located in three buildings set in a row, low and rectangular, with multiple doors opening toward the plaza. Pillars between doors, roof façade, and roofcomb were decorated in cosmological symbols. Exterior wall colors and adornments conformed to the Lakam Ha palette. The buildings rested on a several-tiered platform that rose well above plaza level, giving a southwest view toward the palace and mortuary temples.

Kan Bahlam stood facing the inside wall in a centrally located chamber, flanked by Chak Chan and Mut. Using a hair-tipped pen dipped in black pigment, he quickly made a series of numerical calculations across the plaster. Frowning, he grabbed a rag and wiped out the final figures, made several new entries, and then threw his paintbrush to the floor. It left a train of black blobs where it bounced on the stucco.

"Your newest figures are indecipherable," commented Chak Chan, one of the few nobles who could chide the moody Ba-ch'ok.

"Hrumph!" was all Kan Bahlam would say. He turned and strode outside to stand at the top of the stairway, hands on hips. The breeze had quickened and lifted strands of moist hair hanging at his nape, while the breech clout between his legs swayed.

Chak Chan and Mut came to stand beside him.

"Ah, such a refreshing wind," said Mut. "The air was most oppressive inside."

"Rain is not far off," observed Chak Chan, eyeing the mountainous horizon.

"It is a good thing, for the crops were getting dry. The corn is not far from harvest and will not be as sweet if it dries out," added Mut.

"Such experts at weather and agriculture! Would you were so astute with calendar and cosmic numerology," grumbled Kan Bahlam. "This project is at an impasse. We have made no progress in deciphering the underlying algorithm that will tie historical dates to celestial patterns. I am frustrated!"

"Perhaps there is no unifying algorithm," said Mut.

"Speak not such a thing!" Kan Bahlam's frown darkened, and he glared at his colleague.

"Truly, I do believe there is a model," said Chak Chan. "It is eluding us, slipping by just past our fingertips. It is probably something so obvious that we are overlooking it."

"We have tried dividing calendar periods by solar and lunar movements through the year, and wandering star periodicity, and still no useful model has emerged," said Mut. "What else is there to do? Eclipse tables are not applicable to this type of algorithm. I cannot think of where to go from here."

"We must examine more closely the day counts between historical events, those which most interest our search," said Kan Bahlam. "I sense that within this numerology lies a clue."

"Ah, again we revisit long tables of dates until our minds are roasted," complained Chak Chan.

Kan Bahlam was about to snap at his friend and brother-in-law, but saw two people approaching the stairway from the plaza. Dark clouds swept behind, as though pursuing them, and discharged fat raindrops that splattered noisily on the plaster. The pair quickened their pace as raindrops thickened into a promised deluge.

"It is my brother Tiwol and his new wife," observed Kan Bahlam.

"Ah, yes," confirmed Chak Chan. "She is with child; it shows but slightly."

"My brother loses no time in sowing the dynastic seed," muttered Kan Bahlam, his voice edged with bitterness.

Chak Chan shot a knowing glance toward Mut. Of all the Ba-ch'ok's associates, Chak Chan knew the lingering pain this caused. Just as the pair reached the stairway base, the cloud deities disgorged their contents, and heavy rain pounded the mortals below. The men bounded down the stairways to assist the couple's ascent, all rushing breathlessly into the central chamber, shaking water from their hair and clothing. Mut offered paint cloths for drying. Through the chamber door, the view across the plaza was completely obscured in a thick grey veil as the scent of fresh wetness pervaded the air.

"At least we are now cooled off," Mut offered.

"And drenched in addition," said Chak Chan, vigorously drying his hair.

Kan Bahlam bowed to the visitors, cloth wrapped around his neck.

"Welcome to you, brother, and to your esteemed wife. To what purpose may I attribute this unexpected visit?"

"Let me thank you for the sanctuary, and the drying cloths," replied Tiwol. He turned to make certain that K'inuuw Mat was sufficiently dry. Her hair hung in tendrils, having escaped the turban trying to contain it, and her huipil clung to her body, revealing the swell of her abdomen and blossoming breasts. She nodded and gave a hand sign that all was well.

"You may know that I am acquainting my wife with the structures and activities of her new city," Tiwol continued. "We have completed our tour of the palace and the mortuary pyramids close to it. I thought she might next learn of your Academy of Astronomy and Sciences. Perhaps I should have sent notice of our visit; I hope we do not interrupt you in an important process."

Both Tiwol and K'inuuw Mat looked at the chamber walls covered with stellar symbols and mathematical calculations. Kan Bahlam found it difficult to keep his eyes off his brother's wife, her lithe form and fecundity too clearly revealed. With an effort, he shifted his view toward the chamber walls.

"Our process has come to a halt. Your visit offers us respite from our efforts," said Kan Bahlam. "It is good that we break."

"Just so, for the process is breaking our minds," added Chak Chan.

"We shall be refreshed by the lovely presence of Lady K'inuuw Mat," said Mut. "She brings radiant light to shine upon our dry deliberations."

K'inuuw Mat smiled and bowed her head at the compliment, relieved that it came from Mut rather than Kan Bahlam. She had steeled herself for the encounter, using the chant for protection at every possible moment. Since the marriage feast, she had only seen him at a distance. Now in his close presence in the small chamber, she could feel the magnetic pull creating little flutters in her heart, but she kept her mind calm. She focused attention on the figures spread across the walls.

"It appears that you are working with cycles of the wandering stars," she observed. "What is your objective?"

All three astronomers turned their heads toward the woman, surprise apparent on their faces. Tiwol also seemed nonplussed, for he had not recognized the meaning of the number sequences that covered the mid-portion of the back wall.

"That is true," said Chak Chan. "These are the day numbers for the cycles of each of the five wandering stars. Do you know them?"

"Yes . . . here is 584 for Noh Ek, using his 'big face' name," said K'inuuw Mat, pointing to the top set of number symbols. "Next comes 780 for Chak Ek the red star, then 116 for Xux Ek the rapid star, and 399 for K'awiil Ek the royal dynasty star, and 378 for Ayin Ek the secretive dark star. It appears you are attempting some computation among combinations of their day numbers."

"How do you know this?" Kan Bahlam appeared astonished, eyes wide and lips parted.

"I have received training as a seer on the island of Cuzamil, the abode of Ix Chel and her priestesses," K'inuuw Mat replied. "To make divinations, it was necessary to understand the travels of the wandering stars and what these signified. I have studied the stars for many years. It is a most favorite occupation of mine."

"Just as for me," murmured Kan Bahlam. "Untold nights have I climbed to the tops of pyramids in order to watch their patterns in the sky."

Mut and Chak Chan made comments affirming their interest in celestial studies.

"Then I am most happy to bring you here, dearest," said Tiwol. He hoped to conceal his embarrassment about not understanding astronomy, for it was expected that royal sons and elites have a working knowledge of this science. He was trying to place some context around his wife's newly discovered expertise.

"Tell me more about your work here," K'inuuw Mat continued. "You appear to be involved in a project, what are you seeking?"

Kan Bahlam drew himself to full stature and took a deep breath. This was the last question he had expected from her.

"For some years we have been working to develop an algorithm, to find the key that will connect the cosmic patterns of these important star deities with the history of the Lakam Ha dynasty," said Kan Bahlam. "This would reveal the interconnections between our origins in the misty past, our descent from the creator deities, the founding and growth of our city and polity, the significant events in the lives of our rulers, and perhaps even to project into the future. It is a most daunting project, because we are entering into new territory. We are seeking a pattern of relationships between occurrences in the sky, upon the earth, and in the underground that has never before been discovered."

"It is akin to creating a new language," added Mut. "A new way of understanding and communicating the mystical meaning that is hidden in numerology. Mathematics is a pure language, the dialect of the Gods, and contains the very essence of truth. But that truth is eluding us and creating great frustration."

"The patterns are there, of that I am certain," said Kan Bahlam, with passion thickening his voice. "There is a key that will tie it all together, and reveal the hidden truths. A numerical construct, some number that relates to and connects all the others."

"So this is the algorithm that you seek," concluded K'inuuw Mat. "The numerical key. You wish to use this key to unlock hidden relationships between the periods of the wandering stars and the history of your people."

"Just as you say!" Kan Bahlam exclaimed. His eyes were shining, excited that she grasped the concept and stated it so clearly. He paused, momentarily lost in thought. Tilting his head with a smile playing at the corner of his lips, he sent her a challenge: "What would you suggest, Lady K'inuuw Mat, to help us examine this project in a different light?"

She walked slowly from one wall to the next, studying the symbols and figures, her expression alert and curious. At a few places, she tapped her fingers against numerical figures as if doing inner computations. After gazing intently at the last wall, she turned to face the men.

"Time consists of living beings, the Lords of Time and their many dominions," she said slowly and deliberately. "This you all know well. These Gods, the wandering stars, have purposes of their own and may alter their courses as they will. Cycles of time are not fixed, not absolute in their expressions. There are variations; observe Lady Uc as she cycles through her phases from the tiniest sliver to full roundness and back again to disappear into darkness. We know her cycle varies between 27 and 29 days, and we account for that when recording events. Likewise, the wandering stars have variations in their periods. As astronomers, you work with these in your calculations."

The three astronomers nodded, transfixed by her clear recitation of principles. Tiwol kept a neutral expression and wished he could follow the discussion better.

"From what I can grasp of your calculations, I will suggest keeping in mind two things. These may aid you to see your project in a different light. First, consider the variability of stellar movements, and do not expect an absolute and fixed numerical construct. You will need to work with close approximations. Second, return to using the sacred numbers of our people: 7 and 9 and 13. These numbers are themselves deities; they have agency to act and create and destroy. They tie together the three levels of existence: 7 for humans and the Middleworld, 9 for the Lords of Death and the Underworld, and 13 for the infinitude of the circle and the deities of the Upperworld. In plumbing the depths of these three sacred numbers, you will find revealed the key which you seek."

Kan Bahlam was stunned. In these two suggestions, a young woman who was not known as a great astronomer had opened the door to a vision that immediately coalesced in his mind. He could see patterns involving 7, 9, and 13 that presented vast numerological possibilities. He also caught the essential truth of working with approximations. Absolute perfection might be attained by the Gods but was seldom found in the mortal domain. His intuition told him that she had just opened the door to finding his long-sought algorithm.

In concert, the three astronomers crossed both arms over their chest in the gesture of highest honor, and bowed.

"Well spoken, Lady!" exclaimed Chak Chan.

"Your suggestions do indeed shed new light upon our project," said Mut.

"My deepest appreciation, dear sister-in-law," added Kan Bahlam. "Your insights are nothing less than amazing. You have most assuredly been well-trained at Cuzamil. Of this, I would appreciate speaking with you more."

"It would be my pleasure, Lord Kan Bahlam," replied K'inuuw Mat. She was not at all certain such a meeting would be enjoyable, and turned to Tiwol. He approached her and placed an arm around her waist, holding her to him possessively.

"You are a fount of surprises, dearest one," Tiwol said. "You must not keep your talents hidden from me." He turned to his brother and smiled. "We must not tire my wife, who is with child. Much do I thank you for welcoming her to your Academy and discussing your most intriguing project with her. Little did we guess that she would become such as asset."

Bows and goodbyes were exchanged all around, and Tiwol led his wife down the stairway to the plaza. The rain had passed, and intermittent sunshine lifted waves of mist from the plaster. Kan Bahlam watched as the couple walked through the shifting mist, its tendrils wrapping around the glorious palace and pyramids of the main plaza, glowing and golden in the afternoon sun. There was more to this young woman than beauty, he concluded. And, he wanted to know everything about her.

The long, muscular legs of Kan Bahlam carried him quickly up the palace stairway, two steps at a time. He hurried down the corridor toward the private reception chamber of his father, Pakal. Not waiting for the Royal Steward to usher him in, he made an energetic entrance and greeted the ruler and his chief architect, Yax Chan. They were meeting to discuss plans for Pakal's mortuary pyramid. On a wooden stand in the center of the chamber stood a model crafted by Yax Chan.

"We must begin this construction soon," said Pakal, gesturing toward the model. "As you see, the initial model is based on the pyramid of Kan Bahlam I, my great-grandfather. There is history and continuity in doing this, and it is a splendid structure."

At Kan Bahlam's concerned look, Pakal laughed.

"It is not that I am unwell, son, but that the time has arrived to begin what will be a lengthy project," he said. "Every aspect of the structure and its adornments will carry symbolism, from the shape of the building to the finest detail of carving on pillars and panels. Yax Chan and I have already agreed upon several features, but we need your expertise to properly express the cosmological messages. This structure will communicate the spiritual and historical record of our dynasty, and must contain numerous astronomical and ancestral references. These must also be expressed in the poetry of our calendars."

"It is an honor to be asked," said Kan Bahlam. "But have you not plentiful advice from your calendar priests?"

"For ordinary calendar calculations they serve well enough," said Pakal. "Here, however, my desire is to express a more profound understanding. From what I hear of your work at the Academy, you have tools for such deeper expressions."

"Ah, it is so, we are developing an algorithm that will link our history with the cosmic patterns in a way never done before," Kan Bahlam replied.

"That is what I am seeking. Let us proceed."

Yax Chan demonstrated the features of the pyramid and its temple on the top platform, then began taking off the outer layers to reveal hidden chambers within. He showed that a concealed opening in the temple floor led to a series of narrow stairs that descended steeply, made a switchback, and ended in a small chamber at ground level. A large doorway in the chamber opened to the burial crypt, several steps lower and below ground. The burial crypt was another chamber with a corbelled arch ceiling, just wide enough to hold a huge sarcophagus. The sarcophagus had thick walls and lid; inside was a fish-shaped depression in which the body would lie.

"Obviously the inner chambers must be constructed first," explained Yax Chan. "The sarcophagus and lid will be massive and heavy, impossible to transport down the narrow stairway. Once it is in place, the burial crypt chamber will be built, and then the easement chamber. The pyramid base will have been squared off beforehand, and initial foundation work can proceed at the same time. When the inner chambers are completed, the pyramid will be built from the ground up. At the appropriate point in construction, the stairs will be added. The final phases will involve creating decorative elements and the pillars and tablets containing hieroglyphs and figures."

"Much is yet to be decided," said Pakal. "We are in the early stages, and thought it wise to bring you in now. We must discuss what the glyphic text on the panels will contain. My idea is to place three panels inside the temple on top, giving sufficient space to convey our dynastic and city histories. The outer pillars, there will be six of them, will hold relief carvings of dynastic rulers in costumes of deities."

"The sarcophagus walls will be carved with the entire progression of rulers, from the founder to our present K'uhul B'aakal Ahau. The crypt walls will be painted with figures from our creation heritage, and perhaps others not yet decided," added Yax Chan.

"As you say, this is an enormous project," said Kan Bahlam. "Have you in mind some specific way that I may contribute to it?"

"That I have. It is my intention to go beyond a simple chronological retelling of history," Pakal replied. "The goal is to find symbolic relationships, to place our history in its divine context, to include the actions of the deities and the stars. There are two particular sets of historic events that you can assist me to place within such a framework. The first involves our times of greatest shame and chaos, the inglorious defeat by Kan and destruction of our monuments and shrines. This must be seen within the cosmological perspective, and the actions taken to restore our honor and rebuild structures linked in meaningful patterns. The second is my reconstruction of the portal to the Gods and ancestors. Again, this must be expressed according to higher meanings, to spiritual principles, and link to the future of our people. Once you have found the algorithm that makes the link, our scribes and carvers will create the glyphs that tell the stories. Can you do this?"

Kan Bahlam stood silently, fixated on the model. He knew the two events were the most significant in his father's life. Their proper retelling was of utmost importance. It was the very challenge he sought to master in his work at the Academy. This would be the proving ground, and he did not take it lightly. He drew a deep breath before raising his gaze to meet his father's eyes.

"This will I accomplish," he said.

K'inuuw Mat carefully prepared herself and her household for Kan Bahlam's visit. He had sent an attendant to request a meeting with her, to continue discussing his quest for the algorithm. She made certain that Tiwol would be home that day and sought assurance that Kuy would not be going out. Now that a young noble of Lakam Ha was courting Kuy, the attendant had frequent outings to meet him and visit his family.

Having repeated the chant most of the morning before Kan Bahlam arrived, K'inuuw Mat felt calm and strengthened to converse with him. Both Tiwol and Kuy were present when their visitor arrived, and they spent some time in greetings and small talk before Tiwol retired to his chamber where he worked on pottery, only two doors down from the reception chamber. Kuy had arranged for refreshments on the veranda facing the patio, where mats were set out. She moved to the far end of the veranda to take up weaving on her backstrap loom, a favorite art form of noble women. K'inuuw Mat and Kan Bahlam sat on mats facing each other, and received cups of kob'al from the servant.

"Much do I appreciate your receiving me for further talk," said Kan Bahlam. "Your suggestions at the Academy have offered us excellent options, and we are working on new possibilities in the numerology."

"It is my pleasure to be of assistance in your work," replied K'inuuw Mat. Now that he was so close, her protective screen seemed to waver. She felt her pulse quicken, and the skin on her arms tingled. She tried to push back on the mat and create more distance between them.

"May I say, Lady K'inuuw Mat, that being with child becomes you. Ever beautiful, your appearance is now radiant, the charm of a rare jungle flower in full bloom."

"You are most kind, Lord Kan Bahlam," she said, lowering her face to hide the blush.

"What I say is nothing but sincere and true."

She shifted position, aware that her enlarging abdomen was pushing against her huipil and that he was staring at it. Trying to rearrange the fabric to fit more loosely, she smiled and found no words to reply. Her heart was decidedly beating faster, and she started mentally chanting.

He sighed and looked off into the distance. She read the sadness in his eyes and sensed the pain in his heart. It was not difficult to surmise why, but she wanted to avoid entering a personal conversation. She was determined to avoid knowing him more deeply.

"Shall we speak of your project? I am eager to learn what progress your group is making," she said brightly, seeking to change the mood.

"Just so." Kan Bahlam regrouped quickly; he also wanted to avoid exposing his inner torments. "We have been discussing your suggestions, thinking in terms of numerical approximations rather than absolutes, and using the sacred numbers. Some revelations have come to me, which I believe will lead to the key for the algorithm. First, I must give background about the use of calendars in our city that you may not know. Please forgive me if I repeat information with which you are acquainted."

She nodded for him to continue, noticing that she felt more at ease since the focus of their discussion changed.

"Historians in the early years of our dynasty only had Calendar Round records, the combined dates from the Tzolk'in and Haab calendars that repeat their combinations every 52 years. With these calendars you are familiar. The Long Count calendar was not developed and used consistently until Baktun 8, when K'uk Bahlam I acceded. While K'uk Bahlam is considered the dynastic founder, the first ruler who was fully human, the lineage was actually brought into material form by his predecessor, U K'ix Kan. There is limited information about when his 'birth' took place. Our creation history relates that he had no mother and father, but was simply made and modeled. He was the first person, the first mother-father. His flesh was formed from yellow and white corn, but he was still mostly of the spirit world. He was created by the B'aakal Triad Gods: *Hun Ahau* the Son of First Father, *Mah K'inah Ahau* the Lord of the Underworld, and *Unen K'awiil* the Lord of the Middleworld and keeper of royal blood."

Kan Bahlam paused to make sure she was following.

"I have been learning more about your Triad Gods and creation story," she said.

"The narration of this story was passed down orally through generations, memorized and recited by rulers and carriers of the royal blood," Kan Bahlam continued. "It tells us that K'uk Bahlam acceded more than 1200 tuns after U K'ix Kan, but only provides Calendar Round dates to link these events. Now we anchor births and accessions to the Long Count calendar as well as the Calendar Round dates. To create the links between such important events and the lineage founder who spanned both the celestial and earthly realms, there must be a Long Count date. The accession date of U K'ix Kan is the anchor for all that follows; it allows making the historical-astronomical links."

"So I see," said K'inuuw Mat. "Yes, that would be a critical Long Count date."

"Yet, it is a date not on record, therefore one that must be constructed." Kan Bahlam smiled. "In this is an opportunity, following your suggestion of using approximations. Having only the Calendar Round date for U K'ix Kan actually provides an element of freedom. We have a scope of about 1600 years in which to find significant numerological associations with dynastic rulers leading to my father Pakal, working with the Calendar Round date of U K'ix Kan's accession, 11 Kaban 0 Pop.

"These are large numbers, unwieldy to work with using ordinary calendar calculations. If they were manipulated with an algorithm, then calculations would be easier. I followed your lead by multiplying 7 by 9 by 13 and arrived at the sum 819. This is an intriguing number, because it is commensurable with the cycles of Ayin Ek and K'awiil Ek. I have made initial calculations using this 819 number seeking links between the Triad God Unen K'awiil, U K'ix Kan, and my predecessor namesake, Kan Bahlam I. There are promising results from two sets of Long Count dates that match the Calendar Round dates for U K'ix Kan and Kan Bahlam's accessions. The one I prefer has associations with 364, the computing year, and 116, the period of Xux Ek who is the celestial representation of K'awiil."

"That is promising. It is significant that this number, 819, can find celestial and calendric patterns within historical time intervals."

"It is most promising. This particular pattern merges history, astronomy, and numerology by tying U K'ix Kan to the deity Unen K'awiil, allowing for the conjuring of royal ancestors, and also ties the wandering star aspect of this deity to the first ruler of our dynasty named Kan Bahlam. I am certain that many more associations will emerge from our further investigations."

They both paused, taking sips of kob'al and reflecting. Kan Bahlam felt exhilarated at her understanding of his points; K'inuuw Mat enjoyed exercising her mental abilities to address the puzzles presented. She was becoming almost comfortable in his presence. Their eyes met in mutual regard, and at this moment another idea came to her.

"The cardinal directions could also play a role in deciphering your key," she proposed. "One must not forget the influences of the marking and measuring that set our world into position. There are four cardinal directions, might there also be four calendric stations associated with the 819-day count? You say using 819 makes calculations easier by reducing large numbers. If you also work with the multiples of 819, you obtain similar results but reduce the numbers even more. With four stations for 819 linked to the cardinal directions, you could use a 3276-day count."

Kan Bahlam quickly calculated that 819 times 4 equaled 3276. He shook his head in disbelief as a wide smile curled his sensuous lips.

"An obvious deduction, how did it escape me? This idea inspires a new conceptualization of the 819-day count deity; it can only be K'awiil. As the count proceeds around the four directions, these become the stations or places of K'awiil, the *K'awiil-nal*. So we see the raising of the K'awiil-nal in the order of east, north, west, and south." At her puzzled expression, he explained: "K'awiil is the personification of royal blood. The K'awiil-scepter idol is received by rulers at inauguration, when they ascend the throne. Nal is the word for place; thus the combination is the 'place of K'awiil.' We can add the verb for raising or erecting, walaj, thus the *walaj K'awiil-nal* is the raising of the count that will guide us through the ritual circuit for placement of the earthly representative of K'awiil—the 819-day count—that will provide the algorithm for placing the rulers of our dynasty within meaningful positions within the celestial patterns of the Gods."

"And so you bring together history, astronomy, numerology, and the deities," K'inuuw Mat concluded.

"Yes." Kan Bahlam paused, again thoughtful. "Recently I met with my father and his chief architect. Pakal has requested my assistance in making just such connections in the hieroglyph narrative to be carved in his burial pyramid. It is a monumental undertaking; one dear to his heart, at which I must not fail."

"You will succeed. Of this, I have no doubt. And, you will go on to accomplish even greater things on your own." K'inuuw Mat surprised both herself and Kan Bahlam with her certainty. It was another immediate inner knowing that came from the Goddess Ix Chel.

"Let it be so, Lady," he murmured.

"Please call me by my name," she replied with a smile. "We are family."

"Happily, we are indeed family," he said. "K'inuuw Mat, my dear sister-in-law." The intense look he gave her and strong emanations she felt from his heart left her unsettled as he bade farewell.

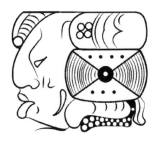

K'inuuw Mat—V

Baktun 9 Katun 12 Tun 1
– Baktun 9 Katun 12 Tun 5
(674 – 677 CE)

1

Fruit hung heavy on trees, papayas bright yellow and mangos rusty red, while fat ears of corn sported dried tassels announcing ripeness. As the harvest sun swing to autumn's midpoint, the place of balance between light and dark, the first child of K'inuuw Mat and Tiwol Chan Mat was born. The child was a girl, a large and vigorous infant who came quickly into the Middleworld as if eager to begin her journey. Everyone was surprised except the mother. K'inuuw Mat had decided to forewarn her husband, hoping to ease him into accepting a daughter. Tiwol brushed off her prediction, emphasizing how they followed prescriptions to conceive a son, and the priestess had confirmed the baby was a boy.

K'inuuw Mat persisted, engaging Tiwol in long conversations about her family's tradition of dedicating a daughter to serve Ix Chel. She tried to explain her sense that Ix Chel had determined the child's gender and claimed her. Although she used every persuasion she could muster, he still refused to accept her foreknowledge and would not make an agreement to dedicate any of their daughters to the Goddess. It was the first time K'inuuw Mat found her husband intractable, and it worried her.

Tiwol was entirely perplexed at this ability of his wife to prophesy. He felt embarrassed that they had produced a girl. He cringed at the thought of his father's disapproval and was loath to face the teasing of his brothers. Chilkay, the Ix Chel priestess who instructed the couple for conception, discussed the process with both parents but could find no glaring mistakes. K'inuuw Mat attempted to explain that the Goddess had claimed the baby, and thought she saw a glimmer of understanding. But, this was a humiliating occurrence for the priestess, and she would offer no support.

Pakal's response was kinder than Tiwol expected. Although Pakal believed in honoring family traditions, and suggested that a future daughter might be given to serve Ix Chel, he stressed the importance of a first daughter for making a political alliance. Even though not the expected son, this child could still serve the dynasty. Pakal visited at the Sutzha River residence when his granddaughter was two days old, his heart once again wrenched by memories, both sweet and sorrowful. When K'inuuw Mat apologized for not bearing a son, he graciously assured that it did not affect his regard for her. Despite the best plans of humans, the deities had their own purposes.

Given this opening, and knowing that Pakal was himself a trained shaman-ruler who undertook journeys and communed with deities, K'inuuw Mat described her experience of Ix Chel entering her womb and claiming the child. Pakal listened attentively; these abilities of his daughter-in-law reminded him of his grandmother Yohl Ik'nal, a highly respected visionary. Although he made no promise that this baby girl might be dedicated to Ix Chel, he agreed to reflect upon her request. He also accepted the name she selected: Yax Chel—Blue Rainbow.

In consultation with Chilkay and the Ah K'inob to calculate an auspicious date for the next birth, Pakal determined that Tiwol and K'inuuw Mat should plan another conception for the following spring. This allowed the mother to nurse her baby over a half-year, giving a healthy start before turning the child over to a wet-nurse. The exact date would be determined by the calendar priests for a birth near the winter solstice. Chilkay admonished the couple to follow her instructions meticulously, and make no deviations even when they thought the fertile period had ended. It was better to miss a conception, and then recalculate timing for another try, than to conceive a child who would not be a boy.

Talol secretly gloated that K'inuuw Mat's child was a girl. It was a small consolation for her own childlessness, made all the more unbearable by the new bride's rapid conception. At least her other sister-in-law, Te' Kuy, was unable to get pregnant since her son's birth more than a year ago. It galled Talol that the evident heir in the lineage came from the second son of Pakal, Kan Joy Chitam. The heir should come from the first son, her husband Kan Bahlam. Of course, the succession had been set before the boy Mayuy was born, progressing from Pakal's first son to the second son, and then to the third son Tiwol Chan Mat, should the older brothers have no male issue. Given Pakal's exceptional longevity, she wondered who would live longest to actually succeed.

Why she hated K'inuuw Mat from the outset sometimes puzzled Talol, when she reflected on it. Perhaps because the woman was young and beautiful, and now had proved to be fecund. At the edges of her memory were the final words of her mother-in-law, Tz'aakb'u Ahau, the beloved wife of Pakal. Called Lalak, the ruler's wife had predicted that the dynasty would continue through Tiwol. Although Talol was not one to give much credence to predictions, those breathed on the deathbed were considered potent. The Gods, however, were changeable and who could read their ultimate intentions.

If Talol were to be honest with herself, however, she must admit that one thing in particular made her hate K'inuuw Mat: Kan Bahlam was obviously attracted her. Why this should be more irksome than his innumerable other liaisons, she was not certain. As far as she could tell, nothing had happened yet between them. But given time she was certain that something would. Kan Bahlam was not a man to deny his appetites for long.

Kan Bahlam had been avoiding his wife, and she was acutely aware of it. They had two primary residences, their palace chambers and a large complex across the Otulum River, east of the palace. He tried to stay in whichever location she was not occupying. When they did happen to spend the night in the same residence, he kept to his own sleeping chamber and never sought hers. She was too proud to go to him. And, she could not recall their last intimacy. She spent her days with women attendants, weaving or painting ceramics, playing music or games, an endless round of boredom.

Now her informants told her Kan Bahlam was consulting with K'inuuw Mat about complicated astronomical and numerological subjects, and the woman had impressed the scholars at his Academy. She wondered how the young woman came to possess such knowledge, and the sharp edge of envy fed her animosity. It was too much to bear. She would find some way to retaliate, to inflict damage upon them both.

Kan Bahlam stood at one end of the ball court, gazing down its narrow corridor between two parallel structures on either side with sloping embankments. Viewing chambers were situated on top of the structures, empty this day because the game was just for practice. When ceremonial games were performed, the chambers would be bursting with noble spectators. The smooth surfaces of the embankments rose from near ground level to above the height of a man, and were used to bounce the ball off and back into play. Both ends of the corridor were open and aligned north to south; one end was located just to the east of the great processional stairway that mounted the north terraces of the palace. The ball court at Lakam Ha was small and simply designed, with only one marker stone placed in the center of the corridor, flush with the ground. The stone's imagery contained motifs for the Underworld: the quatrefoil portal called *Ol* that gave opening to the watery Underworld, Maize God foliations for the resurrection of First Father, and the White Bone Snake symbol that represented the Death Lords. These images spoke of the eternal struggle to defeat death and attain life anew; the story told in the Popol Vuh about the mystery of life repeatedly being reborn out of death.

The tall, heavily muscled Ba-ch'ok shifted his weight from one foot to the other and twisted his torso from side to side, testing the balance of his ballgame gear. Thick cotton padding was wrapped around his pelvis, and a U-shaped yoke made of leather surrounded his waist and lower chest. He wore a knee-pad on this left knee fashioned as a shield with the K'in Ahau face and framed with feathers, and a calf-length leather skirt over his loincloth. Additional cloth padding covered his forearms, and fringed leather anklets flapped above bare feet. Most players wore gloves. The player's costume was completed by a decorative neck collar of shining copper and shells, and an elaborate headdress with deer heads woven on a broad-brimmed hat with cloth strips waving a rainbow of colors.

The heavy padding was necessary to protect ballplayers from serious injury. The balls they used were made from liquid latex taken from rubber trees, heated until the resin formed threads which were wound into a round ball, kneaded and pressed into a mold. The balls were large, generally as wide as a man's forearm, and quite heavy. They bounced readily from either stones or the players' bodies, and could damage unprotected flesh. Once put into play, the ball was not allowed to touch the ground of the corridor, although it could be bounced off the embankments. Players could not touch the ball with hands or feet; it could only be hit with hips, thighs, and forearms. The heavy padding cushioned players when they threw themselves on the ground to use hips or thighs to bounce the ball, when they broke their fall with arms or hands, or fell to one knee keeping the ball in play.

There were regional variations on how the ballgame was scored. In cities with large ball courts, the embankments often had a stone ring set high up the wall on each side. Points were made when the ball was propelled through the rings; each team had its own ring. At smaller courts such as the one at Lakam Ha, rings were not used. The game was won by the team that kept the ball in play longest, preventing it from hitting the ground. The losers were the ones who failed to keep the ball in play. The ballgame could be played between only two opponents, or by small teams of two to five men. A woman of high status would begin the game by tossing the ball down from the viewing chamber.

Two teams of three men each gathered at the Lakam Ha ball court. Kan Bahlam's team included his brother-in-law Chak Chan and his assistant Yuhk Makab'te. The opposing team was headed by Chak Zotz, Nakom of the city and two of his warriors. Kan Bahlam tossed his ball up high against an embankment, and the game began as it bounced down toward the corridor. Chak Zotz moved quickly into position and shoved his hip against the ball, sending it high in the air where it arced and fell, met by Chak Chan's thigh rebounding it up again. It bounced off the opposite embankment and flew an unexpected direction, forcing Kan Bahlam to dive to the ground, breaking his fall with a forearm while swinging his thigh in position to deflect the ball. He grunted in pain from the impact of forearm and hip against the stone corridor. Yelling and grunting, the men continued intercepting the heavy ball, sending it soaring or using the embankments to bounce it into play.

Sweat dripped from Kan Bahlam's forehead and trickled down his back, but intense concentration prevented him from noticing. At one point the ball hit his unprotected upper arm, and he yelped at the searing pain. A bluish bruise began forming quickly, and he spared a moment to hope that it would not turn into a blood clot in the muscle. These large clots were common and had to be removed by slicing the wound open with a knife. The ball hovered over his head and he had no more thoughts of his injuries, using his other forearm to deflect it before it could hit the ground.

The intense physical effort required to play the ballgame made it a sport for only strong and fit men. Those of small stature without much muscle development could not aspire to play. The punishing impacts of ball and ground were hard to sustain for many years, so most players were young men. Kan Bahlam prided himself on his skill in the game, and was a formidable opponent who was nicknamed *ah pitzlal*—the ballplayer. He had maintained his prowess over many years, more than most players.

His abilities meshed with those of his two teammates, and they kept the ball in play for what seemed an interminable time. Chak Zotz matched their stamina, but his warriors started to flag and one misjudged the ball's trajectory, allowing it to hit the ground.

Cheers erupted from Kan Bahlam's team and they raised their arms, making the hand sign for victory. Chak Zotz and his men bowed, and the teams exchanged mutual acknowledgement of a game well played. Had the game been shorter, they would have engaged in another round, but both teams were exhausted. They bid each other farewell and retired to their quarters for post-game recovery. Kan Bahlam thanked his teammates, and then stood alone at the south end of the corridor, gazing thoughtfully along its length. He had observed his father performing ceremonial ballgames on a few occasions. These ceremonial games re-enacted the Maya myth of creation and the saga of the Hero Twins from the Popol Vuh. The Hero Twins played the ballgame against the Lords of Death, using cleverness and trickery to overcome death in the Underworld, allow for the rebirth of the Maize God, and bring about completion of the life cycle.

Ceremonial ballgames expressed the central metaphors that shaped the destiny and history of the Mayas. Players took the roles of the Hero Twins and Death Lords, as the conflict of the teams represented the winning and losing of wagers. The consequences of defeat often ended in sacrifices, followed by the symbolic recovery of the dead First Father from the marker in the floor of the ball court. Ballgame sacrifice served as the ritual climax of struggles between enemy cities, when captive lords were given public execution. These rituals were more common at other cities; in particular, Kan and Pa'chan where captives were tied up tightly and rolled like balls down the stairs of ball courts to their death. In Lakam Ha, Pakal had performed ball court sacrifice in a more traditional way by decapitating captives, commemorating his victory over several allies of Kan. This ritual sacrifice avenged the devastating Kan-inspired attack against Lakam Ha during the reign of his uncle.

Later that evening, Kan Bahlam stretched out with a groan on his sleeping pallet in the residence across the Otulum River. His body was aching from the vigorous ballgame that afternoon and his bruised arm throbbed, but at least no blood clot had formed. His achiness despite taking a long sweat bath followed by a relaxing massage reminded him that he was no longer a youth. His fortieth solar year was approaching, he reluctantly acknowledged. There was no question that he had attained the age of maturity, yet still, he was without issue and had not acceded to the throne. These were depressing thoughts, and he shifted to his side seeking a more comfortable position to soothe his mind and body.

He was dozing off when an arm slipped over his shoulder, the hand tracing down his chest to the lower abdomen. The breath scented of sweet honeysuckle and the warm lips caressing the back of his neck identified his visitor. Before the hand could reach his groin, Kan Bahlam sat up and moved it away; turning to face the young man perched on the edge of the sleeping platform.

"Ab'uk, not tonight. I am not in a mood for this," said Kan Bahlam.

The young man was slender with lustrous black hair, archly tilted almond eyes, and a sensuous face. His lithe limbs were shapely, his hands and feet refined, his manner effeminate. Ab'uk was a noble courtier who was a two-spirit, a man attracted to his own gender. Mayas considered two-spirits a third gender blending qualities of male and female, often having special abilities or favored by deities. They were identified in childhood by their interest in activities of the opposite sex, and often cross-dressed. Being two-spirit was not discouraged. It simply was the person's natural state.

"We have not been together for some time," pouted Ab'uk. "I am yearning for your passions. Your absence dampens my heart."

"My work has demanded all my attention," Kan Bahlam said. "There are important projects that I must accomplish in a short time period."

"Ah, then all the more reason to have a pleasurable break from your labors," Ab'uk purred, reaching to trace his long fingers across Kan Bahlam's jaw. He leaned closer, hand dropping to slide across the hard muscles of Kan Bahlam's chest, bringing his lips up for a kiss.

Kan Bahlam allowed the kiss, but did not return it. When Ab'uk slid his hand down Kan Bahlam's naked body, it was again gently removed.

"Not now, please, Ab'uk," said the Ba-ch'ok. "I wish you no offense. It is not the right time."

"When will be the right time?"

"Not soon, I do not know when. Ab'uk, I do not desire at present to be with a two-spirit," said Kan Bahlam, realizing the truth as he said it.

Ab'uk sat back, his look pained.

"You told me that you had tired of the carping ways of women; that you wanted a lover who allowed you freedom. Have I not done so? It is many moons since I have come to your chambers."

"It is no fault of yours; only that my preferences have changed."

"Changed back to women?"

Kan Bahlam reflected for a moment, realizing that his longing for a woman had indeed supplanted what he felt for the young man.

"So it appears. Yes, I am desirous of loving a woman."

"It is that young woman, your brother's wife!" exclaimed Ab'uk. "Word is about that you find much delight in her company. Think you that I failed to see your attraction at her marriage feast? Your own brother's wife!"

Anger flashed across Kan Bahlam's face.

"Ab'uk, you go too far! By what right do you accuse me, when I have done nothing wrong? I forbid you to spread such rumors; this is despicable and untrue. I have only the greatest respect for Lady K'inuuw Mat. Do not despoil her reputation out of petulance, or allow your jealousy to cloud your mind. I made no promise that you would remain my lover indefinitely. You agreed to our freedom from making commitments."

"Does your passion wane so quickly? You seemed well satisfied with our pleasures." Ab'uk gazed into the distance, his eyes watering. He knew it was foolish to fall in love with the Ba-ch'ok, who soon enough would be ruler of Lakam Ha. He knew he had made agreements about no possessiveness and no expectations. He knew Kan Bahlam's amorous record. But still, he did not want their relationship to end.

"Satisfied I was, wanting something else, I am now," said Kan Bahlam, looking tired. "Be true to the male side of your nature and do not make an emotional scene. Little choice do I have over the volition of my heart. Would that it were otherwise."

"You may count another heart as broken," whispered Ab'uk. He gathered his riotous emotions and made an effort at self-control. He slowly rose from the sleeping platform, held his body erect, and walked toward the door of the chamber. Pushing aside the heavy door drape, he turned to look plaintively at Kan Bahlam, saying: "You know where I am if you want me."

When the drape dropped back into place with a soft whoosh, Kan Bahlam buried his face in his hands.

Slightly over a half-year after the birth of Yax Chel, K'inuuw Mat became pregnant with her second child. In conceiving this child, she and Tiwol followed the Ix Chel priestess' instructions perfectly, not deviating in the least detail. Tiwol was certain the child was a boy, which made him exuberantly happy. K'inuuw Mat allowed herself to hope, almost to believe, but was troubled by Pakal's refusal to allow the first girl to be dedicated to Ix Chel. Better than most, she knew the powers of the Goddess.

Almost at the same time, her sister-in-law Te' Kuy announced that she was pregnant. Since Te' Kuy had miscarried several times, she waited until the pregnancy had passed four moon cycles to make it public. Although the two women had not interacted very much outside of ceremonial gatherings, their common pregnancies drew them together. Te' Kuy invited K'inuuw Mat to visit, and their meetings were so amiable that both sought them frequently. Te' Kuy's daughter, Chab' Nikte, was five years older than Yax Chel and immediately took the toddler under her wing, entertaining her with songs and doll play. The boy Mayuy was a year-and-a-half older than Yax Chel, already sensing that girls' games were not for him, although his sister's songs were drawing him in. The mothers chuckled as the boy wavered between staying aloof and wanting to be part of the fun.

"He is such a well-mannered boy," said K'inuuw Mat. "Others might grab the girls' dolls away to make mischief."

"Already he models himself after his father," Te' Kuy remarked. "Kan Joy Chitam has perfect courtly manners, always courteous and complimentary. Is it not remarkable how soon children begin learning gender behavior?"

"Indeed, quite remarkable. Yet, I have much to learn about children."

"It appears you may have many to learn from," Te' Kuy said, her humor touched with wistfulness.

K'inuuw Mat blushed, hoping her companion was not taking offense. Te' Kuy appeared serene as she passed a hand over her enlarging belly. Having another pregnancy end successfully was her greatest wish, and she did not really care which sex the child would be.

The women chatted about their husbands, happenings in their households, and escapades of their children. Although they had been meeting for several moons, their discussions remained superficial until Te' Kuy's curiosity pushed her to venture into less safe territory. At a pause, while the women sipped kob'al on the veranda, she posed her query.

"My husband mentioned that you visited Kan Bahlam's Academy and provided them with some assistance," Te' Kuy said. "Do you mind if I ask about this? It is something unusual, so I am curious."

"Ah . . . no, I do not mind," replied K'inuuw Mat. "Tiwol was showing me around the city, making me familiar with its buildings and activities. When we visited the Academy, the men were working on astronomical calculations, something I have familiarity with due to my training on Cuzamil. I made some suggestions that seemed helpful to them."

"You are modest. By reports, you helped them solve a mystery that had long eluded them."

"I simply offered a few ideas, ways to think about the dilemma. They took the ideas and extended them through their calculations. My part in this was small."

"It is impressive that you had a part in such esoteric studies. Tell me of your training in Cuzamil."

K'inuuw Mat tried to condense her childhood experiences and family traditions of serving the Goddess into a short and coherent story. She felt uncertain about how much to reveal of her mystical encounters, so kept that part vague. When she described scrying, Te' Kuy appeared fascinated and began asking more detailed questions. As K'inuuw Mat replied, she felt pangs of guilt about not practicing her scrying arts for a long time. The image of her altar in a hidden nook of her residence patio evoked a strong desire to return to scrying.

"Perhaps you would do a scrying for me at some time," said Te' Kuy.

"It is something I have not done recently," K'inuuw Mat replied, feeling hesitant. "My skills are not as great as before, I fear."

"When you feel ready, then we can talk more. I do not mean to place pressure on you."

K'inuuw Mat nodded, feeling insecure since the scrying episode involving Kan Bahlam's face. Though drawn to return to her art, she was conflicted. She determined to avoid scrying for Te' Kuy as best she could. The conversation drifted to other areas, and K'inuuw Mat started to relax until the focus shifted to another family member.

"Have you seen much of our sister-in-law, Talol?" asked Te' Kuy. When K'inuuw Mat gave the hand sign for no, she lowered her voice and glanced around, making certain no servants were in earshot.

"Take heed, be careful of her," whispered Te' Kuy. "I fear she is dangerous, and her mind may not be right. Rumors have spread that she drinks balche in excess, almost daily. This, combined with the strain of being childless and not bringing forth an heir, has made her unstable."

"Oh . . . I am saddened to hear of this," said K'inuuw Mat. "Talol was gracious to me upon my arrival here and provided for my needs. Since then, I have only seen her at gatherings."

"She is deeply troubled by her husband's behaviors. You have heard of these, I assume?"

"Yes, so I have. Are these things said about Kan Bahlam true?"

"To my best knowledge, they are true. He is also not to be trusted." Te' Kuy hesitated, studying her companion's face intently. Again K'inuuw Mat felt a flush creeping up her cheeks and turned her head, hoping it would not be noticeable. Te' Kuy appeared to sense this discomfort, but continued with her warnings.

"It is also rumored that Kan Bahlam is drawn to you. That he is attracted to you, beyond his admiration for your astronomical knowledge."

"This is being said? There is nothing between us. How can this gossip be dispelled?"

"Ah, only with the passage of time as the gossips move to other topics," Te' Kuy replied with a head shake. "That is, if nothing happens to continue their tongues wagging. Dear sister, I am telling you this so you can be forewarned. It is best to keep your distance from both Kan Bahlam and his wife."

"So I will," K'inuuw Mat murmured. "I am touched by your concern for me."

"And for myself and my children, I must avoid contact with Talol, for her presence is poisonous. We will support each other, sister, in finding a safe path through these dangers."

The women shared an embrace before parting. K'inuuw Mat was not certain whether she had made a trustworthy ally, or opened herself for further intrigues.

2

The central chamber of the Academy of Astronomy and Sciences was filled to capacity, several young men sitting cross-legged on floor mats, wearing white turban hats and short skirts of solar priests. Kan Bahlam stood facing them in front of the freshly plastered chamber wall, paintbrush in hand. At his side were Chak Chan and Mut holding pots of paint, while Yuhk Makab'te guarded the doorway. This select group of Ah K'in acolytes was being initiated into esoteric calendar studies, given entry into an elite fellowship of knowledge. They were chosen for their intelligence and dedication. It was the beginning of a new power structure planned by Kan Bahlam and the High Priest, in which secret knowledge buried in astronumerology would be the test of membership. Kan Bahlam envisioned this fellowship extending throughout the region, linking together rulers, elite nobles, and select priests to retain and transfer power. He would extend the network once he became ruler of Lakam Ha.

"You are familiar with the 949-based count that provides links between the Haab calendar and Noh Ek cycle," said Kan Bahlam. "Early in the use of calendars, our forebears recognized the need for a key to draw relationships among the 365-day Haab, 260-day Tzolk'in, 20-day uinal, and 584-day Noh Ek cycle. Noh Ek has been an important wandering star from ancient times, due to its brightness and reappearances on the horizon, rising as Morning Star and setting as Evening Star. At some point in their calculations, our ancestors discovered that multiplying Noh Ek by Haab, and that sum by the 20-day uinal, resulted in a number equal to one Calendar Round of 52 years."

Dipping his brush in a pot of black pigment, Kan Bahlam wrote the equation on the wall.

"The Calendar Round is a good marker for astronumerology investigations," he continued. "It has been in use for nearly four-and-a-half baktuns, over 1,800 solar years. It meshes the Haab and Tzolk'in calendars into a cycle that reaches completion in 52 years, when the day and uinal counts return to their initial combination. Perhaps their most exciting discovery was finding the highest common divisor for the Calendar Round components. Can any of you tell me that number, and explain why it is so significant?"

The acolytes shifted position, some rubbing their chins or furrowing their brows in concentration. They had studied this, but not all could quickly recall the innumerable figures associated with calendar mathematics. One slender man signaled readiness, and Kan Bahlam nodded to proceed.

"The number, Esteemed Ba-ch'ok, is 73," the young man said. "Such numbers that permit calendar scholars to derive highest common divisors and least common multiples are most useful in finding significant links among calendar cycles. This number, 73, is the highest common divisor of both the Haab and Noh Ek cycle. When the Calendar Round is divided by 73, this equals the Tzolk'in calendar of 260 days."

Kan Bahlam smiled and wrote the calculations on the wall.

"Well done. Now let us move to the important derivation of 949, which as you know is the sum of Noh Ek and Haab values. This number was found to reverberate throughout the entire Maya calendrical system in ways that seem almost magical." Kan Bahlam's voice was animated and his expression eager, for to him exploring the wonders of calendars and numbers was second only to star-gazing.

"When we take 18 uinals times 20 days, standard parts of our calendars, we get 360 which is a number highly useful in deriving least common multiples. Using 360 times 949 gives the Calendar Round period and the Tun-Ending period, and guides them to finish their cycles together. It links the Calendar Round, the Haab, the Tun-Ending, and the wandering star cycles of Noh Ek, Chak Ek, and Xux Ek—but we must add 1 day to the Xux Ek cycle to make the formula work."

As Kan Bahlam wrote these numbers on the wall, an acolyte voiced a question.

"Might it be asked, Honored Lord, why adding one day to make formulas work is acceptable? Might the Gods disapprove of altering their stellar patterns?"

Kan Bahlam turned, exchanged knowing glances with Chak Chan, and replied more graciously than the acolyte expected.

"This is an excellent question, young Ah K'in," he said. "Indeed, we might consider ourselves presumptive to take such steps, but even the Gods find need for variability in their works. Does not the moon, Lady Uc, vary in her cycles? Watch the wandering stars over many years, and you will note their cycles range over a span of a few days. We calculate the average days and give that number to their cycles, but it is not absolute. Take the face shown by Lady Uc, sometimes a nubile maiden and other times a malicious and destructive hag. Even our sun shifts his face, sending flares or hiding his glory behind dark shadows during eclipses. The cosmos is made of living beings, and the moods of celestial deities shift. Thus, calendar scholars are in good company when we add variability to our calculations."

"Well stated!" Chak Chan and Mut spoke in unison, bowing to Kan Bahlam. Inwardly, he thanked K'inuuw Mat for setting his thoughts along these lines of reasoning.

"Now, using 949 and 73," he continued, "our predecessors derived another important key number that is useful as the least common multiple of several cycles, using the technique of adding one day in these figures." He wrote the formulas as he spoke.

"Even more significant was using 949 to integrate other calendars with the Long Count," said Kan Bahlam. "These computations served as the basis for using the number 13 in the subdivisions of the Maya Era or Sun, the Great Cycle. We used the beginning of the current Great Cycle, 4 Ahau 8 Kumk'u, for setting the Long Count at 13 baktun, 0 katun, 0 tun, 0 uinal, and 0 kin. The next day, the count was set at all zeros, and the new cycle began.

"Why was the number 13 chosen to demarcate subdivisions of the cycle? Because when used with 949 it brings all levels into resonance with the harmonic symmetry of the cosmos. This is new information for most of you, and advances your status as calendar priests. Now watch as the beauty of this symmetry unfolds."

Dipping his brush again into the paint, Kan Bahlam wrote the sequence on the wall. As each subdivision appeared, the acolytes' eyes widened in amazement. Both 73 and 13 resonated with increasing levels—base 20 numerations with rapidly elongating time periods—of the Long Count to create a mathematically perfect sequence.

Chak Chan took the center position as Kan Bahlam stepped aside. The plan was to change speakers to introduce the new work of the Academy.

"Thus it is, we can admire the genius of using the 949-based count. But it fails to commensurate the cycles of two important wandering stars—K'awill Ek and Ayin Ek," said Chak Chan. "These two deities, bright and clearly visible in the night sky, are conspicuously absent and are vitally important to our relationships with the celestial spheres. They evaded inclusion in the 949 system because their values do not divide evenly into any of the above calendar subdivisions. The work of our Academy for the past few years has been to discover a system that will include their cycles, and that will resonate within the calendars as powerfully as does the 949-based count."

"It has taken much time, and challenged our abilities to the extreme," added Mut. "The elusive algorithm has now been developed, and it holds promise of a masterful tool for linking calendars with celestial patterns and our people's history."

"We have much work left to accomplish," said Kan Bahlam. "Now comes the revelation of this all-important key. You are sworn to secrecy about the number and its potential uses. You are forbidden to speak of it to others outside of our group."

His stern gaze rested briefly on the face of each acolyte, who nodded and gave the hand sign for compliance. They hung breathlessly upon his next words.

"The cycles of K'awiil Ek and Ayin Ek can be divided by 21, but this number does not create resonances throughout the calendar systems as 949 does. It took many trials to find the highest common divisor that allowed parallel resonant patterns. This required using a triple count of the K'awiil Ek cycle. We found that the number 63 was the highest common divisor that worked. To find the link with the Long Count calendar, we looked at the result of multiplying 63 by the calendar foundation value, the kin. This gave the key for the long-sought numerical paradigm: 63 times 13 kins—using the mystical and sacred number 13—results in 819. This number is parallel to 949 in its power to commensurate the cycles of these two wandering stars with the calendar systems. Now you will see the synchrony of these two key numbers within the calendars." He wrote the comparisons on the plaster wall.

"The final linkage produces a very large number of kins (1,195,740) that is the least common multiple of both the 819-day and 949-day counts. It allows us specifically to incorporate the cycles of K'awiil Ek and Ayin Ek into the calendar systems over long time periods. Now these important deities can be integrated. Now another paradigm can be used in seeking the sacred relationships within our calendars, the cosmos, and our people's history."

Kan Bahlam's face became still and his gaze swept past the acolytes, through the door of the chamber, across the broad plaza, and to the distant mountains. The misty contours of temples and pyramids yet to be shimmered before his eyes, as glyphs expressing this astronumerology danced and morphed across their walls. Silence reigned inside the chamber, the acolytes pondering this new information and the Academy colleagues mulling over these concepts. None knew better than Kan Bahlam how much additional work was needed to create the patterns he intended to formulate. He set his intention in a pledge to his vision: he would use this 819-day count for expressing unique and previously unimagined links between his ancestors, the city's rulers, and the Gods of the stars.

Moist air hung heavily in the hushed alcove where the patio met verdant jungle. Silence prevailed until the plop of a heavy drop slipping from drooping leaves resounded on stucco. The birds and monkeys seemed to be napping in the afternoon warmth, reticent to comment on the scene below on the patio. The young woman had been kneeling without movement for some time, her white huipil blending into the contours of the patio, stone altar, and water-filled bowl. She appeared to be another creature of the jungle, yielding to the quiet of autumn.

K'inuuw Mat's heart was not calm, but pulsating with anticipation. She was alone before her scrying bowl, preparing for the first reading she had attempted since coming to Lakam Ha. She had cleansed and ritually purified the scrying bowl, added new water, chanted the invocations to Ix Chel, made an offering of copal and maize cakes. Her scrying stones were spread on the mat in front of the bowl, her hands spread over them palms down, waiting for their signals. Waiting for one stone to speak through emanations to her palms, a subtle tingle or brush of warmth. Though waited patiently, her concentration never slipped. Slowly she moved her palms across the stones in fluid motions, until her right palm hesitated almost on its own above an azure stone streaked with dark green. The signal became stronger, the tingle nearly an itch, as she lifted the stone and held it to her heart. She whispered the scrying chant so softly that none of the jungle creatures were disturbed.

"From the depths, from the dark,
In the mystery of the unseen,
On the surface of these waters,
Show me that which I ask.

In the name of the Goddess,
She, the Knower of All."

She extended her hand over the smooth water that reflected foliage hanging above. Mentally she formed a request for the prophecy she sought.

Great Goddess Ix Chel, my request is to know if this child growing in my womb is a girl or a boy. This I, your humble devotee K'inuuw Mat, ask of your limitless vision that sees what is hidden.

Taking a deep breath, she cast the stone into the calm water and watched as it landed with a splash, sending circles to the bowl's rim. Bouncing back, ripples crossed and re-crossed, gradually diminishing until the surface was again smooth. She watched the surface, waiting for an image to appear, breath bated. It had been so long; would the scrying bowl respond, would the Goddess hear her request?

An image was forming, replacing the reflected leaves with the shape of a baby. The infant turned and its face appeared, but gave no hint of its sex. K'inuuw Mat's heart was pounding now, and she sent mental pleas to reveal more. The infant kicked its bare legs and wiggled, revealing the genitals of a girl. The baby's solemn black eyes stared, her face without a smile, until it morphed into Ix Chel's stern gaze. The Goddess hurled her communication into K'inuuw Mat's mind: *You must dedicate your first daughter to me. Only daughters shall you conceive until I receive my tribute.*

K'inuuw Mat sat back on her heels, bowing her head and crossing arms on her chest. She had expected this from the Goddess, and felt affirmed in both her intuition and ability to scry. Mentally she thanked Ix Chel and gave assurances that she would do everything in her power to prevail over the ruler and her husband and convince them to make the tribute. When she raised her head, the scrying bowl surface was again a reflection of the jungle. She remained in the same position, feeling incomplete. Her need to know about continuing the dynasty through a male heir, the prophecy given by the Oracle of Cuzamil, continued burning in her heart. She firmed her resolution to exhort Pakal, knowing he would be the decision-maker. But she had to know; needed the confirmation from the Goddess. Would it be too audacious to seek the answer through another scrying?

She sang the scrying chant, this time loud enough to evoke twitters from birds in the canopy. From the dense jungles in the distance came the eerie roars of howler monkeys, echoing across mountains as troops awakened and proclaimed their territories. The primal quality of their deep voices caused a shudder in her heart. Disregarding a growing sense of uneasiness, she persisted in her scrying. This time a completely black stone;

smooth and rounded and shining with occult beauty, caused heat in her palm. She reached tentatively and it leapt into her hand, burning the palm. It demanded to be used. With trepidation, she formed her request and cast the stone into the bowl.

Oh Goddess, as I vow to fulfill your tribute, I implore you to show me if I will conceive a boy and bring an heir to Lakam Ha's dynasty.

The black stone landed heavily in the center of the bowl, sending droplets flying onto her face and causing huge ripples. The agitated water seemed reluctant to abate, and she wondered if making this second request was an affront to the Goddess. The air seemed denser, as if rain might spontaneously coalesce from its wetness. It pressed on her skin, coating it with moisture, increased by her perspiration. She waited anxiously for an image to form. The water's surface darkened; became still but remained obscure. Moisture dripped from her nose and chin, but she held position without moving, fixing her gaze on the surface. Something was forming, swirling and dissolving, then regrouping.

Two faces appeared on the water surface, blending into each other, and then separating momentarily before fusing together again. With a gasp, she recognized the two faces: her husband Tiwol and Kan Bahlam. Why did they merge? Why were both faces in the image? Before she could pursue these questions, the two faces dissolved into a baby, a newborn who moved its legs to reveal that it was a boy. Transfixed, she stared at the baby boy, knowing it was her baby. Somehow, both Tiwol and Kan Bahlam were connected with this baby.

The images disappeared, and the scrying bowl was still. She moved from kneeling into a cross-legged sit, rubbing her cramped calves. Rain started coming down in earnest, splattering the bowl's surface and drenching her quickly. She murmured thanks to the Goddess by rote, her mind distracted, her feelings confused and frightened. The baby in her womb kicked hard— the girl, her second daughter. Gently she rubbed her abdomen, soothing the little one.

"You will have a baby brother," she whispered. "Be comforted. You are loved and will be welcome. Your life is important, too."

Rising stiffly while holding her abdomen, she gathered her scrying stones and sitting mats. Pouring rain dripped from her hair, face, and huipil, sibilating into the patio and forming rivulets. As she splashed through puddles and returned to the residence, a memory stabbed her awareness. She recalled the earlier scrying done in her home city, when she asked to see the son of Pakal through whom she would continue the lineage—and saw the face of Kan Bahlam.

In the depth of winter, shortly after the solstice when K'in Ahau showed his face for the briefest time, a second daughter was born to K'inuuw Mat and Tiwol Chan Mat. The girl was named Siyah Chan, Born of Sky. After a rapid labor and easy delivery, K'inuuw Mat gathered strength to face her husband and father-in-law with the Goddess Ix Chel's demand. Tiwol was confused and despondent, unable to understand how this baby could be a girl. Pakal was more thoughtful; his shamanic training enabled him to quickly grasp that other-worldly forces were at work. When K'inuuw Mat met with him, he was already prepared to consider the Goddess' demand. An explanation of the scrying prophecy was the final trigger to his acquiescence, and he nodded with understanding when K'inuuw Mat related that the Goddess would not relent until the first daughter was given to her. Pakal summoned Tiwol and reviewed the situation, directing his son to make the commitment. Pakal reassured Tiwol that the second daughter would serve well for marriage alliances.

A private ceremony was held in the patio of the Sutzha River residence to formally dedicate Yax Chel to the Goddess Ix Chel. Brilliant sunlight broke through a cloudy sky to illuminate the patio, and the waterfall sang joyfully. Songbirds clustered in the high branches and filled the air with lilting melodies. An early blooming hibiscus framed the waterfall in scarlet, as honeysuckle blossoms released intoxicating aromas. Yax Chel beamed with happiness and danced with her mother to celebrate after the short ceremony was completed. Though not yet two solar years old, intuition informed her that something special was happening and she was at the center. Most of her family was there, including her cousins Chab' Nikte and Mayuy who joined in the dancing.

Te' Kuy brought her newborn daughter, born three moons before K'inuuw Mat's new baby. Another toddler born to K'inuuw Mat's attendant Kuy added to the pack of children who played in the patio as the women sat on mats, feasting and talking. Notably absent was Talol, who sent regrets that she felt ill and could not attend. The men clustered in another part of the patio, engaged in their own conversations. Pakal, Tiwol, Kan Joy Chitam, Chak Chan, and Kan Bahlam discussed the early excavation for the foundation of Pakal's burial pyramid, updated by Pakal's chief architect Yax Chan. Details of the underground crypt and the immense sarcophagus it would hold occupied their attention. Yax Chan informed them that he had selected a team of stone carvers who would undertake the complex reproduction of figures, symbols, and glyphs being designed by the city's most accomplished scribes. The glyphs and figures on crypt walls and sides of the sarcophagus would relate the story of Pakal's dynasty, and the sarcophagus lid would depict Pakal's resurrection from the maws of the Underworld as the young Maize God.

Kan Bahlam knew that Pakal wanted three panels carved with a more detailed rendition of dynastic history, from primordial deities to early liminal predecessors, through the historic rulers, and projecting into the future. Pakal's vision encompassed recurrent cycles, through which deities and rulers continued in reincarnated forms. The work of the Academy in developing astronumerology codes linking patterns of the cosmos and dynastic history played an important role in these panels. Kan Bahlam had recently worked out the first set of links for Pakal's life, a pattern connecting him to ancestors and primordial deities. It was too early to discuss this, a few questions still remained.

Kan Bahlam surreptitiously looked toward K'inuuw Mat, wishing he could find a way to discuss it with her. His heart lurched at the beauty of her smile as she held the newborn baby in her lap, whispering secrets known only to mothers and infants. The old, deep ache of his denied fatherhood swelled in his gut. Despair mingled with anger and resentment; the Gods had wronged him. His marriage had devolved into an ugly morass, his wife always suspicious and he repelled by her bitterness. In the clarity of the moment, he realized that he hated Talol. And with equal impact, he realized that he loved K'inuuw Mat. Perhaps for the first time, his heart opened and yearned for closeness, for an intimacy he had never known with a woman. A shock of resolve shot through him—he *would* love her; find a way to her heart despite the consequences.

After the dedication of Yax Chel, Pakal met with K'inuuw Mat and Tiwol along with the Ix Chel priestess-healer Chilkay. Their objective was to plan for the conception of a son, this time with the Goddess' approval. Chilkay advised a period of abstinence, permitting the creative sexual energies to magnify. The time of abstinence should be one solar year, with the Ah K'inob carefully casting auguries for the perfect date of conception. Tiwol frowned at the length of time he must forego his wife's embraces, but had little choice. The future of the Bahlam dynasty might depend upon these prescriptions. The priestess gave the couple several exercises to build their sexual potency over the year. Pakal smiled as he remembered how his wife Lalak had used these techniques in the sexual alchemy that transformed their relationship and led to the birth of their first surviving son, Kan Bahlam.

Pakal found himself dwelling more in the past these days. Perhaps it because he was elderly, having attained seventy-four solar years. He noticed a decrease in his energy and strength, not enough to be debilitating but certainly making him rest more. He had asked Kan Bahlam to assume increasing responsibility for presiding at court sessions and meeting with officials. His oldest son appeared to relish these duties, and carried them out with flourish. He would be an effective ruler, Pakal reflected. And also an ambitious one, to judge by intelligence Pakal had gleaned about his son's future building plans for a grand triad complex.

As homage to the past, Pakal visited the funerary monuments of his grandmother and mother, the two prior rulers of Lakam Ha. Equinoxes and solstices were auspicious times, and as spring equinox approached he planned to visit his grandmother, Yohl Ik'nal, who held special importance for him. She was the first woman to rule Lakam Ha, and she continued the Bahlam dynasty by ascending to the throne after the passing of her father, Kan Bahlam I. It took immense determination and courage to overcome opposition to this succession, as many nobles had resisted, preferring another male with royal blood. Had she not succeeded, rulership would have passed to another noble family, and Pakal would never have become K'uhul B'aakal Ahau. He also acknowledged his mother Sak K'uk with regular visits to her pyramid. For the second time, rulership passed to a royal woman, departing from usual Maya custom. Patrilineal descent was not absolute, but preferred; most woman rulers succeeded their husbands or held the throne for a young son for short periods. Though that was the case for his mother, who only ruled for three years until he came of age, his grandmother ruled in her own right for twenty-two years.

This controversial history spurred Pakal's insistence on male succession from this point on. He would not risk the upheaval and possible rebellion that would occur if he tried to designate a female heir. About his immediate successor, he had no fears. With three sons, all designated as heirs in sequence, he felt certain one would live long enough to succeed. The next generation troubled him, however. He had only one grandson, and life was uncertain for children. This concern compelled him to agree to K'inuuw Mat's plea that her first daughter be dedicated to Ix Chel. Now he waited for her next child; surely a boy. Or so he hoped.

The day of his visit to Yohl Ik'nal's pyramid was sunny, the jungle air steamy. Pakal's attendant Tohom insisted on accompanying him, although Pakal preferred to be alone. Tohom reasoned that he might need nourishment, drink, and a mat for sitting, but Pakal knew the real concern was that he might not be able to walk back over the hills without help. Such it was when one became an old man, he reflected. The walk from the palace to Yohl Ik'nal's pyramid followed the Otulum River going south, toward its origin in the high mountains. Hills rose steeply to the west, just behind where the foundation for Pakal's burial pyramid was being prepared. On the crest of another rise behind these hills was a string of structures, the tallest was a pyramid dedicated to the east, the Lak'in Pyramid. There the solar priests did daily rituals to welcome sunrise. Lakam Ha also had pyramids for rituals to the other three directions. Across the gulch of the river was another rise to a meadow bounded by tall hills, the most eastern one soaring to a steep mountain peak. Pakal knew this was the intended setting for his son Kan Bahlam's planned triad complex.

The river veered in a gentle arc toward the east, bounded by more undeveloped hills covered with lush foliage. The path beside the river became steep and Pakal slowed his pace, breathing heavily. Tohom kept a respectful distance behind and matched his master's pace. Through treetops the roofcomb of Yohl Ik'nal's pyramid was visible, and a series of smooth stepping stones crossed the river to the paved white path that led to its base. The stepped pyramid was built over a natural rock outcropping that had been hollowed for the burial chamber. A small temple sat on top, its four doors opening to a single chamber with an altar carved with Yohl Ik'nal's name glyph. Pakal slowly climbed the stairway, knelt before the altar and offered gifts of amber and copal into the censer. He chanted ritual greetings for honored ancestors as Tohom used a flint to send sparks into the censer, using dried twigs to light a fire. Pungent, earthy copal smoke drifted languidly in the still air.

Pakal had instructed Tohom to remain in the temple, since he wanted to visit the burial chamber alone. He descended several stairs and walked along the pyramid side to a doorway carved into the rock, opening to a narrow passageway with a few steep stairs ending at another doorway closed by heavy drapery. A notch in the door frame allowed the drape to be tied open; light then entered the chamber through the short passageway. Pakal entered the muted interior, always thrilled by its artistic features, though he knew them well. The plastered walls were brilliant red, a symbol of the ruler's *itz*, sacred blood that was shed for the people's benefit. Nine life-sized figures outlined in black and painted deeper red with contrasting whites and pale pinks strode across the walls. The style was from an earlier period, cursive and free-flowing. The figures had slender and supple yet anatomically correct bodies. It was different from the accurate portraits that Pakal preferred, but true enough to recognize a progression of ancestors.

The progression began with Yohl Ik'nal's father Kan Bahlam I, his brother Ahkal Mo' Nab II, and the prior seven rulers going back to lineage founder K'uk Bahlam. All wore elaborate headdresses with feathers reaching the ceiling, and carried shields on one arm while the other arm was outstretched, holding serpent-footed K'awiil scepters. These accoutrements showed they were designated by the Triad God Unen K'awiil as divinely ordained rulers. All the figures faced north and pointed their scepters north, the direction of the spirit world; four figures on the west wall, four on the east wall, and one on the north wall.

Pakal admired the beauty of small details, such as deity faces on scepters, delicate flowers on jewelry, and tiny profile heads on belts. The figures wore elaborate split skirts swinging to the side, decorated loincloths, crosses on waistbands, and diagonally crossed leggings. Heavy pendant necklaces were the only chest adornments. Overall the impression was of power, grace, and animation. Pakal bowed to each ancestor, murmuring their names, before giving his attention to his grandmother.

She lay in the center of the stucco floor, her body well-wrapped and covered with several layers of thick woven blankets. The coverings were completely permeated with red cinnabar, a preparation of mercuric oxide that acted as a preservative. Pakal knew that her body was also impregnated with cinnabar, its red color indicative of the ruler's itz. On top of the blankets were hundreds of jade beads, and the entire form was surrounded by many fine ceramic vessels. Her burial was according to the custom of earlier times. Pakal had pioneered using a sarcophagus for royal burials when interring his wife, Tz'aakb'u Ahau. He envisioned placing his own body inside an inner coffin, then put into the massive sarcophagus his artists were designing.

The divine ruler continued to have responsibilities after death. Preserving the body and keeping it safe through the ages was important in fulfilling these obligations.

Pakal sat on the mat next to Yohl Ik'nal's head, his usual place when visiting her. He chanted greetings and rituals of acknowledgement, assuring her of his continued love and devotion, reminding her of his need for her guidance, given from afar in her celestial residence. She often appeared to him merging from the Vision Serpent's mouth during formal rituals, at which he would let his blood and burn soaked bark paper strips along with copal in censers. He thanked her for this continued support and the katun prophecies she often gave him. This day he was not seeking knowledge, guidance, or predictions for coming katuns. He simply came to honor her, to renew their family connection, to enjoy feeling her presence.

The chamber was warm, and Pakal dozed. Insects buzzed outside, and a lyrical birdsong trebled in the stillness. Pakal began to dream, his chin dropping onto his chest. He dreamt of his beloved wife Lalak, of the Lakam Ha of his youth, of his vision for the great city now nearly completed. Yohl Ik'nal came into his dream, a vigorous young woman of commanding countenance, her face familiar from carvings. She seemed poised to tell him something; her posture emphasized its importance. She stepped to the side, revealing another young woman standing behind her. This woman had an unusual appearance; her hair was yellow as corn silk and her eyes blue as the summer sky. She was tall, nearly Pakal's height, with an oddly square face, tiny nose, and small lips. This woman was surely a foreigner, from unknown lands.

Yohl Ik'nal communicated to Pakal's liminal consciousness.

This is Elie. Do you remember her?

Pakal hovered between dreaming and semi-wakening, trying to access memories. In a flash he recalled his Underworld quest, part of shamanic training in his youth, during which he found the fair-haired woman nearly drowned in the swampy Death Lords' domain. He had helped her escape the clutches of Xibalba, helped her return to the living world again. Mentally he communicated to his grandmother that he did remember Elie.

Good. She has need to communicate with K'inuuw Mat. It is most important; it is critical to the future of our family. Bring K'inuuw Mat here, tell her of Elie. When she sits alone here, Elie will come to her, as I do to you.

K'inuuw Mat? My daughter-in-law? Pakal knew not to question deities and ancestors, but was surprised.

She. She the prophetic one. Bring her soon, Pakal.

He gave assent in the liminal space that was beginning to dissipate. Sounds outside the chamber crept into his awareness; parrots squawking, monkeys chattering, something scratching at the doorway. His eyelids struggled to open, but felt too heavy to move.

"Holy Lord?" Tohom's voice wafted into the chamber. "Much time has passed. Are you ready to leave?"

Pakal shifted and rubbed his knees, aching from sitting crossed and motionless. Dreamily he turned his head toward Tohom, squinting against the brightness streaming through the doorway.

"Help me to rise, Tohom. I am ready to return."

3

Ab'uk stood uneasily in a small reception chamber of the Palace, his palms sweaty and heart thumping. He always felt nervous in the presence of Talol and tried to avoid her. Now she had summoned him to her Palace residence chambers, putting him into a state of serious turmoil. He could not imagine why she wanted to see him. It certainly did not bode well.

She swept haughtily into the chamber wearing an opulent huipil and richly adorned with jewelry. Acknowledging his deep bow, she gestured to be seated upon plush floor mats and called for refreshments. They exchanged courtly pleasantries as servants brought dried figs and papaya slices, along with cacao-laced maize gruel. When the servants departed, her thin face turned toward his, eyes staring intensely as if scouring his soul. A shudder passed through his body as he tensed for her real message.

"We share a common purpose, Ab'uk," she began, voice honeyed. "Just as we have shared a common lover and now share a common wound."

Shock registered on Ab'uk's face before he could collect his reactions. Alarms were exploding in his mind.

"I see you are surprised," she continued. "Perhaps my candor is unexpected. You will find me a generous though exacting ally, and we must begin from a point of honest understanding. It is no secret that you have been my husband's lover. Strangely enough, I find that more tolerable than his liaisons with other women. I hold no grudge against you, Ab'uk. Rather, I am seeking your assistance. Let us become allies in taking revenge against those who bring anguish to our hearts. Let us join forces in bringing salve to our wounds."

Impressions of her haggard, lined face mingled with swirling thoughts as Ab'uk sipped his cacao, buying time to appraise the situation. She was thinner than when he last saw her, with dark circles under her eyes and sagging papery skin forming cowls around her neck. A yellowish hue underlay her complexion that betrayed illness. He recalled the rumors of her excessive drinking. Still, her eyes held the intensity of a jaguar stalking its prey. She was dangerous, and he must proceed with caution. He glanced around at the doorways into the chamber, lifting his eyebrows.

"Do not worry," she murmured. "My servants are well-trained to provide privacy and keep their tongues. You may speak freely."

"Lady Talol, much am I honored by your offer of alliance." Ab'uk chose to go along with her intentions, deciding that to refuse was asking for trouble. "Your honesty in acknowledging our mutual . . . ah, circumstances, is admirable. How may I be of service to you?"

"You have recently been rejected by my husband, is that so?" She gave a colluding smile. "Do not be surprised; I have informants throughout the city. He has tossed you out for a woman, the new target of his lust. She is an outsider, a usurper, not fit to be in our hallowed royal family. She is a sorcerer, a seer trained in that despicable den of witches that reside on Cuzamil. They claim to serve Ix Chel, but really do the bidding of Chak

Chel, the evil old destroyer. This young woman, you know of whom I speak, must be disempowered. Her wicked hold on my husband must be broken."

"Ah . . . this I did not know, of her occult powers," said Ab'uk.

"She has such powers and is a threat to all we hold dear. If she was unable to sustain her spell on my husband, he would turn back to those who pleased him before." Talol gave Ab'uk a knowing look, accompanied by a smirk. "We could salve our hearts, resolve our wounds. This must be done, and you can help attain it."

Ab'uk immediately concluded that the woman as going insane. He was certain that Kan Bahlam would never return to his wife, in fact, knew he detested her. He doubted that K'inuuw Mat was an evil sorcerer, regardless of her seer abilities. Although he did resent how the young woman had displaced him in Kan Bahlam's affections, he had no desire to enter into a plot to harm her. Somehow he had to placate Talol, pretend to join her efforts, and then slip away.

"How do you envision disempowering her, or making it impossible for her to sustain this spell?" Ab'uk asked, trying to sound convincing.

"That is something I am now working on," Talol said. "In all likelihood, I will need to enlist the services of a powerful sorcerer to counteract her powers. I have contacts in outlying villages; there is an old shaman whose abilities are legendary. Whose skills can be bought for the right price. But I will need information about the woman . . . you know who I mean. I will need something of hers—some hair or favorite clothing or jewelry—to use for placing curses. Information about what matters most to her, what her heart secretly craves, any hidden secrets she does not want known, these things are necessary for directing the curses."

"And you want my help to gather such information or things," said Ab'uk.

"Just so! You can accomplish this far better than my attendant women. Any of them would be suspect and provide a link back to me. But you, no one would think of you as my ally. With your court connections and your winning ways, you can extract information. I am certain you can find ways to obtain her things, without anyone suspecting you or me. Yes, you are the perfect one." Talol nodded in satisfaction, sipped her cacao drink, and seemed lost in thought.

"One other thing," she said suddenly, eyes flashing at her visitor. "You must spread rumors to damage her reputation. Spread them around the court, among your circle. Make them juicy so the gossips will grab hold and disperse them widely. You can say that she has made enchantments to trap my husband, casts evil spells on children, led heinous rituals on Cuzamil. Use your imagination. Perhaps even hint at sexual orgies on the island."

Ab'uk suppressed a gasp, and a chill went up his spine. He felt a dark blanket of evil settling around him and dug his fingernails into his palms to keep from lashing out at her.

"As you wish, Lady Talol. I am at your service." Ab'uk forced words out through a dry throat and kept his expression neutral, lowering his eyes. All he wanted was to escape from her presence and figure out a way to avoid this plot.

"Very good. You shall be richly rewarded. It pleases me greatly that we have come to this accord."

Pakal led K'inuuw Mat up the stairs of Yohl Ik'nal's pyramid, past the temple on top and around the side to the doorway carved into the rock. They descended the narrow passageway, stepping carefully down steep stairs and through the doorway into the burial crypt. Pakal tied the heavy door drapery onto the door frame notch, and light crept into the chamber. Pakal's attendant Tohom waited outside, along with another young man assigned to escort K'inuuw Mat on her return.

Even in the dim light, K'inuuw Mat was astonished by the languid beauty of the figures painted on the sides of the crypt. Pakal gave brief descriptions of these processing ancestors and the shrouded figure of Yohl Ik'nal lying on the floor. Mats were in place nearby with a small censer filled with copal ready to light. They had discussed the procedures in advance, and K'inuuw Mat was ready for her encounter with Lakam Ha's first woman ruler. Pakal smiled and bowed, exiting quietly and replacing the door drape.

Hands trembling with anticipation, K'inuuw Mat struck the flint and sent sparks to ignite the twigs in the censer. Soon copal smoke wafted into the semi-darkness, its pungent fumes both comforting and mind-altering. She reviewed Pakal's unexpected visit when he told her about the request passed on by his grandmother. It was a wondrous story; a series of encounters spanning three generations between a strange woman from an unknown land, and the rulers of Lakam Ha. Surely something of vast significance lay within these mysterious encounters, as Pakal intimated. She felt both honored and daunted by being brought into this mystery.

In a soft voice, K'inuuw Mat chanted a prayer of acknowledgement and request, introducing herself to the ancestral ruler and inviting her to come. She stilled her mind and concentrated on becoming receptive to the spirit world. Her body settled into its cross-legged position, and her awareness of physical sensations drifted away. Only her slow, regular breathing remained in consciousness, but soon that too dissipated. She entered a state of pure awareness, alert, open, receptive.

From shimmering sparkles behind closed lids, an ephemeral form began taking shape. The image was a Mayan woman of royal bearing, fully attired as a K'uhul Ahau. From seeing portraits on ceramics, K'inuuw Mat recognized the form as Yohl Ik'nal. The ancestral ruler appeared youthful and vigorous, radiating kindness along with strength. She communicated greetings into K'inuuw Mat's awareness, thanked her for responding to the request, and then brought another form into being, a tall woman with golden hair and blue eyes. The ruler introduced the woman as Elie, and then faded until only the strange women remained in K'inuuw Mat's inner vision.

Elie sent mind-images to K'inuuw Mat: a high plain of stark grasses waving in cold winds, a slate sky with muted sunlight, two adolescent girls meeting by a rocky outcropping and telling each other about vastly different lives. Promises to continue their meetings, changes in their lives that distanced them, yearnings to visit each other. Elie traveled on a huge vessel, propelled by multiple sails across an immense sea to arrive in the lands of the Mayas. She traveled with a sullen man who had much facial hair, who seemed to possess her, but whom she disliked. They set up camp in a city that perched on a mountain ridge; its buildings resembled Lakam Ha but were overgrown with jungle vines and trees. Several workers toiled at removing the overgrowth, collecting artifacts and chipping off wall panels, serving the foreign men who treated them scornfully. These workers had Mayan features but were simply dressed; they had no accoutrements of status. One of the Mayan men befriended Elie; as they interacted a bond developed that blossomed into love. The sullen man, Elie's husband, learned of this and attacked Elie viciously. The Mayan man rescued her and they escaped into the jungles, eluding pursuit.

The next set of mind-images took place in a simple Mayan village of several palapas around a grassy plaza surrounded by high trees and dense jungle. Elie lived in the palapa of the Mayan man, whose features seemed familiar. His mother disapproved of their relationship, there was tension in the village about her presence, and the village shaman viewed her with suspicion. The man remained committed to Elie and they lived as a couple, having three children. Elie became sick after the last birth, and the village shaman refused to intervene with the deities. The local healer was unable to save Elie, and she died. Her spirit was sent to the Underworld, but was unprepared to confront the challenges of the Death Lords. She became trapped in the watery chill of swamps and vermin, her spirit slowly losing strength until she slipped nearly unconscious into murky waters. Suddenly a bright figure appeared on the pathway through the swamps, a young man of arresting presence and great capacity for compassion. He pulled her from the swamps and harnessed the assistance of a huge owl to carry them both out of the Underworld, just before the portal to the Middleworld closed.

Elie returned to live several lifetimes in the Middleworld, her spirit merging into her children in the remote Mayan village. Although these children appeared Mayan, with dark hair and brown skin, some in each generation had blue eyes. Far in the future, one of her descendants with blue eyes became a respected scientist, a woman scholar who studied the history and traditions of her people, and who brought back into light their great accomplishments.

K'inuuw Mat remained in a deep meditative state, internalizing the story told by Elie. Questions surfaced into awareness, and she projected them to Elie.

The girl you first met, this was Yohl Ik'nal?

Elie gave affirmative.

The young man who saved you from the swamps of the Death Lords . . . this was Pakal?

You are insightful, Elie replied.

Who was the man who rescued you, took you to his village? K'inuuw Mat asked.

This man is one of your descendants, through your daughter. Elie's answer was surprising.

What happened to our great city, Lakam Ha? Why was it covered by jungle? Who were those foreign men, whose actions were not honorable?

Elie waved her arm, and a series of images moved across K'inuuw Mat's inner vision. Many foreigners from across the Great East Sea came to the Maya regions and lands of other indigenous people to the north and south. The first invaders were cruel and greedy, seeking gold and plunder, destroying Mayan monuments and art, burning codices. Their priests suppressed Mayan religion and tried to replace the deities with their own One God. Loss of life was widespread through unknown diseases brought by these invaders, whose advanced weapons and warfare tactics overwhelmed the Maya warriors. The nature and organization of society changed drastically, Mayas were pressed into indentured servitude, and Mayan cities were lost to the encroaching jungles.

Wave after wave of foreigners came to the Maya lands, seeking fame and fortune. They built cities modeled after those they came from, often using stones from Mayan structures. They especially preferred using stones from sacred Mayan temple-pyramids to construct their cathedrals and churches.

The Mayas living around these cities soon merged into a hybrid culture, working fields of corn and agave, growing crops and orchards, serving inside households. The foreigners had an appetite for Mayan women and often took them as concubines. Not infrequently, children of these unions were absorbed into the householder's family. A blended race emerged; Elie called them *mestizos*.

During the time of Elie's voyage to the Maya lands, foreign adventurers and explorers began making expeditions deep into the jungles. These intrepid men pursued tales of soaring stone cities half covered by foliage and containing hidden wealth. With the help of local Maya guides, they located numerous Mayan cities long abandoned by former occupants. Some cities were still important sites of spiritual pilgrimage, for the Mayas never completely gave up their native religion. These legendary cities became well-known among foreign countries, and continuing efforts to clear away jungle and restore the stone buildings resulted in increasing visits by tourists, people who sought an experience of exotic places and cultures. A profession of scientists developed who specialized in studying Mayas and other ancient people. Through them, information emerged that revealed the brilliance of the advanced Mayan civilization. The woman scientist with blue eyes, K'inuuw Mat's descendant, was one of these.

K'inuuw Mat tried to absorb all the information Elie imparted, hoping in the recesses of her mind that it would imprint. She still had a burning question.

Can you tell me more about my role in the destiny of the Bahlam lineage?

Elie nodded and continued communicating to K'inuuw Mat mentally.

Through me comes the first blending of your lineage, the Bahlam lineage, with foreigners from the eastern lands across the sea. The mixing of blood—foreign and Maya—happened from our initial contact. But your people of B'aakal remained hidden from their grasp, hidden in dense jungles and high mountains. The discovery of your great city, abandoned for over twenty generations, happened shortly before I came to your lands. Though many of your city left when farming failed and drought prevailed, migrating north to more hospitable climates, the descendants of your Bahlam family stayed. They lived in remote villages, lost their powers and forgot their wisdom. But a few always remembered. Those who remembered are in your direct lineage, through the Bahlam descendant of your daughter, the man who became my rescuer and mate.

It was inevitable that our people would blend. In this way, the Maya people continue. Even though the misguided soldiers and priests tried to destroy your culture and beliefs, and impose their religion, they never completely succeeded. *The invaders burned most of your books, the precious codices with generations of advanced knowledge. But they could not destroy the buildings, where the record of your people is carved in stone. The essence of the Mayas will never disappear if actions are taken during your time to preserve it.*

Elie paused and her startling blue eyes, more intense than a bright summer sky, pierced into the mind and soul of K'inuuw Mat.

This more must I tell you. My dearest friend across the ages, my sister in spirit, Yohl Ik'nal, bid me impart this request to you. The creative genius and boundless willpower of her great-grandson Kan Bahlam is yours to shape and guide. It is your destinies to be together. It is your sacred duty to inspire his architectural work so it preserves the most important and profound aspects of your culture. This she asks of you.

K'inuuw Mat gave consent to fulfill the request of Yohl Ik'nal, even though it confused her. Elie smiled, and as her form radiated love and gratitude, it began dissolving into shimmering mists. In the semi-darkness of the crypt, K'inuuw Mat slowly returned to awareness of her surroundings. The copal incense had burned into ashes, its heady scent lingering. A chorus of green parrots screeched outside, their raucous voices jolting her fully awake. Shifting into a kneeling position, she crossed both arms over her chest and bowed to the floor, in highest homage to the ancestral ruler and her soul sister.

4

Kan Bahlam held his body rigidly as he sat upon the raised platform of the Popol Nah. The benches along the walls of the Council House were crowded with ahauob of the city. Tension filled the air as the messenger continued his report on the recent battle at Imix-Ha. Kan Joy Chitam sat nearest his brother, flanked by the aged Warrior Chief K'akmo, Yuhk Makab'te, Mut, Chak Chan, and Aj Sul the elder Ah Yahauk'ak, military-ceremonial assistant to Pakal. The ruler had relinquished presiding over the Popol Nah to his oldest son, because of declining health.

"It was then, when Balaj Chan K'awiil was ousted from Imix-ha five years ago, that plans were set in motion for yet another intervention by his Kan overlord. The Snake Dynasty could not tolerate this victory by forces of Mutul and Lakam Ha, this challenge to their expansionist agenda. They could not abide the restoration of the rightful Mutul ruler, Nuun Ujol Chaak, to power over his subsidiary city. Now we see the results of these plans. Balaj

Chan K'awiil is returned to the throne of Imix-ha, put back in place as a puppet ruler for the Kan Lords of Uxte'tun. Nuun Ujol Chaak is in hiding, and his location kept secret."

"Will he not return to Mutul and muster forces for retaliation?" asked Kan Bahlam.

"That is probably his plan, but our contacts have lost touch with the ousted warriors. The damage done to Nuun Ujol Chaak's forces was severe. Our estimate is that more than half were killed in battle. Many nobles fled with their families as the battle raged, but some were also slaughtered trying to escape. The warriors of Kan were ruthless and did not spare women and children, or the elderly."

"Such is the Snake legacy," muttered Chak Chan.

"Yuknoom Ch'een of Kan is a power to be reckoned with," growled K'akmo. "He has proved his ability to subdue many cities and extract homage and tribute over katuns. In his 40 years of rulership, this Two-Katun Lord has spread the dominance of Kan widely through our regions. Well do I remember when he defeated Waka' and oversaw the accession of ruler K'inich Bahlam, whom he bonded by marriage to a Kan royal daughter. He established long-term dominance over Cancuen polity far to the south, becoming patron through three generations of rulers, and installing two of them on the throne, the second just earlier this year. In the lower reaches of the K'umaxha River, he or one of his emissaries was involved in the accession of the Amalah ruler five years ago. The tendrils of Kan spread the Snake Dynasty venom too widely for comfort."

"Our warriors soundly defeated the Kan and Imix-ha forces in the battle five years ago that restored our ally Nuun Ujol Chaak to power in that city. We can defeat them again!" Kan Bahlam spoke forcefully, veins standing out in his forehead. He had taken part in this victory and was proud of his prowess.

"Let us mount an attack quickly!" "These scoundrels must be taught a lesson!" "We cannot allow Kan to maintain dominance of K'umaxha River cities!" "We must come to the aid of our ally Mutul!" Shouts of many nobles and warriors joined in cacophony that bounced off the plaster walls of the Popol Nah.

"It is unwise to attack Imix-ha with our forces alone," observed Aj Sul. The elder statesman's deep, booming voice quieted the chamber and drew all eyes to him. "Kan has several allies along the K'umaxha River and could call up their forces. Let me remind you of the toll: Pa'chan, Pipá, Usihwitz, Yokib, Wa-Mut. Three of those cities, as you may recall, were once subsidiaries of the B'aakal polity, our allies. Let us avoid taking rash and ill-founded action."

Kan Bahlam fumed but held his tongue. He fervently wanted to lead an attack against his city's enemies, to once again be in the thick of action with opportunity for taking captives. But, he knew better than to openly oppose his father's respected military assistant. Shooting a glance at K'akmo, he caught the glare in the old warrior's eyes and suspected here was an ally. K'akmo was too old to lead attacks, however, and was in the process of selecting a replacement to recommend to Pakal. No doubt Aj Sul would have a big voice in that selection.

"We shall form a war council to examine our options," said Kan Bahlam, keeping an even voice. "Emissaries must be sent at once to Mutul, accompanied by a small warrior force for protection. They are also to find the whereabouts of Nuun Ujol Chaak and his remaining forces. K'akmo, give me your recommendations tomorrow. I will consult with our K'uhul Ahau, my esteemed father, before finalizing plans. Aj Sul, you will add your wisdom to our deliberations."

Further discussion ensued about the estimated strength of Kan's forces, and their potential augmentation by warriors from Kan allies. Kan Bahlam half-listened to this speculation, knowing that these ahauob must be allowed their time for talking, even if not very productive. His mind was occupied with taking stock of which nobles were most likely to support him, to agree to take action against Imix-ha. He planned to stack the war council in his favor. Still, he had to contend with Pakal's position on this, which he expected would be against immediate action.

His father was getting very old. Although Pakal's mind was sharp, his physical strength had clearly decreased. Lately, he had not been feeling well, due not to any specific ailment but probably a result of lagging stamina from old age.

Surely the old man would not last much longer. Certainly, he had fulfilled his destiny and life mission. He had attained the rare distinction of being a Three-Katun Lord, having now ruled for sixty-five years. Pakal had done enough. Kan Bahlam's own accession to the throne was long overdue. He chafed at the restraints placed on his ambition, his vision for Lakam Ha's future, and his plans for the magnificent Triad Complex.

The afternoon sun cast long shadows across the main plaza. Slowly a dark wedge crept up wide stairways leading to the three tandem buildings of the Academy. The airy lacework roofcombs glowed golden-orange in the warm sunlight of autumn. At the west building, Kan Bahlam stood inside the end chamber, contemplating calculations painted on the rear wall. This small chamber was his personal workspace, where he developed early drafts before showing them to other Academy members. He frowned and rubbed his chin, running the mathematics of the Long Count through his mind once again. This was his initial attempt to put the 819-day count into practical use, to apply its synchronicities to events important in Pakal's life. These calculations would appear as numerical codes on the tablets Pakal was having carved for his mortuary pyramid.

He had developed a set of dates that were linked by celestial cycles of wandering stars. This numerology tied events in his father's life to creation mythology of the Hero Twins. Using a set of four Long Count dates anchored in history and mythology, the calculations began with a ceremony Pakal conducted two years before, on Tzolk'in date 7 Kimi 19 Keh. This ceremony was conjured to complete the appeasement of Death Lords and acknowledge the maturation of the Jeweled Sky Tree, the sacred portal given rebirth by Kan Bahlam's parents. This date was linked by distance numbers to the Hero Twins' appeasement of the Death Lords in mythological times, when they eluded permanent death by using their wits and won resurrection of their father, the Maize God. From that date, the numerology of the 584-day Noh Ek cycle linked with the date Lakam Ha was defeated by Kan. This defeat was the historical and ritual event that needed appeasing.

Using the 399-day cycle of K'awiil Ek, patron star of rulers, he linked Pakal's ceremony to the next important calendar period the ruler would celebrate, the half-katun ending. This date was exactly six K'awiil Ek cycles from the baseline ceremony. He made another link using the 378-day Ayin Ek cycle, connecting Pakal's ceremony to a date preceding the Kan defeat during the reign of Pakal's uncle Aj Ne' Ohl Mat. Text in the glyphic passage referred to the work of the Triad Deity Hun Ahau, One Lord of the Celestial Realm.

Kan Bahlam was pleased with the many significant links this astronumerology provided: Janaab Pakal was intertwined with One Lord, first born of the Triad; the main Death Lords One Death and Seven Death; his ancestor Aj Ne' Ohl Mat; and three wandering stars. Strong associations were made with katun endings through the cycles of Ayin Ek and K'awiil Ek, each close to the length of one katun. The numerology brought together themes of death and resurrection, invoking the Paddler Gods who conveyed souls in their celestial canoe across the night sky and into the Underworld. The link to the Hero Twins had associations with resurrection. Using the 819-day count made these calculations possible, reflected in the code numbers 399, 378, and 584. Those initiated into the select group he was forming would recognize their significance.

Kan Bahlam especially liked the association of both Pakal and Aj Ne' Ohl Mat with the Paddler Gods. If luck was favorable, perhaps his father would not live to celebrate the half-katun ending that was five years in the future.

The sound of voices approaching the stairway drew Kan Bahlam from the chamber. He stood on the top platform and watched as his brother Kan Joy Chitam and K'inuuw Mat began climbing. They appeared to be having a lively conversation, probably talking about their children and families. A twinge of jealousy clouded Kan Bahlam's mood, quickly replaced by his joy at seeing K'inuuw Mat again. She was slender yet shapely, her movements lithe and energetic. After bearing two children, her form still appeared as alluring as when he first saw her at the marriage banquet. He was unprepared by the shaft of desire that pierced his body. Even more surprising was the surge of emotion bursting within his heart.

Is this what love feels like? He wondered. **This immense desiring mixed with immeasurable tenderness?**

Kan Joy Chitam greeted him cheerfully and ushered K'inuuw Mat up the final step.

"Here is our sister-in-law, as I promised," he quipped. "She is eager to hear of your newest calculations, having a mind for such mathematical things, which I do not."

Kan Bahlam had asked his brother to entice K'inuuw Mat into coming for a visit to the Academy. Since they had spent considerable time together during her journey to Lakam Ha and appeared to be good friends, he thought using his brother as a messenger would reduce her reluctance. He sensed that she was uneasy with him, and had been avoiding contact.

The ploy was effective. K'inuuw Mat appeared relaxed and curious. The three entered the chamber, and Kan Bahlam launched into a detailed explanation of how he made the astronumerology calculations to link Pakal with Gods, stars, history, and ancestors. She followed intently, her comments showing that she fully understood his logic. For these moments, the two joined in mutual scholarship and shared wonder. The tension between them was forgotten. Kan Bahlam marveled that it might be the closest he had come to bliss.

Kan Joy Chitam leaned against the door frame, arms folded across his chest. He shook his head at his sister-in-law's intelligence; surely she was smarter than he was, with his inability to understand these complexities. Ah, well, that was not among his talents; he was a courtier and diplomat. These skills would serve a ruler well. Being second in line for the throne did not bother him, for he lacked the burning ambition of his brother. But, he felt assured that his time to rule would come.

Rapid footsteps ascending the stairway caught his attention. He turned to look out the doorway and saw one of his household attendants bounding up the stairs. The breathless man arrived at the platform and spoke through gasps.

"Lord Kan Joy Chitam, your Lady Wife requests that you return home at once. Your son Mayuy has taken ill, and she is much concerned."

"What is his illness?" asked Kan Joy Chitam.

"He has a fever, My Lord. It came on suddenly this afternoon."

The conversation drew Kan Bahlam and K'inuuw Mat out of the chamber.

"What is the trouble?" asked Kan Bahlam.

"It appears my son is sick," replied Kan Joy Chitam. "He has a fever, and my wife wants me home at once." He smiled and spread his hands apologetically. "It is typical of her, at the slightest sign of illness or injury to the children, she becomes distraught. She worries overly much about them. Children will become sick and hurt themselves."

"Still, you must go to her," said K'inuuw Mat. "I understand a mother's concerns. Even if the illness is mild, mothers worry. Please give Te' Kuy my affections and tell her I will visit shortly."

"Those will I convey; she will be most appreciative," said Kan Joy Chitam as he followed the messenger down the stairs.

The two remaining stood silently, watching the receding forms crossing the wide plaza in deepening shadows. The sun, K'in Ahau, was hovering above the western mountaintops, preparing to plunge into his watery nighttime passage below the earth.

"It is late, I must leave soon," said K'inuuw Mat. "My deepest thanks to you for showing me your brilliant new work. Pakal will be pleased; you are making a great tribute to your father."

Kan Bahlam made the hand sign for gratitude and bowed with a smile.

"Before you leave, let me show you a magnificent view," he said. "From behind this chamber, you can see across the plains below. It is a vast expanse, breath-taking in its beauty. Come, it will only take a moment."

She nodded and followed him around the side to a narrow platform that ran the entire length of all three buildings of the Academy. The rear walls of the buildings had no openings. Looking north, she saw the steep escarpment behind the Academy plunging downward to the residential complex bordering the Sutzha River. Although forest trees covered much of the view, she knew that her residence was among the structures. Beyond the escarpment, a vast panorama spread to the distant horizon. Fields and orchards formed a patchwork over gently rolling plains. Clouds over the horizon caught the last golden blush of sunlight, forming magical patterns across the sky. She caught her breath at the soaring beauty of the view.

"Ah, it is magnificent indeed," she breathed.

"I knew you would appreciate it."

The closeness of Kan Bahlam's voice startled her. She could feel his breath on her neck, causing the hairs to rise on the nape. Alarms went off in her mind, and she turned quickly, nearly bumping into his body as he stood close behind her. With widening eyes, she stared up at his face. He was so close that she could feel heat radiating from his body. A wild clash of emotions surged through her, fear mingling with excitement. The magnetic pull she had first felt during the marriage feast returned in full force. It was drawing her body toward his, and she swayed in an effort to keep distance without falling off the platform.

His eyes burned into hers, deep black pools of passion. His lips were slightly parted, and he breathed rapidly. She felt her lips being pulled toward his, beyond her volition. He bent toward her, placing a hand at her waist.

"No!" she cried, quickly turning her face aside. "I must go!"

She tried to step around him, but he caught her wrist. Desperately she struggled to break his grasp, but he grabbed both wrists and swung her against the wall of the building, pressing both her arms up against the cold stones. She twisted her body and swung her face back and forth, but could not break his hold.

"No, no—do not! Let me go!"

He held her firmly against the wall until she stopped moving. Contrary to her will, she lifted her eyes to meet his, their rapid breathing nearly synchronized. Her heaving breasts under her huipil brushed against his chest, bare except for a neck collar. The smell of his maleness filled her nostrils as he slowly pressed his body against hers. His lips found hers, gently at first and then with rising forcefulness. She resisted, then softened and surrendered to a deep, luscious kiss. The feel of his body sent shivers of excitement through her, made her arch her hips into him unbidden. He released his hold on her wrists and slipped both arms around her waist, pulling her even more tightly against him. The kiss lasted an eternity. She did not want it to end.

Finally, she broke mouth contact to murmur against his cheek: "We must not. Let me go. Please."

"You want this as much as I do," he whispered into her ear, tickling with his hot breath. "Admit it. We share this passion."

"Ah . . . no, it is wrong. We cannot."

"We are meant for each other. You know it. It is our destiny to be together."

Her resistance collapsed at these words. How could he know?

With hands now exploring her contours, his touch making her flesh sing, he initiated another long kiss. She melted into him, sliding her hands up his muscled chest, bringing her arms around his neck. The world disappeared, and her heart exploded into his.

"Oh, I am aching for you," he said when the kiss ended. She felt his full arousal and feared he would take her on the hard stone platform.

"Not now . . . how can we . . . oh, no, Kan Bahlam!" She tried to put a little space between their bodies, but he would not release her. His mouth demanded another kiss, and then he loosened his hold and stepped away.

"Not here," he said. "Not now. But soon."

As he used cooling breaths to reduce his arousal, she sagged against the stone wall and willed her heart to slow down. Electricity still crackled between them. She had to divert the energy, somehow.

"How—how did you know we were destined to be together?" she asked.

"From the first moment I saw you, I felt attraction such as never before for a woman," he answered. "Attraction so powerful that it overwhelmed me. Beyond ordinary lust, beyond desire, it is something different and deeper. K'inuuw Mat, I believe that I am in love with you. And, I do not believe that I have ever loved before."

"Oh." Her voice was subdued, and her heart touched. She feared she was feeling the same toward him. This was an emotion far beyond anything she felt for her husband, Tiwol.

"At that first meeting," he continued, "I felt your strong attraction to me. It was so strong that we almost fell into each other's arms, and at your marriage feast! It could only be destiny ordained by the Gods."

"This—this destiny is also something I have become aware of," she said softly.

His eyes widened, and he locked into hers with an incredulous gaze.

"You have?" His voice had dropped to a whisper.

She struggled with a conflicting turmoil of emotions. Since hearing from the phantom Elie in Yohl Ik'nal's tomb that her destiny was intertwined with his, confusion had consumed her. She desperately wanted wise counsel, but was afraid to reveal this to anyone. The flames of desire burst unwanted when she remembered their magnetic attraction. She almost refused to come today. Yet, something drew her inexorably toward him. Now he had voiced the secret she carried. A burden lifted from her soul. She could share it with someone . . . who understood.

She began hesitantly, breaking his gaze momentarily then looking back up into his eyes.

"I was never going to tell you, but . . . several spiritual encounters leave me with little doubt that . . . that our fates are intertwined. It is complex . . . You know that I do scrying, a form of visioning and prophecy. When in my home city I did scrying to see the face of the son of Pakal with whom I would continue the lineage, it was your face—not Tiwol's—that appeared in the scrying bowl. I was shocked . . . and dismayed when I met you and recognized that face."

"That explains why you nearly collapsed when we met," he said thoughtfully.

She nodded, feeling a flush ascend her cheeks remembering it.

"After the births of my two daughters, I felt compelled to learn if I would bear a son. When I asked the Goddess Ix Chel about a son using scrying, the boy's image appeared . . . but there also was a merging of your face and Tiwol's. I do not know what this means; it confuses me. Most recently, when I visited your Holy Ancestor Yohl Ik'nal to fulfill a request passed on through Pakal, she introduced me to a strange foreign woman who has a long connection with your family. This woman, Elie, gave me visions of the future, both perturbing and inspiring. She told me that my destiny and yours are connected, that it is our destiny . . . to be together." Her voice broke into a sob as she said it.

Gently he placed his hand on her arm.

"So it is confirmed, through your own experience," he breathed in relief. "It is not my wishful imaginings."

"No . . . not imaginings. The will of the Gods." She looked up at him, her eyes moist and pained. "How will this destiny work itself out? If we are meant to be together, will this not bring suffering to those around us? I do not want to hurt Tiwol; he is a good husband and father. You are married. I do not see how it can be."

"The ways of the Gods are not the ways of humans. It is not for us to see clearly at present. But we will be together. Our hearts will be united. This I vow, K'inuuw Mat."

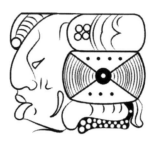

K'inuuw Mat—VI

Baktun 9 Katun 12 Tun 5
– Baktun 9 Katun 12 Tun 6
(677 – 678 CE)

1

A pall hung over the city of Lakam Ha, denser than the mists that gathered in the cooling nights of fall. The sounds of women wailing echoed off stucco walls and across silent plazas. Stone carvers hastily applied their axes, each blow casting sharp staccato notes in contrapuntal rhythm, as they chipped an opening in the floor of a seldom-used chamber in the residence of Pakal's second son, Kan Joy Chitam. Soon the royal family would gather to attend the burial of the venerable ruler's only grandson, Mayuy.

The boy's illness had been short and intense. His small body was ravaged by a ferocious fever, sweat pouring off in rivulets between episodes of severe shaking chills. Nothing the healer priestesses of Ix Chel did was able to help. As Mayuy steadily weakened, the High Priest Ib'ach was called to his side for spiritual intervention, to no avail. The High Priestess Yaxhal also applied her skills, but was no more effective. The priestly leaders of Lakam Ha concluded that the boy's illness was of the spirit, something caused by a deity, a demon or powerful shaman, against which their incantations lacked strength. Just a quarter of the moon cycle passed as he struggled, declined, and succumbed in a nightmare of suffering that enveloped his family and city.

K'inuuw Mat went quickly to be with her sister-in-law when the boy's fever did not resolve in a few days. She spent most of the day beside Te' Kuy, sitting quietly when she was fitfully dozing, holding her tightly when she cried and wailed, restricting her arms to keep her from clawing her face and tearing her hair during episodes of agitation. Maya women often did this self-mutilation during extreme grief to express their utter despair. As Mayuy's final breaths eased away, Te' Kuy was exhausted and semi-delirious. She collapsed into her husband's arms while K'inuuw Mat stroked her hair and murmured prayers for the passing of the soul.

Family members were traditionally buried beneath the floor of the residence, where their spirit would remain connected with those in the house. This particular chamber had been designated for burials; the tiny bodies of four miscarried babies were already in place. Although Mayuy had been tacitly acknowledged as the heir apparent, Pakal had not performed the heir designation ceremony for him; so he was not able to receive a royal burial. Little did this matter to his parents at this point. Their hopes had been crushed. The lineage would not continue through their son. Even more devastating was the loss of a bright child full of joyful energy and potential.

A line of priests holding hand censers led the procession to the burial chamber, trailing a pungent stream of copal incense. Kan Joy Chitam carried his son's body, draped in finest woven blankets with water motifs for the journey into the Underworld. K'inuuw Mat and Tiwol Chan Mat supported Te' Kuy between them. Her tears had not ceased and she was weak from fasting and grief. Pakal and the High Priest and Priestess performed the ritual of interment, casting bouquets of marigolds into the small cyst under the chamber floor, and waving sprigs of basil and vervain around the opening to protect the soul in its journey. Attendants held the two sisters. The youngest, only two years old, was confused and frightened. Chab' Nikte, four years older than her brother, stared wide-eyed in her first encounter with death, trying to process its great mystery in her eight-year-old mind. Most upsetting was their mother's distraught state that removed her emotionally.

Kan Bahlam stood to one side, his face dark and brooding. He glanced across the chamber at his wife, Talol. Her presence added another element of tension, although not attending the burial would have been a serious insult to the family. They were infrequently in the same room these days; he avoided her with a passion and her pride prevented seeking him out. She looked even worse than when he last saw her, with sallow complexion and thin, angular body. Her narrow face seemed viper-like, skin dry and scaly with deep wrinkles. Grey streaks were spreading in her dark hair which was styled on top the head in a small headdress, leaving her scrawny yet sagging neck exposed. As she caught his glance, her thin lips moved slightly into a sneer and her eyes narrowed into slits, sending a bolt of hatred at him across the room. He lowered his gaze and wondered how he had ever found anything attractive in her. Something ominous about her presence troubled him.

The ceremony was drawing to a close as the priests chanted the blessing to send Mayuy's soul successfully on its journey. The icon guardians and objects needed had been reverently placed into the cyst by his father. Later, carvers would cover the opening in the chamber floor and gifts of remembrance would be placed over it by family.

> "The sound of the word of 13 Sky Owl—*Ox Lahun Chan Kuy*
>   brings news, news of the night.
> The sound of the word of Death—*Kimil*,
>   whose touch comes suddenly, portends something new.
> Lords—*Ahau* do their work of 13 days.
> Death is the burden of Moon Woman—*Uc Ixik*.
> Something new happens.
> She brings the blade, sets the foot on the road.
> The wind opens the portal, the celestial canoe drops down.
> The jaguar night sun—*Bahlam Ak'ab K'in*
>   greets the traveler spirit.
> Guides the soul, the White Flower Thing—*Sak Nik Nal*,
>   conducts it on the journey, the path of *Xibalba Be*."

Pakal summoned a select group to his small reception chamber in the palace. The gloomy sky was painted in shades of grey, clouds obscuring the bright face of Ahau K'in. Even the celestial vault reflected his somber mood. Five days had passed since the burial ceremony for his only grandson, and he was deeply troubled. He intended to discuss his concerns about succession and seek the wisdom of the group. These were his closest advisors and most trusted officials, as well as his oldest son and heir, the Ba-ch'ok Kan Bahlam.

The High Priestess Yaxhal arrived first, followed by Aj Sul the priest-warrior holding the title Ah K'uhun. Yax Chan, the chief architect, long time friend and advisor, came in the company of the High Priest Ib'ach. The last to arrive were K'akmo, the venerable Warrior Chief and Kan Bahlam. Pakal greeted each, acknowledged their salutations, and indicated they should take seats on floor mats surrounding his small raised dais. Attendants brought hot cacao-maize drinks laced with spicy chile, for the day was cool with rain threatening. After the drinks were passed around, Pakal ordered the attendants to leave. This discussion was confidential. He had a trusted palace warrior guard the door against eavesdroppers.

"So it is, we have come to a time of difficulty," Pakal began. "The pain in my heart is great over the loss of my grandson, Mayuy. Even greater is the danger we now face, without a male descendant to continue the lineage. We are here to take council, to examine the path ahead. The situation is serious in the long run, although my immediate succession is set through my three sons. My time remaining is limited. When Kan Bahlam succeeds, he will be a man of advanced middle years, and one without children. Should inheritance proceed to my second son, Kan Joy Chitam, he will be even older when he assumes the throne. Due to this tragic event, he has no male successors. It is possible another son could be born, but the problems he and Te' Kuy have experienced with producing children augurs against it. That leaves my youngest son, Tiwol Chan Mat, as the best hope for a male heir. You are well aware of the carefully planned process now in motion to achieve that goal."

The ruler looked at each person present, meeting their eyes and receiving their nods.

"Let us begin a discussion. What say you to this situation?"

"With respect, Holy Lord," said Aj Sul, "can we not consider your oldest granddaughter for succession? Chab' Nikte is an intelligent girl, and given training she might become as gifted a leader as your esteemed mother Sak K'uk and grandmother Yohl Ik'nal. There is sound precedent for female rulers at Lakam Ha."

"There is too much precedent for female rulers in our city," growled K'akmo. "It is a deviation from the common inheritance pattern among our people. Some would argue that each female ruler brings another bloodline into dominance, establishes a new dynasty. Meaning no disrespect, Holy Lord, you have accomplished an impressive deed by convincing our city that your female predecessors in actuality did continue the Bahlam dynasty, and not interject the lineage of their husbands."

A slight smile curled Pakal's lips, and he made the hand sign for "it is so" to his outspoken Warrior Chief, who was candid and to the point.

"K'akmo has succinctly expressed my concern," Pakal responded. "There are ambitious families with pure bloodlines to our founders who covet the throne. Another female succession would be too much for them; they would argue that the Bahlam lineage is not pure enough. Aj Sul, I realize that you naturally support your lineage, the Chuuah family, of which both you and Te' Kuy are members. The Chuuah ambitions for the throne are long-standing, and the lineage is good. But I fear there will be considerable opposition to designating Chab' Nikte as heir."

"Just so," added Yax Chan. "There are rumblings among the noble artisans about lack of a male heir. This is an increasingly influential group, and we need their support."

"With this, I concur, and add that the warriors want a male ruler. They need a strong fighter who will lead them in battles. A woman cannot serve in this way." K'akmo emphasized his point with a hand gesture for strength.

The High Priest raised his hand in an attention-commanding gesture.

"Let there be no doubt that a male heir is essential," he intoned in his deep voice that carried easily across wide plazas. "Therefore, we must assure success for our best opportunity, the coming conception between Tiwol Chan Mat and K'inuuw Mat. Honored Priestess, how go these arrangements?"

"The preparations are proceeding well," replied Yaxhal. "Chilkay, the Ix Chel healer-priestess has been working with K'inuuw Mat for enhancements of fertility. She is residing in the Ix Chel temple during the final two moons before the date determined by the Ah K'inob. The best calendar priests of Lakam Ha did auguries, seeking the most auspicious combination of celestial and earthly qualities, the convergence of stellar patterns and physical techniques for bringing down the spirit of a powerful male, one who will lead and rule successfully. The date they have determined for birth is 3 Lamat 6 Sak on the sacred Tzolk'in calendar, which the Long Count reaches in just over one year."

Pakal, Ib'ach, and Kan Bahlam immediately understood the significance of that date, versed as they were in calendar lore. Lamat was the day sign for one who could deeply analyze and examine everything, able to penetrate into the truth and essence of situations. Sak was the uinal (month) sign that carried qualities of rapid action and swift decisions, with agility for navigating complex and difficult situations. The number 3—Ox was the triad that balanced all activities, the foundation of three hearthstones that underlay Maya society, the numerology of the Triad Deities. The number 6—Uax stood for the sprout, the energies of hatching or emerging anew. The Mayas used the term sprout for a child, a new branch that sprouted from the foundational tree. It implied dynastic progression. All of these qualities were powerfully tied to the abilities needed by a ruler. It made perfect sense.

"An auspicious date indeed," confirmed Pakal. "Think you so, Kan Bahlam?"

"With this date I am in accord," replied the Ba-ch'ok. "It gives a sound configuration for a ruler."

"Now begins the strategic challenge," said Yaxhal. "The priestesses determined on which exact date conception must occur, in order for the child to be born on that selected date. The length of pregnancy is usually 260 days. Thus, conception should take place on 4 Muluc 12 Pax, which is just under two moon cycles away. Several events must occur simultaneously for a successful conception: K'inuuw Mat must be in a state of fertility, with a receptive womb. Tiwol must send strong generative forces into her womb, so the spirit of the child can be drawn from the celestial realm. And, these forces must draw the spirit of a male child—which so far has not happened for them, despite their following prescriptions for a male conception. To further add complications, we all realize that the length of pregnancy varies by several days. Birth on a different day would require recalculations for the qualities of the child, and these might not be as positive." The High Priestess spread her hands apologetically.

Pakal stroked his chin thoughtfully, gazing out of the chamber's small T-shaped window to watch fat raindrops begin spattering the patio outside. The fresh smell of newly fallen rain wafted into the chamber and inexplicably uplifted his mood.

"Less than two moon cycles from now," he murmured. "The time is nearly upon us. What more must the couple do in preparation?"

"In the Ix Chel temple, K'inuuw Mat is being trained in sexual alchemy techniques that will enhance her potency and promote womb receptivity," explained Yaxhal. "During the final moon cycle, she will undergo purifications by steam baths, make devotions and gifts to the deities, and consume special foods and herbs to support her body's readiness for pregnancy. A specially trained Lunar Priestess is working with Tiwol for building his sexual potency, using traditional sexual alchemy techniques for stimulating and then containing arousal. He has been celibate for close to a year, which concentrates creative forces and directs them inward. He will also take select herbs and follow a pure diet, as well as spiritual practices. In truth, we are using every known technique to assure the desired outcome."

"Yes, I well remember these techniques." Pakal smiled nostalgically as memories of his sacred alchemy experiences with Lalak drifted through his mind.

"Well, then it appears all is being done," said K'akmo. "Let us personally do devotions to the Gods for the plan to succeed."

Pakal noticed a scowl on Kan Bahlam's face and sensed that his son was perturbed.

"Kan Bahlam, what troubles you about this plan?"

"It—it appears to be a sound plan," Kan Bahlam replied with uncharacteristic hesitancy. "For the details and techniques of the process I can offer no advice to our esteemed priesthood. But, there is another factor . . . one that could not be known to any of you. With great reluctance do I bring this to your attention. It involves a connection between myself and K'inuuw Mat."

Heads of all present jerked to attention as eyes fixed on Kan Bahlam. Pakal's face remained expressionless, but his son did not miss the terseness emanating toward him.

"In truth, I struggled with saying anything to you about this," said Kan Bahlam. "It is most . . . irregular . . . and mysterious to me. You are aware that K'inuuw Mat does scrying and has a skill for prophecy. Twice in her scrying to ask questions of the goddess Ix Chel, she was shown my face in the reflective water. The first was when she asked to see the son of Pakal with whom she would continue the lineage, and the second when she asked to see if she would bear a son. This second was done recently. She was given the image of a son, but in the same reflection were both my face and that of Tiwol."

He stopped to give the group time for the implications settle into their minds. Expressions on their faces ranged from incredulous to confused. Pakal's eyes were narrowed as he pondered the meaning. Slowly he opened his lids, and his gaze gripped his son.

"You are saying that the Goddess of Childbearing communicated to K'inuuw Mat that you will father the heir to our dynasty." It was a statement, made slowly and deliberately. "Kan Bahlam, over many years you have fathered no children. It appears impossible for you. Why should things be different now?"

"This I also do not understand," Kan Bahlam admitted. "Although I am clearly to be involved, what action the Goddess wants in this situation is unclear. However, I believe it my duty to bring these events to your attention. They bear directly upon the importance of having a male heir."

The High Priest sat with eyes closed, appearing in meditation. Yaxhal's brows were knitted in concentration. Yax Chan broke the charged silence in the room.

"Kan Bahlam, I mean you no insult," he began. "But we must speak the entire truth in this council, for the stakes are great. Among my circle of artisans, Tiwol being one, there are rumors of your desire for his wife. Your reputation for seeking women, unfortunately, is widely known. Not that I wish to imply your account lacks truth, only that you may have ulterior motives."

"Ah, so then . . . you understand my hesitance in bringing this to your attention," said Kan Bahlam. He saw no point in denial. Presently, his motives were sincerely for his dynasty's best interests.

Pakal understood the situation immediately, having devoted his life to serving his people and dynasty. One could have mixed motives and still be acting on a higher plane, for the greater good. He had been there himself. But he pondered how the implication of Kan Bahlam's fatherhood could be realized.

The High Priest immediately opened his eyes and threw light upon this question.

"What we are dealing with here is not of the material world," said Ib'ach. "The deities have knowledge of subtle forces that work in the mystical domain. The embodiment of a soul into human form comes through movements of energies, the *ch'ulel* or life force, the animating essence in Gods, people, and animals. It happens by the drawing down of the ch'ulel from spirit into the flesh. This is not only a physical act, the act of male and female union to conceive a child. It is the flash of spirit light leaving its celestial star and entering the womb to enliven the child. The energies activated during the act of conception are what attract this spirit light, summon this ch'ulel. The stronger these energies, the greater the magnetic pull bringing this spirit into flesh. In this way, Kan Bahlam could father a child—the power of his passionate energies will captivate the ch'ulel that inhabits the soul of the male child who will be heir."

"Ib'ach speaks truly," said Yaxhal. "The ch'ulel of a particular soul residing in the cosmic realm as a star spirit responds to a pattern that matches its own. Many calls are sent forth into the cosmos by aspiring parents to draw down the spirit with qualities they desire for their child. The preparations and techniques we use are meant to augment this call, make it more clear and powerful. But the innate essences of the parents, their own ch'ulel, are the most important factors."

She paused and glanced around at the group; all were listening intently. The workings of the Upperworld, that celestial place of deities and ancestors, remained mysterious to most. It was best understood by the highest ranks of the priesthood, who were now revealing its secrets.

"Consider this well," she continued gravely. "Tiwol and K'inuuw Mat have not succeeded in drawing the soul of a male heir for the Bahlam dynasty. Now, the conception we are planning is critical to accomplishing this goal—especially since we have lost Mayuy, our one hope for succession.

It is possible that despite our maximum efforts, following all protocols, the innate essences of this pair of parents will not be strong enough, will not project the pattern to match the desired soul. Let us consider what Kan Bahlam has said: the Goddess Ix Chel, Mistress of Childbearing and all forms of creation in nature, has clearly shown that he must be involved in the drawing down of a son to Tiwol and K'inuuw Mat. My understanding is that the chance of success is small if he is not involved."

"Sacred Priestess, let me remind you that I have met the Goddess' demand to devote their elder daughter to Her service," Pakal interjected. "Ix Chel made it known through K'inuuw Mat that no son would be born unless this was done. Now it is done. Yax Chel has undergone the dedication ceremony and will be taken to Cuzamil before the onset of her moon blood. Is that not sufficient?"

"It appears not, Holy Lord Pakal. It seems the Goddess has sent another message, one that is meant to help us by revealing the necessity for another essence in this act of creation. The ch'ulel of Kan Bahlam will provide the pattern with the required strength to draw the boy into K'inuuw Mat's womb. My concern is that our plans will not succeed without this element."

K'akmo tilted his head and made a slow appraisal of Kan Bahlam. His studied warrior's eye took in the large well-muscled frame, the tall self-assured stature that often bordered on arrogance, the heavy yet commanding facial features. These left no doubt that here was a man of immense power and magnetism, born for leadership, whose ch'ulel formed a masterful pattern. Whatever the grizzled warrior thought about the Ba-ch'ok's excesses, there was the essence of greatness in his soul.

"Kan Bahlam brings the strength that Tiwol never can," K'akmo observed. "We must carefully consider what our esteemed priestly leaders have said."

"There is one other thing that I can add," said Kan Bahlam softly. "K'inuuw Mat also told me of her visit with our Holy Ancestor Yohl Ik'nal, at your bequest, Father. Visions of the future were given, in which her destiny and mine were intertwined. In some way, we are to . . . to . . ." He hesitated, seeking the right words, careful of underlying meanings. "Our destiny is to . . . bring forth continuation of the lineage . . . together."

Pakal nodded and appeared relieved. His gaze swept around the chamber and through the window, where heavy rain pounded the plaza with furious energy. The steady rhythm of plump raindrops on the stucco roof had a calming effect. It held a promise of continuance.

"This is so," he said. "I did send K'inuuw Mat to commune with my Holy Ancestor and Revered Grandmother. My daughter-in-law did not speak to me of this meeting; perhaps the visions were not yet to be shared. This will I do: seek for myself the guidance of my grandmother in this matter. If Yohl Ik'nal confirms what has been discussed here, then we shall convene again to work out details of how it can be accomplished. In this group, little reminding is needed that no word of this matter shall pass beyond this chamber."

K'inuuw Mat waited anxiously in the austere reception chamber of the Ix Chel temple. Well-worn mats covered most of the floor, only a small altar adding interest by holding an effigy of the Goddess and a wide-brimmed censer. Pale light inched into the chamber through a single doorway, leaving the interior dusky. It was unusual that the priestesses would allow her preparations to be interrupted when just a short time remained. But her visitor was none other than the K'uhul B'aakal Ahau, K'inich Janaab Pakal. The ruler's visit must be about something of utmost importance.

Footsteps approached, and she heard indistinct voices outside. Rising quickly, she turned to the door and recognized Pakal's voice directing his attendant to wait across the patio. The chief Ix Chel priestess' voice informed him she would return in a short time. K'inuuw Mat bowed with arm across her chest as Pakal entered the chamber. He greeted her warmly but did not embrace her as he usually did, mindful that she was in a purification process and must avoid physical contact with men. They sat on mats near each other as she watched him expectantly.

"Forgive this unseemly intrusion upon your sacred preparations," he began. "Nothing but the most urgent matter would compel me to speak with you."

"Is all well with our family? Has anyone become ill?" Anxiety tinged her voice.

"No, no it is not that. Everyone is well, although Te' Kuy continues to grieve deeply. Her sorrow is difficult to behold. Would that I could give her relief."

"Indeed, that is my yearning also. Tiwol is well?"

"Yes. But what I have come to discuss does involve your husband. We are in a serious situation regarding succession, as you understand. This conception for which you prepare is critical to our dynasty's future. So critical that I convened a council of my closest advisors to consider what we should do. Many factors were examined, and some new information brought to light concerning . . . ah, prophecy." Pakal watched her face closely and saw the slightest widening eyes and tensing posture.

"You sense what is being referred to," he said softly.

"How came this information to you?" she asked, almost dreading the reply.

"This I shall speak plainly. Kan Bahlam was included in the council, and he did inform us about the prophecy given by Ix Chel that he would continue the lineage through you."

"He told you what Holy Ancestor Yohl Ik'nal spoke when I visited her."

"That and also about your scrying to see the face of the heir's father. About how both Tiwol and his face own blended together."

K'inuuw Mat covered her face with both hands, bending her head down. Tears gathered and she blinked them back. Her mind was in turmoil and she struggled for composure, remembering her duty to remain serene. Pakal waited, saying nothing, until she wiped the moisture from her cheeks, sighed deeply, and looked back up at him.

"We have done nothing amiss, Holy Lord," she whispered unsteadily. "What this prophecy means in practical, daily life I do not understand. Perhaps it conveys some spiritual process between us, something visible only to the Gods."

"I fear it means something more tangible," Pakal replied. "Let me explain both the concerns and reasoning of the council. This will help you understand the actions we have ordained that will involve you, Tiwol, and Kan Bahlam."

Pakal related details of the council's discussion, emphasizing the importance of ch'ulel in summoning the spirit of a male child, one who would be a strong leader, into her womb. In his relentlessly persuading manner, he drew the necessary connections for these unprecedented actions. When he related his consultation with his grandmother to confirm the message Yohl Ik'nal had given K'inuuw Mat, her eyes widened and a shiver ran up her spine. When he finished the telling, every loop was tightly tied and every objection satisfied. K'inuuw Mat could only sit in stunned silence, eyes closed.

Moments passed that seemed an eternity. Her mind drifted to Cuzamil, to the warm cove waters, the golden beaches, the lush greenery of the Goddess' island where life sprang abundantly, bursting unbidden from every crevice, throbbing with vitality. Deep within her groin sprang also unbidden an intense yearning, as though her womb cried for him—for Kan Bahlam, his face boring into her inner vision. Startled, she flashed open her eyelids as a shiver coursed up her spine.

Pakal was watching her, his face gentle. She found only kindness in his eyes.

"My husband . . . Tiwol, you have told him this?"

Pakal gestured affirmative.

"And . . . and he is accepting of it?"

"Not easily accepting," Pakal replied. "It took a rather long period of discussion to bring him around. His agreement was not easily given. Do not doubt his love for you, because he is willing to follow the council's decree. For indeed it is a decree, and he was given no choice but to comply. When our dynasty is at stake, when our obligations to the Triad Deities and the future of our people weigh in the balance, those with Bahlam blood are required to do their duty. Our lives are not our own to claim, to live as we wish. Tiwol Chan Mat understands this."

"Oh." She tried to control her racing emotions, now a tangle of excitement and sadness. Her heart wept for Tiwol, for she knew he would be deeply wounded. Of course, he would bear it with courage, but she worried about the long-term emotional toll.

"To the more practical matters of this plan," Pakal said, interrupting her reverie.

"Oh, oh yes," she replied, distracted momentarily as images of Kan Bahlam crowded into her mind and evoked again strong urges.

"You will now be instructed by the chief Ix Chel priestess and your own healer-priestess, Chilkay," Pakal continued. "They will reveal the details of how this action is to be carried out. As you can appreciate, this will be kept highly secret. Only a small number of my closest advisors and the necessary priesthood will know. As for the rest of our people, to them any child born of this union will be yours and Tiwol's issue."

She signaled her understanding and agreement. Pakal rose to take leave, and she also stood in respect. They bowed to each other, his arm starting to reach out in a reassuring touch, but he pulled it back. Their gaze met and held for long moments.

"K'inuuw Mat, please accept my most profound appreciation for your understanding of this serious situation. What we are asking of you is no easy action. It is most honorable that you put aside your own needs to fulfill the dynastic destiny. It does naught but raise you in my esteem. You are truly a rare royal daughter."

Pakal turned quickly and left before she could see the wetness in his eyes.

Chilkay and the Ix Chel chief priestess soon entered and settled onto mats with K'inuuw Mat. They secured the door from possible eavesdropping and began.

"The day for conception, as we have determined, is 4 Muluc 12 Pax. This is the mid-winter when all is quiet and the days the shortest. The chilly climate keeps many people inside, helping preserve secrecy. We have a short time period to work with; only one full day counted from sunrise to sunrise. With thirteen periods of light and thirteen periods of dark, we divide these into six sections; three during light and three during dark. In each of these sections, you are to have union with one of the men. The herbs we have given you are priming your womb for receptivity during this time. Thus we are taking advantage of maximal conditions for conception. During your unions, let us remind you to strictly follow the procedures for conceiving a boy, using the prescribed positions. Any variance puts the process at risk."

K'inuuw Mat nodded, having followed these prescriptions twice before. She hoped they would work better this time. But then, her promise to Ix Chel had not been fulfilled. This time was different . . . very different, she thought with a bemused smile.

"One of us will always be present in your household," said Chilkay. "Just outside your chamber. We will usher the men in and out, with enough time between that they do not see each other. Our intent is to remove possible tensions, for it is important to stay calm and centered." The priestess looked intent as she continued. "And, this is very important, Lady K'inuuw. You must not speak about what is transpiring with either man. You must not permit them to speak of it. Any talk will only create strong emotions, and possibly lead to conflict. Remember that maintaining serenity is essential. Keep your focus on the higher purpose of these acts, the great significance for the dynasty and Lakam Ha."

"This do I understand," K'inuuw Mat replied, meeting the priestess' gaze. "Where will this take place? In the Palace chambers?"

"No, for in the Palace it is impossible to escape prying eyes and ears. Too many might observe what is happening and spread gossip," said the chief priestess. "We will use your Sutzha residence. It is more secluded and easier to guard against intruders."

"How . . . where will the men be staying?" she asked.

"Your esteemed husband will remain in a far chamber of your residence," said Chilkay. "He will be attended by a priest selected by Ib'ach, who will himself be in attendance at times. They will assure that Tiwol does not wander about the residence. As for Kan Bahlam, he will come by the narrow path that ascends from below the cascades, not the main path from the plaza. It is unlikely that any will use that path, for it is wet and slippery now. He will also have a priest attendant to escort him and keep the timing accurate."

"Every priest and priestess involved is sworn to secrecy," said the chief priestess. "Both the High Priest Ib'ach and High Priestess Yaxhal have discussed this with them, selecting the most trustworthy to serve."

"Rest assured, Lady K'inuuw, nothing will sully your reputation or that of your husband. Our Holy Lord Pakal is adamant about that. We all have the greatest respect for your service to our city," added Chilkay.

K'inuuw Mat murmured her appreciation, wishing she felt as noble as everyone was making her out. She reviewed the procedures in her mind, making sure all details were etched carefully. She could find no gaps in their planning. Much, however, rested on her shoulders. She hoped she was up to it, especially dealing with the men's feelings—and her own.

"All sounds well-planned," she rejoined to the priestesses. "Will your presence in our Sutzha residence arouse any questions?"

"Not likely," said the chief priestess."With such an important conception underway, none would be surprised that the priesthood was involved."

"And afterwards?" She could not help asking.

"That is in the hands of the deities," said Chilkay. "We will pray and make invocations. You should also offer gifts to Ix Chel and the Triad Gods."

She nodded agreement, but this was not what she meant by afterwards.

2

Dawn seemed reluctant to break on 4 Muluc 12 Pax, as the prior Day Lord struggled to slip off his tumpline and release the daily burden to his successor. Wind howled around corners of pyramids and buffeted treetops, throwing the canopy into a frenzy. Cold rain sliced diagonally across the plazas, pounding walls and streaming through open doorways and windows. Sooty clouds roiled overhead, obscuring the face of K'in Ahau. Faint grayness slowly replacing dark finally hinted that dawn was trying to herald the new day. The unusually chilly storm lashed Lakam Ha, with dangerously high winds that hurtled through the air anything not secured.

K'inuuw Mat shivered as she slipped out from her blanket, pulling the door drape back into place. Even though a corridor overhang gave her chamber some protection, rain was still spattering under the drape and making puddles on the floor. She drew a cape around her shoulders and peered uneasily through the one small window of her chamber. It faced an inside patio and was opposite the wind's direction. The dimly lit patio was drenched as relentless downpour continued. An ominous feeling crept over her, even as her mind advised to remain calm and peaceful.

An Ix Chel priestess carefully chosen for loyalty had replaced her usual household attendant. The young priestess called softly from outside, bidding her come for morning toilet and preparations. They hurried down the rain-drenched corridor to the bathing chamber. Refreshed and warmed by the priestess' massage, K'inuuw Mat returned for a light meal in her sleeping chamber. She burned copal incense and did morning devotions to the Goddess. Her heartbeat was rapid, though, as she waited for her husband to appear.

Though the morning had gained more light, the inside of her chamber remained dim. She thought to request a torch for the wall sconce, but Tiwol appeared before she could. His face was partly shadowed and his expression inscrutable. He moved across the room and folded her in an embrace.

"So much have I missed you," he breathed into her ear.

"And I, you," she replied as their lips met.

It happened so quickly, she had no time to react. They were lying on her mat, and joined in fierce union, more forceful than she remembered. Her mind went blank, and she became immersed in the familiar pleasures of his body. One small part of awareness was careful to maintain the correct position for conceiving a boy, which was the most natural anyway. However, there were small details of where her legs and feet should be placed, and she attended to them. Afterwards, they lay in each other's embrace. It felt so normal; she nearly forgot what was to follow.

Their initial time together passed quickly, and they joined again. When she stroked his face, his eyes were hooded. He said nothing, although toward the period's end she felt his tension. When the priestess called for him to leave, he moved away without looking back at her; his body held stiffly upright. Just as he exited through the drape, she saw his fists were clenched.

Remorse flooded through her, and tears sprang to her eyes. She could not possibly imagine how difficult this must be for him. Cold fingers of doubt crept around her heart. Had she done wrong by agreeing to the arrangement? Would this damage their relationship beyond repair?

A voice called at the door, this time she recognized it was Chilkay. Pulling a cape around her body, she went with the priestess for cleansing to prepare for her next encounter. There was no sight of Tiwol, for he must now be sequestered in his distant chamber with a priest stationed outside. Her mind felt numb, and she tried to keep it that way.

Back in her chamber, skin tingling with the freshness of rosemary and passion flowers from the bath, she pulled the cape tighter around the transparent shift hanging loosely from her shoulders. Chilkay had added sweetly scented herbs to the censer, which glowed softly in the semi-dark. Though the priestess had offered a wall torch, K'inuuw Mat declined. She both dreaded and yearned for who would appear; best to keep the setting dim.

Rain pounded so hard that she did not hear him enter. Sensing a presence, she spun around and felt an immediate burst of electricity between them. Kan Bahlam seemed huge standing at the doorway, nearly filling the space. Shadows hung over his face, but she caught the blazing fire in his eyes. Her heart buffeted her chest, making her gasp. An unbearable throbbing passion arose in her groin and flashed up through her body. It was impossible to speak.

In two strides he covered the distance between them, grabbed her roughly into his arms and kissed her like a man taken to his limit, and then pushed beyond it. The momentum shoved her against the wall, his body pressing hard into hers. She arched against him, hands sliding up his muscled shoulders, and kissed him back in wild abandon. Their wordless, urgent passion blanketed the world, making everything distant and meaningless. Only this depthless kiss, the meeting of their heated bodies, the struggle even to breathe was real.

He slid the loose shift off her shoulders and lifted her onto the sleeping pallet, quickly tossing off his loincloth and short cape. Their joining was an explosion of unbelievable sensation that seemed to include every part of her body, mind, and soul. Only pure life force, ch'ulel, seemed to exist as their crashing energies converged and melded into oneness, their hearts throbbing and bodies pulsating in perfect synchrony. Even their rapid gasps for air followed the same rhythm. As violent as his passionate joining was, hers matched with equal force. Some primal power, far more ancient and primitive than human purposes, took over. They soared among the stars, crashed as ocean waves over craggy boulders, exploded as volcanoes finally allowed release.

It was like nothing she had ever experienced. This awareness slowly emerged as they lay beside each other, spent after an exhilarating climax. He was so still she wondered if he was asleep. Her fingers moved through his loosened hair, feeling dampness. He turned his head and looked into her eyes with an expression so full of love it awed her.

"Your hair is wet," she whispered lamely. It seemed so mundane after traveling the cosmos.

"The rain is heavy, and I would not wait for them to dry it completely," he murmured back.

She continued gazing into his eyes, devouring his face, as if to re-imprint it on her mind in this new context. She realized she hardly knew him, even though she had just shared his naked soul . . . and body. Unbidden, her hand caressed his cheek and traced the sensuous curve of his mouth. It made her fingers tingle.

"You know I love you," he said.

"Yes. But I do not understand it."

"There is little to understand. It is destiny, it simply is."

"But . . ." She stopped herself, remembering they were forbidden to talk about the situation.

He smiled, lifting her fingers to kiss the tips.

"My heart is perfumed by your being," he whispered. "You are all I dreamed and more. Just being together, being able to love each other, is enough . . . for now."

An aching spread in her heart, that yearning she had come to know for him. Her mind struggled to suppress thoughts of hurting her husband. Perhaps Kan Bahlam followed these thoughts, for he groaned softly and lifted onto one elbow, leaning to find her lips in a long, luscious kiss. Desire ignited inside her again, as if her womb cried to be satisfied, to be filled by his seed. She slid hands along his sides and allowed the exquisite pleasure of exploring his body. His hands moved likewise over hers, torching her sensations that demanded to be satisfied.

They joined again and again during the time period allowed that morning. It seemed their passion would never be satiated. She had not imagined she could desire a man so much, or be so completely fulfilled by one.

Wind and rain continued throughout the day. The storm kept Lakam Ha residents inside and quieted the creatures of the jungle. Susurrations of constant raindrops created a hypnotic sound, adding to the surrealistic world in which K'inuuw Mat found herself. She was enveloped in this gray shroud that masked everything normal and ordinary. The priestesses brought her food and drink, which she hardly touched, guided her to the bathing chamber and back, ushered in and summoned out the two men from her chamber. She wanted to remain hypnotized, semi-conscious, detached from her usual emotions. Otherwise, she could not bear it.

Pale daylight gave way to night, winds howling more ferociously and rain unrelenting. It was so dark inside that she allowed one wall torch set in a sconce. Dancing flames cast eerie shadows across the walls, adding to the strangeness. When she was alone, she stared into the flames to numb her mind and feelings. Except when Kan Bahlam came.

Her time periods with Tiwol were the most difficult. She could sense his mounting anger, though he worked hard to contain it. He seemed on the verge of speaking, but held his tongue. She tried making light talk once, but his icy gaze silenced her. When they joined, a few times he whispered her name in a voice nearly breaking. It caused her heart stabbing pain and brought tears to her eyes. She tried to tell him that she loved him, but the words choked in her throat. Would he believe her? Was it even true?

The final time period with Tiwol began just after the middle of the night. He delayed arriving until near the end, and she was worried. When he came, he murmured "Let's finish this." Their joining was perfunctory, and he left quickly, as though eager to remove himself from her company. She cried afterwards and dozed fitfully. The High Priestess Yaxhal came to waken her for the last period with Kan Bahlam. Her haggard face evoked the priestess' empathy, drawing murmured reassurances during the cleansing. Yaxhal dabbed astringent herbs gently to soften her swollen eyes.

"It is almost over, Lady K'inuuw," Yaxhal said kindly. "You are most brave. All will be well."

She felt exhausted, waiting in the chilly chamber for Kan Bahlam. How could her body go through yet another session of such passion? Irreverently, she wondered if his three times climbing up the slippery, rain-drenched cascades path would wear him out and dampen his desire. When he arrived, however, she felt his energy just as strong as before and realized she underestimated his stamina. Soon she found she had not given herself enough credit, either. All sense of tiredness evaporated when he wrapped his powerful arms around her, tilting her chin up for another soul-searing kiss. Their bodies met with undiminished desire, and their ecstasy remained unabated in repeated joining together.

Kan Bahlam was reluctant to leave, she could tell. How he knew their time was drawing to an end, she did not know. Perhaps all his training in calendars and time-keeping had attuned his senses to this. Now she saw a tinge of anguish flicker in his eyes. He sighed deeply and held her tight against his warm body. She snuggled into his form, a small sigh escaping her lips.

"This is more difficult than I thought," he said, lips brushing her ear.

She stroked his forehead and brushed back a long strand of hair. She felt an impending loss, a tear in the new fabric woven tightly around her heart. She could not keep the forbidden words escaping her lips.

"What will happen? For us, for everyone?"

"Shhh," he placed a finger on her lips. "We must not speak of this." He cupped one hand along her cheek, tracing the angle of her neck. Then he lay back, looking up at the ceiling.

"This one thing I do know," he whispered. "This is not an ending, but a beginning. Our purpose together has only been launched."

She exhaled slowly, tried to shift focus and brought to mind their purpose, though it seemed distant and unreal. Even as she recalled the last few intense days, and the memories of joining with Kan Bahlam seared across her mind, she was surprised by a sensation of warmth deep inside her womb. The smiling face of Ix Chel flashed across her inner vision. In that moment she knew that the ch'ulel of a soul had entered, and that she had conceived . . . a boy.

3

W omen's voices mingled with laughter floated down the palace corridor. Several ceramic whistles warbled close harmonies, accompanied by gourd rattles. Two servants entered the doorway into Talol's main reception chamber, carrying cups of warm cacao-chile beverage, frothy and bitter-piquant. The mornings continued chilly, although the harsh winter was waning and the promise of spring smiled in budding flowers. At one side of the chamber, a small group of women sat on mats working back-strap looms, weaving bright geometric patterns. Talol sat alone on the wall bench at the other side, a servant working on her hair and headdress.

Much more is required to give her any semblance of attractiveness, thought Ab'uk from his mat with the women. He was sewing finished fabric into a dress and admired his design. Weaving and making clothes was a favorite occupation. The women accepted him as a two-spirit, one of male gender who more closely identified with being female. He fit into their group readily, wearing a square-neck huipil with short sleeves that hung straight from shoulders to below the knees. His hair was styled in the feminine manner, long tresses braided and wrapped at the side in several loops. As did most of the women, he wore a short turban decorated with ribbons and shells. It was easy to mistake him for a woman, with his small, slender shape and delicate features.

Stealthily he ventured another glance at Talol, quickly dropping his eyes as her stare turned toward him. He focused intently on making even stitches with a bone needle, humming the tune played by the whistles.

Desperately he hoped she would ignore him; even more, that she had forgotten the charge given several moons before. But if she did not forget, he had a plan.

The servant finished and touched Ab'uk on the shoulder when passing out. She gave the hand sign for "go" and tilted her head toward Talol. Ab'uk tensed, sensing that the charge was not forgotten. Trying to mask his reluctance, he put down the sewing and rose from the mat, crossing the chamber to bow before the thin form on the bench. Talol gestured for him to sit on the bench beside her. For a few moments, they sat in silence. The women playing whistles stopped, and Talol ordered them to continue their songs. Ab'uk realized the music would muffle the conversation he knew was inevitable.

"Your weaving goes well," Talol said dryly. "You have quite a talent for clothing."

"Your words are kind," Ab'uk responded. "Many here are talented weavers."

Talol frowned but did not reply. She glanced toward the women across the chamber, who appeared engrossed in weaving and listening to music.

"You have other talents, however," she said. "Have you put them to use on the mission we discussed some moons ago?"

A shiver ran up Ab'uk's spine, but he kept his demeanor calm.

"There have emerged certain possibilities," he said cryptically. "Carefully have I considered the method of obtaining . . . that which you requested. The way appeared to me recently."

"That is so? And what might that way be?"

Ab'uk looked toward the women, hesitating. Talol signaled him to continue, whispering that they would not be heard.

"The lady's husband is renowned for his pottery, and I have developed an interest in advancing my skills in ceramic work." Ab'uk kept his voice low, with his back toward the women. "Therefore, I have requested to study with him. He has accepted and I am to begin in several days time. It is an exceptional opportunity . . ."

He did not need to elaborate, for she immediately caught his meaning and smiled.

"Ah that is so," she chirped. "A perfect opportunity to . . . accomplish your goals."

He lowered his eyes, aware of the bitterness of his feelings. How had he become caught up in this dreadful plot? If anything came of it, he might be incriminated. If nothing came of it, she would surely seek revenge for his betrayal. The outcome looked dismal either way.

"I hear the lady is not well," Talol murmured. Ab'uk nodded and she continued: "The pregnancy appears to make her sick. Perhaps it is not settling well into her womb. At times the mother's body does reject the baby; there is something not compatible with their spirits. This might be the case."

So you hope! Ab'uk thought. The evil hag probably wanted both mother and baby to die. If she managed to have a village shaman cast the death spell on K'inuuw Mat, it would weight mercilessly upon his soul. He must find some way to deflect this crime, even if he became endangered. Although his plan was not fully formed, and much depended on what he observed once inside the lady's household while studying with her husband, he was determined to undermine Talol's intentions.

Within several days Ab'uk was invited by Tiwol Chan Mat to begin studying pottery-making in the studio at the Sutzha residence. Ab'uk came to the residence every day at first, watching and imitating Tiwol through each step of preparing and seasoning the fine clay used by master potters. When the exact mixture of clay and volcanic ash was properly moistened with water, the supple material was rolled into long, slender strands and these were coiled and stacked. Then they were pinched and pulled into the desired shape. The coiled clay strands were slowly smoothed with wet hands, a difficult process because the potter had to move around the form, taking care to keep the walls even in thickness and slope. It was tedious and back-tiring work, done while kneeling on the floor. Once shaped to satisfaction, the pot was air dried to prevent cracking. This process depended on the air being less humid; spring to early summer was the best season. When the pot was judged properly dried, it was fired under low heat in an oven.

Shaping the form, whether a tall straight-sided cup for drinking or a squat, rounded bowl for food, was an art in itself. Many different shapes, including wide platters and lidded bowls with feet, were in the Maya repertory. But, most exciting was planning the decorations, executing the drawings of figures and glyphs, and selecting the paints. Plant and mineral sources provided a range of colors: red, orange, yellow, blue, green, black, and white.

Maya ceramics were often polychrome or black on a colored background, with a wide range of metaphysical and magical creatures as well as portraits of rulers, nobles, and deities. A marked increase of imported fine polychrome vases began early in Pakal's reign. Ceramic styles from trade regions influenced Lakam Ha tastes, although the typical locally produced pottery remained popular. This style was an orange slip with monochrome or polychrome designs of red on orange in mostly geometric patterns. Tripod plates with wide everted rims were common. Tiwol's pottery style took a departure from this, introducing new shapes and colors. His vases, cups, and plates had more decorations and colors, with only modest rim eversion.

Tiwol's preference was monochrome reds and blacks over a cream or pale orange slip, typically with a linear red trim on necks, bases, and ridges. Often he used fine gray or black pastes that were incised or fluted and left unpainted, the carved surfaces offering harmonic contrast. To finish pottery after firing, resins were rubbed against the surface to create a glossy appearance, without the use of glazes.

Ab'uk became engrossed in the artistic process and nearly forgot his assigned mission. One morning as the sun neared apex, he was shaping wet clay into forms on the veranda of Tiwol's work chamber. Looking up from his work, he saw a woman coming across the patio, moving slowly and seeming a little unsteady. As she neared, he recognized K'inuuw Mat. Her customary vigor was missing, she appeared wan, and her color was pale.

"Lady K'inuuw Mat!" he exclaimed, starting to rise.

"Do not stand, Ab'uk," she said. "You are involved in a critical phase of your work. Please do not ruin it by stopping now."

Of course, she would understand that a potter cannot abandon a wet pot being shaped. He thanked her and continued working as she walked past and into the chamber. His gaze took in her rounded belly, protruding noticeably under her huipil. Its weight already caused her to walk in a wider gait maintain balance. Doing some quick mental calculations, he was surprised that the pregnancy seemed so large at what could only be its fourth or fifth moon. It was clear that this pregnancy was taking a toll on her health.

The doorway to the chamber was behind Ab'uk, and he tried to concentrate so he could hear. At first only muffled voices came to his ears, then Tiwol spoke loudly.

"You should not have come without an attendant. Where is Kuy?"

K'inuuw Mat said something about Kuy needing to be with her child.

"Well then, another attendant. It is not good for you to walk out alone."

To Ab'uk, Tiwol's voice held an edge of irritation. K'inuuw Mat said something else he could not make out, and then Tiwol continued.

"What is it you want with me? I can be of little help."

"It is just that I am worried." They had moved closer to the door, and Ab'uk heard clearly. "I have not before been so sick. I fear something is wrong."

"Call for Chilkay, then. Tell her to bring more herbs. I have my work here to do. These things are women's concerns."

Ab'uk was astonished at Tiwol's tone. He sounded brusque and angry, hardly what one would expect of a man who just fathered the long-anticipated male heir to the throne. Certainly, that was what all the priesthood was saying, although they had predicted unsuccessfully twice before and Ab'uk had his doubts. But something was different this time. At the least, Tiwol could show some sympathy. His wife was suffering with this pregnancy and deserved support. It sounded as if she might be crying.

"Come, I will walk you back to your chambers." Tiwol seemed to relent a bit, his voice softer.

They came past Ab'uk with Tiwol holding K'inuuw Mat's elbow, steadying her gait. She leaned against him as he paused, turning his head to Ab'uk and asking him to keep the paints moistened as soon as he could leave shaping his pot. Ab'uk looked up to nod, and he saw K'inuuw Mat full face as she stood close to him. Her eyes were wet with pronounced dark circles underneath, her cheeks hollow and complexion pallid, her neck and arms thin. In sharp contrast was her jewelry; he was captivated by the simple white shell earrings she wore. Small and delicate, three scallops hung on progressively larger loops of silvery material. A short necklace of tiny white conches encircled her neck.

Her eyes met his, and she appeared puzzled. He quickly spoke to cover his embarrassment over staring, both shocked at her appearance and transfixed by her jewelry.

"Forgive me for staring, Lady K'inuuw Mat," Ab'uk said. "I am impressed by your beautiful jewelry. Where did you find it?"

"Ah . . . yes, the shells, they are from the island of Cuzamil," she replied with a faint smile. "You know I was there as a young girl. These are my favorites from my time there. Thank you for admiring them."

He bowed his head, and then lifted it to watch as the pair walked slowly across the patio. Two clear impressions were left in his mind. First, the shell jewelry was perfect as an object belonging to K'inuuw Mat that was precious to her and often touched her body. It was exactly the object that Talol had charged him to obtain from her household. The second impression was less clear but equally compelling: there was some type of discord surrounding her pregnancy that went beyond her sickness.

Ab'uk frequented the marketplace over the next several days. Since the weather was drier, merchants came frequently to offer their wares at the central plaza of the city. At the north edge, they placed mats on the ground, organized in several rows. More affluent merchants used thin poles to hold canopies over their mats, giving shade on hot days and protecting goods from rain. Mats were spread with a panoply of goods from faraway regions, coastal to high mountains. There was obsidian, chert, and flint mined from mountains, copper from southern river deltas where metalworking was known, and occasionally silver or gold from northern regions around Teotihuacan. Spices and exotic foods including dried fish and shellfish spread salty or pungent aromas, with an array of sharp implements such as stingray spines and bone needles. Rows of pottery in exuberant polychrome styles offered elites expensive vases and plates to impress guests. Precious and semiprecious stones sparkled in the sun, from the myriad shades of green found in jades to the red corals and white shells of the coast.

The market always offered happy diversion for Ab'uk, and he lingered over fine embroidery and fabrics, colorful feathers, well-thrown and painted ceramics, and especially jewelry. He noticed a new vendor, obviously doing well since he had a large canopy over his mats. The trader was from coastal regions along the K'ak-nab and said he often obtained shell jewelry from Cuzamil. Ab'uk described the earrings and necklace worn by K'inuuw Mat, and the merchant soon located similar small scallops and conches among his wares. To make the design that Ab'uk wanted was costly and he bargained energetically, but the merchant knew the value of his goods. Finally, Ab'uk settled on a price he could afford for one earring in the design he wanted. The merchant seemed puzzled, but Ab'uk explained it was to replace one earring lost from a pair, very dear to the lady concerned. He paid with cacao pods, the standard unit of exchange. It badly depleted his reserve. But, he now would have a replica of K'inuuw Mat's earring, one that had never been worn by a woman. One that would provide no target for the shaman's curse.

Chilkay offered more herbal tea to K'inuuw Mat as they sat on mats in the small reception chamber. The tea was a mixture of boiled ginger root and steeped guava bark, both known for anti-nausea properties, used to settle the stomach after vomiting and aid digestion. It seemed to K'inuuw Mat that she had consumed an ocean of this concoction and it still did not completely stop the nausea. In her first two pregnancies, she had experienced a short period of mild nausea, no more than one moon cycle. After that, she felt healthy, hungry, and full of energy. Not so with this pregnancy, now nearing its sixth moon cycle. Her appetite was poor, and her stomach upset most of the time. She was losing body weight while the child grew at an alarming rate. She had carried both the previous babies high and inside, so the pregnancies barely showed at a similar stage. This time, her abdomen protruded nearly straight out from her breastbone and hung heavily, straining ligaments and stretching muscles.

She groaned as she shifted position, trying to find a modicum of comfort. Taking the cup of tea, she slowly forced it down, swallow by swallow. A belch escaped as she finished drinking.

"Oh! There simply is no room in my stomach," she muttered. "When will this get better? I have never been so miserable."

"Such a large baby, this augurs for it being male," replied Chilkay, trying to be reassuring. With a practiced eye, she looked at K'inuuw Mat's belly again. A question was forming in her mind, one she had not considered yet. Rarely had she seen a pregnancy this large in the sixth moon cycle. The protruding shape of the abdomen was also unusual. The severe and lengthy nausea and vomiting meant that the internal bodily changes maintaining pregnancy were extreme. The question found its expression—might K'inuuw Mat be carrying twins?

"Lady K'inuuw, might I trouble you to lie down for an examination of your abdomen?" she asked.

"Another examination? Is anything wrong?" K'inuuw Mat thought that Chilkay had examined her much more than was normal. Ruefully she admitted that she felt anything but normal and complied with another groan, as Chilkay arranged a cushion under her head.

The priestess lifted the huipil and ran her palms across K'inuuw Mat's distended belly. Multiple stretch marks made angry red lines across the lower part. None had appeared during the previous pregnancies. She probed gently to trace an outline of the baby's form, trying to identify the hard bulge of its head contrasting to the soft one of the buttocks. After some prodding and pulling, she was satisfied that the head was downward, just over the pubic bone. That was good; a breech birth with a huge infant would be extremely dangerous. She bent down and placed an ear over what she imagined was the baby's back, listening and counting. The heartbeat was distinct and strong, in normal rapid rhythm about twice an adult's pulse rate.

"The baby is well placed and his heartbeat is normal," she stated. "Now please turn on your right side, and breathe as quietly as you can."

The priestess made several more adjustments of the baby's position after K'inuuw Mat had changed position. She identified its outline again and pushed it gently forward, trying to make room along the ribcage. In the small hollow that appeared, she placed her ear and listened intently. She was seeking a second heartbeat, one that had a different rhythm from the louder pattern. Distantly she heard the mother's own heartbeat, easily identified as it was much slower. She strained to hear, intensified her focus. For an instant she thought she heard a second rapid heartbeat, but lost it.

"Lady K'inuuw, can you please hold your breath a few moments?"

When K'inuuw Mat stopped her breath, Chilkay pressed her ear more firmly in the hollow. There it was! A soft, nearly inaudible pattering sound, very rapid. This faint heartbeat was faster than the large baby's, but still within normal range. She listened a moment more to confirm until the mother gasped and drew in a deep breath.

Chilkay helped K'inuuw Mat move back to sitting and smoothed the huipil over her huge belly. The lady's eyes held a worried expression.

"The deities appear to have been most generous with your conception, My Lady. They granted you not one, but two babies. You are carrying twins. I was able to hear a second heartbeat, deeper inside and a bit faster. No wonder your abdomen is so large and you have persisting sickness."

"Oh! Twins!" K'inuuw Mat's eyes enlarged and her hands flew to her abdomen. "Two babies . . . oh, is this not unusual . . . and dangerous?"

"It is unusual, but I have delivered a few twins over the years. Having twins does increase the danger of birth complications, but your risk is less because you have already borne two babies. Twins are most dangerous with a first pregnancy. It is possible that your labor will begin sooner than expected; this will alter the solar priests' calculations. I must discuss it with them."

"We must tell Tiwol . . . and Lord Pakal," said K'inuuw Mat.

"Yes, and several others," Chilkay responded.

K'inuuw Mat immediately thought of Kan Bahlam. She thought too often of him, and tried to push memories out of her mind. Although he had sent multiple requests to visit her, she had declined to say she was feeling unwell. In truth, she felt emotionally unable to be in his presence. Her trepidation was increased by the continuing tension with her husband. Tiwol's anger simmered just below the surface, and she dreaded doing anything to further provoke him.

"At once I will bring word to Lord Pakal. Do you prefer to tell your husband?" asked Chilkay. "It will be good to have the Ix Chel chief priestess more involved in your care, and seek the assistance of the High Priest and Priestess to keep you safe."

"It is best for you to tell Tiwol." K'inuuw Mat's voice was choked and she felt tears burning against her eyelids. "This has been a most difficult time for him."

"As you request." Chilkay was aware of their strained relationship. She hesitated, but felt it must be said. "Lord Kan Bahlam will want to know. I shall convey the information to him. He asks about you often, you know. He even comes to see me at the Ix Chel temple to learn of how your health fares. He wants greatly to visit you."

"Ah . . . I cannot see him. This is more than I can bear." Tears now were creeping down her cheeks.

"It is understandable. Should things change, perhaps I can arrange a meeting at the Ix Chel temple . . . that none will know about."

K'inuuw Mat dropped her head, wiping at the tears. She gave the hand sign for "no" but felt unable to speak.

"One other precaution must be taken for your wellbeing," Chilkay continued. "You have been informed that the birthing must take place in the palace, in the royal birthing chamber where the Honored Ancestor Lady Tz'aakb'u Ahau gave birth to Pakal's sons. Our Holy Lord has so decreed. You were to move into your palace residence chambers during the final moon of your pregnancy. But now, we must provide closer supervision throughout the remainder of the pregnancy and labor might begin early. It will be prudent for you to relocate to the palace residence as soon as possible."

"So soon?" It pained K'inuuw Mat to leave the secluded comfort of the Sutzha residence, and she was troubled about undergoing childbirth in what amounted to an observation chamber. She knew that Pakal, the royal family and several elites, as well as select priesthood would be present for the birth. This tradition had been explained, but she felt childbirth should be an intimate family experience. "Is it really necessary?"

"Yes, My Lady, it is," replied Chilkay. "This residence is too distant, the climb up from these cascades too difficult. We cannot wait until there are . . . urgent needs. It simply is not safe for you to remain here."

Tears were now falling in earnest, and K'inuuw Mat did not try to hide them. Chilkay called a servant to fetch Kuy to come comfort her mistress.

Word spread rapidly throughout Lakam Ha that Pakal's daughter-in-law was pregnant with twins. Only one prior set of twins had been born to the royal family, several generations earlier, and just one child had survived more than a few days. The story made for juicy gossip, the danger rising with each re-telling. More generous-minded citizens included Lady K'inuuw Mat in their offerings and prayers that all would be well. Kan Joy Chitam and his wife, Te' Kuy, came to visit several times after their sister-in-law had moved to the palace residence. Te' Kuy no longer openly grieved the loss of their son, but sadness still hung upon her. She seemed to bear no jealousy toward K'inuuw Mat, and sincerely gave congratulations on the pregnancy that might produce two males to continue the dynasty. While K'inuuw Mat resided in the palace, Tukun her former attendant was assigned to aid Kuy so a noble woman would remain close by. Ix Chel priestess-healers stayed in adjacent chambers in shifts throughout the day and night.

Tiwol told her that he would remain in the Sutzha residence and watch over their two daughters' care. This would allow him to continue his pottery projects, and also provide more space in the palace for the attendants and priestesses to stay near her chambers. She did not question his choice, although she would prefer that he and the girls be closer. When Tiwol came to visit, they kept conversation superficial and she spent most of the time focused on the children. These brief moments were the highlight of her days sequestered in the palace chambers. The two small girls brought such delight, and she missed them terribly. Tiwol appeared bemused at the situation of her carrying twins; it was as though he could not sort it out in his mind. She noticed a subtle change in his demeanor, a slight softening although he still felt emotionally remote from her.

Pakal came frequently to see her, taking her hand and telling stories about his wife's several pregnancies and births. He was kind but firm about using the royal birthing chamber. This momentous event was so important that the leaders of the city must witness it. She tried to ask that only family be present, but he demurred, saying it was most important to keep the tradition. She usually felt bolstered by his positive manner; he appeared convinced that both babies were male and the birth would go well.

Chilkay and the chief Ix Chel priestess came every few days to assess her condition. As the pregnancy advanced into the seventh moon cycle, the nausea finally eased and her appetite was better. Although hungry, she could eat only small meals as the enlarged abdomen pressed upward against the stomach. After this improvement seemed stable for a time, Chilkay broached the subject of visiting Kan Bahlam. He pressured her to plead his case, saying he would behave with all propriety. K'inuuw Mat worried that servants might overhear, but Chilkay assured her they were sent on errands. When she finally relented, Chilkay made arrangements for a palanquin to carry her to the Ix Chel temple for a purification ceremony and extended examinations by the healers. During that time, she would be sequestered for a period in a special chamber with a hidden entrance, known only to the highest priestesses. No one would see Kan Bahlam enter or leave.

The palanquin ride was more tiring than she expected, and she needed help getting into and out of it. The purification ceremony occurred first, priestesses brushing her body with sprigs of basil and pay-che, and then wafting copal incense over all body surfaces while chanting for Ix Chel's blessings. She was next taken for examination in a different chamber, tended by Chilkay and the chief Ix Chel priestess. The priestesses confirmed that the pregnancy was progressing normally, and again identified two separate heartbeats within her womb. Chilkay led her through a concealed passageway into the special chamber. There she was settled onto thick floor mats and propped up with several plush pillows to allow ease of breathing. Thankfully, K'inuuw Mat relaxed back onto the pillows and found reasonable comfort.

She felt both anxious and excited. She had not seen Kan Bahlam for seven moon cycles. Even through her prolonged illness, she had yearned for his presence, almost against her will. She had tried to shut him out of her mind, with small success. Soon he would be here.

A concealed stone panel on one wall of the chamber creaked and moved, surprising her. She had thought it part of the wall mural. Now it slid on a smooth pivot stone, and Kan Bahlam stepped into the chamber. She caught her breath as he stood there, devouring her with his eyes. Quickly he moved across the chamber and fell to his knees at her side, grasping both her hands and pressing them to his lips. Head bowed, he covered her palms with kisses, sending unexpected thrills up her arms.

"Ah, most precious, I have so missed you!" he murmured.

Looking up, his dark eyes met hers and burned into her soul.

"Are you well now?"

"Reasonably well, yes," she managed to reply.

"You look glorious to me; your beauty shines as a butterfly."

"Is your vision gone, Kan Bahlam?" she asked with a smile. "I am monstrous, deformed and huge. This hardly resembles how you last saw me."

"You could not be more beautiful," he breathed softly. "My eyes have hungered for your sight, my heart an empty vessel begging to be filled with your presence, my ears deaf until hearing your sweet voice."

"Please do not say such things. This is not proper; you agreed to behave."

"Forgive me. My heart is bursting. I am so grateful that you have received me."

She tried to withdraw her hands from his grasp, but he would not let go. The heat of his strong hands coursed into hers and made them tingle. The pure life force in him was reassuring and enlivening. She allowed her fingers to intertwine with his. Tentatively, he freed one hand and placed it gently on her belly.

"This is quite huge," he said. "I am sorry to have caused you suffering."

"It was no fault of yours," she replied. "Such is the burden of women."

"No, I feel responsible. This have I brought upon you."

"You only did your duty," she reminded him. "You were charged to be part of this conception. In any event, these babies may not be of your seed."

"Think you so?" He seemed pained at the idea.

"You have no issue to my knowledge. Over many years, it is said."

"This is a different situation, one ordained by the deities. The powers of the Goddess can overcome any human limitations. You know this is true."

She nodded and allowed the realization to re-surface in her awareness.

"As you say, this is different. This pregnancy is different than my others. Something indeed has come from you, has entered into me that is shaping these babies." She laughed, tossing her head back. "Very well, Kan Bahlam. I will grant you the blame. Does that satisfy you?"

He smiled in return, relaxing and settling down into a cross-legged position. He continued to caress her belly and exclaimed when he felt a strong kick against his hand.

"This babe has acknowledged me!" he said. "Yes, I am deeply satisfied. You have given me more than I dreamed possible."

"It has not yet happened," she reminded him. "There is danger with the birth of twins. Much remains unknown . . . and undetermined. And, you cannot publically claim the child . . . or children."

"Let us deal with that in the future. For now, know that I am always with you, in my heart and my awareness. Daily I pray for your safety and wellbeing. Ask anything of me, and it is yours."

She smiled her appreciation and longed to feel his embrace, the reassurance of his strong arms around her. She knew he would not come closer unless invited. Finally, she could no longer resist.

"Hold me," she whispered.

He moved quickly but carefully, wrapping her in a gentle embrace and cradling her head against his shoulder. Her abdomen prevented a full meeting of their bodies but the electrical energy coursed between them. He kissed her cheek, and she turned her face toward him for one long and full kiss. It was almost more than she could bear, taking her breath away. With pounding heart, she slowly pushed him away.

"We must not," she murmured. "But thank you. Feeling you next to me bolsters my courage." She did not add how much it thrilled her heart.

"You are beloved to me, beyond measure," he whispered. "I will stay beside you through this when the time comes. I will always be there, to help however I can."

"You will be at my labor? In the royal birthing chamber?"

"Yes, the entire royal family will be there."

She tried to digest this, now understanding what Pakal meant by the witnessing. She was simultaneously reassured and dismayed. At least she would have his strength to draw upon.

"Then I shall see you there," she said. "But not before. We must not attempt to meet again."

"This I understand," he replied. "Please accept my eternal gratitude to have these few moments with you. Know that I love you, beyond all measure and without condition."

"Thank . . . thank you," she breathed as tears threatened. "You . . . you are dear to me."

Footsteps sounded outside the chamber with a discreet call to alert them the time was over. Kan Bahlam kissed her palms again, touched her cheek and lightly caressed her abdomen. He rose and left silently through the stone panel of the wall mural, closing it behind him. The mural slid into place as if nothing had ever happened.

4

The last days of the ninth moon cycle approached, leaving the priestess-healers astonished that labor had not begun. They marveled that K'inuuw Mat's abdomen continued to stretch as the babies grew. She feared it might explode. It was nearly impossible for her to sit up from reclining, or to stand without help. Chilkay fashioned a sling braced around her shoulders to support the lower abdomen. Even aided by the sling and two helpers, K'inuuw Mat could not walk steadily and waddled about awkwardly. She slept an unusual amount, resting on one side or another, always uncomfortable and short of breath, and never felt refreshed. She could barely eat, taking mostly maize liquids and a few bites of fruit.

She was desperate for this pregnancy to end. Despite being apprehensive about labor, she now pleaded daily with Ix Chel to have it begin. Finally, three days before the auspicious date selected by the Ah K'inob for the male heir's birth, she noticed early signs of labor. Her chronic backache became sharper from time to time, and she felt her womb tightening. No fluid had escaped from the birth sac yet, which usually made labor more rapid. Regardless, she was heartened that the process was in motion.

Chilkay was relieved and alerted the priestesses and attendants. It was too early to convene witnesses in the birthing chamber, and better for K'inuuw Mat to have peace and privacy until labor was more advanced. The day wore on without much change, and darkness fell. Sitting beside K'inuuw Mat with a hand resting on the womb to gauge strength of contractions, the priestess began to worry. The womb seemed unable to activate properly, as though it lacked muscle tone. This was not surprising, since the womb had been stretched almost beyond capacity. The question was whether it would gain enough strength to push the babies out. She kept her concern to herself, deciding to wait through the night. There was no need to take action at present, as long as the babies' heartbeats remained regular.

The sun rose to initiate a new day, streaming brightness through the T-shaped window of the chamber. K'inuuw Mat moaned as another contraction mounted, and Chilkay was encouraged that it felt very firm. She checked the babies' heartbeats after the womb relaxed; all was well. The morning passed, and Chilkay was relieved by another priestess. She discussed the labor process with B'akel, the chief Ix Chel priestess, before taking rest in an adjoining chamber. They decided to administer herbal remedies that would strengthen contractions if labor was not progressing by late afternoon.

During the afternoon Pakal and Tiwol visited to offer encouragement. K'inuuw Mat was happy to have them nearby and clung to Pakal's hand. It was gratifying that Tiwol sought her other hand and held it firmly, pressing his thumb into her palm as he often did in intimate moments. She smiled at both men, trying to control a grimace when labor pains arose. They could both see that labor was not intense, having been through previous births. After they left, she involuntarily thought of Kan Bahlam and wished for his strong presence. She knew labor was not progressing normally.

Pakal and Tiwol conferred with the chief Ix Chel priestess, who told them she was planning to give herbs that would strengthen labor contractions. She advised gathering the selected priesthood in the birthing chamber, to cleanse the chamber of negative energies and begin activating protective forces. The men asked when birth might happen, and she replied it was too soon to predict. She would delay the move to the birthing chamber until labor became more active, but well before birth was imminent.

Chilkay prepared herbal concoctions for stimulating labor: Small branches of rue with leaves steeped in water, squeezed and strained would aid contractions. Grated ginger root steeped in hot water until very strong would help restart delayed or desultory labor. A trumpet tree leaf infusion acted as a sedative and drew excess water out the body, while a decoction made of nine ants that ran up the trumpet tree (not down) boiled in a cup of water then strained would help with difficult childbirth. These were combined in a lukewarm drink and given several times during the four quarters from sunrise to sunrise. The sun was low in the west when the treatment was started and continued through the night. By the next dawn, the herbs had taken effect and labor was in full force.

Contractions of unimaginable power consumed K'inuuw Mat, wrenching cries of agony from her throat. Sweat poured from her face and chest, and she panted like a wounded animal. Between contractions, priestesses wiped her face and skin, applied cool cloths to her forehead, urged sips of herbal concoction. She slipped into semi-drowsing when the pain let up, arousing to acute awareness of the forces wrenching her body apart with the next wave of pain. At the height of the next contraction, the birth sac burst and clear fluid seeped down her thighs. The chief Ix Chel priestess called for a litter to bring her to the birthing chamber. Chilkay sent attendants to notify the royal family and elites who would witness the birth.

Kan Bahlam lounged back on mat and cushions on the veranda of his palace residence courtyard. He kept mostly to the far chamber, trying to avoid Talol who was also staying at the palace. On this second day of K'inuuw Mat's labor, he waited outside for the summons to the birthing chamber, needing fresh air. It was hard to stop worrying; rumors flew around the palace corridors that the labor was extremely difficult. Each day he made offerings in a ceremony to Ix Chel and Unen K'awill, Triad Patron God of the dynasty. When he thought about K'inuuw Mat suffering while bearing the children—his child, at least one, he believed—a sharp dagger pierced his heart. It was beyond frustrating to feel so powerless.

Footsteps sounded behind him on the veranda, evoking a flash of annoyance that it might be Talol. Twisting to look over his shoulder, he saw Ab'uk approaching. He was surprised; it was over a year since he had seen his former lover. Moving to sit cross-legged, he signaled Ab'uk to join him on the mats. Partly his friendliness was out of relief that it was not Talol.

"Greetings, Ab'uk, what purpose brings you here?" he asked.

Ab'uk grasped his left shoulder and bowed before sitting.

"It is good to see you again, Lord Kan Bahlam. You appear well."

"As well as may be under the circumstances. I expect to be called to the birthing chamber soon."

"Ah, yes, the labor is problematic," Ab'uk said. "We are all concerned for Lady K'inuuw Mat. May the Gods and Goddesses protect her."

"Indeed, may they do so."

Ab'uk looked all around the courtyard and veranda. He saw no one and asked, "Are we alone?"

"To my knowledge we are, but that might change at any time."

"Then I shall speak quickly and softly," Ab'uk continued in a low voice. "Do all in your power to keep Lady Talol away from the birthing chamber. She harbors ill intentions toward K'inuuw Mat . . . I fear she would damage the Lady and her babies."

Kan Bahlam was on full alert. He glanced around and dropped his voice.

"What say you? She intends harm?"

"Yes . . . I-I hesitated to tell you, for I am uncertain about her plans, it is something I overheard . . . in her ladies' court."

Ab'uk had struggled mightily about informing Kan Bahlam, fearful that his own part in Talol's plotting would bring him disaster. Just to know about a plot to harm or kill one of the royal family, and not to report it, was treason. His complicity had gone too far to be overlooked, and he doubted he could argue his way out. It was now two moon cycles since he purchased the shell earring at the market and gave it to Talol. She was well pleased, remarking that she remembered the Lady wearing such earrings at a ceremony. Her ability to recall details was frightening. Talol rewarded him with expensive jade and cacao beans; blood money he felt ashamed to take but could not refuse. At first, he believed nothing would come of the shaman's curse, but now with a problematic childbirth, he was afraid. He had no desire to harm K'inuuw Mat who had always been kind and considerate to him. Her husband had taught him excellent pottery making skills. He felt compelled to give warning, even in dissembled form.

"How does Talol intend to harm Lady K'inuuw?" asked Kan Bahlam.

"Much to my regret, I do not know her precise plans," lied Ab'uk. "My fear is that she will bring evil forces into the birthing chamber. She deals with . . . village shamans . . ."

Kan Bahlam seemed intent on grilling Ab'uk, but a servant entered with summons to the birthing chamber. As he stood to leave, Kan Bahlam shot a thunderous glare at Ab'uk.

"Get more information," he growled. "Find a way to bring it to me quickly."

The royal birthing chamber was spacious, with a labor bench and birth platform built in the center. The platform was at the foot of the labor bench, making the transition into birth position easy. A strong rail between two posts allowed the parturient woman to grip and support herself, while a carved-out section in the base of the platform formed a birth basin. The priestesses were able to slide hands below, into the basin, to guide the baby out the birth canal. Others could stand beside the parturient woman to support her, and provide pressure on the abdomen to push the baby down. Benches lining one wall of the chamber permitted the royal family and elite guests to sit during the process. An altar placed in one corner provided space for priests and priestesses to conduct rituals. It stood beside the small T-shaped window that admitted some light. Large bowls filled with warm water stood along another wall. Soft woven cloths were stacked next to the bowls.

Incense burners were already lit when K'inuuw Mat was carried by litter and lowered onto the labor bench. Priests seated on floor mats chanted softly and replaced copal incense, using the purest white sap that gave off a slightly sweet, clean odor. Chilkay and B'akel took positions on either side of the labor bench, while other priestesses stood ready with water and cloths. Cushions were placed under K'inuuw Mat's head, permitting her to see those seated on the wall bench. Between contractions, she noted that the High Priest and Priestess were already seated, as was Pakal, Tiwol, Kan Joy Chitam, Te' Kuy, and a few other of Pakal's closest courtiers and their wives. Searing pain from the next contraction forced her to lie back and close her eyes. She tried not to cry out, but Chilkay whispered in her ear to scream if needed, all would understand and sympathize. Chilkay coached her breathing and provided circular rubbing movements across her abdomen, which gave slight pain relief.

Some time passed before she looked again, between contractions, at the bench. She saw Talol there and had an involuntary shudder. Even in her distracted state of consciousness, she sensed an evil presence, some harmful intent. She removed her gaze and determined not to look at the thin, haggard woman again. But, where was Kan Bahlam? She sensed his presence during the next contraction, a presence so powerful that it penetrated through her haziness and pain. A tiny smile curved her lips, greeting his presence. She felt reassured.

The day passed slowly and the sun dipped toward the western horizon. K'inuuw Mat felt the contractions easing slightly, and breathed deeply in between, trying to bolster her strength. Fatigue was creeping into her limbs, and she dozed whenever possible. Chilkay pressed a cup to her lips with the concoction, urging her to drink as much as she could. B'akel exchanged a concerned look with the High Priestess Yaxhal. Motioning another priestess to take her place, B'akel signaled to Yaxhal to join her outside the chamber. Unbidden, Kan Bahlam slipped out to meet them.

"How bad is it?" he asked.

"Serious, if labor does not become strong again," said the chief Ix Chel priestess. "Yaxhal, you must implore our Triad Deities to help. We have pleaded with Ix Chel; either the Goddess cannot do more, or she has her own purposes."

"Certainly, I will set to rituals at once," said Yaxhal. "Let me summon an attendant to instruct my priestesses in the temple. I will request proper offerings brought here, which I will use inside the chamber, at the altar."

"Cannot you do more to hasten the labor?" Kan Bahlam glared at B'akel. "Surely there is more help you can provide her."

"We are doing all we can, Lord Kan Bahlam," she replied.

"Hruumph!" He stomped off down the corridor. He did not fully understand, but knew he had to get Talol out of the birthing chamber. She was evil and intended harm. He found a palace servant whom he ordered to summon his wife, Talol, to meet him at their residence chambers. He waited there, anger simmering. Soon she appeared, a rail-like apparition drifting along the corridor, almost floating. He could barely look at her face, but forced himself to meet her cold eyes.

"You asked to see me, Kan Bahlam?" Her voice was thin and reedy.

"So you have heard, so you have come," he spat. "Whatever you are doing or have done, I will not allow it to happen. If you bring harm to Lady K'inuuw Mat, I will kill you with my own hands."

Talol appeared surprised, then amused.

"Your concern betrays you, Kan Bahlam. You do not deceive me; I know you love her," she hissed. "You bastard! You do not frighten me."

He grabbed her wrist and twisted it sharply, evoking a cry of pain. She pushed against him with her other hand. He jerked her toward him, grasping her throat tightly.

"Stay away from her, Talol. Keep your venom to yourself. You would do well to have some fear. If you return to the chamber, I will forcefully remove you—and have you restrained." He shoved her from him and she staggered against the wall.

Her eyes narrowed and she rubbed her wrist, gasping for breath.

"Stay away!" Eyes blazing with fury, he spun around and walked quickly down the corridor.

"I will have revenge," she muttered under her breath, but he was out of earshot.

Darkness was falling as Kan Bahlam hurried back to the birthing chamber. He immediately sensed that the situation had changed. The room was charged with excitement. He saw the priestesses had positioned K'inuuw Mat on the birth platform. She held onto the bar as two priestesses supported her on each side; a third priestess encircled her waist with both arms and pushed downward on her abdomen. Chilkay crouched in front, arms extended underneath to guide the child's head out and slide its body into the birthing bowl. K'inuuw Mat pushed and strained with each contraction, sweat pouring from her face, uttering sustained grunts. Tiwol was kneeling beside Chilkay; fingers twisted tightly together, breath bated. Kan Bahlam slid into his place on the bench and stared, transfixed. He had never before witnessed a birth, and it stunned him.

From between K'inuuw Mat's thighs a bloody wrinkled ball appeared. Another long push and the head emerged, smeared with mucus and blood. Chilkay ran a finger around the neck, making sure the cord was not twisted there, then grasped the head and turned it slightly to ease one shoulder out first, then the other slid out. With a final push, the baby's body dropped into the priestesses' hands. Others brought wet cloths and began cleansing, wiping out the baby's mouth and nostrils, rubbing feet and back. Silence hung heavily in the room, no one moved. It seemed an eternity, and the baby neither moved nor cried.

Tiwol, who was very close, gasped.

"It is so pale! Is the baby dead?"

A shrill cry answered his question, as the tiny form started waving arms and legs. The cries were birdlike, high and chirping. Chilkay finished cleaning the baby and presented it to Tiwol and those on the bench. The child was a girl, with skin so pale it was nearly white, and wisps of light yellow hair.

"She is an albino," Chilkay pronounced slowly. "She is filled with magic. She is *juntan*, beloved of the Gods."

The other priestesses helped K'inuuw Mat lie again on the labor platform, once the afterbirth was discharged and the umbilical cord tied and cut. They cleansed her and wiped sweat from face and body. Her abdomen still remained large, only slightly diminished after discharging the tiny girl.

"My baby," she gasped. "Bring me my baby."

Chilkay brought the baby close, showing all parts, turning her carefully. The baby was moving energetically and continued her high, chirping cries.

"Is she normal? Is she healthy?" asked K'inuuw Mat.

"She is healthy, and normally formed, and yet different. She lacks pigments that give color to skin, hair, and eyes. Such albinos are born rarely among our people, but have been known since antiquity. She is very special, my Lady. She came in the liminal time between light and darkness."

"Ah . . . she is beautiful," crooned K'inuuw Mat. "So delicate, so pure and fine. Let me hold her."

Chilkay wrapped the baby in a soft blanket and placed her in the mother's arms. Turning to the witnesses, she explained what came next.

"It will take some time for Lady K'inuuw Mat's womb to reorganize and settle tightly around the second baby. When that is accomplished, labor will start up again. It is best for her to rest now and take sips of liquids. This is a good time for you also to refresh yourselves and rest, take some food. When labor resumes, you will be called."

Tiwol lingered as the others left the chamber. He approached his wife, bent and kissed her forehead. She smiled up at him, cuddling the baby.

"The next will be a boy," she whispered.

"What matters is that this beautiful girl is safely born and healthy. She is a rare gift from the deities. Let me hold her when you are done; I want to press her against my heart and welcome her into our family."

The night reached mid-point before labor commenced once again. Torches were placed in wall sconces and cast wavering light. K'inuuw Mat had slept, watched carefully by substitute priestesses while Chilkay and the B'akel rested. When summoned back to the chamber, Chilkay listened for the baby's heartbeat and assessed how far it had dropped into the birth canal. She was pleased that the heartbeat was normal, and the head firmly lodged below the pubic bone. Together the priestesses offered thanks to Ix Chel and prayed that birth would occur soon. Contractions kept mounting in length and intensity, drawing anguished cries from the mother. Chilkay reassured her that this was good; they wanted labor to progress rapidly because it was so prolonged. The longer the labor, the more risk of illness to mother and danger to baby.

The royal family and other witnesses returned, except for Talol and Te' Kuy. Kan Joy Chitam offered apologies, saying his wife was too exhausted and emotionally fragile to undergo additional strain. Kan Bahlam eyed the door warily, preparing for Talol to enter, relieved that she did not appear. Tiwol knelt beside his wife for a time, caressing her face, until the priestesses asked him to sit on the bench.

The silence of deepest night was broken only by K'inuuw Mat's cries and soft murmurings of the priestesses. At one point her cries changed into deep groans, and she began pushing, straining so hard that her face turned red and the blood vessels on her temples seemed ready to burst. Chilkay motioned to bring her again to the birth platform, where she gripped the bar with white knuckles during pushes. Between contractions she sagged in exhaustion, held up by priestesses on either side. With every push, a priestess wrapped arms around her belly and shoved downward, trying to help expel the baby. Time passed with agonizing slowness; it seemed the ordeal would never end. It was clear to B'akel that K'inuuw Mat's energy was failing, and may not last to push out the large baby. It was possible that the baby was too large to pass through the birth canal. This possibility, the most severe complication of labor, had been discussed among the priests and priestesses.

There was an extreme course of action they could take in situations when babies could not pass through the mother's birth canal. Certain healer-priests were trained in using knives for surgical procedures, such as cutting out embedded spears or lancing festering wounds. Among these, one had specialized in the most desperate measure taken when childbirth failed and the mother was at the point of death. Using a finely honed obsidian blade, the priest would cut a long incision from the mother's navel to above the pubic bone, open the abdomen, cut through the womb, and remove the baby through this opening. They knew that the mother would not survive this surgery, and the baby had a small chance of living. It was the final, last-moment action when all seemed lost.

This priest was called *Ah Ch'ak-taj*, He of the Cutting Obsidian.

B'akel made a hand sign to Chilkay that asked "is it time?" Both knew what this meant. Chilkay had her assistants lift K'inuuw Mat back onto the labor bench and made another examination of the baby's movement into the birth canal. She felt inside with cleansed fingers, noting the head had molded markedly and elongated, trying to squeeze through the narrow space of the pelvic bones.

"There is some progress," she whispered. "Much molding, it may yet be possible to pass through."

"It is prudent to have the Ah Ch'ak-taj on hand," B'akel whispered back. "I will confer with Pakal and Tiwol."

She left, signaling the two men to accompany her. Outside in the corridor, she advised they prepare for the worst and have the Ah Ch'ak-taj at hand, even though there was still hope the birth would happen naturally. Pakal nodded grim agreement; Tiwol nearly collapsed and could not respond. Pakal called Chak Chan to come out and assist with Tiwol, have him walk outside in the patio and collect himself. He ordered a servant to bring balche since he doubted sedating herbs would be enough for Tiwol if this final desperate measure was necessary. Pakal fervently hoped it would not be, but felt compelled to take extreme measures to save his dynastic heir. He returned and knelt at the altar, immersed in prayer, asking the priests to burn more copal.

Kan Bahlam watched and figured out that desperate measures were being considered. Terror twisted through his gut and profound guilt gripped his heart. If she died, it would be his fault. His heartbeat was deafening in his ears, drowning out the groans of the woman he loved. Hideous images flooded his mind of her belly being ripped open, blood streaming and pooling beside her, life seeping away and leaving her blanched and motionless.

He leapt off the bench and ran outside before the agonized cry could form in his throat. He stood shuddering, gasping, clenching his fists. His back was toward the patio, and he did not hear Tiwol and Chak Chan approach until a hand roughly grasped his shoulder and spun him around.

"This is your doing!" Tiwol yelled in his face. "You are killing her! She never had trouble having my babies!"

"Oh Gods! This cannot happen—she must not die!" Kan Bahlam cried, voice breaking.

"If she does, it is on your soul. I should never have agreed to this . . . this despicable arrangement . . . I hate you!"

Tiwol lunged toward his brother and grabbed his neck with both hands. Kan Bahlam resisted, stepping back and then dropped his hands, defenseless. Chak Chan pushed hard against Tiwol and broke them apart. The brothers stood, eyes locked, chests heaving.

From the corridor two men approached, a servant bringing the Ah Ch'ak-taj to the birthing chamber. The tall, muscular priest held a bundle of wrapped obsidian blades. They stopped and stared at the three distraught men. Moving with jaguar swiftness, Kan Bahlam pulled the bundle from the priest's hands and grasped one long, thin obsidian knife out, dropping the rest to the floor making a clattering sound. He held the blade point under his breastbone, one hand extended out toward Tiwol.

"Kill me. Take my life for hers. I do not want to live if she dies."

Slowly he moved the hand holding the knife toward his brother, offering him the handle. Tiwol stood frozen, shocked to the core. The others remained motionless. Only the heavy breathing of the brothers and the piteous moans from the birthing chamber filled the charged air. Tiwol reached a hand toward the knife handle, moving as though in slow motion. Flickering torchlight glinted off the polished blade surface, playing along the sharp edges like sparks. He grasped it from Kan Bahlam, holding it in stabbing position. Kan Bahlam let his arms fall back, spread wide, and arched his bare chest forward. Tiwol poised the sharp point of the obsidian blade a hand's breadth away; one rapid stab under the ribcage and upward would pierce Kan Bahlam's heart.

"No." Tiwol's hand holding the knife dropped. "You will see this ordeal to its end. I will not spare you her suffering. If she dies, brother, I shall take up your offer."

The priest quickly reclaimed his knife and backed away. The frightened servant scurried off down the corridor. The three men stood as frozen, although hot blood coursed through them. Cutting through the tension came a priestess' voice.

"Kan Bahlam, Lady K'inuuw is calling for you."

He bounded into the chamber and fell to his knees beside the labor bench. The others followed and stood just inside. He was startled by how pale she appeared, and terrified as torchlight shadows turned her eyes into skull-like dark hollows.

"Help me . . ." Her voice wavered, so weak it was hard to hear.

He grasped her hand. It felt far too cold. Wrapping his fingers around it, he leaned close.

"Yes . . . yes, I am here, I will help you."

"Give . . . give me your strength."

"It is yours. All my strength is yours." He willed the power of his pounding heart, his hot coursing blood, his aching love to flow into her. She placed her other hand on top his; he enfolded both her chilly hands in his large warm palms. Closing his eyes, he summoned every fiber of his being to pour out life force into her. Moments passed, her breath seemed shallow. He would not let her die. The power of his will would fill her with life.

"K'inuuw! K'inuuw, you can do this. Feel my strength within you. It is there. Use it."

Suddenly she drew a great breath and cried out as an immense contraction seized her womb.

"Aiyeee! He is coming!" she screamed. Her face contorted as she pushed with ultimate force.

Chilkay, B'akel, and other priestesses sprang into action as the crown bulged at her vulva. They had Kan Bahlam help lift her to the birth platform. She had no strength to hold onto the bar and would have fallen if his arms were not supporting her. Chilkay realized they needed this muscular man to help push out the baby. She ordered two priestesses on each side to hold K'inuuw Mat up, while Kan Bahlam used his huge biceps and forearms to push down on the upper abdomen. She gave a few quick instructions to the astonished man, who rapidly understood what they wanted him to do.

They worked as a team, Kan Bahlam shoving down vigorously while the priestesses staggered keeping their burden upright. Every time a contraction hit, Chilkay called "Push!" and the team did their tasks. Squatting at the birth basin, Chilkay watched as the baby's head slowly protruded more from the birth canal. Everyone present leaned forward, transfixed with the mysterious process unfolding before their eyes. Tiwol was on his knees, just behind Chilkay.

"Just a few more pushes, My Lady!" urged Chilkay. B'akel lined up priestesses with cloths, ready to move the moment needed.

When contractions eased, K'inuuw Mat sagged against Kan Bahlam's chest. He kept both arms folded around her, holding her firmly but making sure she could draw deep breaths. The top of her head rested under his chin. He kept focused on flooding her with life force and energy.

"I . . . I cannot . . ." Her voice came faintly to him. He bent his head and brushed lips across her ear. "You can. You must, for all who love you. Only a little more . . . now, push hard!"

She strained again, feeling the pressure of his arms helping move the baby. Searing pain tore through her vulva and she felt a sudden movement, as though something released. Now she pushed again and again, driven by animal instinct and involuntary, primitive body imperatives.

"The head is out!" exclaimed Chilkay. The baby's cranium was amazingly elongated, both from genetic traits and excessive molding. Grasping and turning it, the priestess pulled and simultaneously placed a finger inside to check the cord and shoulder position. All was normal; she pulled again with one long finger crooked into the baby's armpit. The shoulders were wide, but with Kan Bahlam's pushing and her pulling, she managed to help them twist and slide under the pubic bone. One final push and the baby's body slipped out with a gush of blood and fluid. The afterbirth followed almost immediately, as though the womb could not wait to be rid of its burdensome contents.

Priestesses cleansed the baby's nose, throat, and face, wiping vigorously with damp cloths. Chilkay made certain the womb was clamping down to control bleeding, and helped ease K'inuuw Mat back onto the labor bench. Other priestesses came to cleanse the mother and place warming blankets over her shivering form. Only when assured that the mother was out of danger, did Chilkay realize that pale morning light was winking at the small window. The new day had begun, exactly the day prognosticated by the solar priests for the birth of the dynastic heir.

Kan Bahlam stepped away from his position beside K'inuuw Mat, although he desperately wanted to gather her in his arms and rain kisses over her face. Lusty wails from the baby caught his attention, and he moved closer for a better view. He knew the outcome from the look on Pakal's face. The elderly ruler was smiling more broadly than he had ever seen, and Tiwol looked elated. B'akel was holding the baby, proudly showing off the genitals of a boy who seemed enormous compared to his tiny twin sister.

His feet touched the ground, the grandson of K'inich Janaab Pakal and the son of K'inuuw Mat and Tiwol Chan Mat, the dynastic heir Ahkal Mo' Nab. His birth was recorded as:

Baktun 9, Katun 12, Uinal 6, Tun 5, Kin 8 on the sacred calendar day 3 Lamat 6 Sak.

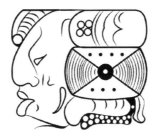

K'inuuw Mat—VII

Baktun 9 Katun 12 Tun 7 – Baktun 9 Katun 13 Tun 10 (679 – 702 CE)

1

The royal court of Lakam Ha was packed with ahauob and warriors. Important news had arrived from a scouting expedition sent to discover what happened during recent battles between forces of Kan and Mutul. Previous reports brought information of Kan's victory over Imix-ha two years ago, when the Snake Lords ousted Nuun Ujol Chaak, Lakam Ha's ally, and re-seated his half-brother Balaj Chan K'awiil on the throne. Nuun Ujol Chaak had returned to his dynastic throne at Mutul, but now it was feared that worse had befallen the rightful Mutul ruler.

Kan Bahlam sat on the double jaguar-headed throne of the palace court. He presided for his father Pakal, who was growing weaker as he aged and often deferred duties to his oldest son, the Ba-ch'ok. Representatives from the expedition now bowed before him, prepared to deliver their report. K'akmo, the grizzled Warrior Chief of Lakam Ha, stood near the throne along with the noble assistants and other officers.

"It is with great regret that we bring this information," said the scout spokesman. "A terrible defeat has been delivered by forces of Kan to our ally, Mutul. Kan ruler Yuknoom Ch'een and that usurper Balaj Chan K'awiil combined their forces to overcome those of Mutul. Nuun Ujol Chaak and his Nakom, Nuun Bahlam, were captured and have been taken as prisoners to Kan's capitol city, Uxte'tun. Mutul is in turmoil, many warriors and nobles killed or captured, monuments destroyed, wealth looted. Balaj Chan K'awiil has been proclaimed ruler of Mutul, but in truth, he is a vassal of Kan. They are bragging about how this victory is revenge against Lakam Ha for our support of Nuun Ujol Chaak. He is calling his victory *witzaj b'aak*, a mountaining of bones exactly as was done when our forces first defeated him."

"On what date did he do the witzaj b'aak?" asked Kan Bahlam.

"By our reports, that date was 11 Kaban 0 Zotz."

Kan Bahlam did rapid calendar calculations in his mind, a skill few had mastered. Being a consummate mathematician and astronomer, he at once saw the significance of this date. He leaned back and rubbed his chin, looking around at the ahauob in the court.

"Perfectly timed revenge," he said. "How many of you recall the date when my father Pakal rescued Nuun Ujol Chaak and brought him here to our city for sanctuary? It was shortly after the attack against Imix-ha in which my uncle Bahlam Ajaw performed a witzaj b'aak and created a mountaining of bones from defeated warriors. Balaj Chan K'awiil has a long memory and excellent astronomical knowledge. This is a direct parallel; his ritual was timed to take place exactly one katun after his half-brother arrived in Lakam Ha."

"Exactly twenty tuns," muttered K'akmo, who had been with Pakal for this battle. "It seems long ago, yet I remember clearly when we escorted Nuun Ujol Chaak into Lakam Ha."

"It is clever for Balaj Chan K'awiil to throw this back in our faces using celestial and calendar numerology," observed Chak Chan. His astronomical training allowed him to appreciate the associations created.

"We must avenge this insult!" exclaimed Aj Sul, always eager for action.

"Would that I could again lead our forces against the usurper and his Kan allies," growled K'akmo. "But my limbs grow feeble with age, and I must defer to our Ah K'uhun, Aj Sul. Who better than a seasoned warrior-priest to lead us into a righteous battle?"

Many voices were raised in support of Aj Sul, who had been designated to assume the Warrior Chief role after K'akmo retired. There was strong sentiment for taking action, particularly among the warriors who had not seen battle in several years. Kan Bahlam permitted their heated exchanges and then raised his hand, bringing them back to order.

"It is so; we shall call a war council," he said. "I will consult with my father Pakal, along with K'akmo, Aj Sul, and their assistant warrior leaders to decide our timing and plans. The snake dynasty will again be shown that they cannot attack our allies without consequences."

He grilled the messenger for additional details, the royal scribe diligently recording these in the codex kept at ready during court sessions. Time was required to get Lakam Ha forces prepared for battle, and plan strategies for attacking Kan forces occupying Mutul. Since Mutul was a considerable distance from Lakam Ha, many days would be needed for travel. Although traveling south by canoes along the K'umaxha River would make the journey faster, there was danger from hostile cities along the river who were Kan allies. It might be necessary to travel mostly overland, which was much slower due to thick jungles and mountainous terrain. Whether the warriors traveled by river or overland, they were compelled to delay until after the approaching rainy season which made such journeys too hazardous.

After discussing plans for warrior trainings and setting up the war council, Kan Bahlam called the court session to an end. As the nobles and warriors dispersed, he walked outside to the terrace along the throne room's west face. From this vantage point, he gazed across the expanse of the main plaza, busy with people going about their daily tasks. At the far end of the plaza were canopies of merchants and rows of colorful mats spread with various wares. He drew a deep breath, inhaling faint aromas of incense and savory stews. Sounds of the jungle carried over the murmur of conversations: squawks of parrots, twitters of songbirds, distant roars of howler monkeys. He was ruler over this magnificent city, in all but actual accession. He sensed that his father did not have much longer to live; already Pakal had outstripped every other Lakam Ha ruler in longevity. This thought led him to shift his gaze toward Pakal's funerary pyramid now under construction.

"How goes the pyramid-temple for my father?" he queried Yax Chan, Pakal's chief architect who was standing beside him, along with his courtiers Chak Chan, Mut, Aj Sul, and Yuhk Makab'te.

"Progress has been good this season," said Yax Chan. "The crypt holding his sarcophagus is completed, except for wall decorations. The outer sarcophagus and lid are in place, but yet need carving. As the pyramid's outer walls are built from the ground upward and backfill put in place, the stairway ascending from the crypt is also being constructed."

"Excellent. How much longer is needed to complete it?"

"Perhaps another two years," replied the architect.

"Will that be too long?" asked Chak Chan. "How fares your father's health?"

"He is well enough," said Kan Bahlam. "He tires easily and prefers to avoid court sessions and adjudications, but still hopes to conduct the Katun-13 ceremonies in five years."

"Ah, that may be an overly ambitious plan," observed Yuhk Makab'te.

"Just so," added Mut. "Not that one would wish our beloved K'uhul Ahau to enter the road, but his departure cannot be far in the future."

"We are well into the process of planning majestic transition ceremonies for Holy Lord Pakal, with grandeur never before equaled at Lakam Ha," said Aj Sul.

Kan Joy Chitam appeared from the chamber where he had hovered, listening to the conversation, and joined the group of men.

"Planning our father's departure once again, brother?" he chided, swatting Kan Bahlam's shoulder lightly. "You should not have much longer to wait. How are the preparations?"

"All proceeds well," said Kan Bahlam. He appeared unruffled by his brother's prod. "Let us hope that preparing for attack against Kan forces at Mutul will not detract from completing Pakal's monument and ceremony. What think you, Aj Sul?"

"We have the resources, Lord Kan Bahlam," replied the Ah K'uhun. "Lakam Ha's population has steadily been increasing, for many are drawn to live and work in our great city. With careful planning, men for both projects will be sufficient."

Kan Bahlam nodded in acknowledgement, and bid his companions farewell for the time. He had other concerns on his mind and returned to his palace chambers to await a visitor. He had summoned the one person who could provide the information he needed on two fronts—Ab'uk.

In the small reception chamber of his residence, Kan Bahlam sat on floor mats attended only by his steward. He relished the quiet of having the residence to himself; he had commanded his wife, Talol, to leave the palace and confine herself to their residence across the Otolum River. After their confrontation during the birth, he made it clear he did not want to see her again. But, he needed information about her schemes.

The steward ushered in Ab'uk, who bowed deeply and then sat on the mat as Kan Bahlam indicated. They exchanged pleasantries and drank cups of kob'al. Ab'uk seemed wary but also gratified to be summoned by the Ba-ch'ok.

"Ab'uk, you may be of assistance to me," said Kan Bahlam. "There is information I need concerning the activities of my wife, Talol. You keep company among her lady courtiers still?"

"Not at present, Lord Kan Bahlam," replied Ab'uk. "She disfavors me now. In truth, I am afraid of seeking her presence. She bears me ill-will . . . for reasons you may guess."

"Indeed. She knows you informed me of her intention to harm Lady K'inuuw Mat."

"Yes. She believes that I have foiled her plans in some way . . . not that I had the power to do this." Ab'uk hoped he would not be pressed for details.

"It is important for me to know how Talol plans to inflict harm," Kan Bahlam persisted. "You mentioned using a village shaman, no doubt to place a curse on the Lady. How was that to be accomplished?"

"I . . . I fear you will punish me . . . hate me . . ."

"Do not fear, Ab'uk. You brought warning alerting me of danger during the birth. That shows your true allegiance. You can prevent future harm and become my ally in protecting K'inuuw Mat. But you must reveal details."

"She . . . Lady Talol, threatened me and forced me to obtain something from Lady K'inuuw Mat, some personal object . . . with which to empower the curse," Ab'uk confessed. "But instead I had a copy made of an earring in the market, and told Lady Talol it belonged to Lady K'inuuw."

"Ah, clever of you. But now Talol knows something went amiss, for the curse did not cause the intended harm . . . or death." Kan Bahlam shuddered remembering how close K'inuuw Mat came to dying during her labor. "But you no longer are trusted by Talol."

"Yes, and I avoid her but fear she will exact revenge upon me."

"And she still intends to harm K'inuuw Mat," Kan Bahlam concluded. "She would also harm me, if she can find a way. Have you friends among Talol's women, someone you can use to gain information?"

"Perhaps. But her women may not be in confidence about her plans."

"Do your best to glean what information you can. I am placing you under my protection and will have a guard assigned. Ab'uk, I do appreciate your assistance in this."

Kan Bahlam placed a hand on Ab'uk's shoulder, and the young man shivered at the touch. Yet, he knew the Ba-ch'ok's heart was given to another. Ab'uk struggled with his feelings, jealousy contending with devotion. He realized the time of their intimacy had passed and could not be regained. Regardless, he would help as he could.

"On another subject," Kan Bahlam continued. "Do you continue to study with Tiwol?"

"From time to time I return to his studio for advice and additional practice," said Ab'uk. "My ceramics are much improved by his instruction. Recently I showed him a bowl, and it pleased him well."

"How fares Lady K'inuuw Mat and the babies?"

"The Lady is still weak, but her health improves steadily. The boy is growing rapidly and crawls everywhere; he is trying to stand and will walk soon. The beautiful pale girl is not so physically advanced, but her eyes hold spirit knowledge far beyond a babe's. She is indeed a remarkable child. Have you not visited recently?"

"No . . . my duties have demanded much time," said Kan Bahlam. "I should be most happy to visit soon, would you convey my request to Lady K'inuuw?"

"As you desire, Lord Kan Bahlam," said Ab'uk. "But why not send your steward to ask?"

"Ah . . . it suits my needs better to send you, to make the request . . . less official." Kan Bahlam hoped that K'inuuw Mat would recognize the informality of the visit and see him alone, rather than as the heir and acting regent.

"Then I will convey it to the Lady at once, and bring her reply."

"This do I appreciate. May all be well with you, Ab'uk."

The reply brought by Ab'uk a few days later was not what Kan Bahlam wanted. K'inuuw Mat had agreed to receive him but made it clear that she would have attendants present, and that Tiwol would be working in his studio. He had not seen her alone since the birth; his few visits during her recovery were brief and in company of priestesses or attendants. It was apparent to him that she was keeping distance between them.

The day was warm and clear when he arrived at the Sutzha residence, where K'inuuw Mat received him on the veranda of the patio bordering the waterfall. Her primary noble attendant Kuy was present, along with two young women serving as nursemaids for the twins. The two older girls were playing near the pool formed at the waterfall base. When the steward announced his arrival, Tiwol appeared from the studio door at the far end of the veranda and came to meet him. Ruefully he wondered who else might show up to form a crowd.

"Greetings, Kan Bahlam," said Tiwol, his voice cool. He bowed and clasped his shoulder in formal honoring of rulers. Kan Bahlam bowed back and signaled to be at ease. "I hope these days find you well and in good spirits."

"Indeed they do, thank you, brother," replied Kan Bahlam. "I am told your family is thriving and your wife regaining health. For these, I am most grateful."

Tiwol smiled and spread his hand toward the children.

"It seems my family continues to grow," he said more warmly. "For this, I am blessed by the Gods. You have served us all well, and I am appreciative."

The allusion to Kan Bahlam's role in making the birth successful did not escape him, and he smiled back to his brother.

"One could do no more for his family," he said. "I am happy to have been of assistance."

He glanced quickly at K'inuuw Mat, who remained seated on a mat during the brothers' exchange. She appeared in better health than at his last visit, with color in her cheeks and bright eyes. Her slender form had filled out slightly but still appeared fragile. She moved as if to get up, but he quickly protested.

"Do not rise, Lady K'inuuw. I wish not to make this a formal occasion, simply a family visit. With permission, I will sit beside you in a moment, after speaking with your husband."

She settled back on the mat and he continued the conversation with Tiwol, asking about his current ceramics projects. Tiwol was working on a large set of burial pottery commissioned by the ruling family of Sak Tz'i. He planned to take the set himself to the nearby city, to provide careful supervision of transport. Part of the way was by canoe along the Chakamax River near Lakam Ha, to its convergence with the mighty K'umaxha River. Sak Tz'i was a short distance downriver, close to the larger river's bank. Kan Bahlam cautioned his brother of possible hostility from Pakab, a city along the river long aligned with Kan. He urged taking several warriors along with traders on the journey. Tiwol inquired about the situation with Imix-Ha and Mutul, and they discussed recent events. Then Tiwol excused himself to return to the studio.

After Kan Bahlam sat beside K'inuuw Mat and they exchanged pleasantries, and he greeted Kuy, he allowed his eyes to fully take in the domestic scene. It was a bittersweet experience; one he yearned to have yet seemed denied by fate. The two older girls played with ceramic dolls and wooden animal toys, engrossed in a little drama of their own making. He figured they would be five and three years old now. Babbling sounds from nearby made him shift his gaze to the twins, each with an attendant beside them on large mats, surrounded by fabric toys. He looked intently at the boy, Ahkal Mo' Nab, trying to determine who he resembled. At just under one year old, the child's chubby face seemed indeterminate to Kan Bahlam. The boy had a large nose, straight forehead and elongated cranium, and tilted almond eyes, but so did nearly all noble Maya children. His lips were full, but that was also typical. It was too soon to determine who he resembled, Kan Bahlam concluded.

The girl, Sak'uay, appeared wispy and almost surreal with her creamy skin and corn-silk hair. She seemed half the boy's size, with slender limbs and a narrow face. When he caught her eyes, he gasped. They were nearly colorless, having only a slight rosy tone. Yet he felt an uncanny depth in her gaze, and was again startled when she smiled fully at him and babbled something known only to her. He nodded back and returned the smile, which seemed to delight the girl, who laughed in trilling cascades resembling birdcalls.

"She seems to enjoy your company," said K'inuuw Mat.

"It is certain that I enjoy hers," Kan Bahlam replied. "Her name is wonderfully suited—Sak'uay, White Spirit. I am still amazed, and profoundly affected, by their births."

Kan Bahlam shifted position so his back blocked Kuy's view, though she appeared preoccupied for the time with her weaving. Quickly he grabbed K'inuuw Mat's hand and pressed the palm to his lips. Still holding her hand, he murmured softly so only they could hear: "It sweetens my heart to see you appearing so well. You are more beautiful each time I behold you. I am aching to be with you."

Her eyes widened and she snatched back her hand, whispering to stop saying such things.

"Thank you, I am feeling quite well," she said more loudly than necessary. "Chilkay tells me that my body has almost recovered from childbirth and loss of blood that followed. She brings me herbs to build my blood and selects the most nourishing food to restore strength. What a treasure this Ix Chel priestess is for our people. Kuy and my attendants could not provide more caring attention."

Kuy looked up upon hearing her name, smiled at her mistress and returned attention to the intricate pattern she was weaving on the backstrap loom.

"Yes, our city is blessed with most accomplished healers." Kan Bahlam resumed normal conversational voice and chatted about other attributes making Lakam Ha a vortex of culture, art, science, and politics in the region. He mentioned work proceeding on Pakal's monument and the excellence of stone carvers in precisely fitting the large limestone blocks of the pyramid. Design for a crypt built below ground level deep inside the pyramid, the huge sarcophagus carved from a single stone slab with a close-fitting lid, an inner fish-shaped structure cradling the ruler's body, and intricately decorated walls were part of the plans. Once the crypt and sarcophagus were in place, a narrow stairway would be constructed ascending to the upper pyramid temple, giving the only access to the burial chamber. He described elaborate plans for Pakal's burial rituals already being developed by the priesthood.

"And afterwards, you will become B'aakal K'uhul Ahau," K'inuuw Mat said.

"I desire not to rush this event," he replied with reasonable sincerity. "Already I have assumed much of the ruler's work."

"But you are eager to begin your own project, to build the triad group you envision. I understand it is frustrating to be delayed."

"Ah, many things delay this work. Soon a military campaign will be launched against the Kan puppet set on the throne of Mutul. Other conflicts are simmering among allies that we must assist. Diplomatic visits are necessary that will take me away for some time. So, you see . . ." He spread his hands in a gesture of resignation.

She laughed and tilted her head in a way that wrenched his heart. He could barely restrain his arms from gathering her up against him. She seemed to notice his intense feelings, shifted position and called to the nursemaids to be careful that the twins did not swallow any pebbles or twigs. He sighed and gazed again at the twins.

"Tell me about Ahkal," he said. "You have watched other children grow, how seems he?"

"Ahkal is very developed for one so young," she responded, relieved at changing focus. "He has such a strong will, and demands what he wants immediately . . . ah, as babies can through cries and fussing and grabbing. You can see how large and strong he is; he stands with ease and seems ready to take steps at any moment. I believe he is most intelligent, though of course I am a mother."

"He is born to rule," observed Kan Bahlam. "Already he possesses a commanding presence. One can only imagine how he will be in a few years! You understand, he will be acknowledged as soon as possible. Once I become ruler, I must designate Kan Joy Chitam as Ba-ch'ok, for this was decreed by our father. Should my brother still have no male children, which I believe will be the case, then I will order a ceremony to acknowledge Ahkal as bearer of the royal blood. It is announced through this ceremony that he will be next in succession, after Kan Joy Chitam. Your son, our . . ." Kan Bahlam caught himself quickly. "Our ruler, your son will become our ruler. Of this I am certain."

Sudden screeches from the older girls drew everyone's attention. They were fighting over a doll and tearing off its clothing. Kuy slipped out of the backstrap loom and rushed over to help settle the tiff, and the twins' attendants were busy keeping their charges from crawling toward the entertaining bedlam. Kan Bahlam saw an opportunity and seized it.

"K'inuuw, find a way to meet me. Somewhere away from your household. It torments me that I cannot hold you, kiss you, talk to you alone."

"No, Kan Bahlam, no. This I cannot do, please do not ask."

"Why not? What harm a few moments together?"

"There is too much risk . . . we will be seen by someone. I will not cause my husband any more pain."

"Ah, K'inuuw, beloved, I am pleading . . ."

"Stop." She lowered her voice to a whisper, making sure the distraction was still happening. The two girls were both crying as Kuy lectured them on proper sisterly behavior. Attendants were holding the squirming twins who raised their own cries for freedom.

"Kan Bahlam, listen." Her voice was low and firm. "You know I care deeply for you. You know I am eternally grateful for your saving my life. What we have shared is precious beyond belief. But now we must be completely proper toward each other. I love Tiwol and will not hurt him again. Do not ask, or I shall not even see you here."

The years following the twins' birth were turbulent ones for K'inuuw Mat, and her brush with death gave cause to reflect upon her own mortality. The difficult pregnancy and birth, along with the lengthy recovery period, made her aware of changes in her body. Although now capable of performing daily routines, she lacked vigor and her stamina lagged. Perhaps it was due to emotions strained to the breaking point, she mused. Never had she been so conflicted, so confused about her feelings and thoughts. It nearly fractured her heart to dismiss Kan Bahlam so firmly, to place barriers between them, but she recognized the necessity. Gradually her relationship with Tiwol was mending, his affection returning and his trust being rebuilt. He delighted in the twins and showered them with love equal to the other girls; never did he mention any doubts about their parentage. Most likely his closeness to his brother would never be restored.

She had told Kan Bahlam that she loved Tiwol. It was true, she reflected, that she did love her husband. But she knew, she could not deny, that she also loved Kan Bahlam, even though she refused to say the words to him. How could she love two men and desire intimacy with both? These thoughts troubled her deeply and went against what she believed. A film of sadness overlay her apparent calm, a yearning that could not be answered. She dreamt of him, and often found herself immersed in memories of their passionate, tender, and courageous moments together. How he gave her strength to fight for her life, and impelled the boy's delivery through sheer determination, would be forever emblazoned in her heart.

Kan Bahlam infrequently came to the Sutzha residence to visit. She sensed it caused him as much anguish as it did her, fueling the desire both felt but could not express. Only when playing with the twins did he seem relaxed, for he had an intense interest in their development and showered them with affection. Perhaps it was her imagination, but she thought Ahkal resembled Kan Bahlam more as the boy approached his second solar year. Sak'uay doted on her uncle and created songs which she sang for him exclusively, her sweet voice captivating his heart. At times her songs brought tears to his eyes.

He appeared to be using Ab'uk as a messenger to stay in closer contact with her, for the young courtier visited every few days. Ab'uk had formed a special relationship with Tiwol through their mutual love of ceramics, and Tiwol invited him along on the trip to Sak Tz'i to deliver the burial pottery, where clients could be cultivated. Ab'uk also brought strange admonitions from Kan Bahlam, warning her to eat only food prepared in her residence kitchen palapa by women she trusted. This included food given to the children, which sent cold fingers of fear clutching her heart. She interrogated Ab'uk about the basis for these precautions; he reluctantly revealed that Kan Bahlam suspected his estranged wife, Talol, of scheming to harm her or her family.

K'inuuw Mat had not seen Talol since the ordeal of her labor, and remembered the foreboding sense of evil she felt then. She instructed her cooks to only use fruits and vegetables taken from their residence gardens or meats brought by hunters working for Tiwol, and not to accept any gifts of foods from others. Still, she was disinclined to believe her sister-in-law would try to poison her family's food. She wanted to believe the best of Talol, who had suffered much grief. However, an incident happened that changed her views.

Once word was about the city that K'inuuw Mat had recovered from the difficult childbirth and was enjoying good health, her other sister-in-law Te' Kuy, wife of Kan Joy Chitam, came with a request. Te' Kuy was still troubled over the death of her son, and the pronouncement by priests that a spiritual illness ended his short life. Her mother's intuition hinted that the death was not natural, that it was caused by evil intent. She desperately wanted information that might confirm or refute this, and asked K'inuuw

Mat to do a scrying to find out. It was something that K'inuuw Mat wished to avoid, but Te' Kuy's continuing torment melted her defenses and she agreed.

She chose an auspicious day and time, prepared as usual with offerings to Ix Chel and purifications, and selected the stone that spoke to her sensitivities. She asked the scrying bowl to show who, if anyone, had taken action to end the life of Mayuy. The face that appeared, clear as if reflected in a mirror, was that of Talol. Settling her startled emotions with additional meditation, she asked a second question of the scrying bowl: How had the act been accomplished? A series of images swirled across the placid water, an elderly village woman concocting a shamanic curse using a toy taken from the boy's chamber, the curse invoking lethal fevers that no priestly rituals could resolve.

K'inuuw Mat was shaken to the core and bewildered about what to do. She knew this act was treason and punishable by death. Would her divination by scrying be taken seriously? Did her duty to Pakal, and to the dynasty, compel her to reveal this to him? Now she became seriously frightened about the risk to her own children, especially to Ahkal. She decided she must tell Pakal, and also Kan Bahlam, Te' Kuy, and Kan Joy Chitam.

Through Ab'uk she sent a request to Kan Bahlam to set up a meeting of the involved parties. Before this, she confided the scrying information to Te' Kuy who could only give thanks that her suspicions were confirmed, although her fury was beyond measure. In the meeting, Pakal listened carefully and gave credence to K'inuuw Mat's ability at scrying, for he had already experienced her accuracy. Kan Bahlam's expression was thunderous, ready in his anger to execute Talol immediately. Only his father's stern admonitions to await the course of justice held him back. Additional evidence against Talol was brought by Ab'uk, who was present at Kan Bahlam's request. Ab'uk had learned from his confidant among Talol's women that she was concocting poisons, against whom the woman did not know. However, the herbs Talol had gathered were among the most lethal and could not fail to kill whoever consumed them.

Pakal rendered his verdict: Talol would be executed if she could not prove her innocence. Already the evidence weighed heavily against her. She was placed under house arrest, surrounded by guards, until Pakal could schedule an adjudication to hear her evidence. This session never happened; Talol took her own life with her poisons.

As the fall equinox drew near, signaling the drier period of autumn before onset of winter rains, Tiwol set off on the journey to Sak Tz'i accompanied by Ab'uk. They needed two canoes for carrying warriors, attendants, gifts, and the burial pottery carefully wrapped in thick cloths and packed into bundles. When overland travel became necessary after going as far as possible on rivers, the bearers would use tumplines across their foreheads to carry the pottery and other goods. Tiwol expected the trip would take at least a moon cycle to complete, since he wanted to visit ahauob in Sak Tz'i to generate more business for himself and Ab'uk.

Warm, sunny days of autumn lulled K'inuuw Mat into a comfortable routine. She spent time weaving with Kuy and other attendants, supervised lessons of the older girls, played with the twins on the veranda, entertained other noble women with music and conversation on the patio, conferred with servants and cooks about meals and household management. From time to time her steward arranged visits to Pakal and the home Te' Kuy. She and her sister-in-law had become close after the tragic events they shared. She received Kan Bahlam on occasion, but always with several attendants and the children present. Since Talol's death, she noticed his mood seemed lighter. Still, the intense fire she detected in his eyes when they met hers was unsettling. He behaved impeccably, though the charged undercurrent between them never failed to excite tingles deep inside her.

At times her reveries turned to recollections of the prophecy given by the Oracle of Ix Chel at Cuzamil. Reflecting on events in her life, she saw how one part of this prophecy had played out, the continuation of the royal dynasty at Lakam Ha. Though it was small comfort, she also understood the enigmatic image given by her scrying bowl, the face of Pakal's son with whom she would produce the heir. Her own prophecy through scrying had proven correct, but she could never have imagined the way in which it came to be. The entangled relations with the two men she loved troubled her deeply. Although she could seek more insight through her scrying bowl, she lacked courage to face its answers.

Something more was part of the Oracle's prophecy, and that eluded her completely. She had long ago memorized these words:

"A destiny beyond your own awaits. A people's legacy depends on you.
In the high court of royalty shall your life unfold.
Rulers shall seek your wisdom; leaders your guidance.
Through you shall dynasties abide."

The part of the prophecy about rulers seeking her wisdom and leaders her guidance, and the people's legacy depending on her, was beyond her comprehension. It was true that she had given small assistance to Kan Bahlam in discovering the code for his numerological quests, and was taken into confidence by Holy Ancestor Yohl Ik'nal about a future destiny of the lineage, but these fell short of the Oracle's sweeping predictions. It all seemed too much for her mind to engage, so she abandoned the effort to seek meaning. Her intuition nudged the fringes of awareness, however, hinting at events still nascent.

Walking beside the pond, soothed by sounds of waterfall and jungle at dusk, she felt an odd fogginess creep over her mind. The equinox sunset cast long golden streams across the patio, bathing the veranda in rosy warmth. All the children were inside the dining chamber having their evening meal, their lilting voices blending with loud buzzing insects making a final pass before dark. There was an eerie stillness filling her ears, almost blocking out sounds. Although somnolence tried to claim her, a part of her mind was screaming alerts.

Across the patio she saw her steward emerge from the reception chamber followed by a solemn procession. First came Pakal, walking slowly and supported at either elbow by his attendant Tohom and Kan Joy Chitam. Curiously, he appeared much older than the last time she saw him, although it was only a few days. Te' Kuy and Kan Bahlam were next, followed by the leading courtiers and family: Yax Chan, Aj Sul, Chak Chan, Mut, and Yuhk Makab'te. Behind them was the Ix Chel priestess-healer Chilkay. For once, her steward did not announce the visitors, his face stricken. When the procession reached her near the pond, she thought her pounding heart would drown out any words. But Pakal's voice roared in her ears.

"There is no easy way to say it. Your husband—my son, Tiwol Chan Mat, is dead. He was killed during the return trip from Sak Tz'i. Warriors from Popo' attacked the canoes on the Chakamax River, only a day's journey away. It is . . . my immense sorrow to bring you this news." Pakal's voice choked and he sagged between his assistants.

Kan Joy Chitam continued.

"Our warriors were outnumbered; several were killed or taken captive. Ab'uk was wounded, not seriously. They were able to recover Tiwol's body and bring it back . . . it is now in your palace residence. My heart is breaking, dear sister. Forgive me for bearing this information to you."

Te' Kuy came quickly from behind and wrapped K'inuuw Mat in her arms, murmuring condolences. Kan Bahlam stood discretely behind, face scowling and fists clenched. The others surrounded her, giving hugs or patting her shoulders.

"You will stay with us for a few days," said Te' Kuy. "You must not be alone now. We will take you to see Tiwol before bringing you to our residence. The children will remain here, under Kuy's care."

In the semi-darkness the scene swirled within K'inuuw Mat's vision, blurring and reforming as tears poured down her cheeks. She buried her face on Te' Kuy's shoulder and allowed grief to flood over her. Chilkay came to her side, giving assurances that herbs would be given later to ease her sleep and emotions. Thankfully, shock created its own form of emotional numbness as she walked with the procession from her Sutzha residence to the palace. Viewing Tiwol's body seemed like a dream, surreal in the wavering torchlight of the palace residence chamber. His wounds must have been on his trunk, for his face appeared perfect and calm, as though asleep. She knelt beside the bench, tears dampening his blanket as she embraced him and placed soft kisses on his cold lips and cheeks. Te' Kuy and Chilkay helped her rise and guided her out of the chamber, where in the shadows she sensed Kan Bahlam's form. There was the faintest comfort she felt in his strong presence, but she could not think or speak.

Pakal conducted burial rites for Tiwol. The elderly ruler had recovered some vigor and his voice rang clearly as he spoke the invocations for a successful journey through the Underworld, defeating the Death Lords, and rising to the sky as a star ancestor. Tiwol's burial crypt was inside the modest pyramid adjacent to his mother's mortuary pyramid; these two smaller structures formed a line west of the tall pyramid under construction for Pakal. The city remained in mourning for six moon cycles, to honor the son of their K'uhul Ahau with repeated chanting and ceremonies at his pyramid.

K'inuuw Mat remained with her sister and brother-in-law for the first moon cycle, then relocated in the palace residence at Pakal's request. He wanted to spend time with his grandchildren, especially the presumptive heir, and walking down the incline to the Sutzha residence was difficult. She was content about this because it was too painful to stay at the beautiful home by the waterfall and pond, full of so many memories of Tiwol. Te' Kuy brought her children often to play with their cousins, and provided welcome distraction for K'inuuw Mat.

Ab'uk visited frequently after his recovery; his leg wounds healed quickly, and he offered as much detail of the attack as she requested. Tiwol had fought bravely along with the warriors, but they could not defeat the superior Popo' forces. After Tiwol was stabbed in the chest with a lance, he fell into the river. This prevented the enemies from taking his body back to Popo' for display during victory ceremonies. As the Lakam Ha ruler's son, he was the prize captive, dead or alive. Instead, they dragged away several noble warriors and attendants. After the enemy departed, Ab'uk insisted his remaining warriors search downriver to recover Tiwol's body so it could receive proper burial at home.

She thanked Ab'uk and came to enjoy his chatty visits conveying palace gossip and happenings among the artistic community. After two moon cycles had passed, Ab'uk brought a request from Kan Bahlam that she receive him, an event she had been contemplating with mixed emotions. She decided she was ready to see him, though not alone. Her palace attendant Tukun had taken over many of Kuy's duties, since the noble companion from Uxte'kuh was again pregnant. K'inuuw Mat was happy for Kuy and her husband and found Tukun an efficient household organizer and congenial companion.

Kan Bahlam's visit aroused familiar feelings, to her surprise. She thought her grieving for Tiwol would suppress the magnetic charge between them, but it felt as strong as ever. No doubt he sensed it also, but he sought no physical contact and kept conversation proper. He expressed sorrow over her loss, asked how she fared and how the children were doing, especially the two older girls who understood more than the twins did. She inquired about his projects at the Academy, his duties as acting regent, and his plans related to regional politics. Tukun sat dutifully close to her mistress, nodding and interjecting comments at times. As the visit drew to a close, Kan Bahlam stretched out his hand toward K'inuuw Mat and leaned closer. Although his proximity set off waves of warmth within her body, she hesitated before placing her hand in his. It seemed a brotherly gesture, and Tukun did not catch the undercurrents.

"Dear sister, soon I shall leave with warriors to assist our ally Mutul, to restore the rightful dynasty to the throne," he said. Her palm was pulsing against his, currents shooting up her arm and making her heart flutter. He closed his hand around hers and continued: "After this campaign, which will take at least one year, it is my vow to avenge the death of your honored husband, my brother Tiwol Chan Mat. I will undertake an attack on Popo' and make them regret their despicable raid on our trading party that offered no threat to them. Popo' lords will rue the day they awakened the anger of the Bahlam dynasty. This I promise you."

She had difficulty concentrating on his words with so much electricity passing through their clasped hands. She could not break the grasp.

"Upon my return from Mutul, with my father's concurrence, we will conduct a ceremony to designate your son, Ahkal Mo' Nab as bearer of the royal blood. I am certain Holy Lord Pakal will be pleased to announce this succession plan, for it has been largely of his making. Nothing gives me more happiness than anticipating the acknowledgement of your son . . ." His eyes met hers and he formed the word "our" soundlessly on his lips. ". . . as the next heir in line for the throne after Kan Joy Chitam. This also I promise you, K'inuuw Mat."

In the depth of his black eyes was the passion of yet another promise.

2

The year of Kan Bahlam's absence passed more quickly than K'inuuw Mat expected. His brother Kan Joy Chitam assumed the acting regent role with his family spending more time in the palace. As spring blossomed and luxuriant growth sprouted, she requested permission to return to the Sutzha residence for the long, warm days of summer. Pakal acquiesced, extracting promises of frequent palace visits. She preferred the quiet of her secluded residence and delighted in spending time outside in the patio, watching the children play and listening to the melodic waterfall. Her oldest daughter Yax Chel was in her eighth solar year, growing tall and slender with a keen mind and flair for ritual. The girl created little ceremonies for her siblings with props and costumes, which they all relished. It reminded K'inuuw Mat of the promise to dedicate the girl to Ix Chel. Her moon flow would begin within a few years, calling for a visit to Cuzamil, island of the Goddess.

Siyah Chan, the second daughter, was six solar years old and had elegance fitting a royal offspring, her movements graceful and fluid. She would make a most desirable match to secure future alliances. Sak'uay, the first-born twin, flitted like a pale butterfly on slim toddler legs, dancing in sun rays and singing to frogs in the pond. Her fine yellow hair was unlike any her mother had ever seen, fanning out as she twirled like a cape. When she went outside, attendants applied light-colored clay to her face and limbs to block effects of the sun. Chilkay had advised that the child's pale skin lacked pigment to protect from sunburn, and would form serious blisters unless shielded. Ahkal Mo' Nab, the second born twin brother, towered over Sak'uay for he was unusually tall. His sturdy legs and thick trunk promised to become admirably muscled and strong as he grew. During their rituals, he usually played the God or ruler who was being honored, a role that seemed natural to him. Even so, he was kind and gentle with his sisters and never took advantage of his size.

Whenever K'inuuw Mat examined Ahkal's features, which she did frequently, she remained perplexed about whom he resembled most. Beyond doubt, his body took after Kan Bahlam, but his face was such a blend that she always saw both men reflected there. Perhaps as he grew into adolescence, his maturing features would give better indication. As unlikely as it may be, she was convinced that Kan Bahlam fathered this boy not just through ch'ulel, soul essence, but also physically.

As the year ended and messengers brought word that Lakam Ha's warriors were soon returning from Mutul, she was surprised at how much she anticipated seeing Kan Bahlam. The amount of time she spent thinking of him and worrying about his safety also surprised her; it was unseemly. Surely she should be mourning Tiwol longer than two years. Indeed, she did miss his gentle and supportive presence. Passing by his studio, stabbing pain pierced her heart and reminded her of this loss. She regretted that the children now had no father, even while she tried to pour her love into that gap. Especially the boy; Ahkal would need the guidance of a strong male model. Sometimes she tried imagining how, and if, Kan Bahlam would fill that need.

Word came that the Lakam Ha contingent had returned victoriously with few casualties, and Kan Bahlam was uninjured. The messenger, a palace attendant, also conveyed a request from the Ba-ch'ok for a visit at the Sutzha residence. He came the next day and she received him on the patio veranda on a warm, sunny late morning.

"It is my great pleasure to see you returned and in good health, Lord Kan Bahlam," she said.

"No greater than mine to conclude this campaign," he replied, "and to be again in your gracious presence."

They exchanged bows, clasping their left shoulder in the courtly Maya acknowledgement. Upon hearing Kan Bahlam's voice, the pack of children descended upon him, squealing and laughing. He had become a favorite with them, for he always played or told stories. He and K'inuuw Mat sat for a while, children climbing over him and begging to hear about his adventures. He regaled them with dangerous treks through jungles, barely avoiding jaguars and tales of brave warriors doing heroic deeds to assist the rightful ruler of Mutul. They marveled at the size and grandeur of the venerable Maya city far to the south, with its soaring pyramids and vast plazas spread over a huge area, surrounded by swamps and cultivated fields as far as the eye could see. Of course, the swamps were full of crocodiles and poisonous frogs and tall stilt-legged herons, making for tantalizing stories.

"Did you restore the rightful ruler of Mutul?" asked Yax Chel.

"Yes, we did re-seat the historic dynasty, but unfortunately our ally Nuun Ujol Chaak had been killed," said Kan Bahlam. "He was a prisoner of Kan for a few years. We were able to throw out the enemy forces that occupied Mutul and place his son Hasau Chan K'awiil on the throne. He will be an excellent ruler, for he is ambitious and clever."

"Just as you are!" exclaimed Ahkal. "You will be our ruler soon, Mother says."

"Does your mother also say that I am ambitious and clever?"

"Oh, very much so!" added Yax Chel.

"Then you must thank her whenever she compliments me," Kan Bahlam laughed.

The older girls talked about their activities for a time, and Sak'uay snuggled into his lap. He urged her to sing for him, to which she happily complied. K'inuuw Mat was touched at the obvious affection her children felt for him, and how thirsty he was for family experiences. His years of childlessness must have been difficult.

The children's attendants came to summon them for the noon meal, and they reluctantly followed with promises to return soon. Kan Bahlam offered a hand to assist K'inuuw Mat to rise, inviting her to walk with him near the waterfall. Her personal attendant remained on the veranda, occupied with weaving. Towering trees hung liana-draped branches high above the patio, climbing the steep hillside bordering the river cascades. Around the periphery, broad-leafed plants nodded and flowering vines trailed, populated by chirping tree frogs and humming insects. The waterfall was running lower during summer, making delightful burbles where it fell into the pond. Across the smooth pond surface away from the waterfall, skating insects danced in overlapping circles.

Kan Bahlam stopped close to the waterfall and breathed in the fresh, moist scents of cascading waters. K'inuuw Mat stood close to him, keenly aware of magnetic forces radiating from his powerful body. Her pulse quickened as his masculine scent filled her nose.

"This place is so lovely," he murmured. "It is a rare gem. You are fortunate to live here."

"That is so, and I am grateful. How fortunate that your father built this residence for his beloved wife, Lalak," she replied.

"Hmmm." Kan Bahlam seemed deep in thought. When he spoke, his eyes gazed into the distance. "This business of warfare puts me in mind of one's mortality. Warriors are always killed on each campaign; someday it could be me. Other battles will be forthcoming soon; I must exact revenge against Popo'."

"Surely not soon!" she exclaimed. "You have just returned. Much did I worry about your safety while you were away."

He turned to her, placing hands lightly on her upper arms. She tingled at his touch.

"You worried about me?"

"Every day," she breathed, meeting his eyes. "Thanks be to the Gods for your safe return."

Their eyes met and locked; she felt drawn into the pools of darkness sparking an inner flame that danced in their depths.

"Our lives are uncertain, K'inuuw Mat. We must not allow them to slip away. Let us find happiness in whatever time remains. You know how deeply I love you. How much I love the children. Now I am asking that you consent to become my wife."

"Your wife . . . to marry?" She gasped as her heart lurched. "Is it not too soon? Would this be proper . . . to marry your brother's widow?"

"Entirely proper and fitting, it is not an uncommon practice," he replied firmly. "And, it is not too soon. We have waited over two years; that is long enough for mourning. We both know that we are destined to be together. The ways of the deities as they work out our destinies are not always kind, and we cannot understand them. I can only give thanks to the Gods—selfish as it may be—that now there are no obstacles to our union."

She drew back but he grasped her arms more tightly, pulling her toward him.

"I . . . I do not know . . . Tiwol's death was a terrible accident . . . but . . ."

"You have no blame, no responsibility in this. You followed the most honorable path after our . . . our moments together, refusing to be alone with me. I have great respect for your behavior, although I burned with desire to be with you. There is no guilt, no blame now. K'inuuw, come to me."

He closed his arms around her, holding her tightly against his chest where she buried her face against the warm skin. Moments passed as her mind tossed in turmoil, feelings of guilt mingling with hope and fueled by rising desire. A knowing from deep within, a burst of intuition, told her he was right. She had behaved properly and fulfilled her obligations as a wife and a bearer of the royal lineage. A knot in her chest suddenly released and a bursting sensation arose in her heart. She lifted her face and looked hungrily into his.

"Kan Bahlam . . . my beloved . . . I consent to become your wife."

He kissed her with overwhelming passion, and she returned the kiss with equal zeal. She wrapped her arms around his muscular chest and pressed her body against his, freely and with abandon never before possible. Their very souls met and merged in a lingering embrace.

Kan Bahlam obtained Pakal's approval for the marriage and requested they be allowed a simple, private ceremony. It did not seem fitting or timely to plan a lavish public ceremony, to which Pakal agreed, while insisting that the High Priest and Priestess officiate because it was a royal wedding for the heir. Less than half a moon cycle passed until the ceremony was set up, to take place at the Sutzha residence. They invited a small group of their closest courtiers and attendants and planned to host a feast for them and the royal family afterwards. They followed the basic marriage ritual used among Mayas for untold generations: when the man received and ate food prepared by the woman at her home, they entered the state of matrimony.

K'inuuw Mat needed help from her cooks to make the maize cakes embedded with dried fruit and nuts, and enjoyed learning the process. She felt a sense of accomplishment when the cakes she made, about the size of her palm, actually stuck together and did not crumble. She also brewed a small batch of kob'al, a mildly alcoholic drink made of toasted maize and fruit juice, which was a more complicated process but worked out fine. When the guests had assembled on the patio, including the High Priest and Priestess, she came forth from inside her chambers carrying a tray with maize cakes and cups of kob'al. Kan Bahlam stood near the waterfall, looking resplendent in white loincloth trimmed in red embroidery, a sun God pectoral and short cape, and feathered headdress. Chak Chan stood to one side of Kan Bahlam.

K'inuuw Mat walked carefully across the patio, balancing the tray as Kuy followed. Both women wore simply cut huipils falling from shoulder to below knee, of the finest white cotton with multicolored borders in geometric patterns. Around K'inuuw Mat's neck was the lovely jade and white shell necklace and in her ears were tiny white scallop earrings from Cuzamil, proclaiming her ties to Ix Chel. Arriving to face Kan Bahlam, she offered him the tray with shining eyes. He took a maize cake and cup of kob'al, smiling at her as though his heart would erupt. He took a big bite of the maize cake and chewed thoughtfully; she waited breathlessly. A wicked gleam in his eye made her fear he would spit it out. But, he smiled and took another bite, washing it down with swallows of kob'al.

"It is good," he declared.

"These have you made by your own hand, Lady K'inuuw Mat?" intoned the High Priest.

"Yes, by my hand were made the cakes and drink," she replied proudly.

"These have you taken by your own free will, Lord Kan Bahlam?" said the High Priestess.

"Indeed, that is so!" Kan Bahlam said enthusiastically.

"Thus has it happened," the High Priest continued. "Lord Kan Bahlam has eaten food and drink made by Lady K'inuuw Mat, in her own home. By the traditions of our people, they have committed themselves in marriage. Let this sacred union be attested by those present, it is so, they are married."

Cheers and claps greeted the pronouncement, joined by the children's exclamations. The twins each attached themselves to one of Kan Bahlam's legs, bouncing in their enthusiasm though not quite understanding everything. The older girls hugged their mother, joyful tears in their eyes. They realized this marriage would bring her happiness after the tragic loss, and were thrilled to have Kan Bahlam as their father. The afternoon passed in exuberant feasting, dancing, and celebration. Pakal stayed until the sun dipped behind the escarpment, needing two assistants to help him climb up to the plaza. After darkness fell and all the guests left, and the children were taken to their chambers by attendants, K'inuuw Mat and Kan Bahlam retired to the sleeping chamber to fulfill their long-delayed passion in a night of delirious rapture.

True to his word, Kan Bahlam arranged the ceremony denoting Ahkal Mo' Nab as bearer of the royal blood. He assisted Pakal to conduct the ritual, done in the small courtyard in front of the Sak Nuk Nah, the sacred shrine which held the portal to the Gods. Ahkal stood proudly in ceremonial attire and followed instructions for processing around the courtyard, then joining his grandfather Pakal who was seated on the double-headed jaguar throne inside the sacred chamber. Kan Bahlam led the boy in reciting the creation story of B'aakal, which was required knowledge for those given this designation. It was a long recitative, full of occult wisdom and naming of Gods and ancestors, more than a child could commit to memory. Kan Bahlam had practiced the recital with Ahkal several times, helping with pronunciation and schooling the boy on how to maintain a regal presence.

Ahkal performed well and seemed to relish acknowledgement of his important status. Already he showed signs of natural authority. His mother and sisters, along with the elite nobles and royal family of Lakam Ha, focused intently as he repeated after Kan Bahlam the final stanza of the recitative.

"It was accomplished, in the Fourth Creation,
    the birth of a son from a man and a woman, Halach Uinik, real people,
    the progenitors of the B'aakal lineage.
The son, the ruler, Holy B'aakal Lord, K'uk Bahlam I,
    whose blood flows through all rulers of Lakam Ha.
And in this way the Triad Gods, the three sons of Ix Muwaan Mat,
    created the B'aakal lineage, the founders of Lakam Ha."

Drummers began a soft cadence as priests and priestesses chanted the titles for the B'aakal K'uhul Ahau, K'inich Janaab Pakal. Assistants near Pakal lifted ornately wrapped bundles and presented these to Ahkal, as the ruler spoke: "Ahkal Mo' Nab, son of Tiwol Chan Mat and K'inuuw Mat, you are now designated as bearer of the sacred blood of Ah K'uk Bahlam Ahau, our lineage founder. You have correctly recited the names of the Gods, retold their history, and given account of their days. You are acknowledged as bearer of the royal blood. In recognition of this, you will carry the symbols of rulership as have all leaders of B'aakal. This is your right and heritage."

The assistants opened the bundles which held a carved flint K'awiil scepter and a ceramic K'in Ahau shield. K'awiil was the patron deity of Lakam Ha rulers, the youngest Triad God. K'in Ahau was the Sun Lord, the celestial expression of First Father—Hun Hunahpu, creator deity of the Maya people. For this occasion, a smaller version of the scepter and ceramic shield were made, a size that could be carried by a boy nearing his fifth solar year. Ahkal glanced at Kan Bahlam, who signaled him to pick up the icons. With deliberate movements, the boy took the scepter in one hand and the shield in the other, and then followed Kan Bahlam, the High Priest and High Priestess in a slow procession around the courtyard. Ahkal held his head high, making his feathered headdress dance, and extended the icons out at arms' length, walking solemnly behind and keeping eyes focused forward. Drums took up a brisk tempo, accompanied by high ceramic whistles and lilting wooden flutes.

All present cheered as Ahkal finished the circuit and returned the icons to Pakal. The elderly ruler arose with difficulty from the throne, crossed both arms over his chest and bowed in the gesture of ultimate respect. Silently, the nobles and priesthood followed suit. Ahkal Mo' Nab had crossed a threshold and was transformed into a new status by the ritual. It was understood that he was now in line to become a future ruler of Lakam Ha.

K'inuuw Mat entered the palace chamber used by Kan Bahlam and his architects as a workshop. A model of Pakal's mortuary monument was set on a bench, and on the chamber wall were drawings of the upper temple with its six pillars as well as the sarcophagus lid and sides. Artists had been working on designs for decorating these, outlines painted in black onto the stucco wall. Kan Bahlam and Mut, his assistant who was a skilled painter and stone carver, stood near the wall in deep contemplation. They turned as she entered and bowed slightly in greeting.

"We are stymied, my dear," Kan Bahlam said. "Mut and I disagree about how to depict my father on the sarcophagus lid. Mut prefers the usual style of a standing ruler in magnificent attire, looking regal and powerful. I favor something unique, an image that conveys core beliefs of our people about rulership and ties into broader themes. What think you?"

K'inuuw Mat walked closer to the wall and studied the preliminary sketches of a typical appearing ruler. She closed her eyes and summoned images conveying the eternal themes of birth, death, and regeneration.

These to her were at the core of a ruler's destiny, the covenant with the Gods. The idea of death as new birth gave a sense of continuous cycles in which the past, present, and future became one in an eternal flow. She kept seeing the form of an infant in the posture of emergence. With a laugh, she shook her head.

"My noble lords, you will not like what my imagination conjures," she said. "But you have asked, so I shall reveal it. I agree, Kan Bahlam, that our great ruler deserves unique depictions. A standard portrait simply does not have power to convey his essence. The art of our city, as I have observed over the years, is different than other Maya cities. It is realistic, free-form, flowing, and graceful. Themes are mostly about lineage and relationships with the deities. To my mind, these themes should continue in Pakal's memorials."

"To these ideas, we have no objections, do we Mut?" said Kan Bahlam. His assistant signaled concordance. "But, what might we not like?"

"The image of Pakal in the posture of an infant, emerging from the maws of the Underworld monster," said K'inuuw Mat. "In this he is being re-born, returning from death to life, with the promise of renewal for his people. Perhaps with additional imagery of resurrection such as the celestial bird or the Wakah Chan Te' and sky band motifs." She spread her hands in the sign for offering.

"An amazing idea!" exclaimed Kan Bahlam. "That is deeply evocative of lineage renewal and a compelling juxtaposition of life, death, and new birth."

Mut wrinkled his forehead, eyes closed in concentration.

"Hmmm, let me think," he murmured. "Yes! That would be an immensely symbolic image. However, I believe Pakal should appear as a young man in the height of his powers, a young Maize God with accompanying iconography. His hands, feet, and jewelry should convey a sense of motion, of arising from the monster's jaws. I could make his pectoral appear to be swinging. Such imagery suggests that Pakal's reign, his dynasty, is eternal. Death becomes life, ancestors become heirs."

"Just so! Let us find other images to expand those ideas . . . the sacred Jeweled Sky Tree must be there. What about having the tree behind Pakal, as though he were ascending up its trunk to the Upperworld?" added Kan Bahlam.

"That is good; it makes him appear to be sprouting from the earth, emerging through a new birth, and connects him with the ritual aspects of ascending through dimensions using the tree," said Mut.

"We must add the double-headed serpent; the traditional symbol of rulership," said Kan Bahlam. "And images of K'awiil with the smoking axe embedded in Pakal's forehead, reiterating he is chosen and beloved by the God of dynastic succession."

"Adding symbols of ritual bloodletting would bring in themes of royal sacrifice in order to renew agriculture cycles and bring forth new life for the people," said K'inuuw Mat. "A stingray spine would serve that purpose."

They continued offering ideas as Mut took a hair-tipped brush, dipped it in black pigment and began drawing images on the plastered wall. After he completed the image of a youthful Pakal attired as the Maize God, emerging from the monster's jaws and seeming to float upward along the Wakah Chan Te' axis, all stood back to reflect.

"Mut, this is perfect," said K'inuuw Mat. "It eloquently merges iconography of death and birth, vigor and fragility, time and eternity."

"We need more ties into succession and dynastic themes," observed Kan Bahlam. "Mut, I agree you have captured key ideas for the sarcophagus lid, but we need to consider the sides, the walls of the crypt, and the upper temple. My dearest," he turned to K'inuuw Mat, "have you other images to suggest for these elements?"

Discussion turned to ways of depicting dynastic continuity and intergenerational substitution, the idea that the father turns into the son, the ancestor becomes the descendant. K'inuuw Mat proposed that the piers of the temple on top be used to emphasize parallel dynastic events. Just as Pakal was shown dying and being reborn on the sarcophagus lid, so would Kan Bahlam appear being born to his parents on the temple piers. Each of the two inner piers, flanking the central doorway, would depict one of Kan Bahlam's parents—Pakal and Tz'aakb'u Ahau—facing the doorway holding an infant in the same flexed, supine pose on the sarcophagus lid. The infant, Kan Bahlam, would have a serpentine foot characteristic of baby K'awiil. These life-size figures prominently located on the central piers would command the attention of visitors, proclaiming the parents' honored status. Other elements including a sky band frame and zoomorphic pedestal would also tie piers to sarcophagus lid.

When Mut envisioned the piers, he noted that the pyramid-temple would be painted red-orange and the standing figures on piers painted hues of red, so the infant could be painted in blues and greens. This would make the portraits stand out when viewed from a distance. Adding figures of dynastic founder K'uk Bahlam I and ancestor Kan Bahlam I on adjacent piers, also holding baby K'awiil would give further emphasis to dynastic continuity.

Many other ideas were considered, including molded stucco figures of nine prior rulers on the walls of the burial crypt, and carved figures of Pakal's closer ancestors on the sarcophagus sides. While the rulers on the walls appeared as vigilant sentinels of dynasty, the ancestors on the sarcophagus walls could be depicted in active poses as fruiting trees sprouting from verdant earth, nurturers who confirm and uphold the future lineage. Pakal's mother Sak K'uk and father Kan Mo' Hix would be featured as a pair at the head and foot of the sarcophagus, framing the birth and death of their son. The foot of the sarcophagus faced the entrance to the crypt, first visible to visitors, making a poignant intergenerational statement.

One additional element was planned to link Pakal to his people. They would make a small cut-stone tube, called a psychoduct, following a long course from one inner pier across the floor of the temple, then descending along the left side of the interior stairs to the crypt. From there it would continue to the south side of the sarcophagus. This tube from Pakal's entombed body to the outside of the pyramid would permit the ruler to communicate with his people in the Middleworld and bring sunshine into the depths, thus reuniting the spheres of living and dead.

It was a complex architectural and artistic affirmation of ancestors as embodiments of the transformative power of death.

Mut used an open wall space to capture their ideas, writing furiously to keep up. He kept muttering as he wrote: "Amazing! Totally unique . . . ancestors blend into descendants, embody death as transformation . . . Parent, child, and ancestors converge . . . it is all here, lineage, renewal, accession, sacrifice."

"Pakal as a vulnerable infant yet an immortal being, a God and a human, and infinite rebirth for the dynasty," mused Kan Bahlam. "With this am I well pleased."

He reached toward K'inuuw Mat, who stood beside him, and enfolded her in his arms. Caught off guard, she laughed and melted into his strong body. He bent and gave her a solid kiss that lasted long enough for Mut to turn around and smile.

"It appears your husband appreciates your suggestions, Lady K'inuuw," he observed wryly.

"Indeed I do!" exclaimed Kan Bahlam. "There is much more to accomplish, and my beloved wife can give more inspiration. Pakal wants inscribed panels all across the back wall of the temple superstructure telling his dynastic chronology, and recounting major events in which his predecessors carried out sacred obligations. This hieroglyphic presentation must include numerological links to cosmic patterns and deep history, and stretch into the future. This may take several years. But for now, let us finish the designs for sarcophagus, piers, and crypt walls and get stone carvers to work quickly. We have not much time left, I fear."

As the final days of Pakal's long life were ebbing, and the city initiated a prolonged mourning process with slow drumming and plaintive wailing in the main plaza by the ruler's palace residence, he sent a summons to K'inuuw Mat. She had already moved with her family into Kan Bahlam's palace chambers to be nearby. Pakal's attendant Tohom conducted her to his chamber, where he lay alone for the moment, having sent away the priesthood that was in constant attendance during this time. She understood at once that he intended a private conversation, for her ears alone. Tohom left as she knelt beside Pakal's sleeping bench, discreetly drawing heavy drapes across the door.

"Here I am, Holy Lord," K'inuuw Mat murmured, leaning close to his ear to be certain he heard.

Pakal's head was propped up by several pillows and his breathing was raspy. He turned slowly to look at her and smiled. Even the ravages of extreme age could not erase the nobility of his features, and the light shining from his eyes belied outer weakness.

"Glad am I . . . to see you." Pakal's voice had a diaphanous quality as the words slipped out between breaths. "Lalak—my wife—said to look . . . to Tiwol. But it is you . . . your deeds . . . that fulfilled our need."

"With Tiwol, and . . . Kan Bahlam," she added.

"Just so . . . I am grateful." Pakal paused and looked into the distance, a liminal glow in his eyes, as though he was already seeing into the spirit dimension. "The future of our dynasty . . . of our people . . . will be difficult . . . tragic. This have I seen . . . in youthful visions. You must help preserve . . . our great culture. Help Kan Bahlam achieve this . . . in his works, his Academy. Let our high attainments not be lost."

"This will I do, Holy Lord. Have you guidance for how I may help?"

"Holy Ancestor Yohl Ik'nal . . . will guide you. Ask her . . . to show you the ways."

K'inuuw Mat bowed her head and silence surrounded them, except for Pakal's noisy breathing. She reached to place a hand over his, surprised at how cold his boney fingers felt. He squeezed back faintly and their fingers entwined. Eyes closed, Pakal seemed drifting into sleep but she remained beside him, keeping still. She thought the pauses between his breaths were getting longer. After a particularly laborious breath, he roused and again looked at her.

"Our Maya people . . . our wisdom, will not be extinguished." His voice sounded stronger. "Even the royal blood . . . of our dynasty . . . will endure. Through you . . . your children . . . we continue. Ask Yohl Ik'nal . . . and Elie . . . they will show you."

"As you request, so shall I do," she replied. Images of the pale-skinned foreigner with corn-silk hair and sky blue eyes drifted across her inner vision. She gave a start upon recognizing the similar coloring of her daughter Sak'uay. She must reflect on this later.

"Then I am content." Pakal sighed and his eyes closed again, yet she waited. When he spoke once more, it was merely a breathy whisper with eyes still closed.

"They come . . . the Paddler Gods . . . I am ready . . . to board the celestial canoe . . . Ah, Lalak, soon we are joined . . . once again."

K'inuuw Mat stayed beside Pakal until his steward Tohom peered through the door drape, asking by hand sign if she was finished. Pakal showed no sign of awakening as she gently removed her hand from his, and she nodded. Tohom assisted her to rise as several priests and priestesses entered the chamber, tending incense and chanting soft prayers.

3

K'inich Janaab Pakal, K'uhul B'aakal Ahau, revered ruler of Lakam Ha for sixty-eight years, "entered the road," *och-b'ih*, on the date commemorated in many panels and glyphs.

Baktun 9, Katun 12, Tun 11, Uinal 5, Kin 18 on the sacred calendar date 6 Etznab 11 Yax.

(August 31, 683 CE)

His burial rites were the most extended and extravagant ever witnessed in the Maya world. Dignitaries and ahauob from the entire region and far beyond came to honor the greatest ruler of their epoch. Citizens of Lakam Ha extended hospitality, housing visitors in their residences and preparing for prolonged feasting and ceremonies. Kan Bahlam and his brother Kan Joy Chitam oversaw the rituals and held court for visitors. The High Priest was in charge of burial preparations and the High Priestess arranged processions, music, and dancing. K'inuuw Mat, as wife of the Ba-ch'ok, was responsible for organizing feasts for elite visitors.

An elaborate embalming procedure was done for Pakal's body while it remained in his palace chamber. After the body was cleansed and ritually purified by baths in herb-infused water using basil, Pixoy (bay cedar), and Kaba Yax Nik (vervain), three layers of preservative substances were applied. First was a thick layer of cinnabar, red mercuric oxide, which was sealed with natural resins from copal trees and plant agglutinants. After these hardened, a layer of clay mixed with ashes was applied. Once this dark brown layer dried, another application of cinnabar was made and sealed. This process required several days, during which drumming and chanting continued, with offerings of copal incense and cacao placed before altars in the adjacent courtyard.

Pakal's body was ritually dressed and placed on a litter. His only clothing was a loincloth of finest white cotton, decorated with symbols of sky, earth, and water to signify his mastery over all three realms. Around his neck and upper chest he wore a jade pectoral collar and multiple strands of jade jewelry. In his ears large square jade earplugs had prongs extended forward, dangling white shells. Around both wrists were multiple jade wristbands, and his fingers were lavishly adorned with jade rings. In each palm was a jade icon, one sphere and one square signifying his powers as a maker and modeler of earth and cosmos. A mosaic mask made of jadeite and shells covered his face, eyes formed by white shells with black obsidian irises. Inside his mouth was an Ik shaped jade, the symbol of wind and breath, bringer of life.

The final elements of Pakal's sarcophagus and burial crypt were completed during the embalming process. Although carvers had been working on these for some time, they needed to finish quickly. The intricate designs were exquisitely drawn and mapped onto the stone sarcophagus lid, sides, and base but the hasty final carving left tool marks and outline painting readily visible. On the lid, Pakal was portrayed as both the Maize God and K'awiil, in the moment of rebirth from the Underworld. His reclining, youthful body assumed a birth pose as it hovered in the maw of the Underworld Monster. From the behind Pakal's trunk a large World Tree—Wakah Chan Te' rose to affirm that by his death the world was once again centered and renewed. The eternal tree was resurrected to continue providing of life and abundance to the Maya people, spanning and connecting the three worlds. The celestial bird soaring above the tree emphasized Pakal's link with the cosmos. Deity heads emerging from the double-headed serpent bar creating branches of the tree denoted his command of life-death forces and his ability to commune with the Gods.

On the sarcophagus sides Pakal's ancestors were carved, shown emerging from cracks in the earth as fruiting and flowering plants, also reborn alongside of Pakal. On the border of the lid and on its six legs images were carved of non-royal nobles, immortalized as celestial bodies by the Ek sign. The titles of these star-Lords included Aj K'uhun, Sahal, and Yahau K'ak. They emerged from quatrefoil openings along a sky band that represented the cosmos itself, overlooking Pakal's transit through the "white road" of the Celestial Caiman, and then into the Underworld to overcome the Lords of Death.

A smooth, womb-like coffin was carved inside the sarcophagus. This inner structure had a fish shape, flaring around the upper body but narrow around the ankles, widening slightly like a fishtail for the feet. This structure was painted with red cinnabar for further preservation and to symbolize the rising sun bringing light to the world. On the walls of the crypt were nine ancestor figures; lineage affirmations and guides through the nine levels of the Underworld. They would assist Pakal in his struggles with the Death Lords.

Many mortuary offerings surrounded the sarcophagus for Pakal to use in his Underworld trials. These included ceramic bowls and pottery, figurines, flint implements, shells, jade, amber, and obsidian.

On the day chosen for interment of the ruler, Lakam Ha's main plaza was packed with people. Warriors formed two lines to open a pathway for the burial procession moving from the palace to Pakal's mortuary pyramid. First to appear from the palace stairways were musicians and dancers, enacting themes from Pakal's life. Several lines of priests and priestesses followed, carrying censers that emitted waves of copal incense. Drummers were stationed on the palace stairways to keep solemn rhythm as the litter bearing the ruler's body slowly descended, carried by four strong warriors. The litter was simple with an open canopy, allowing ready view for those nearby. Immediately behind the litter walked the royal family, headed by Kan Bahlam. Elite nobles, courtiers, and warriors followed and behind them came notable artisans. At the base of the steep pyramid stairway, musicians and drummers continued to play while the priesthood ascended the stairway and took up stations along its entire length. Tall incense burners shaped into faces of Gods and supernatural beings lined the stairway, curls of smoke snaking upward in the still morning.

When Pakal's litter arrived at the stairway, silence fell upon the plaza. The High Priest and Priestess stepped forward on the upper platform of the pyramid and delivered litanies to honor their venerated ruler. They called upon the Triad Gods and other deities to provide sustenance and blessings upon his journey. Drums returned to beating a dirge, and the priesthood chanted as the litter bearers carefully made their way up the stairs. They carried the litter at an angle to maintain footing and keep it level. At the upper platform they passed between inner piers depicting Pakal and Tz'aakb'u Ahau holding Kan Bahlam as baby K'awiil, entered the temple chamber, and then began the difficult descent through the narrow interior stairway passage. Attendants carried torches in front to light the way; the stairway down to the burial crypt was completely dark, deep inside the pyramid interior. Other attendants waited in the small chamber facing the crypt, some holding torches while others inside the crypt prepared to move the ruler's body from litter into sarcophagus. The space left between the immense sarcophagus and the crypt walls was tight, only the width of one person on each side. Scaffolding had been built to allow lowering of the huge stone lid onto the sarcophagus.

The attendants waited until the royal family had gathered in the small chamber, filling it to capacity. They watched as the ruler's litter was passed to crypt attendants, who carefully moved his body until they could lower him into the womb-shaped interior. They positioned the body supine, face upward, limbs extended. The sarcophagus was positioned inside the crypt so the ruler's head pointed north, the direction of the Upperworld. The north end of the crypt was slightly elevated for better viewing; the ruler's feet at the south end were closest to the chamber. The attendants then squeezed out, and the royal family entered the crypt and paid respects to Pakal. Once they finished and returned up the narrow stairs, elite nobles and palace attendants could have turns visiting the crypt, followed by a steady stream of residents and visitors.

The visitation process to the venerated ruler's tomb continued for several days, allowing repeat visits for those who desired. As the time approached to seal the tomb, the extraordinary process of companion sacrifices, called a mukah event, was carried out. Only the most revered rulers were granted this extreme offering of human attendants to serve in the afterlife. It was considered a great honor to accompany their ruler in his journey, an ultimate act of devotion and eternal dedication. The five companions, most from Pakal's household, volunteered their lives out of love for their ruler. Three were adults and one an adolescent. One attendant desired her child to accompany her. These companions were heavily sedated before ritually sacrificed; their bodies used symbolically as gifts of ch'ulel, essential life force. After ceremonies were completed, the five bodies were fit inside a stone box just large enough to hold them all, placed in the small chamber facing Pakal's crypt.

As visitors began leaving Lakam Ha, after prolonged feasting and rituals honoring Pakal, Kan Bahlam completed Pakal's interment. He had workers lower the lid from its scaffolding into place until it rested perfectly over the sarcophagus walls. The slits left between were sealed completely with white stucco, preventing insects and debris from entering. He organized a contingent of workers to quarry stone and rubble for sealing his father's tomb. Load after load was laboriously carried up the tall stairway to the superstructure temple using tumplines. Then these loads were carried down the narrow, switchback stairway into the depths of the pyramid. A large triangular shaped stone had been placed during initial construction inside the small chamber, for later use sealing off entrance into the crypt. Workers now strained to move it into position, finally accomplishing closure of the crypt entrance. After this, repeated loads of stone, rubble, and earth were emptied to fill the small chamber. As workers gradually filled the stairway up to the temple floor, they placed offerings along the way, final gifts for their beloved ruler. A large limestone slab with pairs of drill holes on each end was set over the opening to the stairway; the drill holes would allow later lifting of the slab. Kan Bahlam conducted a ceremony to commemorate sealing the tomb and to activate the tube through which he would now communicate with his father.

Kan Bahlam's accession as K'uhul B'aakal Ahau took place 133 days after Pakal's death. He was enthroned in the Sak Nuk Nah, where he put on the white headband while seated on the double-headed jaguar throne in Lakam Ha's most sacred shrine. On the wall behind the throne was the beautiful portrait of his father's accession, with Kan Bahlam's grandmother, Sak K'uk, offering the drum major headdress of rulership to her son Pakal. Elaborate ceremonies and festivities surrounded the installation of the new ruler, aged 49 years, who quickly set to work on projects that would leave his own mark on the city. Many monuments, panels, and murals would soon proclaim his accession date.

Baktun 9, Katun 12, Tun 11, Uinal 12, Kin 10 on the sacred calendar date 8 Ok 3 Kayab (January 10, 684 CE)

One of his first official acts was to designate his brother Kan Joy Chitam as Ba-ch'ok, following Pakal's earlier setting of dynastic progression. Kan Joy Chitam still had no male children, so Kan Bahlam felt reasonably certain that Ahkal Mo' Nab would become heir designate, as implied through the bearer of royal blood ceremony. In his heart, Kan Bahlam wanted K'inuuw Mat's son—who he considered his son—to be Ba-ch'ok, but he could not go against his father's wishes.

Mut and other carvers were at work on the long hieroglyphic passages for three tablets in the posterior chamber atop Pakal's pyramid temple. Before his death, Pakal had provided some of the text for the tablets, but Kan Bahlam created the major part of this dynastic narrative. It would take another four years to complete, after which the pyramid-temple dedication would take place.

The East Tablet contained a katun history for Lakam Ha, from Katun 13 Ahau (514 CE) to the first one celebrated by Pakal, Katun 1 Ahau (632 CE). The twenty-year katun periods identified the ruler who celebrated the period endings, linked to accession date. The text began with Ahkal Mo' Nab I, the sixth ruler who moved the dynastic seat from mythological Toktan to Lakam Ha. Each ruler celebrated katun endings through offerings to the Triad Gods and ritual adornment of their effigies. Pakal's grandmother Yohl Ik'nal became the first women ruler, succeeding her father Kan Bahlam I. The narrative emphasized events during her son's reign, the defeat and sacking of Lakam Ha by Kan, the snake dynasty of Dzibanche and Uxte'tun (611 CE). The ruler and leaders were killed, and the sacred shrine—Sak Nuk Nah was destroyed, causing the portal to the Gods to collapse. This shaped events that brought Pakal to the throne. The text included difficult times in which Pakal's mother Sak K'uk and her celestial counterpart Goddess Muwaan Mat ruled the city, and the Gods could not be properly honored.

The Central Tablet continued the pattern of katun ending celebrations, now with Pakal as ruler. Rituals became more elaborate and detailed as Lakam Ha recovered and grew in prosperity. With each successive katun ceremony, he provided increasingly complete offerings and adornments to the Triad Gods. By Katun 12 Ahau (652 CE), his second katun ending ceremony, the Sak Nuk Nah was rebuilt and the portal to the Gods re-established. Pakal properly adorned the Gods. When Pakal performed his third katun ending for Katun 10 Ahau (672 CE), the three Gods were able to re-seat themselves and the Wakah Chan Te' matured. The spiritual charter of Lakam Ha was restored and communication renewed with cosmological realms. Pakal's many accomplishments in architecture and warfare were commemorated. The coming katun was named for "Shiny Ten Lord, deathly year." It was to be a time of death, for Pakal, his wife, and son Tiwol would die in that period.

The West Tablet had a remarkable shift in narrative and was completely constructed by Kan Bahlam to highlight the mysteries of his astronumerology. It began with predictions about future events, stating that at the next katun ending, Katun 8 Ahau (692 CE), the deities would be appeased, whether or not Pakal was still alive. The next prediction jumped 140 years ahead, seven generations into the future, stating that deities for both B'aakal and Matawiil would receive complete adornments. Astronumerology was used to link the ascendance of a mythical predecessor 1,246,826 years earlier with Pakal's accession, and then to a deep future 4,772 years ahead when the dynasty would continue with a "person of the mat . . . person of the wind" tending to spiritual obligations. The time intervals between these events used Noh Ek, K'awiil Ek, and Ayin Ek cycles with intricate numerology that brought together the death and resurrection of Hun Hunahpu, Pakal, the Paddler Gods, and Aj Ne Ohl Mat, the historic ruler whose reign saw Lakam Ha's defeat by Kan. Pakal was able to use the portal to the Gods that he had reconstructed to conjure these future and past interconnections.

Interwoven through these religious actions were historic events, Pakal's political maneuvering, military victories, the hosting of Nuun Ujol Chaak, and the restitution against Kan. The inscriptions concluded with the death of Pakal's wife, Tz'aakb'u Ahau, and Pakal's own death eleven years later. The final passage would record the accession of Kan Bahlam, closing with the words that he "offers devotion to the B'olon Te' Nah—Nine Tree House, the tomb of K'inich Janaab Pakal."

When spring arrived with dry weather, Kan Bahlam embarked on the campaign seeking vengeance against Popo' for the death of his brother Tiwol. Although the terrain between the cities was steep and mountainous, the war council planned a mostly overland route to take advantage of surprise. If their forces traveled by river, they would be detected by traders and possibly attacked by expeditions from hostile river cities. Scouts had been dispatched the prior fall to locate paths through the jungles, and before the main forces set forth, a crew was organized to clear foliage off the paths or cut new ones if needed. The distance was not great, easily covered in a few days. Following intense training of warriors during a moon cycle, the Lakam Ha forces departed shortly after spring equinox, led by Kan Bahlam and Aj Sul. Kan Joy Chitam remained in the city as administrator. He had no inclination toward being a warrior, preferring courtly duties.

K'inuuw Mat did not have long to worry about her husband, for his forces returned victorious after less than half a moon cycle. They paraded noble captives through the streets and displayed booty taken from Popo' although the ruler was left at his defeated city. Kan Bahlam chose to keep Yuknoom Bahlam on the throne after forcing him to acknowledge subservience to Lakam Ha, and imposed heavy tribute obligations. Enough Popo' warriors were killed to seriously reduce future threat, and their warrior chiefs taken as captives. It was a major victory, and Lakam Ha celebrated enthusiastically.

The following spring Kan Bahlam performed an important calendar ritual. The Long Count Calendar arrived at the point for a Tun 13 ritual, marking the count of tuns moving from 12 to 13 as the current year bearer transferred his burden to the next. While not as important as katun changes, this tun count of 13 had cosmological meanings: 13 was the number of the endless circle that represented spirit, and served as the basis for the sacred Tzolk'in Calendar with its 13 by 20 count that set ceremonial cycles. Scribes recorded the event in calendar codices.

Baktun 9, Katun 12, Tun 13, Uinal 0, Kin 0 on the sacred date 10 Ahau 3 Zotz (April 24, 685 CE).

This was his first bloodletting ritual since becoming ruler. At dawn, he performed the ceremony in the Temple of Solar Priests situated at the north border of the main plaza. In keeping with Pakal's philosophy of including commoners in sacred calendar rituals, the people of Lakam Ha were invited and flooded the plaza. A select group of elite nobles climbed the pyramid stairs behind Kan Bahlam to witness the ruler's sacrifice and offerings. K'inuuw Mat was among the few inside the temple chamber as her husband, ritually purified and with altered consciousness from hallucinogenic and pain-relieving substances, sat before a ceramic bowl and used a stingray spine to draw blood from his genitals. Strips of bark paper caught the itz of the K'uhul Ahau; the paper burning in copal censers transformed it into an undulating Vision Serpent. After the ritual, Kan Bahlam informed his people of the Vision Serpent's message, one of continued prosperity and growing regional influence for their city.

Kan Bahlam was now free to begin his own ambitious building program, its complex design the fruit of nearly a katun of intellectual and astronomical effort. He intended to make it clear through his constructions, in full public view to both nobles and commoners that Creation had recurred at Lakam Ha. This message would be set in stone at a site just west of Pakal's funerary monument, nestled at the base of K'uk Lakam Witz—Fiery Water Mountain. The tall mountain rose south of Lakam Ha, its highest peaks framing the site, and from its base came the life-giving waters flowing across the plateau on which the city perched. The location was a perfect natural world expression of the deep symbolism in Maya Creation and the origins of B'aakal.

On a warm, clear summer evening he took K'inuuw Mat to the site. Attendants had placed mats on the gentle curve of a large hill that would hold the main temple of the Triad Group he planned to construct. Hand in hand they climbed in twilight, the sun's last rays streaming rosy-golden behind Pakal's pyramid and stars beginning to twinkle in the east. They sat close together as he described what he envisioned.

"Here will be the three temples, serving several metaphysical purposes," he said. "They will symbolize the hearthstones of Creation as well as those in every household, arranged as the triangle dangling from Turtle Constellation. We will be able to see it soon in the night sky. Just as the three cosmic hearthstones, the celestial triangle was set by the Gods at the beginning of Creation, and the hearth serves as center of our households, so these three temples will become the center of B'aakal polity."

"What a magnificent symbol!" exclaimed K'inuuw Mat. "It will be easily recognized by all, from the most humble to the priesthood and ahauob. Stories of Creation and the three cosmic hearthstones are told over every Maya hearth, by every family, as they gather in the evenings."

"Just so. All will be reminded that Lakam Ha is a renewed Creation, where a new cosmic order was established through our dynasty. On this hill where we sit will be the largest and tallest of the three temples. It is dedicated to Hun Ahau, First Father-Sun God, first born of the Triad. The building's position on top of this hill is aligned to sunrise behind its roofcomb. I have other ideas for solar alignments that express dynastic and cosmic relations. These I will show you as the building progresses."

K'inuuw Mat turned to look east and saw The Fish-Snake Constellation on the horizon. The eastern terrain gradually sloped down until reaching the edge of the escarpment, where two rivers cascaded steeply, one forming the waterfalls and pond of her Sutzha residence. Immediately below the hill was a residential complex across from the palace, situated low enough that it would not block the sunrise.

"It is a perfect location," she said. "It will capture the magic of sunrise."

Kan Bahlam smiled and leaned to kiss her cheek before continuing. He had dismissed the attendants, knowing that the later moonrise would give enough light to return to the palace.

"Now look south toward the peak of K'uk Lakam Witz. Do you see that small flat rise just above the level ground? That is where the temple of Unen K'awiil, Baby Jaguar our dynastic patron will be situated. As Triad God of the earthly realm, his temple will be lower than the celestial Sun God's but higher than the temple of the Underworld deity. Its location on the mountainside evokes parallels with the conjuring done by the Primordial Mother to birth the Triad Deities at sacred mountains of Matawiil."

K'inuuw Mat could barely see the outline of a shelf near the mountain's base, not high enough to set the second temple above the first. She nodded and touched his upper arm, fingers thrilling to the curve of his hard muscles.

"There, farthest west, will be the temple of Mah Kinah Ahau, Waterlily-Jaguar Sun of Underworld domains and warfare. His temple will be lowest, symbolizing its location in the watery realms of Xibalba. It will be situated to reflect both solar and lunar phenomena, important in battle and dynastic accomplishments."

"This third temple will be closest to Pakal's burial monument," K'inuuw Mat observed, watching the last thin streams of pink clouds fading in the west, backlighting the roofcomb. "It is a good location for sunset alignments."

"We plan to build this temple for lunar alignments also," said Kan Bahlam. "Much precision is required to correctly locate doors, calculate angles, and make openings in walls of the temples. Mut, Yuhk Makab'te, and Chak Chan have worked for years with me at the Academy to design the temples. Ah, K'inuuw, I am happy to finally begin this great work that I have dreamed and planned for so long."

She slid her hand up his shoulder and touched his cheek, causing him to turn and lower his head for a deep kiss. She savored the sensuous feelings coursing through her body and wrapped her arms around him. He pulled her into a tight embrace, the warm skin of his bare chest igniting against her neck and arms. Both wore typical summer garb, her dress a thin sleeveless huipil while he wore only a loincloth.

"And I am happy to be here with you as your wife," she murmured after their kiss ended.

He chuckled and replied: "We are fortunate. May we long continue to delight in each other. Never did I believe being with one woman would bring such satisfaction."

"I am glad you have changed your ways," she quipped.

"Perhaps I shall never outlive my disreputable past," he said, laughing. "Yet, see how I have improved, all due to you."

"I humbly accept your praise, although I do believe the Gods and your father had a hand in this." Thinking of Pakal, she remembered his final request of her, to aid Kan Bahlam in preserving Maya accomplishments for the future. Shifting so she could lean back against his chest, she waved a hand toward the open meadow below the hill.

"There, in the center of the three temples, you will create a plaza, I suppose?"

"Exactly; it will hold many people during ceremonies at the temples," he said. "There will be an altar in the middle and stairways from all three temples will descend to the plaza. This creates a vortex moving from the Sun God's temple to Baby Jaguar's temple, and then to the Underworld Sun-Waterlily Jaguar's temple. As the vortex swirls with ch'ulel during rituals, it converges into the center altar. Very powerful!"

"So I can well imagine. Have you considered the temple adornments, what might be depicted and communicated there?"

"Yes, to some degree. I want the messages to go beyond recounting dynastic history, for this is well-accomplished in my father's mortuary monument. Also, I intend these to express my accession and rulership, to emphasize my place in the lineage."

"As is fitting." K'inuuw Mat reflected for a moment before continuing. An idea occurred to her, and she wanted to speak it clearly. "Lakam Ha has a unique Creation Story, framed by a special relationship with the Triad Gods and their ancestors. Although this story is memorized and retold by royalty during bearer of royal blood ceremonies, I have not seen it painted on murals or carved on tablets. Perhaps it is written in codices, I do not know. Would these three temples, dedicated to the Triad Gods, be a suitable location to have the story inscribed, carved in stone for posterity?"

"Ah, K'inuuw, indeed you have the gift of a seer," Kan Bahlam replied. "Similar thoughts have occurred to me. B'aakal's Creation Story has been written in codices, which bearers of the royal blood study in preparation for the ceremony, but these books are fragile and may not last through future eras. I have pondered how to include our Creation Story in the complex astronumerology that will be used to make dynastic linkages with deep past, distant future, and celestial patterns. You must discuss these ideas more with me. As you say truly, perhaps the best way to preserve our history, mythology, and sciences is through carving them in stone."

"Although carving in stone does require space and resources. So, it seems necessary to be selective about what to express in this medium, and what to preserve in other ways," she mused.

"Yes, the glyphic text must be carefully chosen, as space inside the temples will be limited. So, my dearest, we have quite a project ahead of us!"

They laughed as he drew her backward until they lay side by side on the mats, gazing westward at the night sky. Overhead the full panoply spread from horizon to horizon, filled with brilliant twinkling lights against an indigo dome. The sheer immensity of stars made it difficult to discern patterns of constellations, although the milky arc of the Celestial Caiman was readily apparent. K'inuuw Mat focused on segments of sky until she recognized the Turtle Constellation with its belt of three adjacent stars, and its two brighter stars dangling below.

"I see Am', the Turtle Constellation!" she exclaimed.

"Yes, the celestial hearth triangle is nearly overhead," said Kan Bahlam. "Look to the far north and you will see Noh Ek just beginning to rise as Evening Star. K'awiil Ek and Chak Ek in the mid south, farther above horizon, will be in near conjunction with the moon when she rises later. Can you identify some background constellations?"

"Hmmm . . . I see the frog-water monster Imix, to the north of Am' . . . and I believe that is the peccary Chitam at the far south horizon."

"Good! Now tilt your head back and look east, you will see the fish-snake Kan Chay just leaving the night sky."

Arching her neck and rolling eyes toward her brows, she caught a glimpse of the serpentine star alignment, but lost balance and rolled into his arms. Laughing, he hugged her as she nuzzled his neck. After several long kisses, both felt urgently arising desire. He slipped his hand up her short huipil, touching the places that produced ecstatic sensations.

"Should we . . . do this on the Sun God's hill?" she gasped.

"It is not his hill yet; for now it is still mine," breathed Kan Bahlam, his mouth brushing hot against her lips.

"But . . . attendants . . ."

"They are gone. Soon the moon will rise, almost full . . ." He loosened his loincloth and lowered his body onto hers. "Now is our time for love."

K'inuuw Mat walked beside the Otolum River past the place where it ran underground into the aqueduct bringing water into the palace. From the aqueduct entrance, going up-river it ran freely as a narrow waterway, curving around the hill which supported Yohl Ik'nal's burial temple and disappearing into the base of K'uk Lakam Witz. She paused to survey construction underway just west of the river. The foundations were being put in place for Kan Bahlam's Triad temples, several-tiered platforms rising to the central plaza. Already workers were clearing ground for the base platform on the largest hill for the Sun God's temple. She smiled remembering the night she and Kan Bahlam sat on that hill, observing the night sky, planning the Triad temples, and losing themselves in glorious love-making.

Her purpose this day was to visit the tomb of Holy Ancestor Yohl Ik'nal, making offerings and seeking guidance as Pakal had requested. The temple still stood as a lone sentinel atop the modest hill, although construction had begun on a long rectangular structure at the base, next to the river. She followed the path that ran beside the river, turning onto a branch leading over a short-span bridge to the stairway rising up to the temple. Today she brought especially fine offerings of amber and seashells from Cuzamil and planned to burn rare white copal incense at the altar. Although she had made several pilgrimages to this shrine since Pakal's death, none had been completely successful. The rituals and offerings had given her access to the spiritual essence of Yohl Ik'nal, whose presence she could feel quite strongly, but the Holy Ancestor had not materialized into a spirit form she could communicate with.

She had with her one additional offering, the most precious thing in her possession. This she would use if all else failed. It was a small strip of bark paper permeated with a few drops of her first moon flow, collected many years ago on Cuzamil. She recalled how her mother and the Ix Chel priestesses emphasized the power of first moon flow: whatever she requested of Ix Chel, the Goddess could not deny. It was that important, she concluded, to use this invaluable object to gain the guidance of Yohl Ik'nal.

K'inuuw Mat placed offerings on the altar inside the small temple superstructure, reciting words of ancestral honoring. She went around the side to the crypt entrance, slipping past the heavy drape and kneeling on mats beside the shrouded form of Yohl Ik'nal. She placed the white copal in a censer and struck a flint sending sparks to ignite the twigs already there. Copal smoke curled in the semi-darkness as she chanted invocations. Stilling her mind, she focused on being receptive to the spirit world as she settled into a cross-legged position. Quickly a sense of the ancestor's presence came to her, but again no form took shape. She waited, repeating requests, holding a calm center. After some time, she realized her precious offering was necessary. From a pouch tied to her sash, she removed a dried darkened bark strip. She chanted prayers to Ix Chel and reminded the Goddess of their covenant. With great deliberation, she placed the bark strip into the censer.

A momentary blaze of fire cast flickering light inside the crypt, soon fading as the bark strip burned to ashes. K'inuuw Mat whispered a final plea: "Holy Ancestor Yohl Ik'nal, here have I gifted you my own first moon blood, my most precious possession, for I must receive your guidance. Your son Lord Pakal sent me, he who is now also a Holy Ancestor. You must show me how to preserve our people's great wisdom and accomplishments for future generations. This is my request, this is my plea."

She called to Ix Chel, invoking the Goddess' powers to fulfill the request. Again she used breathing and inner focus to still body and mind, and soon passed from physical sensations into a state of pure awareness. She became intensely alert, open, and receptive. Although her eyes were closed, she saw through inner vision the form of Yohl Ik'nal materializing as though taking shape from copal smoke. The youthful appearing ancestor in full royal regalia nodded to her and communicated into her mind.

"You have summoned me by the power of your Goddess and moon blood. Your request is familiar to me, and herein will you be given the answers you seek. To preserve Maya wisdom and knowledge, three approaches are needed. The first involves our scribes, those who write upon codices and vessels and murals. Every scribe family must commit to continuing this sacred skill through all generations. Sons and daughters must be trained and make copies of earlier work, adding to the corpus according to their times. Each generation some works must be hidden, placed in dry caves or sealed in vessels in burial crypts under household floors. Knowledge of these places must remain secret, passed down through each family.

"The second involves the oral traditions of our shamans and healers. This knowledge and wisdom must also be a sacred family obligation, passed down through generations. The most adept child in the family is chosen by the elder, who imparts training and dedication. Some esoteric skills can never be written; only intimate knowledge and experience can retain these. The families must understand and commit to maintaining the oral traditions.

"The third is to create a record of our people, history, and knowledge through stories carved in stones. You understand the importance of this and have joined with Lord Kan Bahlam to advance the process. To give you a long viewpoint of how important these records are, I am summoning the foreign women you met once before, named Elie. She has perspective from her times that go beyond mine."

With these words, Yohl Ik'nal moved to the side, and another form appeared in K'inuuw Mat's inner vision. It was the pale-skinned woman with golden hair and blue eyes, from a land far across the endless sea. The resemblance in coloration to her twin daughter was striking, except that Sak'uay had transparent amber eyes.

"Greetings, Lady K'inuuw Mat," communicated the ethereal form of Elie. "I have seen through spirit eyes your pale daughter who gives descent to the Bahlam lineage of my Mayan rescuer and companion, father of my children. She is a lovely and intuitive girl. Much has happened in your life that was foretold, you may recall from our prior meeting."

K'inuuw Mat communicated that she did remember it well, and Elie continued.

"At that meeting I informed you of a foreign people who come to Maya lands to conquer and plunder. This was several hundred years before my expedition, and I was quite familiar with this history. These people, called Spaniards, also sought to convert the Mayas to their religion based on a God who would not tolerate other deities. They systematically tried to destroy all writings and artifacts about Mayan beliefs, including burning all codices and idols that could be snatched from Maya homes and shrines. Mayan language was almost lost; over many years of subjugation, the language of the Spaniards was spoken. But some of your people retained knowledge of spoken Mayan and written hieroglyphs in ways described by Yohl Ik'nal.

"It is of critical importance that additional records be created and preserved that are less susceptible to loss and destruction. The most eloquent testament to the greatness of the Mayas is in the monuments and pyramids, temples and palaces of your cities. These speak more profoundly than ceramic idols or codices. This is the work of Kan Bahlam that you are charged to assist.

"You must influence him to place the most important knowledge, science, and mythology of your people into carved stone monuments. These withstand the erosions of time and are not easily destroyed. In a later age, many people will once again learn to read your language. They will be wonderstruck by your cities of stone. They will be astonished at your people's wisdom and accomplishments. Thus will your great culture be preserved."

K'inuuw Mat bowed, arm across her chest, hand clasping her left shoulder. She sensed the spirit forms of the two women beginning to dissipate, but needed more.

"You are aware of plans Kan Bahlam and I discussed about carved tablets in his Triad Group temples," she communicated, sensing their affirmation. "Is there more? Is something yet missing?"

"Encourage Kan Bahlam in spreading numerology and codes he is developing," came from Yohl Ik'nal. "He sees these as methods to extend his power, to build a cadre of elite nobles in a brotherhood of influence. Such is the view of men and rulers. In truth, these codes establish a hidden language of Zuyua, one that initiates can perpetuate through generations in times of extreme oppression. And, do not overlook a lineage of healers who will sequester knowledge of herbal and plant medicine and remember spiritual foundations of healing arts. This also must continue through dedicated families.

"To you has been given great responsibility. You are resourceful; find others who will assist. Always remember, K'inuuw Mat, that you too are juntan, beloved of the Gods and Goddesses. Receive my blessings and my love."

Yohl Ik'nal raised both hands, palms outward toward K'inuuw Mat in the timeless gesture of blessing. K'inuuw Mat spread her hands wide, palms open to receive, and felt the surge of energy throughout her body. Slowly the two forms melted away and she was alone in the darkened crypt.

4

The island of Cuzamil shimmered brightly, white beaches flanked by waving palms set against dark sapphire seas. Nothing appeared different from K'inuuw Mat's memories; white-robed priestesses, their loose hair tossed by soft breezes, escorted pilgrims along sandy paths surrounded by verdant tropical plants. The small city's central plaza and low structures seemed unchanged, but she knew this would not be true of the people. Her aunt

Yatik, an Ix Chel priestess, had released her spirit to join the ancestors, as had her mother Chelte' in Uxte'kuh. The High Priestess ruler of Cuzamil and the Ix Chel Oracle were both new since her time there. But her fellow acolyte Olal, now a respected Ix Chel priestess, welcomed her with open arms.

Yax Chel, her oldest daughter, was now twelve solar years and showing signs of puberty. K'inuuw Mat wanted the girl to begin her moon flow on Cuzamil, as she had done. It was fitting since Yax Chel would be dedicated to serving the Goddess as promised, and would remain on the island. The other two girls were brought on the trip to receive the blessings of Ix Chel and perhaps have prophecies for their lives made by the Oracle. For K'inuuw Mat, it felt as if a long cycle was reaching completion. Her heart sang to be on the sacred island once again.

For Yax Chel, it was the realization of a dream from her earliest memories, something for which her life had always seemed consecrated. She did not know about the initial resistance in her Lakam Ha family to this tradition, and her mother chose not to reveal it. The girl was best served by emphasizing the continuous, many-generational dedication of the eldest daughter in their maternal lineage to Ix Chel. Siyah Chan, two years younger than Yax Chel, was delighted with finally seeing and experiencing an island. Lakam Ha had many rivers and ponds, but to cross waters as wide and endless as this eastern sea, the K'ak-nab, was miraculous. Sak'uay was approaching her eighth solar year and found the island a mystical paradise. She communed with spirit essences of boundless waters, exotic plants, shell-strewn beaches, and many unusual forest and sea creatures. Despite her mother's precautions to cover her pale skin with clay creams, she could not resist swimming and exploring beaches which caused repeated sunburns. She was grateful for the healing arts of Olal, who smeared her reddened skin with soothing aloe and herbs.

Within two moon cycles on the island, Yax Chel began her first moon flow and saved this precious first blood, the same as her mother had done. All the family was thrilled by Yax Chel's ceremonies; along with a collection of girls she was honored as a young maiden, now capable of the sacred gift of motherhood. The family remained another two moon cycles, for the High Priestess had scheduled an initiation ritual for girls who were dedicating their lives to the Goddess, and the Oracle of Cuzamil would be receiving supplicants during that time. The sweet beauty of the initiation ritual brought tears to everyone's eyes and tugged at K'inuuw Mat's heart—both for memories of her yearning to serve the Goddess, and the coming separation from her oldest daughter who would fulfill that dream.

During this time, K'inuuw Mat met with the Cuzamil High Priestess-Ruler and leading healer priestesses to discuss preserving their healing traditions into an uncertain future. She revealed her visionary experiences with ancestors and the guidance given, which the priestesses understood perfectly. Their own prophecies had warned them of a coming patriarchy when men would strive to take over the island. They were not surprised that foreign people would come to their lands and try to overthrow their culture and steal their wealth. Over the course of several meetings, plans were formed to create a resilient network of Cuzamil-trained healers who dedicated their families to transmitting healing arts through generations. Even when not on the island, these families would carry this knowledge into deep jungles or remote mountains to assure it would never be lost.

K'inuuw Mat did not seek another consultation with the Oracle for herself; she felt well directed about her life by Yohl Ik'nal and Elie. She did bring her two younger daughters for prophecies with some trepidation, recalling how traumatic her long-past experience had been. Perhaps it was the years passing or her familiarity with prophetic processes, but she found this encounter much less intimidating and more supportive. She wondered if somehow the person who gave over her body and consciousness to channel Ix Chel might make a difference; even though all remnants of persona were supposed to be obliterated by extensive austerities, cleansings, and ritual intoxicants.

The Oracle's predictions for both her daughters were optimistic. Siyah Chan would marry a noble from an important polity city, have several children to continue that ruling lineage, live a healthy and fulfilling life, and seal close alliances into the future. Sak'uay received special attention from the Oracle, who remarked that her appearance was gifted by the Primordial Mother Muwaan Mat, for purposes of deep future unfolding of the Maya people. The girl would remain in Lakam Ha, marry a local noble, and eventually their descendants would be among the few who would never leave the region. Her mystical ties to the waters, land, creatures, and deities around her home would persist through generations, reaching into a distant, nearly unimaginable future.

K'inuuw Mat felt satisfied by the Oracle's prophecies. Her return to Cuzamil was more than she had anticipated, and she had a sense of fulfillment. Cycles came and cycles turned, and this cycle in her life was complete. Although their leave-taking of Yax Chel brought tears and sadness, the women of the Bahlam ruler's family returned to their lofty mountain home with many happy memories and propitious futures.

The next several years passed quickly, dominated by building construction and temple dedications for Kan Bahlam interspersed with a series of battles against Popo' and Kan ally Amalah. When the ruler of Popo' reasserted his dominion and refused tribute demanded by Lakam Ha, Kan Bahlam led another attack in which the ruler Yuknoom Bahlam was captured and later killed. The city was left in chaos but rebounded quickly with the next ruler, K'inich B'aaknal Chaak assuming the throne within a year. The main theme of this young ruler's 27-year reign was conflict with Lakam Ha and vying for dominance in their region, particularly gaining control over travel along the K'umaxha River. Kan Bahlam could not have known it at the time, but his humiliating defeats of Popo' would lead to dire consequences for Lakam Ha after he was no longer ruler.

Kan Bahlam extended his domain farther eastward by raiding Amalah, a small city that had long been allied with the Kan Lords of Ka'an. Thirty years earlier, the Amalah ruler locally nicknamed "Hawk Skull" had received a "second crowning" one year after assuming the throne, this time overseen by the ruler of Kan. On the same standing stone that commemorated this event, Kan Bahlam had carved the record of a "third crowning" he had overseen. This victory brought Lakam Ha's influence close to the territories claimed by long-time enemy Kan.

In between these battles, Kan Bahlam dedicated his father's mortuary pyramid as winter solstice arrived. Relief carvings of figures on the six piers of the superstructure temple and the three long hieroglyphic tablets in its interior chamber were completed. Sumptuous feasts and high ceremonies were held to honor the great K'inich Janaab Pakal, longest reigning ruler of Lakam Ha. Just two years later, Kan Bahlam's own grandest construction, the three-temple complex for the Triad Gods was nearing completion. He planned extensive ceremonies timed to coincide with the most significant calendar event in a lifetime—the ending of Katun 12 and beginning of Katun 13.

The three temples were strategically placed to create an earthly mirror image of the star cluster forming the hearthstones of Maya Creation. Each temple was devoted to one of the Triad Gods, Patron Deities of Lakam Ha. Temple size, height, and monumental motifs expressed characteristics and powers of the Triad God who "possessed" the structure. In Lakam Ha's unique mythological history, the Triad Gods were born on sacred mountains in Matawiil, so the temples of the Triad Group formed artificial mountains. Their interior shrines were called a *pib nah*. Pib nah meant both "underground house" and "sweat bath" which implied hidden rituals, purification, and the birth process. Each temple had the same architectural layout: a main entrance opening onto a central chamber, and two side doorways leading into small rooms on either side. At the rear of the central chamber was an enclosed shrine, an inner sanctum that held tablets carved with hieroglyphs and images.

The tablets were divided into three sections: hieroglyph text on the left, images of Kan Bahlam doing ceremony in the center, and continuation of hieroglyph text on the right. On either side of the doorway to inner shrine were two tall panels portraying life-size images of the ruler, ancestors, or Gods. The two small rooms had shorter walls constructed with openings at strategic points to invoke cosmologic phenomena. The text and images of each temple were germane to the deity it belonged to, conveying the associated symbolism, history, mythology, and astronumerlogy.

The temple of the First-Born Triad God, Hun Ahau, had Upperworld celestial and solar associations. It was the largest temple and sat atop the highest hill. The temple of the Second-Born Triad God, Mah Kinah Ahau, was tied to the watery Underworld domain and to warfare. It was second in size and situated closest to ground level. The temple of the Third-Born Triad God, Unen K'awiil, represented the earthly Middleworld realm and ruling dynasties. It was smallest in size and located on a hill of middle height. These three realms had numerological affiliations respectively with 13, 9, and 7—numbers with strong links to the 819-day count. To emphasize this point, Kan Bahlam began each tablet of the three interior shrines with an event linked to the 819-day count.

When visitors climbed the stairway and approached the temple, they passed by inscribed balustrades flanking the top steps. The balustrades announced which God "possessed" the temple, giving dates when each God "touched the earth" and was born at Matawiil, followed by the dedication date, Kan Bahlam's titles, and his parents' names. In a sense, Kan Bahlam was giving birth to each Triad God through the pib nah symbolism. His own "God-taking" apotheosis was achieved through these creations. He was depicted on all three interior tablets as a youth on one side and mature ruler on the other, in dress symbolic of the deity, surrounded by text and images further drawing connections with the Gods.

All three temples were dedicated on the same date, inscribed on the balustrades.

Baktun 9, Katun 12, Tun 19, Uinal 14, Kin 12 on the sacred calendar date 5 Eb 5 Kayab (January 10, 692 CE).

In the ritual progression for dedicating the temples, movement was from east to south to north, starting with the Sun God Hun Ahau's temple, progressing to the temple of Unen K'awiil, and finishing at the temple of Mah Kinah Ahau. The narratives on the hieroglyph texts of the three temples told the Lakam Ha Creation Story. Divided into three parts, the first temple told of beginnings of the ruling dynasty and continued to the accession of Kan Bahlam II, the current ruler. Text on the panel in the second temple recorded his parentage, naming his mother Ix Tz'aakb'u Ahau "The Matawiil Noblewoman," stressing her bloodlines back to the original lineage progenitors in mythological Matawiil. Text on the third temple panel connected Kan Bahlam with warfare and conjuring the Triad Deities, again noting his youth ritual, accession, and parentage. In these texts he built in astronumerology with links to the wandering stars and sun, the 819-day count, and numeric codes embedded in calendar intervals that would be recognized by initiates in Zuyua.

Kan Bahlam effectively constructed an "astronumerology canoe" that, akin to the Celestial Canoe in which the Paddler Gods convey deceased to the Underworld, would carry forth into rebirth the religious charter of B'aakal. Text and icons combined with astronumerology to reinforce the same messages: the white headband ceremony of Muwaan Mat was fundamental to the religious and political charter of Lakam Ha. Subsequent generations of rulers all tied on the white headband to continue this covenant.

Kan Bahlam's dedication of the Triad Group was the continuation of where his father left off after opening the portal at the Sak Nuk Nah, but here it was done through a public architectural portrayal of Re-Creation. K'inuuw Mat's heart burst with joy as she watched her husband conduct the elaborate rituals, starting at daybreak and continuing until sunset. Tall incense burners with two-tiered deity heads wearing elaborate headdresses, set on symbolic decorative bases, lined either side of the Temple of Hun Ahau stairway. This innovative censer style was favored by Kan Bahlam, and he had them produced copiously. Nearly fifty incense burners released curls of pungent smoke into the still morning air as the ruler, elite nobles, and priesthood climbed the stairway to perform "creation and activation" rites for the effigy of the God of the temple. The group dedicated the pib nah to the God and placed precious offerings inside the shrine. Musicians and dancers enacted themes related to the Triad Gods in front of crowds filling the plaza. After completing the dedication, Kan Bahlam stood at the top platform and retold that portion of the B'aakal Creation Story to the people.

In solemn procession, the ruler and contingent moved to the next Triad God temple and repeated the rituals. K'inuuw Mat remained close to her husband, among the elites selected to accompany him to the top platform of each temple. Only Kan Bahlam and the main priesthood went inside the interior shrine. She was not dismayed, however, for her husband had given her a private exposition of the shrines a few days earlier. She was thrilled and impressed by how he guided his scribes, artists, and stone carvers in depicting the imagery and creating the text to convey the Creation Story and link it to his personal history. Even more astonishing was weaving in the puzzles to trigger awareness of the 819-day count and esotericism of Zuyua.

Had she ever doubted it, this profound and enormous creation would convince her of his genius.

The sun was setting behind the superstructure roofcomb of Pakal's mortuary temple as the rituals for the third temple reached completion. At the winter solstice the sun descended directly behind the center of the roofcomb, but now it had moved slightly north. The sun has risen just past the peak of K'uk Lakam Witz, in close alignment with the second temple. After final invocations, the ruler led his people down the platforms, past the palace, and into the main plaza for feasting. Ceremonies and celebrations continued through the next three days, with additional adornments of the Gods' effigies which were then placed into small crypts built into the floor of each temple, along with offerings of jade, shells, stones, cacao, and copal. The crypts were covered by stone slabs to protect and hide these gifts to the Gods. On the final day, Kan Bahlam performed the ultimate sacrifice by offering his royal blood to the deities. This sacred ritual was observed only by select priests and elites, who assisted in the process of bloodletting from thighs and genitals, collected droplets of blood on bark paper to burn in censers, and witnessed the ruler's experience of the Vision Serpent.

K'inuuw Mat knew her husband was psychologically and physically prepared, his senses altered by hallucinogens, but it still pained her when he deftly used the stingray spine perforator to draw blood. She realized that royal women were occasionally expected to draw blood from tongue or earlobes, but this had not been asked of her. Perhaps Kan Bahlam wished to spare her, since her first arranged marriage was not intended to make her K'uhul Ixik, Holy Lady the ruler's wife. For this she was grateful.

It was a season of grand ceremonies for Lakam Ha. Only two moon cycles later came the Baktun-13 calendar rituals, the most important ones that would occur in Kan Bahlam's lifetime. He performed the katun-binding ceremony in the Sak Nuk Nah, sacred shrine housing the portal to the Gods. The interior courtyard was filled with elite nobles, priesthood, favorite artisans, and high-ranking warriors while the remainder of Lakam Ha's citizens spread across the main plaza. Although they could not see inside the palace and into the courtyard, they would attune their senses to the sacred events taking place there, events that would impact their city's future.

Kan Bahlam and K'inuuw Mat were sequestered in underground chambers until time for the ceremony, passing through tunnels constructed by Pakal that led to the central throne room of the Sak Nuk Nah. He was attired as Maize God-Yum K'ax, the First Father-Hun Ahau deity; she dressed as the Mother Earth Goddess, Ix Chel-Ix Azal Uoh. After the royal couple reached the throne chamber, they walked to the outside doorway and lifted arms in blessing, evoking cheers from the crowd in the courtyard. Musicians joined with drums, conches, whistles, and wood clackers. Kan Bahlam recited the tradition-steeped passage for katun-ending ceremonies.

"It is the k'altun, the stone seating, the binding of the tun.
It is the tribute, the celestial burden, the earthly burden.
As in times of the ancestors, as in times of the Gods.
The gifts are given, the names are called, the days are kept.
It is the penance of the Holy Lord, K'uhul Ahau.
Now shall we seat the stones of the katun, the precious k'altun.
It is the k'altun of 13 Ahau 8 Uo.
It is the twelfth katun. Thirteen becomes ahau.
The patron of the katun is 13-Ahau, Oxlahun Ahau."

The priestly chorus repeated the last three lines, for these demarcated the new katun by naming the presiding ahau, specific dates, and numeric components of the time period. They chanted the name of their ruler: K'inich Kan Bahlam, K'uhul B'aakal Ahau. They called him "Beloved of the Gods," *Juntan K'uh*. When the ruler took his seat on the double-headed jaguar throne, they brought bloodletting implements along with three wrapped bundles, gifts for the Gods. Drummers kept a steady beat while copal smoke burned in multiple censers. K'inuuw Mat presented one by one the bundles to her husband for opening, as he recited invocations for each.

"Lords of the First Sky, Lords of the Jeweled Sky Tree, born of the earth and celestial vault, the shining precious gem tree reaching from Middleworld to Upperworld, it is this your son Kan Bahlam who makes the offering, who gives the gifts. Here are your jewels, your adornments, your hats, all that is required for your dressing. Although you are already perfect, and your beauty and radiance are beyond compare, yet you rejoice anew when those of your creation return the favors with precious, resplendent offerings, remembering, re-creating. Receive, Holy Lords, these offerings."

He opened each bundle and lifted the contents in succession, calling the name of the deity and describing the gifts.

"6 Chan Yoch'ok'in—sky possessor who enters the sun—to you I offer necklace and earspools of rosy spondylus and red coral carved with sun glyphs. For Hun Ahau is the hat of the Sun Lord—K'in Ahau with yellow and red feathers and sun discs on a tall white crown studded with stars. May these be proper and pleasing.

"16 Ch'ok-in—emergent young sun—to you I offer necklace and earspools of gold beads and amber, carved with sun and moon glyphs. For Mah Kinah Ahau is the hat of the Underworld Sun, the Waterlily Jaguar of watery realms, with blue and white feathers and shell discs along the headband and fish motifs on a jaguar-head top. May these be proper and pleasing.

"9 Tz'ak Ahau—conjuring lord—to you I offer necklace and earspools of dark green jade and obsidian carved with conjuring glyphs. For Unen K'awiil is the hat of feathery white plumes and jaguar skin bands, decorated with shiny mirrors and ahau face glyphs on its tall dome, symbols of royal patronage. May these be proper and pleasing."

These offerings were taken by attendants and placed behind the throne, where they would be later buried in a crypt built into the chamber floor. Drumming intensified as Kan Bahlam, already in an altered state, prepared for bloodletting with assistants providing implements. Once blood-soaked paper was burning in the censer, he sat with closed eyes and the drumming ceased. All remained silent and waited as the ruler communicated with the copal smoke Vision Serpent, detectable only through his inner visioning. His eyelids barely separated as the undulating serpent gradually morphed from the smoke, its iridescent scaly form glittering, slit eyes glowing red, and elaborately foliated jaws gaping wide. He watched the serpent sway and curl, fading back into smoke and then resuming its visionary form. The jaws opened and closed several times, and then a head emerged from the widespread jaws. It appeared to be the face of his ancestor and namesake, Kan Bahlam I, his great-great-grandfather. He attuned his awareness to the ancestor, open to receive communications.

Kan Bahlam I gave predictions for the coming katun. This 20-year period would be one of mixed fortunes for Lakam Ha, successful harvests bringing prosperity and polity affairs remaining in balance for the first half. Kan Bahlam was given premonition of his life ending, and his brother Kan Joy Chitam's subsequent rule falling upon troubled times. By the advent of the next katun, however, the new ruler—his son, in his mind—Ahkal Mo' Nab would restore the city's dominance in the polity and create more impressive buildings with tablets recording and preserving their history and accomplishments. The katun period would end on a high note, and that was what he would emphasize to his people.

The Katun-13 calendar ceremonies were recorded on tablets at Lakam Ha.

Baktun 9, Katun 13, Tun 0, Uinal 0, Kin 0 on the sacred calendar date 8 Ahau 8 Uo (March 18, 692 CE).

5

"Mother, see what I have just made!" exclaimed Sak'uay as she rushed over holding a ceramic cup in her hands. The cup was painted with dancing jaguars and hummingbirds in a vine motif, a wide band around the rim covered with hieroglyphs. The figures were red and black against a creamy slip, the band red-orange with white glyphs.

"How beautiful!" exclaimed K'inuuw Mat. "You have learned well working with Ab'uk in the studio." Ab'uk had become close to the ruling family through his loyalty during the traumatic events of the twins' birth and his exposure of the betrayal by Kan Bahlam's deceased wife, Talol. After Tiwol's death, K'inuuw Mat invited Ab'uk to use the ceramics studio for his work. He had found satisfying intimacy with another two-spirit man, and they shared a residence.

"Ab'uk is an excellent teacher; he says he learned these skills from my late father. I tried to make a similar design to the last few ceramics Father made."

"And so you have, it is much like Tiwol's work."

K'inuuw Mat admired the cup, turning it around to view all sides. The glyphs were well-rendered in a sure hand following the cursive style favored in Lakam Ha. She also admired the beauty of her pale daughter, now a maiden of 17 solar years. Sak'uay retained her willowy quality, with slender limbs and long fingers, though now her body had filled out. Her light yellow hair was braided against the neck with tufts hanging over forehead and ears. Often she wore dark-colored headdresses for contrast, but today her head was bare. The color of her eyes changed depending on lighting, and perhaps emotions. Today they shined clear amber with rosy hints.

Ab'uk joined them, wiping clay from his hands on a cloth hanging at his waist.

"Indeed, Sak'uay does fine ceramic work and her painting talent is outstanding," he said. "She could make a good profit from her creations, just as Tiwol did. Would that please you, Sak'uay? Shall we engage merchants to trade your work after you have completed a collection?"

"That would well please me," the young woman replied. "I am not certain, though, that this is the effort most important for me to undertake. Ab'uk and Mother, I must tell you both that I am much drawn to the writing of hieroglyphs. These I find more fascinating than making ceramics. Might it be possible to study with a scribe?"

Royal and elite children were taught to read and write hieroglyphs, but the scribe occupation was usually undertaken by the artisan class. Scribes were needed to record in codices the political and ceremonial events of rulers, to detail trade and tribute transactions, to keep track of astronomy and celestial patterns, to create calendars, or to send messages between cities. Scribes were key in designing text for tablets, panels, lintels, and other monuments. Once scribes finished writing these monumental texts, stone carvers used them as guides to create the incised versions.

"It is not usual for a royal daughter to become a scribe," said K'inuuw Mat thoughtfully.

"But, Mother, you have said the times to come will be unusual," Sak'uay replied.

"That is so. It is good to think outside our typical ways, to consider new things. You do have a talent for writing hieroglyphs."

"Beyond doubt, she writes glyphs better than most of my students," said Ab'uk. "She knows more glyphs and reads more codices than any. Perhaps she has a calling to be a scribe."

"The work of scribes is of utmost importance," added K'inuuw Mat. "Have I mentioned the program Kan Bahlam and I are undertaking to organize families of scribes to deliberately preserve written texts into the future?"

"You have spoken of this," said Sak'uay. "You made reference to the uncertain times to come, which is more reason to add to these scribal efforts."

"Let us discuss your desire to become a scribe with Kan Bahlam. If he concurs, then we will find a teacher soon."

Sak'uay was content, for she well knew her step-father's fondness for her and had no doubt he would agree. K'inuuw Mat smiled to herself, knowing what her daughter was thinking. She reflected on how her children had grown and created lives of their own. Her second daughter Siyah Chan was now 19 solar years and arrangements had been negotiated for her marriage with a royal son in Pipá, a nearby city. Located on northeast plains near the K'umaxha River, this city had been contested between Lakam Ha and Kan for many years. This marriage would tighten ties between the two cities, making continued alliance more likely. Although it troubled her that the loyalties of Pipá rulers had been known to shift, she realized this risk was inherent in a royal daughter's role.

Her son and Sak'uay's twin brother Ahkal Mo' Nab had been out of her household for several years. When he reached eight years, he went to the High Priest's temple for training received by all royal sons. There he learned history and sciences, had access to the impressive library of codices maintained by the priests, and underwent initiations into shamanic practices necessary for potential future rulers. Ahkal was now a tall, solidly built and muscular young man who greatly resembled Kan Bahlam. He was intent upon becoming a powerful warrior, and now trained in battle skills. In this he also resembled Kan Bahlam more than Tiwol. She became more convinced with time that Kan Bahlam was her son's father.

Kan Bahlam had emphasized his warrior role in recent monuments, a departure from the usual depictions of rulers at Lakam Ha. A new temple recently completed at the base of K'uk Lakam Witz, quite close to the Temple of Unen K'awiil in the Triad Group, portrayed Kan Bahlam as a warrior king with a kneeling captive from Popo' that commemorated his victory over that city. Another unique monument commissioned by Kan Bahlam was the singular standing stone that held his likeness, set on the upper stairway of the Temple of Hun Ahau, largest of the Triad Group. When she first viewed this monument with its spectacular solar phenomenon during summer solstice, it took her breath away.

She recalled the experience vividly. On a warm mid-summer afternoon, Kan Bahlam brought her, with a small group of his closest courtiers and priests, to the plaza of the Triad Group. It was the first summer solstice since the temples had been dedicated. His goal was to show them the solar alignment illuminating bonds between humans, nature and the cosmos, as well as dynastic progression. They stood at the base of the stairway leading up the Temple of Hun Ahau, watching as the flaming orb dropped behind the superstructure temple of Pakal's burial pyramid. At a magical moment, the sun rays entered the west window of the anterior corridor and streamed through it, exiting the east window and casting golden beams across a distance onto the upper platform of the largest Triad temple—exactly the spot where Kan Bahlam's standing stone was placed. The monument lit up like golden flames, illuminating the ruler's face and body. All watching were transfixed as light shimmered then gradually faded when the sun fell behind the western mountains.

The message was a powerful one: Kan Bahlam was highlighted as the heir of Pakal, receiving the Sun God's light through his father's monument, inheriting the right to rule and the power of his now-legendary father. Since

Kan Bahlam wore attire on the standing stone symbolic of his ancestral lineage, it emphasized his legitimacy to continue the dynasty. It was an ultimate statement of the transfer of royal power.

A few priests were stationed at the small altar in the plaza center, to view the sunset from a different angle. As they watched, the setting sun rays pierced the center of the roofcomb on Mah Kinah Ahau's temple, sending a stellar burst of sunbeams through its filigreed pattern.

The next morning at sunrise he brought the group to observe additional solar relationships. The solstice sun rose precisely over the northeastern edge of the top platform of the Temple of Hun Ahau, viewed from the entrance to the Temple of Mah Kinah Ahau. This point was just north of the K'uk Lakam Witz ridge. At the sun's zenith, it appeared rising directly over the mid-roofcomb of the Temple of Hun Ahau.

Additional light patterns played out in Mah Kinah Ahau's temple, third of the Triad Group. Just after sunrise, light entered the northwest right door and streamed diagonally across the floor, piercing the dark interior. Broad at first, the ray was made narrow by consecutive wall edges partially blocking it, until it became a thin beam of light striking the corner of the southwest chamber. Any icon or statue positioned there would be illuminated. Only the most precise architectural design could create this phenomenon. One priest was stationed directly in the center of the building; as the light beam moved, his form was fully illuminated by dazzling morning rays. At future rituals Kan Bahlam would stand there, creating maximal impact.

Other phenomena occurred at nadir sunrise in the late fall. Light flooded into this same temple, first illuminating the room to the south of the inner sanctuary and soon reaching the entrance doorway into the sanctuary. The sunlight then streamed into the sanctuary to shine upon the tablets on its back wall. These tablets portrayed war symbols and depicted Kan Bahlam as a warrior ruler. At equinox, the sun rose at a low point on the horizon between the highest mountain peak and the first Triad Group temple, the tallest of the three. Sunlight entered the middle doorway of the third Triad Group temple at an oblique angle, flooding into the main chamber until it became a thin knife of light reaching into the southwest corner. This allowed Maya astronomers to recognize the exact days of vernal and autumnal equinoxes. At zenith passage, the sun rose directly over the roofcomb of the first temple, a wide beam of light entering the northeast doorway of the third temple, and advancing toward the southeast corner of the sanctuary. At winter solstice, the sunrise was centered over the highest peak of K'uk Lakam Witz and the roofcomb of the second temple. Shafts of light entered the middle door of the third temple, streamed into the main chamber and aligned with the medial walls that opened into the sanctuary.

There were also lunar alignments, especially relevant to the temple of Mah Kinah Ahau, the Underworld Sun-Full Moon. The rising moon at maximum southern elongation aligned with the temple, and at northern elongation could be seen setting over the temple roofcomb. At these points the moon seemed to hang in the sky, called lunar standstills. Kan Bahlam had timed additional bloodletting rituals to the lunar elongation following a new moon in conjunction with the sun, midway between the solstice and zenith. These rituals were done several months after the initial Triad Group dedications.

As the rainy season drew to a close in early spring, Kan Bahlam received messengers from Mutul with news that Hasau Chan K'awiil was planning a campaign against Kan in retribution for his father's death and the city's defeats at the hands of the Snake Lords. Meeting in the Popol Nah and holding council with ahauob and warrior leaders, he decided to join his ally in this endeavor. K'inuuw Mat was not pleased with this plan.

In the early evening, she and her husband enjoyed their meal on the veranda of their palace residence, facing onto the interior courtyard. The air was fresh with recent rain and stars were just appearing above. K'inuuw Mat relished these moments together, with no courtiers or administrative demands on her husband, and the children, now young adults, off at their own pursuits. But tonight she was troubled.

"Must you lead the forces to join with Hasau Chan K'awiil? It is a long trip and dangerous with several enemy cities along the K'umaxha River," she said.

"It is best if I give leadership to our forces," Kan Bahlam replied. "I am well impressed with this young Mutul ruler and will enjoy meeting with him. It demonstrates our commitment as a long-standing ally."

"Sending your Nakom and main Yahau K'ak, Aj Sul, is not sufficient? There are many seasoned warriors among our forces."

"That is true, but it is some time since I have seen battle, and desire to join our forces."

K'inuuw Mat watched his expression carefully, noting his enthusiasm and physical vitality. Her heart thrilled at his still well-muscled body and the magnetic attraction that he emanated. Even at sixty solar years, he was a magnificent man. But, his age did concern her.

"You have seen many battles and had great victories," she said. "None would question your accomplishments as a warrior. But, my dearest, you are no longer a young man. I fear that going into battle at your age is too risky. My heart wishes that you not go."

Kan Bahlam threw back his head and laughed. He reached over and laid a palm against her cheek, cupping her chin.

"How sweet for you to worry about me. Do not fear; I am a weathered warrior and know some tricks about protecting myself. I will be surrounded by my warriors. And, I am eager for some action. A strike against Kan will give me satisfaction. You recall that Kan's ally Popo' captured six of my vassals only three years ago, in defiance of my demands for tribute and homage. When Popo' ruler B'aaknal Chaak had sculptures made commemorating this on his ball court, he referred to me as *ah pitzlal*. Not in admiration but as a derogatory title, implying that I was no more than a ball game player. Defeating his ally will be a slap in his face, one that I relish."

K'inuuw Mat sighed and took his hand in hers, kissing his palm.

"Such are the ways of men, of warrior-rulers," she said. "You seem set upon this venture, so I shall not argue. I will pray that the Gods keep you safe."

Grasping her hand he pulled her gently into his arms, wrapping her in his warm embrace. After a few lingering kisses, he murmured in her ear: "Send the attendants away early. I want you all for myself tonight."

The warrior forces of Lakam Ha left soon afterwards, led by their K'uhul Ahau K'inich Kan Bahlam II. Several hundred warriors made up the contingent, with Aj Sul as warrior chief and with Ahkal Mo' Nab joining for his first battle. His mother did not try to dissuade him, for she well understood the obligations of future rulers and her son's appetite for battle. This gave her additional cause for worry, and her devotions to the Triad Deities and the Earth Mother Ix Chel were intense. Messengers carried information back to Lakam Ha during the campaign, and she learned of the decisive victory accomplished by Mutul, to which Lakam Ha forces contributed. Colorful stories were told by messengers of Hasau Chan K'awiil leading troops into battle under the standard and effigies of Mutul. After several days of fighting, Kan forces were routed and many captives taken, including Kan ruler Yuknoom Yich'aak K'ak. The Mutul ruler returned to his city enthroned on his battle palanquin with a towering jaguar image at his back, and a long string of bound captives dragging behind. Ceremonies were held to commemorate this victory, including sacrifice of the Kan ruler and several ranking nobles and warriors.

The latest messenger brought word that Kan Bahlam had been wounded, though not mortally and was now returning home carried on a litter. Ahkal Mo' Nab was uninjured and had earned admiration for his ferocious battle skills, taking a captive himself. Remnants of defeated Kan forces had straggled back to their city, which would never regain its prominence as a great military power.

The decisive battle took place in mid-summer, and by the passage of a moon cycle Lakam Ha forces returned, bringing Kan Bahlam still on a litter. Immediately K'inuuw Mat summoned Ix Chel healers to attend his wounds. There were some minor gashes on his forearms, but the most worrisome was a stab wound in his left side, partly deflected by the ribcage but penetrating deep into tissues. The healers were concerned about damage to internal organs, although active bleeding had stopped. Kan Bahlam's recovery was slow, and he always had varying degrees of pain in the left side. After several moon cycles, he was able to resume ruler responsibilities from his brother Kan Joy Chitam, who presided during his absence and recovery. But to K'inuuw Mat's assessment, he never regained his former vigor.

Kan Bahlam had two smaller structures built immediately north of the Temple of Mah Kinah Ahau. In the closer structure, a low temple on two platforms, he placed a collection of the double-tiered deity incense burners that he so favored, richly decorated and full of symbolism. He had stone carvers make an exquisite tablet that depicted him dancing out of the Underworld on the surface of the cosmic ocean. Perhaps it was done in anticipation of his death.

On the tablet, Kan Bahlam was shown triumphantly emerging from Xibalba after his defeat of the Death Lords. He was performing the toe-heel dance steps that were foundational to Maya dancing, and his richly adorned kilt swayed with his movements. On this elongated loincloth was the image of the Underworld Sun-Waterlily Jaguar in its skeletal form. In his headdress were the K'in Ahau face of the Sun Lord and a symbol of the Wakah Chan Te', the Jeweled Sky Tree. Kneeling beside him was his mother, Tz'aakb'u Ahau, presenting him the K'awiil scepter effigy, symbol of spiritual transformation. She was attired in the mat skirt and shawl of royalty and watery reeds, wearing an earth monster emblem on her quetzal feather headdress. The symbolism of both their costumes identified them with the risen sun on the surface of the supernatural ocean. Kan Bahlam became First Father, and his mother became the Primordial Mother and progenitor.

Two side panels of hieroglyphic text described Kan Bahlam's otherworldly accession as recreating the mythic event in which Primordial Mother Muwaan Mat gave birth to K'awiil and presented him to First Father, an event that took place over 900,000 years before Kan Bahlam's time. The moment he grasped the K'awiil scepter from his mother, he completed his resurrection into the Upperworld, becoming an ancestor in the stars. It was fitting that the female essence was what helped him over the final hurdle in his apotheosis, bequeathing to him ecstatic spiritual consciousness that completed his transformation into an infinite star deity.

Kan Bahlam's work had been accomplished. He had recreated the spiritual charter of Lakam Ha, reunited the city's Creation Story with earth and sky through architecture and symbolism of the Triad Group, and brought his dynastic contributions to prominence. The overarching theme of equivalence—all things and times are one—permeated his creations. The cycles came and went, all repeated and all became one.

The creative genius of astronumerology, secret Zuyua codes, and brilliant architect of the Triad Group died not long afterwards. These Triad temples not only recorded events that brought about the Creation of the Maya World, but replicated these events in their physical locations, imagery, and ritual function. When the Milky-Starred Sky Tree, the Celestial Caiman centered the cosmos at the moment of Creation, it became the Raised-Up Sky Tree. As it stood erect over the largest Triad temple, the scorpion constellation hovered just above the mountains south of the Triad Group, and the Celestial Canoe entered the Underworld.

The great ruler Kan Bahlam II was seated in the Celestial Canoe with the Paddler Gods and mourning animals exactly as all rulers before him. In this same manner would all great souls to come. He "entered the way" on the date commemorated by many glyphs on his monuments.

Baktun 9, Katun 13, Tun 10, Uinal 1, Kin 5 on the sacred calendar date 6 Chikchan 3 Pop (February 20, 702 CE).

As Kan Bahlam's life was ebbing, K'inuuw Mat and Kan Joy Chitam had a burial crypt prepared inside the Temple of Hun Ahau. The passage into the crypt was dug into the side of the pyramid's hill, rather than entering from the temple superstructure as had Pakal's. Kan Bahlam was interred in full ritual as befitted rulers, and after a period of visitation and mourning, the passage was filled with dirt and rubble, and the entrance concealed for all time.

K'inuuw Mat—VIII

Baktun 9 Katun 13 Tun 16 – Baktun 9 Katun 14 Tun 10 (708 – 722 CE)

1

Lakam Ha was in a celebratory mood as the city prepared for another royal wedding. The recently designated Ba-ch'ok, Ahkal Mo' Nab was to marry an elite noblewoman from a local family named Men Nich. The match was selected and the marriage arranged through joint efforts of K'inuuw Mat and her brother-in-law Kan Joy Chitam, who had acknowledged her son as his heir. Kan Joy Chitam succeeded to the throne four moon cycles after the death of Kan Bahlam. During the first five years of his reign, the polity remained relatively peaceful except for occasional skirmishes with Popo' raiding parties.

Kan Joy Chitam was fifty-seven years old when he became ruler, and lost no time making his mark through building projects. He began significant modifications to the northern gallery of the palace, remodeling the buildings and main entrance. The stairway was broadened, rising grandly to the doorways above, and the panels enhanced with additional carvings. The chambers of the narrow buildings were used for installation of subordinate political offices, positions that grew exponentially in most polities around this time. It made a bold political statement of Lakam Ha's regional influence with its theatrical design and focus on dominance. He would not dedicate these constructions until many years later.

On the back wall of the central building, the ruler would install a large sculpted panel with a lengthy inscription that recorded much of his life history. It commemorated his accession with a beautifully sculpted portrayal of his father Pakal on the left, offering him the drum major headdress of rulership, and his mother Tz'aakb'u Ahau offering the K'awiil effigy of divine ancestry. Between them, Kan Joy Chitam sat on the double-headed serpent bar iconic of Maya rulership and command of cosmic forces, his head turned toward his father. The message was clear: The great ruler Pakal himself installed his son, passing on the rightful inheritance of the dynasty.

Within two years of their marriage, Ahkal Mo' Nab and Men Nich had a son named Upakal K'inich. K'inuuw Mat was delighted with her grandson and pleased that an heir appeared so soon. With her second daughter now married and living at Pipá, her thoughts turned to a match for the youngest, Sak'uay. Given the young woman's unusual appearance, this might not be easy. Some Mayas held superstitions that albinos were in league with evil spirits, servants of the destructive old Moon Goddess, Chak Chel. Some men would not find her attractive with her moonlight-touched skin and strange translucent eyes. Her yellow hair was enough to turn heads and draw startled stares from those who had not seen her before.

An experience Sak'uay reported turned K'inuuw Mat's thoughts to future events, even as it raised her concern about finding an accepting husband. The day before summer solstice when the plaza of the Triad Group would be filled with people for ceremonies, Sak'uay went to the complex to conduct her own personal ritual alone. After devotions at the central plaza altar, she climbed the stairway of the Temple of Hun Ahau to watch the sunset light up Kan Bahlam's singular standing stone monument. She sat just below the monument, eyes watching the distant superstructure of Pakal's burial pyramid where the last rays would stream through to illuminate Kan Bahlam's figure. Her vision suddenly became hazy and the humming sound of many voices filled her ears. These voices were singing a strange melody with foreign words that she had never heard. Shifting her gaze toward the plaza, she saw through a haze that a group of white-attired people formed a half-circle in an arc between the first and third temples. Instead of bright red-orange buildings, the temples were grey stone and appeared partially overgrown, some parts collapsed. The group, both men and women, held their arms extended outward with upturned, open palms. It seemed they were performing some ritual that involved giving and receiving blessings. Their blurry faces caused her a start—they all had pale skin similar to hers. She then noticed that some had yellow or light brown hair, while others had dark hair. They were obviously not Maya people.

A blaze of sunlight hitting her eyes yanked her from the vision. She looked with clear view at Kan Bahlam's figure glowing golden in the sun's last rays. Transfixed, she watched until the glow faded and then glanced down at the plaza. It was empty.

That evening she joined her mother for a meal and described her unusual vision. They were living at the Sutzha residence, since the ruler's family occupied their former palace chambers. They preferred it, ever soothed by the quiet complex and lovely patio by the waterfall and pond. Sitting on mats near the pond, mother and daughter enjoyed the warm evening air and softly buzzing insects.

"This is a remarkable vision, Sak'uay," said K'inuuw Mat. "It seems you have seen into the future. These people must be foreigners who are visiting our city in distant times."

"Why did the temples seem deteriorated? I also had a sense that no one lived in our city then."

"It must be in times to come, in the very far future. Perhaps our people left Lakam Ha and had not lived there for many generations, so the city was not maintained."

"Why would our people do that?" Sak'uay appeared disturbed.

"Ah, my dearest one, many difficulties are to come for our people. I have been shown this in visions of my own. But this is not soon, not in your lifetime or several to come."

"What of the people? Who were they, and why did they look similar to me?"

K'inuuw Mat paused and thought about her encounters with Elie. Immediately she knew that her daughter must be taken to the shrine of Yohl Ik'nal and learn about the family's long-standing supernatural relationships to the foreign woman with blue eyes and yellow hair.

"What I can tell you now," K'inuuw Mat said, "is that our people, our family, will have complex future relationships with pale-skinned foreigners. There have been spirit encounters, visions given to your ancestors and to me linking us to these foreigners. From this vision given to you, I understand that it is time to introduce you to the threads that weave our lives together. And, to the woman whose spirit form has communicated this."

Sak'uay looked at her mother with widened eyes, gasping: "You have encountered pale foreigners before?"

"Yes, and you must not be frightened of them. Some will become part of our family. Let us plan for a visit to the tomb of your ancestor Yohl Ik'nal, for she is the one who imparted to me this knowledge and these visions."

Sak'uay seemed eager to make the visit. But, K'inuuw Mat was even more concerned about finding a suitable husband for her extraordinary daughter. A few days after solstice ceremonies were over the two women went to the modest old pyramid across the Otolum River. Sak'uay had only been once before, as a small child, and marveled at the evocative portraits of her ancestors in an archaic style. They did the requisite rituals and offerings, and settled to await the former ruler's appearance. As if anticipated in advance, when Yohl Ik'nal did manifest in gossamer spirit form, she had the other woman already with her. Sak'uay was enthralled by the pale woman who resembled her, except for the startling blue eyes. Communications among the woman flowed readily by mind-thoughts.

"You have brought your daughter, the one I mentioned before," said Yohl Ik'nal. "She is the one through whom our family lineage continues into the far distant future."

"Yes, she is called Sak'uay," replied K'inuuw Mat.

"Sak'uay, White Spirit, it is fitting." Yohl Ik'nal gestured toward the wispy form beside her. "Here you meet another one who is a White Spirit but of a race formed of such colorations. She is called Elie, although that is not her full name. There is much for you to know, beloved daughter of daughters, and yet all cannot be known. The future is shaped by decisions every person in the lineage has made and will make. These decisions are buffeted by circumstances all around. What I see ahead is one path, there could be others. Perhaps your mother, with her prophetic abilities, can do scrying for confirmation. First let me tell you of how this began, how my beautiful soul-sister Elie and I came to know each other."

Yohl Ik'nal related the story to Sak'uay as she had earlier told K'inuuw Mat. She included the contacts that happened during the lives of her daughter Sak K'uk and grandson Pakal. She affirmed that this link would continue through the daughters that would descend through Sak'uay's side of the family. Turning to Elie, she asked the foreign woman to communicate more and answer questions.

"You have an important role, Sak'uay," said Elie. "With your scribe training, you have already created codices full of Maya knowledge. You must continue doing this all your life, and hiding many of these in safe, dry places. It is important to write your own family's history, including what happened with your ancestors and now with me. Someday these hieroglyphs written on bark-paper will be discovered and translated by those who most need to learn what they contain . . . by your own future descendants, who will reawaken to who they really are. Imagine the power of learning you are born of an exalted royal lineage, a family that brought to heights one of the greatest Mayan cities. The pyramids and complexes of Mayan cities will rise through the jungle for an indeterminable future time. The Mayas of that time, the future descendants of your family, will still be walking among ruins of these cities."

"Would people of the future come to our cities and wear white clothing to perform rituals?" asked Sak'uay. "People with pale faces and light hair?"

"Yes. I am aware of your vision, and it is exactly this. My people, originally from lands across the huge sea, and others of their race will find their way to the lands of the Mayas. They will be drawn to learn and study and honor Maya culture. They and the Mayas of that time will restore the cities and preserve the codices, ceramics, idols, and artifacts of the Mayas. It is a future of great promise."

"Then I must marry and have children," Sak'uay reflected. "I must pass down the scribe tradition. I was not certain before that I would marry."

"That is your decision, but much rests upon it," said Elie. "Let me show you another potential future that draws us together. If you marry and your family remains living close to Lakam Ha, at that time when my life brought me to your region, events can transpire that bring me in contact with your descendants. Our lineages can merge, and children born of this joining can carry forth both our destinies. Although I do not see all the details clearly, this I do know: a kind man of your family will rescue me from abuse and take me to his village home. We will love each other and have children; it seems he is a descendant of yours. From this merging of lineages will come scientists who study Maya culture and make discoveries. But the greatest discovery is their own true heritage."

"Ah, however, only if I do have children," said Sak'uay. "I see it is most important."

K'inuuw Mat was surprised that her daughter had considered never marrying, and relieved that now her mind appeared to have changed. She also realized that continuing the lineage was crucial. Yet, another question troubled her, one about her son.

"Holy Ancestor, may I ask something of the destiny of my son, Ahkal Mo' Nab?" she inquired of Yohl Ik'nal. "You have made me aware that difficulties are approaching for our people. There was an allusion that our civilization would fall and our cities abandoned. Is the time for this collapse coming soon? How will my son fare should he become ruler?"

"Rest assured, the time is not soon," said Yohl Ik'nal. "Ahkal Mo' Nab will become another respected and strong leader of our city. He will build more complexes to further inscribe in stone for posterity the history and cosmology of the Mayas, of the Bahlam dynasty. After him, his sons will rule and also create impressive works. The major decline is in the next generation, and it happens without strife. The land loses its hospitality, the region becomes unlivable, and the people move on. It is not so for every Mayan city, but Lakam Ha is beloved of the Triad Gods and blessed by their beneficence."

"There are much darker times to come," added Elie. "You have been given a sense of this time when avaricious foreigners invade the Maya lands in search of gold and treasures. The aftermath is even worse, when their priests attempt to convert the Mayas by destroying the culture and inflicting atrocities. The Mayas are a resilient people, and will retain much of their rich heritage. People like your daughter's descendants are most important to this."

"A point of caution, K'inuuw Mat," said Yohl Ik'nal. "The present ruler is soon to fall upon hard times, and Lakam Ha will be subjugated for some years. Your son will restore its glory. Protect your family when the danger arrives."

"From where comes the danger?" asked K'inuuw Mat.

"From the most contentious city in the region, Popo'."

"Thank you, Holy Ancestor. Your revelations are deeply appreciated, and I will do all I can to prepare."

The ephemeral spirit forms began dissipating, and the visitors repeated chants of gratitude. Soon the mother and daughter were alone in the crypt, bowing with foreheads to the mat beside the shrouded form of their ancestor.

2

Ab'uk sped across the great plaza to the path descending along cascades to the Sutzha residence, plunging recklessly down uneven surfaces. Heart pounding and breath rasping, he forced his aging legs nearly beyond their capacity. Reaching the residence entrance, he called out between gasps as his trembling limbs threatened to collapse. When a servant appeared, he commanded she summon the ladies of the house at once. K'inuuw Mat and Sak'uay appeared quickly at the doorway.

"Holy Lady, the attack you foresaw from Popo' has begun," Ab'uk said. "Even now enemy forces are entering the city. Come quickly; I will guide you both to a safe hiding place in the jungle".

"What of my son and his family?" K'inuuw Mat asked.

"Ahkal Mo' Nab will fight. His family has already been taken into hiding. Come, come quickly! There is little time."

K'inuuw Mat dismissed the servants to their own homes where there would be less danger of being taken captive. Grabbing mats and shawls, the two women followed Ab'uk through a little used trail leading east into the foothills. In the distance they heard shouts and cries as battling forces met. Struggling through vines and brush, Ab'uk used his long knife to cut away obstructions as the trail narrowed and rose. After some time, the jungle canopy blocked all sound except bird and monkey calls, and humming insects. All three were exhausted when the trail ended at a steep cliff. Ab'uk pushed aside draping lianas and ferns to reveal a cave entrance, and led the women inside. It smelled dank and droplets fell from the ceiling, but at one side the floor was higher and sandy. There they spread the mats and sat to rest.

"It will be best for me to go back and see what is happening," said Ab'uk. "The sun will not set for some time, and I will return with food, water, and information. You may need to remain here tonight and tomorrow."

When Ab'uk returned to the city, he took a different path and veered south to pass through a large housing complex that filled the area between the Sutzha and Otolum Rivers. The maze-like passages among residences provided ample places for hiding, but he saw no enemy warriors. Residents of the complex had either fled into the jungle or sequestered themselves in hidden corners of their houses. He crept through eerily deserted passages until from a rise he could see the palace and main plaza. Cries, screams, and thumping noises reached his ears, though still at a distance. He could see many warriors battling near the ball court and in the open area between the palace and the triple structures of the astronomy academy. From his perspective, he could not determine which forces were prevailing.

In the midst of battle, Ahkal Mo' Nab had an up close if not more definitive view. After Lakam Ha trumpeters had sounded the alarm, he quickly arranged for his family's safety while donning padded war vest and leggings. Grabbing his shield, spear, and knives, he ran toward the main plaza and joined other warriors as the Popo' forces climbed onto the plateau from the Sutzha entrance. He found Aj Sul, Mut, and K'akmo for a hurried council to plan protection for the ruler Kan Joy Chitam, who was not a warrior. A small contingent of warriors was sent to defend the ruler and make sure his family was hidden.

Ahkal Mo' Nab and his forces sped to engage the enemy, first throwing spears into approaching ranks while dodging their missiles. Once face-to-face with enemy warriors, they used stone axes embedded with sharp chert points swung in large circles, smashing into heads, chests, and thighs and splattering blood onto the stark whiteness of the plaza. If axes were parried or broken, warriors drew long obsidian blades for slashing and stabbing opponents while deflecting blows with leather shields. Those in the rear ranks kept throwing spears toward the steady stream of enemy warriors entering the plaza.

Men grunted, screamed, and howled as blood flowed freely. Many from both sides fell motionless or writhing in agony. The Popo' standard bearer appeared at the rear of their ranks, his banner waving in bright sunlight. A phalanx of Lakam Ha warriors tried to drive through enemy lines to bring down the Popo' standard, but they were turned back. It soon became obvious that Lakam Ha was outnumbered, even with more warriors arriving at the plaza. Steadily they were pushed back toward the palace, where the Lakam Ha standard bearer stood on the wide east stairway into the palace.

Glancing back toward the palace, Ahkal Mo' Nab saw his uncle Kan Joy Chitam next to the standard bearer, surrounded by a ring of warriors. A flash of admiration washed over him; even though unable to fight his uncle determined to take a stand with his forces. Just then an enemy warrior stabbed his arm, and Ahkal Mo' Nab returned the blows, slashing furiously with a short knife in one hand and long dagger in the other. His dagger found its mark as he plunged it through the enemy's throat and slowly the man fell backwards, eyes wide with surprise as lifeblood gurgled from the wound. Deflecting other enemies' weapons, parrying and thrusting, Ahkal Mo' Nab and the Lakam Ha forces were relentlessly pushed back until they were at the base of the palace stairways.

They struggled there for what seemed an eternity, more men falling and more blood pooling on the stairs and plaza. The enemy horde formed a semi-circle, pinning Lakam Ha warriors against the stairways. Another Popo' group broke away and flanked the defenders, finding a path to ascend the north stairways and enter the palace. Shouts and thumps showed they encountered Lakam Ha warriors inside the palace, but soon the Popo' warriors appeared behind Kan Joy Chitam and his standard bearer. The ruler turned and raised his hand, giving the signal for surrender. A shout from leaders on both sides relayed the command to their forces, and fighting stopped.

Breathing heavily with a stream of blood dripping from his arm, Ahkal Mo' Nab reluctantly released his weapons and dropped them to the ground. He gazed helplessly up the stairs to observe the Nakom from Popo' along with ruler B'aaknal Chaak ascend to face Kan Joy Chitam. The Nakom grasped the standard and threw it down, trampling on it. Two Popo' warriors grabbed Kan Joy Chitam by the shoulders, ripped off his royal adornments and headdress, and pushed him to his knees. They bound his hands behind him and replaced his ear flares with strips of white cloth, signifying that he was a captive. A wail of despair rose from the throats of Lakam Ha forces while those of Popo' cheered.

B'aaknal Chaak turned to face the warriors below, raising his arms for silence.

"Thus is defeated the mighty, the proud Lakam Ha," he intoned. "Thus is our honor assuaged and our vengeance fulfilled, for the dastardly attacks of this city upon us. Thus is the position of overlord and vassal upturned; now shall Lakam Ha pay tribute to Popo' and defer to our demands.

"Warriors of Lakam Ha! Surrender your weapons, return to your homes, plot no more against us and we will leave you to live another day. Do not interfere with the retribution we require against that ah pitzlal, your despicable ruler Kan Bahlam, for his injuries to Popo' in the past. His standing stone image shall be destroyed; his temples desecrated. Oppose our just retaliations, and you will suffer death and more destruction.

"Your current ruler, Kan Joy Chitam, we shall bring back to Popo' to live as a captive. He will receive treatment worthy of an Ah K'uhul, but must undergo humiliations to remedy the wrong-doing of his predecessors. He will march through our streets in bondage for important ceremonies; he will bow before the Popo' rulers and acknowledge subservience. If you value his life, you will not attempt to recover him. Perhaps we will return him in some years' time; that remains to be seen. My stewards will establish the necessary tribute from your city. See to it that tribute is given generously and whenever required.

"Those are our conditions. Accept them, keep them, and we will depart your city in two days time. Thus has this ruler, this K'uhul Popo' Ahau—K'inich B'aaknal Chaak, spoken."

The date of Lakam Ha's ignoble defeat was carved on monuments in Popo'.

Baktun 9, Katun 13, Tun 19, Uinal 13, Kin 3 on the date 13 Akbal 16 Yax (August 20, 711 CE).

3

I n the years following Kan Joy Chitam's capture, life at Lakam Ha returned to some semblance of normal. Ahkal Mo' Nab as Ba-ch'ok took over governance and fulfilled the ruler's obligations to perform ceremonies at calendar endings, doing the required self-bloodletting sacrifice, giving bundles and adorning the Gods. Several times each year an envoy from Lakam Ha was sent to deliver tribute to Popo' consisting of cacao pods, fine woven fabrics, ceramics and jewelry, obsidian and flint blades, and various crops including maize, peppers, squash, and fruit. This steady outflow of goods and food created a leaner lifestyle in Lakam Ha, with less feasting and fewer luxury goods. Building projects were put on hold since Popo' required workers to aid their own construction during the dry season.

It did not make much difference in K'inuuw Mat's life, since she had been living more simply before. What did impact her deeply was losing part of Kan Bahlam's heritage. On first viewing the utter destruction of his standing stone monument, broken off at the base and shattered into multiple fragments, she wept uncontrollably. Together with Sak'uay, she did repeated rituals to purify the spot where the monument had stood. She asked stonemasons to restore the monument, only to learn it was impossible. Gathering the fragments, she bestowed blessings on them and had a crypt built at the foot of the Pyramid of Hun Ahau, on whose stairway the monument once stood. With her son, daughter, and the High Priestess, she conducted ceremonies to inter the fragments, attended by most nobles and warriors of Lakam Ha.

She felt fortunate that Popo' warriors had inflicted minimal damage to the panels and pillars of Kan Bahlam's Triad Group. Though they chipped away small pieces here and there, they apparently spent their fury demolishing the standing stone monument. Eager to return home, they abandoned efforts on the pyramid-temples early. Touch-up paint and plaster patches were able to restore almost all the images and glyphs.

Happiness came again with the birth of her next two grandsons. Men Nich gave birth two years apart to vigorous boys named after previous rulers in reverse order of B'aakal succession.

Kan Bahlam III – his feet touched the ground on Baktun 9, Katun 14, Tun 1 (713 CE).

K'uk Bahlam II – his feet touched the ground on Baktun 9, Katun 14, Tun 3 (715 CE).

She had another cause for happiness when Sak'uay came with unexpected news. In the aftermath of the Popo' defeat, she had devoted little attention to finding a suitable husband for her daughter. Now it appeared that the young woman had accomplished this herself. Sak'uay told her mother that a noble scribe, one of her colleagues with whom she had collaborated for several years, recently approached her with a proposal of marriage. His name was Chik, and K'inuuw Mat was aware that he came from a good, though not elite, family.

"Much do we have in common," said Sak'uay. "We studied scribal arts together, and have assisted each other practicing and developing our skills. As we became closer, I told him about your visions and the mission to preserve Maya knowledge for the future. He feels strongly about this and is eager to join the effort creating codices. He will be a great asset, for there is much work to do."

"As long as he is dear to your heart," said K'inuuw Mat. "That is most important. It is also well that you share the same profession and can work together on the codices project."

"Chik is also a skilled hunter," said Sak'uay. "In his forays into the jungles, he discovered many caves; some are suitable for hiding codices. He has taken me to several, and we already have plans to use a few of these."

"Excellent! It pleases me that your part of this work is advancing. Inform Chik that he may come to ask my approval of your marriage."

The marriage ceremonies were performed three moons later. Ahkal Mo' Nab as oldest male in the family and acting ruler, gave consent and stood in place of a father for the simple ritual attended by a small group. Te' Kuy and her daughters were there, bearing bravely the aftermath of her husband Kan Joy Chitam's capture. The most recent tribute bearers were permitted a few words with him, confirming he was still alive and being treated decently. Yax Chel and Siyah Chan came for their sister's marriage; both were satisfied with their lives as different as these were; the first now a leading Ix Chel priestess on Cuzamil, the second as wife of a regional city noble with several children. Chak Chan and assistants of Kan Bahlam attended, as well as the younger generation of warriors and courtiers associated with Ahkal Mo' Nab. One young warrior, Chak Zotz, had risen rapidly to attain titles of Yahau K'ak and Sahal, becoming the designated Nakom-Warrior Chief as Aj Sul advanced in age.

Ab'uk was given an honored place as close confidant to the family. He and K'inuuw Mat reminisced about the numerous crises they weathered together, reliving the aftermath of the Popo' attack when Ab'uk returned to the cave. He had provided vivid description of the battle, her son's bravery as a warrior, and the capture of the ruler. Since the Popo' forces planned to remain at least two days, he brought dried fruit and maize cakes, showing the women a nearby creek where they could drink and cleanse. They spent three nights in the cave, a memorable experience of discomfort, worry, and apprehension over jungle creatures. After Ab'uk reported the invaders had departed, they gratefully returned home to the mourning city.

Chik and Sak'uay remained with K'inuuw Mat in the Sutzha residence by her request. She had no heart for living alone in the house by the waterfalls that held so many memories. The quiet presence of her unique, intuitive daughter was such a comfort, and she found Chik to be quick-witted and amusing, an excellent story-teller as they enjoyed lingering twilight on the patio. His ability to remember tales related through generations served as an asset in creating codices of their people's history. One evening K'inuuw Mat was struck with the idea of telling the stories of women, the wives and mothers and daughters and sisters who would rarely be mentioned in carved monuments or painted panels. To relate the stories of women in the royal family, however, she would need to accomplish two things: communicate again with Holy Ancestor Yohl Ik'nal, and reveal the truth of her twin daughter and son's parentage.

The first was easier to do. K'inuuw Mat and Sak'uay made several visits to Yohl Ik'nal's tomb for visioning episodes with the first woman ruler. The scribe brought writing materials to make notes for accuracy. They obtained details that would later be inscribed in a codex. The challenges facing the first woman ruler intrigued them; they rejoiced at Yohl Ik'nal's visionary abilities that saved her city from defeat. Both remarked on the extraordinary efforts made by Sak K'uk, daughter of Yohl Ik'nal and second women ruler, to face the Death Lords and gain an alliance with Primordial Mother Muwaan Mat. Through the Great Goddess' intervention, Sak K'uk held the throne until her son Pakal was of age to ascend. Even after that Sak K'uk remained as co-regent for several years. The intertwining lives of Pakal and his wife Lalak provided a tale of overcoming emotional obstacles and discovering inner strengths; it particularly charmed Sak'uay as an affirmation of true love.

Telling her own story to her daughter was difficult for K'inuuw Mat. After a faltering start as they sat alone near the waterfall, she relaxed into the gentle and accepting demeanor of the young woman, whose translucent eyes seemed to pierce any veil yet were completely devoid of judgment. Sak'uay's ethereal nature felt simultaneously infinite yet immediately present. So K'inuuw Mat held nothing back in the re-telling of her relationship with Kan Bahlam: how they were magnetically attracted, yet tried to resist; how their minds and spirits joined in astronomical and celestial explorations;

the tensions created in the family and with Tiwol; the tragic loss of Kan Joy Chitam's son and heir; and the exceptional plan agreed upon by Pakal, his key advisors, and the priesthood to assure a male heir through her.

As K'inuuw Mat described the conception, difficult pregnancy, and life-threatening labor, tears rose in both women's eyes. Sak'uay was impressed at how Kan Bahlam's willpower and strength brought forth the birth of her brother, snatching her mother from the jaws of death. She expressed thanks to the Goddess Ix Chel that her own birth as first of the twins was not so troublesome. Then she listened to the unfolding of this drama, including the change in Kan Bahlam's character and Tiwol Chan Mat's death on a trading expedition. As the tale ended happily with the marriage of her mother and Kan Bahlam, she sighed. A scribe could not hope for a more compelling story to inscribe in the beautiful icons of glyphs and figures.

They agreed that the stories in what they began calling "The Women's Codex" could be shared with Chik, but it would remain known only to the three of them. Ahkal Mo' Nab would receive no benefit learning about his dual fathers, nor would it serve dynastic history. Let the stone monuments, panels, and pillars portray succession in the accepted manner. In any event, the dynasty was continued through Pakal's sons and grandsons. But, Sak'uay requested that she alone write in The Women's Codex, so its execution would come solely from a woman's hand. Chik readily accepted his wife's desire.

The rhythm of life at the Sutzha residence continued in its leisurely pace as years passed. True to her pledge, Sak'uay lost no time having children, well aware that she was already considered in her middle years and childbearing would become increasingly risky. A boy and two girls were born over the next five years, all healthy and of normal Maya appearance. It appeared the albino inheritance would skip this generation. K'inuuw Mat was happy that her residence once again resonated with the joyful sounds of children.

When Chik and Sak'uay completed codices, they prepared the fragile wood and bark paper books for storage that would last through long time periods. First, a clean white cotton cloth was wrapped around the book, making several layers. Next, a cotton cloth permeated with insect repelling solutions made from powdered annatto leaves and hog plum bark were used, wrapped tightly over the first cloth layers. After that, a latex coating was applied and carefully sealed; making sure not the tiniest hole was left unfilled. The bundled codex was tied securely with strong yucca fibers to hold the layers in place.

The scribe pair took their bundled codices, often along with ceremonial objects such as seashells, obsidian and jade stones, or ceramic icons, sequestered in pouches as they set off into the jungles towards caves previously identified. Usually, they traveled several days to reach remote areas that were infrequently visited. Their goal was to place the codices in small, hidden caves that no one would find of interest. It was most important that the caves have no water, either dripping through ceilings or trickling across the bottom. Also, the caves must be small, offering no space for people or animals to take up residence. Once they found the right cave, they squeezed far enough into it to dig a hole in the floor large enough to hold the codex bundle. Most commonly they used hard flint knives to carve a square piece of stone out, using that as a lid once the codex was inside the hole. Then they placed dry sand and rubble around the codex and ceremonial objects, replaced the stone lid, and scattered cave debris over the top to conceal the opening. Outside they performed rituals to clear and purify the space, and make it invisible to those wandering nearby.

4

Ahkal Mo' Nab stormed into the council house with his courtiers in tow and breathing hard to keep up with their Ba-ch'ok's long strides. The nobles, artisans, and warriors already sitting on the benches lining the walls jumped to their feet, bowing low with right arm clasping their left shoulders in acknowledgement. When he reached the low platform at the head of the long rectangular chamber, he slumped heavily onto the jaguar pelt mat and glared at the assembly. Necessity required him to involve many more people in making decisions than his nature would prefer. Even lesser nobles and craftsmen felt they should have a voice in policies. While he recognized the advantages of cultivating these alliances, it irked him that royal authority had to be shared now. It was not this way in times of his ancestors, even Pakal the Great. Ruefully he recalled that wealthier merchants even felt entitled to have minor throne rooms in their household chambers. He had presided over installations of several such upstarts into their positions as junior officials.

It was a sign of the new times—times of shared governance, widely distributed wealth, doling out political power to maintain equanimity and ensure cooperation. He blamed much of this on his uncle, Kan Joy Chitam, who was not strong enough as a leader, failed to keep a well-trained and ready warrior contingent, and got himself captured by Popo' so a new Lakam Ha ruler could not be seated while he was still alive. Even while captive, his uncle "performed" several acts as Lakam Ha ruler, including witnessing the accession of a ruler at Wa-Mut nearly four years later and "installing" a junior official at Lakam Ha only two years ago. These activities were overseen by Popo' leaders, and Lakam Ha was required to acknowledge them.

And now Ahkal Mo' Nab was forced to relate to the council the latest Popo' insult.

"Honorable assembly," he began as he straightened to a regal posture and tossed back his head, staring down his long nose. "It is with regret that I inform you, these despicable, degenerate despots at Popo' now demand that we provide a ceremony in which our captive ruler will perform a dedication. In effigy or in person, I am uncertain. It is a dedication of the palace chamber which he had built many years ago, the renovated north gallery. Why should such a thing be? Only to humiliate us. Only to force their will upon our city once again. It is insufferable!"

He paused for some moments, eyes sweeping the chamber, and then called for their voices.

"Who wishes to speak? Shall we comply or resist?"

Chak Zotz, the young newly appointed Nakom-Warrior Chief, sprang to his feet.

"Let us not suffer another insult!" he cried. "Let us resist! Our warriors are better trained now; we can fight and prevail against this heinous villainy!"

Others in the council echoed these sentiments: "Restore our honor!" "Defeat the cowards!" "Remove this stain by eradicating our enemy!"

The elder Warrior Chief, Aj Sul, who was well past his prime, expressed a moderate view.

"It is so, our forces are strengthened, yet most are not battle-tested. Hot-blooded youth yearn for action to exercise their skills, but we must consider the larger view of experience and numbers of warriors," he advised.

"Our ranks have increased, and ardor adds greatly to prowess in battle!" Chak Zotz exclaimed. "I am thirsting for revenge upon these vile dogs! Let us revive our self-respect."

A leading merchant rose with a disparate view.

"It is regrettable that we are offered another insult," he said. "But we continue at a disadvantage. Did not our latest envoys to Popo' bring information on the strength of their forces? Were we not told that our tribute allows fewer of their men to labor in construction and the fields, so more can train as warriors? We must be realistic. Lakam Ha does not have matching forces, even though our warriors are now better prepared, thanks to the admirable efforts of our Nakoms. I advise caution, Honored Lord."

"Well spoken," added a minor noble artisan. "Even though Holy Lord Kan Joy Chitam completed those structures, he has not yet done their dedication. Perhaps it is his personal desire that this dedication take place now. It all due respect, let us honor our ruler's intentions."

Heated discussion broke out among the council members, arguing both viewpoints. After allowing members to release some steam this way, Ahkal Mo' Nab took charge again.

"What say you, Aj Sul?" he asked the Warrior Chief. "You have seen much combat in your years of service. You were Ah Yahau K'ak, Fire Lord to my grandfather Pakal. How would the forces of Lakam Ha fare against Popo' at this time? What is the prospect of victory? Tell us most truly, for we must not risk our city and people to another defeat. Although the terms of tribute are galling, these have given us peace and a comfortable life."

"Ah, my Lord, when you put it this way, I am given cause for reflection," said Aj Sul. "It is true that our warriors are stronger now than at the last attack, but still our numbers are no match for theirs. We have been drained of manpower over the years and strapped between tending their fields and our own. Yes, we might win temporarily. But I fear in a longer siege we might not prevail. There would be risk of loss. This I cannot deny."

Voices of other youthful and eager warriors joined in.

"We are capable!" shouted a young warrior. "Give us an opportunity to show our bravery!"

"With respect, Honored Nakom, we are eager to turn our axes and blades against this evil enemy!" "Our cause is just; we shall prevail!"

"Be not rash," advised a respected stone carver, an artisan of high repute. "Consider the consequences of another ignoble defeat."

"While our ruler still lives, we should abide by his decisions," said Chak Chan. "Kan Joy Chitam is our K'uhul B'aakal Ahau, designated in succession by Pakal. We must honor our great ancestor ruler's intentions and maintain proper dynastic order. This is the way of our tradition, our keeping covenant with the Triad Gods."

Chak Chan, elderly brother-in-law of Kan Bahlam and cousin by marriage to Kan Joy Chitam, carried weight in the hierarchy of influence. Other voices of moderation echoed his sentiments. Ahkal Mo' Nab recognized the prevailing attitude was toward cooperation with the demands of Popo' for this ceremony.

"Much do I appreciate the viewpoints of all assembled," he said. "These will I take under consideration with my key advisors, including the perspectives of our High Priest. We must ascertain the desires of our Triad Gods; discern their wishes for our city's actions in this matter."

When the acting ruler met later with this small group, the council's sentiment against battle was upheld. Although Chak Zotz fumed, he did not press resistance. Ahkal Mo' Nab, also lusting for vengeance, smarted even more once the terms for the dedication were presented by a Popo' messenger—they intended to bring Kan Joy Chitam back to Lakam Ha to perform the ceremony in person.

Under the hot midsummer sun, the main plaza of Lakam Ha was filled with people for the palace north gallery dedication. A large contingent arrived from Popo' several days in advance, including impressively armed warriors and the ruler K'inich B'aakal Chaak with his son K'ak Bahlam. The Popo' nobility was given an entire wing in the palace with numerous servants to attend their needs. Additional chambers were given over to house their warriors who kept close surveillance. Many Lakam Ha households were pressed into service to host Popo' nobles and warriors. Kan Joy Chitam was allowed to reunite with his wife and daughters in the ruler's chambers of the palace, recently vacated by Ahkal Mo' Nab and his family. The city's mood was an odd mixture of celebration and somberness. Commoners rejoiced that once again there was opulent feasting and impressive ceremonies; nobles kept up congenial appearances while most harbored resentment.

K'inuuw Mat and her family attended several feasts and were in front ranks for the dedication ceremonies. She could only imagine how her son Ahkal Mo' Nab suffered under this blow to his pride and authority. With admirable restraint, he kept silent on political subjects and performed the necessary courtesies to the noble oppressors. He was given no time alone with his uncle; probably for the best in her view.

Kan Joy Chitam was quite old, having reached his mid-seventies and enfeebled by his years of captivity. He moved slowly and spoke in a querulous voice but carried out the rituals well, making a short speech and performing chants during offerings of copal and elements to the Pahautuns of the four directions. In the festivities that continued into the night, a few clashes occurred between young men of the two cities with minor wounds but no deaths. Warriors of both cities intervened to keep order, working with unexpected cooperation.

The ruler left instructions that the dedication be recorded on a tablet placed on the wall of the north gallery. He met with stone-carvers to explain his wishes for imagery depicting his father Pakal and mother Tz'aakb'u Ahau on either side of him, offering the symbols of rulership. Glyphs between the three figures gave dates of the dedication and names of protagonists, recorded much of the elderly ruler's life, but avoided any mention of his city's subjugation at the hands of Popo'.

The dedication date of the palace north gallery was carved on this tablet.

Baktun 9, Katun 14, Tun 8, Uinal 14, Kin 15 on the date 9 Men 3 Yax (August 14, 720 CE).

Satisfied with Lakam Ha's submission during the dedication ceremonies and provision of ample hospitality, the Popo' contingent departed two days afterwards. Despite pleas from the ruler's family, begging that he remain as he was old and infirm, K'inich B'aakal Chaak took Kan Joy Chitam back with him. Perhaps he feared that leaving the ruler would lead to a resurgence of resistance, or was reluctant to upset the balance that served him well for nearly ten years. But the uneasy accommodation was disrupted within the year.

Messengers brought word to Lakam Ha that Kan Joy Chitam had died, though they could not obtain the exact date from their Popo' sources. The circumstances of his death were also mysterious; it was not clear if he died of old age or was killed. Popo' declined to return his body for royal interment, much to his family's distress. As quickly as possible following this news, Ahkal Mo' Nab organized his accession to the throne. He had waited too long for an opportunity to formalize his leadership. The city enjoyed another occasion of feasting, celebrating, and impressive rituals as K'inuuw Mat's son became K'uhul B'aakal Ahau at the age of forty-four years. Shortly afterwards he designated his oldest son Upakal K'inich as Ba-ch'ok, named on the stucco pier of the new Temple of the Lords, one of six temples he would build during his reign.

The date of Ahkal Mo' Nab's accession was carved on monuments and panels.

Baktun 9, Katun 14, Tun 10, Uinal 4, Kin 2 on the date 9 Ik 4 Kayab (January 3, 722 CE).

5

Summer solstice was her favorite time of year. K'inuuw Mat relished the long, warm sunny days, the lingering sunsets that brought Lakam Ha's red-orange buildings to flame, and the clear star-strewn night sky. Some of her happiest moments were during summer's height; she would always cherish the night of passion with Kan Bahlam on top of the Sun God's hill.

His memory filled her as she walked up the platform stairs leading onto the plaza of his Triad Group. Glancing at the roofcomb of Pakal's temple, she gauged time remaining until sunrays came streaming through the top chamber to highlight the middle stairway that climbed the tall Pyramid of Hun Ahau, Sun God. It would be there in moments, so she hurried up the stairway as quickly as her creaking knees would allow. She planned to stand in the place where the broken foundation of Kan Bahlam's standing stone remained. Pain stabbed her heart once again when she thought of the monument's vengeful destruction by the warriors of Popo'.

It had been a unique stone monument, carved in the likeness of Kan Bahlam in regal splendor, the first and only standing stone in Lakam Ha. Now only a stub remained. She had ritually interred the fragments when she found that stone-workers could never reassemble it. The image of the monument standing proudly before the Sun God's temple, its fine bas relief carvings glowing golden in the solstice sunset, would be forever emblazoned in her mind. Indeed, in those moments Kan Bahlam did become Hun Ahau—First Father, the Maize God, the Sun God.

She positioned herself to stand just in front of the foundation stub, facing the plaza which the three temples surrounded. Lifting her face to look across the plaza, she positioned her hands in the "break sign" with both arms flexed at her sides, right hand palm up in the receiving sign at waist level, left hand raised with palm outward in the blessing sign. This was the hand sign of creation, used for all bringing forth or birth events, whether of universes or creatures. It signified daybreak and breaking through into new levels. This gesture, always seen in depictions of the Hero Twins and rebirth of their father the Maize God, encompassed the universal experience of bringing forth and cycling anew.

Sunrays radiated through the temple chamber, creating a burst of brilliance that streamed across from Pakal's temple to Kan Bahlam's east temple where K'inuuw Mat stood. Her face was wreathed in a golden glow that spread over her entire body. The hint of a smile curved her lips as her eyes held the distant vision of a future yet to come.

These magnificent stone structures with their inscribed tablets filled with Maya history, cosmology, and astronumerology codes would still be standing in lush jungles as the Long Count continued unfolding into unimaginable eons ahead. Maya wisdom and knowledge would be preserved through the deep traditions embedded in the soul of the people. Someday foreign people would discover Maya civilization and remain astonished at its accomplishments. Someday the Maya descendants of her people would reclaim their heritage, would remember and relearn the high culture that went into hiding to survive. Someday her own descendants would return to this Triad Group and perform ceremonies. Even when blended with other people and cultures, the Maya essence would continue, for her people understood the nature of existence as cycles—to be born was to die, and to die was to be reborn.

THUS IT IS

Afterword

The date of K'inuuw Mat's death is not recorded at Palenque. For purposes of this story, it is given as November 30, 722 CE (9.14.11.2.13 on the date 2 Ben 11 Muwaan). This would have been a little under a year after her son Ahkal Mo' Nab III acceded, and a half-year after she stood in the place of Kan Bahlam's standing stone at summer solstice. The only known portrait of K'inuuw Mat is on the Tablet of the Slaves, commissioned by her son K'inich Ahkal Mo' Nab, who is being seated into rulership in the center of the tablet. She is sitting on his left, holding up a K'awiil effigy on top a Sun God disc. Tiwol Chan Mat is portrayed to his son's right, holding up a drum major hat with long arching feathers.

Ahkal Mo' Nab III ruled for over fourteen years. There is little record of the first part of his reign, possibly due to continued political hostilities with Popo' (Tonina) and the new ruler's need to consolidate power after a difficult succession. Beginning around 730 CE there is evidence of renewed warfare in the region, much of it instigated by the ruler and his warriors against neighboring cities. One can be certain he extracted revenge from Popo' for the humiliation imposed by that city.

The Tablet of the Slaves records several early battles and conquests, emphasizing the participation of an important warrior and Sahal named Chak Zotz. This tablet portrays Ahkal Mo' Nab between his parents, Tiwol Chan Mat and K'inuuw Mat, as they offer him symbols of rulership. It was discovered in a building complex called Group IV, where Chak Zotz resided. He was important enough to have his own small throne room, where the Tablet of the Slaves was placed. Though portrayed on the tablet, he is not the main focus. Chak Zotz had several personal military victories including the capture of three lords, attacks on Popo' and a subsidiary city, and capture of a Sahal of Yokib (Piedras Negras) ruler Yo'nal Ahk in 725.

Building and dedication of several temples are attributed to Ahkal Mo' Nab between 731 and 734 CE. Temple XVIII, located west of the Cross Group, describes on doorjamb panels the essentials of his birth and accession, linking them to Muwaan Mat's enthronement 3,025 years earlier. In Structure XVI, part of a modest building complex just north of the Temple of the Cross (Sun God's Temple), archeologists found an intriguing carving with perhaps the most unusual portrayal in Palenque. The fragment that survived depicts three men standing above a kneeling figure with an immense cloth bundle on his back. This figure is named as Ahkal Mo' Nab; he grasps the bundle with outstretched arms while his assistants help. Glyphs are lacking to explain the scene although it appears related to tribute, perhaps connected to long-term subjugation to Popo' (Tonina).

Temple XIX, south of the Cross Group (Triad Group) and directly facing the stairway ascending the Temple of the Cross, has several remarkable monuments carved with high quality and refinement. The long, vaulted structure has two parallel galleries with only a single small doorway opening to the Cross Group. Several square piers divided the two galleries, but the construction was faulty and it collapsed in a fairly short time. Buried in rubble, the piers, masonry platforms, and benches inside were excavated beginning in 1998.

Inside the single doorway of Temple XIX stood a pier with a stunning portrait of Ahkal Mo' Nab. The thin, fine-grained limestone slab was collapsed and broken when excavated, and only half of its surface has been recovered. The ruler stands in the center with two kneeling attendants, wearing a fantastically designed costume of an immense cormorant. He stands within the gaping mouth of the bird's head, constructed as an elaborate back-rack. The symbolism connects the ruler with Muwaan Mat, Triad Progenitor, and Matawiil, place of mythic origin of his dynasty. Other icons and glyphs relate to dynastic succession and the Sun God.

Another notable monument is a rectangular altar-like platform with sculpted panels on two faces, each having lengthy hieroglyphic text in Palenque's calligraphic style and a row of seated figures. The glyphs record mythical and dynastic events. One side shows enthroned ruler K'inich Ahkal Mo' Nab flanked by six high-ranking courtiers as the ruler leans forward to receive the white headband of rulership. The other side has three figures and accompanying glyphs relating to the Triad Gods and dedication of the structure. As the central figure, he sits before a throne cushion and cradles a massive bundle of coiled rope in his arms, and the other two hold ceremonial poses. The scene is related to rituals done by Ahkal Mo' Nab.

Temple XXI was built adjacent to Temple XX (Yohl Ik'nal's temple), also oriented toward the Cross Group. It contains a small masonry platform with another masterpiece of carving by the same team of artisans. The scene depicts K'inich Janaab Pakal on the central throne, handing a feathered bloodletter to his grandson Ahkal Mo' Nab sitting on his right. On his left is his great-grandson Upakal K'inich, who succeeded after Ahkal Mo' Nab.

Both heirs wear elegant leafy capes and confer with fantastical rodents, as the hallowed great ruler conveys fundamental duties of rulership.

In 731 CE, the 13th ruler of Copan, Uaxaclajuun Ub'aah K'awiil (Eighteen Rabbit), erected a monument that makes reference to Palenque. One of a pair created late in his reign, Stela A had glyphs on one side listing the emblems of Copan, Tikal, Kalakmul, and Palenque. The traditional reading of these glyphs is that representatives or possibly the rulers of these cities took part in important rituals at Copan. If so, then Ahkal Mo' Nab III would have visited Copan. Other interpretations suggest that these city emblem glyphs, along with directional glyphs for the four skies and quarters, were used as metaphors for the whole world. The Copan ruler was asserting his hegemony over the world and control of the most powerful cities in it. This was an effort to bolster his waning power; seven years later he was captured and killed by his prior vassal state, Quirigua.

Upakal K'inich became ruler around 741 and added "Janaab Pakal" to his name, a clear evocation of his legitimate right to succeed. He is also called Pakal II. The only recorded date associated with him is 9.15.10.10.13 on the day 8 Ben 16 Kumk'u (January 29, 742 CE), when he invested a subordinate official as a K'an Tok lord. Inscriptions on the K'an Tok Tablet from Temple XVII relate that several individuals were "installed into the office of K'an Tok" by various rulers of Palenque between 435 – 768 CE. Holders of this office were members of the royal lineage, though its significance is unclear. Upakal K'inich Janaab Pakal and his brother K'inich K'uk Bahlam II were among the rulers who installed officials as K'an Tok.

During his reign a Lakam Ha "princess" named Lady Chak Nik Ye' Xook (also called Ix Xok) was sent to marry into the dynasty of Oxwitik (Copan). She is thought to be the granddaughter of Ahkal Mo' Nab, and daughter of Upakal K'inich. It is likely that Copan sought this union to bolster their faltering dynasty. Her marriage to K'ak Yipyaj Chan K'awiil (Smoke Shell) occurred in 742 CE. When her husband ascended to the throne seven years later, she became the queen of Copan, and mother of Copan's 16th ruler Yax Pasaj Chan Yooat (Yax Pac). Having a royal woman from Palenque as mother was obviously important to him, for he named her on several inscriptions while his father is rarely mentioned. Kinship ties to Palenque served to legitimize late Copan rulers as their local authority diminished.

Around 745 a panel fragment found in Popo' recorded a defeat of Lakam Ha under ruler Tuun Chapat. On this fragment is the image of a bound prisoner accompanied by the Palenque emblem glyph, but the name of the presumed ruler was on an adjoining stone, now missing. There is no way at present to know if it was Upakal K'inich, who died about 750 near the age of 40 years.

The middle of the 8th Century is a poorly documented time at Palenque. Between 741 and 764 there is no archeological evidence of new buildings or tablets. The important katun ending in 751 (9.16.0.0.0) is not recorded at Palenque, although it was prominently celebrated at the neighboring city of Pipá (Pomona). On the stela carved for that occasion, ruler K'inich Hix Mo' Bahlam was assisted by someone named K'inich Kan Bahlam, Holy Lord of B'aakal. This provides evidence that Kan Bahlam III, thought to be a son of Ahkal Mo' Nab, was ruler of Lakam Ha by 751. Speculation about why a Lakam Ha ruler would assist a historical rival during a katun end ceremony leads to the supposition that Pipá had subjugated Lakam Ha. It is possible that Kan Bahlam III spent time in Pipá in exile, or was forced to perform vassal duties.

The accession date of the next Lakam Ha ruler is known. Pakal's great-grandson K'uk Bahlam II ascended the throne on 9.16.13.0.7 on the date 9 Manik 15 Uo (March 8, 764 CE). He was a brother of the prior two rulers, all sons of Ahkal Mo' Nab III. He was named after the dynastic founder who lived four centuries earlier. This last clearly documented ruler continued to reign for about 20 years, after which Palenque's lengthy history quickly falls into silence.

K'inich K'uk Bahlam II commissioned some minor construction projects in the palace, including modifications to the unusual square tower built by his father. At the base of this tower he placed the Tablet of the 96 Glyphs, perhaps inserted into one step of a small stairway. The tower stairway faces onto a small plaza that opens to House E, the Sak Nuk Nah—White Skin House created by Pakal. The small ornate tablet commemorated K'uk Bahlam's first katun (20 years) as ruler, retelling the dedication of House E by Pakal and accession of two subsequent rulers. The text ends by declaring that K'inich Janaab Pakal, who had been dead for a century, "governed over" his great-grandson's first katun anniversary in 9.17.13.0.7 on the date 7 Manik 0 Pax (November 24, 783 CE).

Perhaps the revered ancestor did oversee the occasion, since his portrait on the Oval Palace Tablet set over the throne in House E looked out onto the plaza, towards the Tower steps where the Tablet of the 96 Glyphs once was seated.

There is another mention of K'uk Bahlam II on the fragmented K'an Tok Tablet found in Temple XVI, where his name appears with the date 768 CE at the end of a long list of Palenque rulers who installed officials into this position. Although the dedication date for the K'an Tok Tablet is not known, the style matches other monuments carved during his reign.

Mystery surrounds the last person connected with the ruling dynasty as well as the abandonment of Palenque shortly after 799 CE. A small, ornately carved bowl of fine grey paste from the Tabasco plains, called blackware, was uncovered near the ground's surface in front of an entrance to a residential compound known as the Murciélagos Group (Group III). This type of inscribed ceramics was very rare, suggesting the bowl was a treasured object of some elite family. The style and source of the vessel date to the end of the 8th Century.

On the bowl the inauguration date of a man called Wak Kimi Janaab Pakal was inscribed: 9.18.9.4.4 on the date 7 Kan 17 Muwaan (November 17, 799 CE). This nobleman has not yet been placed in the family history of Palenque or linked to the ruling dynasty. His first two names, Wak Kimi, translate to "Six Death" which is a calendar date. Some Mayanists suggest this implies growing Mexican influence, because taking day names was common in their culture. But it also has a long history among the Mayas. By adding on the illustrious name Janaab Pakal, this obscure leader was evoking the city's past glories. Perhaps he was a descendant of K'uk Bahlam II or Upakal K'inich. Much of the blackware vessel text remains undeciphered, but what is understood may name the last known ruler of Palenque.

The last dated reference to Palenque (around 814 CE) appears on a clay brick from Comalcalco, a city far northwest of Palenque at the edge of the Maya regions. Historically allied with Lakam Ha, Comalcalco (Nab'nahotot) grew and increased its influence around this time. Most of the inscriptions found there cluster near the end of the 8th and beginning of the 9th Centuries. The inscription on the clay brick refers to a "Holy Lord of B'aakal" without any specifics; it might refer to a current or earlier ruler.

The Abandonment of Palenque

As the Maya Long Count Calendar rolled into Baktun 10 (10.0.0.0.0) the once magnificent city Palenque was abandoned over a relatively short time period, its soaring pyramids, broad plazas, and large complexes left to bear mute testimony to a high culture. Although some neighboring cities, including Tonina (Popo') and Yaxchilan (Pa'chan), continued to function for several more generations, very few survived after 850 CE. Rapid abandonment of cities in the region was a devastating and widespread pattern, with drastic reduction of population. The phenomena underlying this "collapse" include climate change, population overgrowth, endemic warfare, and decreasing food and water supplies along with disease. Archeologists have documented the presence of these factors in the 7th and 8th Centuries.

The driving factor for Palenque seemed to be rapid population growth. Settlement archeology reveals clear indications of phenomenal growth in population density between 770 – 850 CE in the central Palenque area. There was a near doubling of population in the century leading up to the collapse. In a city situated on a narrow ridge with limited level land, only the elite compounds and ritual centers had the best conditions, including fresh water sources. Houses of lesser nobles and commoners perched on hillsides or at the mountain base, with problematic crowding and reduced quality of the water supply.

The increasing population of elites who claimed political and religious privilege made severe demands on workers and resources. Burgeoning families of rulers and high officials led to competition and conflict, reducing the cohesion of the community. Warfare between cities increased as they competed to obtain resources and status. As their world tipped out of balance, rules of authority were severely undermined; commoners lost confidence that their rulers could satisfy their covenant with the Gods and maintain the equilibrium of the cosmos.

Drought occurred during this time, affecting crops and reducing food supply. Some cities suffered effects of deforestation as they cut excessively to produce fire for making limestone plaster, essential for building. At some critical point, commoners could no longer bear the burden of supplying elites with food at their own families' expense, and began leaving. There is no evidence at Palenque of an epidemic or of violence near the end. Some have suggested that the population departure from the central city was an organized and orderly process, implying the work of a council. A group of elite leaders, now a mix of nobles and royalty, sitting in council and calmly assessing the situation, is one possibility. After deciding the area could no longer support living in the city, they ordered an evacuation and carried it out peaceably.

A few people continued living at Palenque after the elites left. They occupied some of the prominent structures with easy water access, and might have been remnants of Palenque nobility or squatters from elsewhere. A few distinctive potsherds found in the palace and Group C complex were Fine Orange wares dating after 850 CE; very different types of pottery than that made at Palenque. Even these few lingerers abandoned the city before 1000 CE, and the jungle quickly reclaimed terraces and hillsides while grasses grew on crumbling plazas. Soon the Palace, temples, pyramids, and residential complexes were submerged under a dense green canopy and lost to memory.

Mayas continued living in the region, though their population was much less than at Palenque's apex. When the Spanish founded the town Santo Domingo de Palenque in 1567, the local Mayas appeared to have no cultural memory of the people who built the ruined stone cities buried in the jungles. They called the strange buildings and vaulted aqueduct the *otolum*, "Houses of Earth." That name lives on today as the Otolum River, the stream that passes by the palace and the Cross Group.

The ancient Mayas were a mystical and visionary people, trained in shamanic arts and profoundly connected with beings in multiple dimensions of existence. Interactions between living humans, supernatural beings of the Upperworld, and demonic lords of the Underworld were very real and immediate. In this context, the words of respected Mayanists, father and son team George and David Stuart, reveal hints of prescient knowledge among the royal dynasty at Palenque. Ruler's names were reused in a remarkable pattern. Names from founder K'uk Bahlam I to the midpoint—the reign of K'inich Janaab Pakal—were used after that in reverse order up to the last documented ruler. The symmetry is not perfect—especially with the women rulers Yohl Ik'nal and Sak K'uk. But it is uncanny, as noted in the Stuart's words (David Stuart & George Stuart: **Palenque: Eternal City of the Maya**. Thames & Hudson, 2008, p. 238).

"The overall king list suggests a closed system. With K'inich K'uk Bahlam's installment on the throne, would the Maya of Palenque have understood that he was, as a mirror of the founder, 'the last' king? We hesitate to think that Maya dynasties were predestined to end by themselves, given that the Maya collapse was a real phenomenon that came about through a combination of environmental, economic, and political factors."

Yet might not it be?

Field Journal Synopsis (1994 – 2004)

Francesca Nokom Gutierrez (Franci) is a young Mexican archeologist who was born in the town of Palenque, situated near the entrance to the ruins of ancient Lakam Ha. She is of mixed heritage, a mestizo with Mayan and Spanish ancestry. Her paternal grandmother grew up in Tumbala, a small, isolated Maya village deep in the jungles surrounding Palenque. Franci was the first in her family to obtain a university degree, specializing in Mayan archeological restoration, which both pleases and distresses her parents. While they are proud of her, they fear she will not marry a local man, might never marry at all, or might move far away to Mexico City where she earned her doctoral degree.

Franci keeps a field journal during her archeological projects, recording events and her reactions. In May of 1994, Franci is working with a team in the Palenque ruins, cleaning and stabilizing the structures as part of a project to maintain Mexico's cultural heritage. The team makes an unexpected discovery; a hidden and previously unknown substructure in the pyramid adjacent to the Temple of the Inscriptions where famous Palenque ruler K'inich Janaab Pakal was interred. Inside a sealed chamber of the Temple XIII substructure was an unopened sarcophagus that held a royal skeleton, completely permeated with red cinnabar, a preservative used by ancient Mayas. The skeleton was identified as that of a woman, the first Mayan "queen" ever found, and dubbed "The Red Queen." This experience made Franci fascinated with royal women of Palenque, and she began learning as much as possible about these Mayan queens. Although archeologists concluded that this royal woman was connected to Pakal, there were no hieroglyphs in her tomb to identify who she was.

Franci's grandmother Juanita Nokom looked exactly like ancient Mayas who lived in Palenque, except she had sky-blue eyes and her cranium was not notably elongated. Juanita promised to tell Franci the story of her blue eyes, which Franci also inherited, but wanted to wait until her granddaughter was married. Juanita made hints that Franci needed to discover her true self by listening to the "lightning in the blood." There was also some mysterious, possibly scandalous, history surrounding her grandmother's family in Tumbala. Franci tries to learn more, even asking the local priest who knew her family well, but could not find the specifics.

Ten years after the discovery of The Red Queen's tomb, Franci was given an assignment by her university to study with researchers in Mérida, Yucatán who were using new techniques to examine skeletal evidence.

Strontium isotopes studies showed that The Red Queen did not grow up in Palenque, but in a nearby region, making it less likely that she was the mother or grandmother of Pakal. The evidence pointed toward his wife; however, DNA studies were underway for confirmation.

While in Mérida, Franci meets British linguist Charlie Courtney, working as a visiting professor at the university where Franci is temporarily studying. Charlie's specialty is Mesoamerican dialects and archaic Spanish; with much in common and immediately attracted, they form a friendship. Franci's grandmother becomes seriously ill, so she goes to Palenque town. Just before she dies, Juanita gives Franci a box she kept hidden with secrets only for Franci's eyes. In the box is an old Spanish book from colonial times, and the charred page of an ancient Mayan codex.

Franci needs Charlie's help to read the Spanish book, but they had to call in an epigrapher to decipher the Maya hieroglyphs. The archaic Spanish book, written in Chilam Bahlam style of a Mayan village spokesman, gave the usual dire predictions for disasters after the Spanish conquest, but ended with hints of a scandal surrounding the arrival of a foreign woman in the village who was taken in by a local family. The Mayan codex page, written near the time when ancient Lakam Ha was abandoned at the end of the 8th century, referred to the final clearly identified ruler of Lakam Ha and spoke of leaving a legacy in caves and crypts. The scribe appeared to be a woman of royal lineage, but only part of her name was legible: Sak or white.

Franci and Charlie embark on a search to unravel Juanita's genealogy and learn the secrets of the family scandal that occurred in Tumbala. They search Catholic church archives in Palenque town first, and are able to find marriage and baptism records from Juanita to a great-grandmother who was somehow unusual. It appeared that this woman, called Ele Naach, was a foreigner. Her daughter was baptized in the Palenque church, and the father was a Tumbala villager named Francesco Nokom Tzuk, who could be traced to Juanita.

But there the trail runs out. Franci and Charlie realize they need to visit Tumbala and search its archives, ask questions of locals, meet with members of Juanita's family, and possibly consult the village shaman. Taking leaves from their positions, they find a truck bringing produce from Tumbala to the Palenque market, and arrange a ride back to the village.

Field Journal

Francesca Nokom Gutierrez
Tumbala, Chiapas, México

March 29, 2004

Charlie and I bounced along with crates of oranges, squash, onions, and carrots in the truck bed as the antiquated vehicle chugged noisily along a narrow dirt road heading deep into the Chiapas jungles. Impressive potholes caused teeth-jarring bumps and elicited distressed squawks from hapless chickens inside wooden cages. When the truck swayed our backs were thrown against its wooden side rails, but at least these kept us from tumbling out. Still, we considered ourselves fortunate to have made arrangements with a Tumbala villager returning from Palenque town to his isolated jungle home. My family is from Palenque town, so it was not hard to locate the market, though getting cooperation from the truck driver was a bit challenging.

We were on a quest to discover what secrets my Mayan grandmother Juanita Nokom had left behind in her home village, Tumbala, when she left to marry my grandfather in Palenque town. It had taken us a week to make arrangements for absences from our positions at UADY, the university where we both work in Mérida. Now each with two weeks leave, we hoped to unravel the clues we had uncovered doing genealogical research in the archives of the regional Catholic Church in Palenque. There we traced Juanita's lineage back three generations to her grandmother born in Tumbala in 1874.

Though Juanita died a few months ago without revealing her secrets, she did leave me invaluable documents that pointed to the trail. These included an old leather-bound book, its faded maroon cover typical for Spanish colonial times, the first page dated 1886. But, it was written in an undecipherable Arabic alphabet, words that seemed a Chol Maya dialect when I sounded them out, written in archaic Spanish letters. I had no hope of understanding it.

Luckily I had recently met Charlie Courtney, a British linguist specializing in ancient Mesoamerican languages, and he helped translate the book which used an archaic Spanish alphabet, phonetically forming the Mayan words. It was written by a Chilam Bahlam, the prophetic "Jaguar Spokesmen" that every Mayan village had. It recorded a K'altun Count, one traditional method of following 20-year time periods called katuns for recording the village history. Between Charlie and me, we determined that the count started around 450 CE and followed the history of ancient Palenque, called Lakam Ha, until it was abandoned around 900 CE. Then the account continued with descendants of Palenque Mayas who moved into the jungles and formed small villages. Though the book did not say which village, we surmised it was Tumbala. The account ended near the date written on the first page, which we estimated about 1880.

I clearly remember how riveting it was when Charlie reached the end of the book and read the final passages: "It says, roughly translated, that the woman arrived, she had suffered much, she was taken in by . . . someone in the village, not clear who. This created some kind of problem with the village priest who seemed to want her thrown out. If I'm reading it right, it hints at something unusual in the village, some kind of scandal. Related to this woman, who appears to be a foreigner."

Our archival research at the Palenque church led to identifying the foreign woman in the ancestry of my grandmother Juanita. The woman was called Ele Naach, an unusual Maya name that Charlie thought combined her given name in a foreign language with the Mayan word for "far" as her last name. In the church records, on September 27, 1874, the daughter of Ele Naach and Francesco Nokom Tzuk of Tumbala was baptized, and her name was Ximina Nokom Naach—the grandmother of my grandmother Juanita.

Once we arrived at this point, however, our trail ran out. The prelate of the Palenque church advised that a village elder would be our best bet, someone who remembered the story about the foreign woman. He could recall the village priests in the past mentioning a scandal that was still gossiped about in Tumbala, but did not know details. He also said we might need to find the village shaman; though the church disapproved, almost all Maya villages had one. The shamans were often the best memory-keepers in Mayan culture.

The Mayas have fascinated me since childhood. My family is part Mayan on both sides, marrying into Mexicans of Spanish descent. This blend is called *mestizo*, and the majority of contemporary Mexicans have this mixed blood. My father often acted as a volunteer tour guide for friends when they visited the nearby ruins of ancient Palenque, one of the greatest Mayan cities perched partway up the escarpment of the Sierra Madre de Chiapas mountain range. I was the first in my family to attend university, and I continued through graduate studies to attain a doctorate in archeological restoration. Naturally, my focus was ancient Mayan civilization, and I've participated in two important archeological projects at Palenque: the 1994 discovery of the Red Queen's tomb in Temple XIII, and the excavation of the chamber with throne and alfarda in Temple XIX. Currently, I'm doing a special study in bio-archeology with Dr. Teisler on the Red Queen at UADY in Mérida.

That's how I met Charlie, because he is a visiting professor at the same university. We hit it off right away, and after my grandmother gave me her hidden treasures, our relationship has grown through his help. Maybe it's even becoming romantic, which will thrill my parents. They despair that I'll ever marry due to my advanced education and faculty position in Mexico City. When they met Charlie, they liked him and no doubt harbor some hope. My grandmother Juanita often told me that she would reveal the secret of her blue eyes when I got married, but she died too soon. Juanita had intense, sky-blue eyes that stood out in her dark, narrow highland Maya face. Among my family, I'm the only one who inherited these blue eyes, although my skin color is more like my Spanish ancestors.

There were two other items in the well-sealed box that Juanita gave me. Tucked at the end of the archaic Spanish book was a separate single page that appears to be made of bark paper. The ancient Mayas made paper out of pounded bark, smoothed and coated with a thin layer of plaster. These were formed into multiple-page codices that opened in accordion fashion. The single page I had was charred around all four edges, indicating that it probably was rescued from burning. In the years after the Spanish conquest, Catholic friars attempted to convert Mayas and eradicate their pagan beliefs, including burning all the codices and religious icons they could find. This partly burned page was covered in Mayan hieroglyphs written in the flowing, calligraphic style of Lakam Ha, the Mayan name for Palenque. Charlie asked an epigrapher colleague, Miguel Sosa, to translate the glyphs and he gave the following rendition.

"Then it happened, on the back of Katun 15, the Lord is Ho'lahun Ahau.
"He ties on the white headband, the K'inich Kan Bahlam, K'uhul B'aakal Ahau.
"He is seated on the jaguar throne.

"It was the completion of the Temple of the Lords, the Progression of
    Rulers,
        the payment of tribute in cotton and cacao.
"The time of its rising, the Square Tower of Solar Observations.
"The time of travail that was foretold is soon upon us.
"Now shall we go into the forests, into the hidden places.
"Now shall our lives be changed.
"In these times shall she leave the hidden legacy;
"Daughter of father K'inich Kan Bahlam,
        daughter of mother K'inuuw Mat,
        granddaughter of K'inich Janaab Pakal.
"In the caves, in the crypts, in the distant secret places,
"For those who will know."

We were excited beyond imagining! This appeared to be a remnant
of an authentic Mayan codex written near the abandonment of Palenque at
the end of the 8th century CE, during the "Maya collapse." Unfortunately, the
scribe's name was almost obliterated by burning, with only the initial name
glyph "sak" remaining. Sak, which means white, is commonly used in ancient
Mayan names. We knew it was written by a woman, since the feminine
pronoun was used. Most scribes were men, but women occasionally were
taught scribal skills. We swore Miguel to secrecy until we could uncover
more information about the codex and Spanish book. The final item left
by Juanita was a square-shaped jade stone with a glyph carved on the
surface and a small hole at top center, so it could be worn as a pendant. The
epigrapher Miguel told us the glyph, composed of two connected images,
was the name Lakam Ha, "Place of Big Waters." This was the ancient Mayan
name for the city Palenque, dominant city of B'aakal polity.

I placed these precious items in my locker at UADY with climate
control to preserve the fragile book and codex page from deterioration.
Charlie and I speculated a little about the enigmatic hieroglyphic message
on the codex page.

"She calls herself a granddaughter of Pakal," I said referring to
the scribe.

"I didn't know Pakal had other grandchildren besides Ahkal Mo' Nab,"
replied Charlie.

"Neither did I. But inscriptions on panels or tablets are concerned
with dynastic rulers. Most are sons, and they wouldn't mention non-ruling
daughters or granddaughters."

"Peculiar that she says her father was the second Kan Bahlam. I thought he never had any children."

"That's what the epigraphic history of Palenque says." I reflected for a few moments, dredging my memory to review the Palenque dynasty. "We know from what she wrote that her mother, K'inuuw Mat was the wife of his younger brother Tiwol Chan Mat. Makes me wonder about what drama might have played out in those far-ago times."

Later that day . . .

Tumbala is a typical outlying Mayan village that has been lightly touched by modern civilization. The narrow dirt road filled with potholes is nearly impassable during the rainy season, and few venture so deep in the jungle at any time. It took us nearly six hours to get there, six miserable hours jostling around with vegetables and chickens, coated with dust and throats parched. We brought along minimal supplies in our backpacks, taking occasional sips of tepid water and munching energy bars. Our gear included a tiny tent and sleeping bags, in case we couldn't get accommodation in a village palapa.

Dusk was falling when we paid the truck driver and asked about a place to stay. He just shrugged and walked off, decidedly unhelpful. A few villagers stood outside their palapas, the oval structures with stucco walls and palm-thatched roofs that serve as homes for most Mayas. None approached us, so we walked slowly down the dirt street, taking note of two cross streets that ended near the encroaching brush. We followed the last cross street and found it led to what served as the village square. The largest palapa seemed a bit nicer than others, so we approached it and called greetings in Spanish.

"Hola! Buenos tardes. Por favor, puede hablar con nosotros, somos visitados," I said loudly, peering through the open doorway. I was politely requesting that someone come talk with us, as we were visitors.

An elderly Mayan man came to the doorway, thin and stooped, attired in off-white manta tunic and calf-length pants. His grey-streaked hair hung loosely around his shoulders and his feet were bare. He glared at us under bushy brows from a classic highland Mayan face.

"Que quieren?" he said in good Spanish, asking what we wanted.

"Is there a room we can rent for the night?" I asked. "We are doing research, and want to remain in Tumbala for a few days."

"Research? No one does research in Tumbala," he replied. "Go to Palenque."

"We just came from Palenque. What we want to learn can be found in Tumbala."

"Then you do not want to learn much," he said with a chuckle. "Not much happens in Tumbala."

"We are seeking to learn about the family of my grandmother, who was born in Tumbala," I related, feeling a bit more hopeful.

"Your grandmother?" He peered more closely at me, then looked at Charlie's sun-reddened face and laughed. "Surely this red one has no family from Tumbala."

"No, you are right, he does not. My grandmother, now having passed on to the realm of ancestors, was Juanita Nokom."

He grunted, and I caught a shadow cross his eyes. Long moments passed as he seemed to consider this information.

"You will not find what you seek," he murmured. "Best you return to your city. Are you from Palenque town, or from Mérida? No matter, tonight none will take you back. Best you come into my hut, no one else will give you a place to sleep or food to eat." He sighed wearily and gestured us to enter.

Inside the floor was clean-swept, hard-packed dirt with a three-stone hearth in the center. The walls were composed of thin tree trunks held together with rope and partially filled with plaster in between. A space was left between upper walls and thatched roof for air flow. I recognized this as the cooking palapa, and realized they must have another for sleeping. A flat metal plate was balanced on the three stones, and beside it an older woman was kneeling, making tortillas. At one edge a large pot simmered, emitting delicious odors of stew and herbs, probably some combination of beans, turkey, tomatoes, squash, and mixed spices. Two hammocks were stowed drooping from their wall hangers, which could later be strung across the palapa walls. A rickety table and two chairs, along with a bench covered with cloths, baskets, and tools were about the only other items inside.

"Bienvenidos," he said. "Welcome to my home. Here is my wife Isabel, I am called Beto. We will share our meal with you, though it is not much. Tonight you can sleep here in the hammocks. It will be hot, but better than outside with the insects and bats."

"Thank you very much," I replied. "It is our pleasure to meet you and your wife. We cannot say how much we appreciate your helping us, your hospitality. I am Francesca, and this is my friend Charlie. He is from England."

Charlie smiled and expressed his gratitude in flawless Spanish, causing both Isabel and Beto to turn and stare at him. Charlie speaks fifteen or so languages, and sounds like he was born in Madrid. Not Yucatecan Spanish, but easy for any Spanish-speaker to understand. Beto gestured to place our things by the hammocks and went outside to soon return with a couple of crates for us to sit. Isabel served the stew in clay bowls and placed tortillas in a warmer for us to use as scoopers. A small clay bowl with salt and ceramic cups that Beto filled with juice accompanied the meal. Simple as it was, Charlie and I later agreed it was among the best meals we'd ever had.

After the meal, Beto invited Charlie outside for a smoke, and grudgingly included me. He no doubt saw me almost as a foreigner, a woman outside her proper place, more like a modified man. I was only too glad to accept a cigar, since the smoke helped keep mosquitoes and other biting insects at bay. Though neither of us normally smokes, taking a few short draws on our cigars, enough to keep them lighted, and blowing smoke at our tormentors was a pleasure.

"Juanita Nokom. That name I have not heard for many years," said Beto.

"Did you know her?" I asked.

"Yes, yes, we all knew her. All of us of that age."

"Can you tell me . . . what you know about her?"

"Different. Strange. Always apart from the others."

"Can you say more?"

"She left, we knew she would leave. The village was not for her."

"What of her family, the ones who stayed here?"

"Her brother, her sister, they stayed. They were older. Juanita was born late, her mother Itzel, too old the midwife said for more babies. Bad thing, Itzel died. The other children, they were normal. Juanita, not so."

"How not so?" I was curious why Juanita never talked about her village family, and never wanted to visit them. I did not know her mother died in childbirth.

"The ones with the blue eyes. They were never normal." He squinted at me, shaking his head. "You have the blue eyes. That is why you go away, do this research in the big cities. Bad thing, the blue eyes."

"Did Itzel have blue eyes?"

"Yes, and her sister Xuxa also. Maybe it would have been normal for Juanita, with her mother dead, no one with the uay mark to raise her. But Xuxa took over, she raised Juanita and gave her the strangeness. So she was not normal."

"The uay mark? What do you mean?" I knew that uay meant spirit companion in Mayan, but was perplexed at how Beto was using the word.

"The blue eyes, they are the uay mark. Not normal. Our people do not have blue eyes . . . ah, well those who marry with the Spanish, the light-skinned ones, sometimes they get blue eyes, but not the same. These blue eyes, Juanita's eyes, they came from . . . that woman, the foreign woman."

Now I was really excited and glanced at Charlie, who was puffing thoughtfully at his cigar. I don't think he even noticed the acrid bite of the smoke.

"Don Beto," I said carefully, using a title of respect, "this is very important information for me. I need to learn of this foreign woman, and what Xuxa did to make Juanita strange. Please tell me all you know."

"Xuxa . . . they went into the jungle. No one knows where. Sometimes they were gone for days. It was not normal, not safe. But they were never harmed. Not good for women to go into the jungle, alone. Not normal."

"What did they do in the jungle?"

Beto puffed on his cigar, blowing smoke in a thin curl into the darkness. Without city lights, the village was enveloped in inky blackness. Dim lanterns from doorways cast rusty halos that dissipated in a few feet. I wondered if Tumbala even had a generator.

"This, I do not know," he finally said. "Ancient things, forbidden things. Father Justo talked to them, said they did things of the Devil. But they did not listen. Maybe they lost their souls."

Beto crossed himself in Catholic style and murmured a prayer.

"Who would know what they did?"

"This is not good," Beto retorted. "Not good to ask such things. You should return to Palenque town tomorrow."

Charlie spoke up, attempting to move the conversation to a better tone.

"Don Beto, we are scientists. We study the practices of the ancient Mayas. We have tools and experience that protects us, makes us strong against such bad things. For our research, we must learn of such things."

Beto shook his head, muttering some words about *la locura*, our craziness.

"Maybe Tata Kayum . . . if he will speak to you."

"Tata Kayum?" asked Charlie.

"He is h'men . . . you know?"

"Yes, we know," Charlie replied. H'men was a village designation for a type of shaman.

"Maybe tomorrow. We will see."

"Don Beto, we want to speak with him," I added. "Tomorrow is good. What others of Juanita's family still live here?"

"The children of her brother and sister . . . their children, there are several. None has blue eyes, Dios gracias."

"May we meet some of them? Tomorrow, will you introduce us?"

"It is late," he said. "You are tired from your travels. I have spoken much already. Let us go to our sleep. Tomorrow may find another thing of interest."

He rose, and I knew I couldn't push any further. My mind was whirling with what I'd already been told, trying to process memories from talks with my grandmother that might provide clues. Charlie and I bid Beto good night and retired to our hammocks for a restless sleep, unaccustomed to the sling and sway of our hanging beds.

March 30, 2004

The next morning we woke early to the raucous cries of green parrots, scarlet macaws, brown jays, spider monkeys, and a hoard of chirping insects. The jungle seemed just outside our palapa, which it indeed was. Isabel made breakfast of tortillas and plantains, but we had to do without coffee. Juice was our drink, or well water into which we dropped purification tablets. It appeared there was no electricity in Tumbala, thus no refrigeration. Isabel pointed us to an outdoor washing area, a stall made of thin poles tied with rope near the well. We pumped the mechanical handle to draw water and took turns doing a quick wash-up with a home-made soapy substance that smelled vaguely of tallow.

Beto joined us later and took us to a palapa complex on an adjoining street where he said Juanita's relatives lived. Word had spread about us through the village, and many locals watched curiously as we walked. Five palapas crowded around an open dirt area in which chickens and turkeys foraged recently thrown corn, and pigs wallowed in a puddle of mud. Rope lines strung from two poles held drying laundry. Two palapas were cooking-style and the others had solid stucco walls for sleeping. Several children from about age two to ten played nearby already streaked with dust and all barefoot. Though it was early, the heat was oppressive.

Two men and a woman approached, and Beto introduced us to Juanita's niece and nephews, my second cousins. The men seemed to understand Spanish, but the woman was either too shy or spoke only Mayan. They related no memory of Juanita, who left the village when they were very young. I asked about their parents, Juanita's sister and brother, but both were deceased. Were there any other relatives? No one could think of any, except those who married into the family. It seemed this was a dead end, so I expressed my pleasure at meeting my relatives and we bid good-by. As we left the complex, I glanced inside a palapa and caught the eye of a young woman who appeared in her early twenties. Something in her expression grabbed my attention, but she quickly made a hand signal to leave and bowed her head. Her features were evocative of Juanita's from a picture when she married my grandfather. I made a mental note to try and make contact with this young woman later.

Back on the street, I asked Beto if he would take us to meet Tata Kayum, the h'men. He shook his head sadly, saying the h'men was not at home and no one knew where he had gone or when he would return. I suspected he was avoiding us, but decided to try another tact. I knew that every Mayan village had an assigned priest who would make regular visits to say mass and perform rituals such as baptisms, marriages, and last rites. These priests had village assistants, called deacons, who kept up with religious observances between visits. The maroon-covered Spanish book my grandmother left me might have been written by some early version of a deacon, someone who knew both Spanish and Mayan and could write. Clearly, the writer had Maya training as a Chilam Bahlam and was knowledgeable of ancient Maya customs. Perhaps finding the current deacon might lead to the trail of this earlier counterpart.

"Don Beto, who is the present village priest?" I asked.

"Ah, there have been several successors to Father Justo," he replied. "It is hard work, coming to Tumbala, not many priests continue. Let me think, let me think. No, no, he was before the current one . . . ah, names escape me as I get older . . . ah yes, Father Ricardo. He is the last one. Father Ricardo. But he has not come for a long time, many months."

"Father Ricardo," I repeated. This priest must be from another parish, because our Palenque prelate had not mentioned his name. "What city does Father Ricardo come from?"

"Hmmm. San Cristóbal? I believe that is it."

San Cristóbal de las Casas is a lovely mountain city southwest of Palenque with a heavy European influence. I've visited there several times to enjoy the crisp mountain air; situated on an 8,000-foot peak the city is filled with espresso shops and bookstores. A huge cathedral faces the main plaza where upscale restaurants offer international cuisine and boutique hotels host tourists from around the world. Certainly the city has a large parish and could send out traveling priests to Mayan villages.

"Do you know when he will come again?" I asked.

"No. He does not make a regular time to visit."

"Does he have an assistant living here, a deacon?"

"Yes, that is Marco."

"Can we visit Marco? Could you please take us to him?"

Beto heaved a big sigh, as though we were too burdensome to bear, and muttered: "Yes, yes, I will take you to him."

Going in the opposite direction of Beto's palapa, we followed him to another side street and arrived at a large complex having two cooking and sleeping palapas. Beto called greetings and a Mayan man came to the door who he introduced as Marco, the village deacon. Marco invited us inside and we were impressed to see an actual wooden desk and chair, along with four other chairs and several storage cabinets all of varnished wood. In the tropics, any wood not covered with varnish will soon become food for bichos.

"So, you are our visitors from Palenque town," said Marco. "How may I be of assistance?"

His Spanish was excellent as befit his station. As a deacon, he could read and write both languages.

I provided background on our search, deciding to go a step further and reveal the antique Spanish book my grandmother left me.

"We believe this book was written by an early deacon of Tumbala," I explained. "But he was writing in Chol Mayan translated phonetically into archaic Spanish. He wrote in the style of a Chilam Bahlam. Do you have any knowledge of such previous records?"

"No, I have never heard of such a thing," said Marco. "All the records I have here are written in regular Spanish. Well, as far as I know. There are some very old records that I have never looked at; no reason to do so."

Charlie perked up immediately and asked: "Would it be possible for me to look at those old records? I'm a linguist and can read archaic Spanish. These might be useful in our search."

Marco paused to consider Charlie's request. I could see that, as the most educated person in the village he was intrigued to meet a linguist. And, it was a diversion from what must be a very boring and repetitious routine.

"Why not? Father Ricardo has never forbidden showing the old records. What harm? It is good to be helpful; our Lord was most helpful to all types of people. Come, bring your chairs close to the desk and I will put the oldest records there."

Marco rummaged around in the most distant cabinets, looking on the two lowest shelves. He pulled out five dusty volumes and shook them, brushing off powdery crumbles from around the edges.

"Bichos!" he grumbled. "One can't get rid of those pests. I spray insecticide from time to time, but they keep coming back."

I saw Charlie shudder at the casual way these precious ancient documents were treated, and hoped the bichos had spared most of the pages inside. The books were leather-bound in faded tones of blue, gold, and maroon without lettering on the covers; typical for old Spanish records. We were both holding our breath as Charlie opened the first, and let out a relieved sigh as the pages turned without falling apart. Although nibbled around the edges, most pages appeared intact and covered with elegant curlicues of archaic Spanish.

"Dog's Bollocks!" Charlie exclaimed in British slang for "great find." He grinned at me and his golden curls bounced, making him too cute for words. "We're on to it, Franci. A regular gold mine, in similar Spanish to your grandmother's book. Marco, can you let me have a notebook or some paper and a pen? I'll need to take notes and we don't have those supplies."

Marco complied with a spiral notebook and two ballpoint pens. He leaned over Charlie's shoulder and scrutinized the web-like lines of indecipherable Spanish, at least to his eyes.

"If you find something that would be important to The Church, please make a note for me," Marco requested.

"I'll do my best," Charlie replied, though I doubted he knew what The Catholic Church might consider important. We settled into another long session combing through tedious records, looking for anything that might pertain to Juanita's great-grandmother Ele and her descendants. The earliest books were dated 1881 – 1885, the time frame that interested us. Charlie poured through pages of church records, which mostly contained reports of the village priest's periodic visits, accounts of current populations, illnesses and deaths, and logs of gifts presented by villagers in lieu of money for church donations. Births and baptisms seemed particularly important, and the records noted which baptisms were done in Tumbala, and which had to take place in Palenque town because of the village priest's absence. It made sense that church records would focus on the salvation of native souls by Catholic baptism, as was their belief. In similar vein, marriages were designated by town or village where they took place. With a typically Spanish concern for minutia, villager attendance at Holy Days of Obligation services was dutifully recorded. Any disputes between villagers that the priest mediated were described in painstaking detail.

After over two hours, Charlie rubbed his eyes and sighed. Marco brought bottled water for us to drink; Beto had long since left. Charlie had started with the most recent date, 1885, and now only the oldest book dated 1881 remained. As he slowly turned its pages, I was losing hope that the old Spanish church records would reveal anything helpful. But, on the next page turn, Charlie grabbed the spiral notebook and started writing. I watched in fascination as his bold handwriting covered the page. He said nothing, continuing to scan the rest of the pages, and then closing the book carefully.

"We have some information," he said to me as Marco drew closer, curiosity marking his features. "Here is what I was able to translate:

"In the year of our Lord 1873 returned to Tumbala one resident Francesco Nokom Tzuk who was away for a year working for British explorers. He had in his company a British woman who was known only by her given name Ele. She refused to speak more of her situation or origin. She would not be returned to her people, and the Nokom family gave her shelter. Francesco Nokom, who was a single man, took her as a wife, but they declined to be married in The Church. The case of Francesco Nokom Tzuk will be taken to the regional prelate for possible excommunication."

"There are our people, Francesco and Ele!" I exclaimed.

"These are the ancestors about whom you are seeking information?" asked Marco.

"Yes," I replied. "This tells us when the foreign woman came to Tumbala, and something of her circumstances."

"So she was British," "Charlie observed. "Accounts for the blue eyes. In that time period, the latter 1800s a number of European adventurers came to Mexico and Central America, didn't they?"

"Yes, in the aftermath of the international success of Stephens and Catherwood's *Incidents of Travel* books. They published *Incidents of Travel in Central America, Chiapas and Yucatan* in 1841 and soon the books were selling out, making the American journalist and British artist considerable money. These were the travel books of the time, and Europe had wanderlust for adventure in exotic tropical locales," I added. "Most of the explorers of that era were not archeologists, but more like adventurers out for treasures. They absconded with as many artifacts as they could carry and fueled the black market for archeological relics. It makes us modern archeologists very sad."

"Women weren't heading out on such adventures by themselves, I don't think," Charlie said. "Stands to reason that the British woman Ele accompanied a male explorer, probably her husband. Their expedition must have gone to Palenque ruins, and Francesco Nokom must have been among their native workers."

"Right! And something happened . . . what did the Chilam Bahlam say? Something about the foreign woman who arrived at the village having suffered much. . ."

"So Francesco rescued her from the British group who were mistreating her . . . or just her husband doing it, and took her to his village where she could hide safely."

"Where she decided to stay," I continued. "She didn't want to return to them. And, it appears she and Francesco must have fallen in love . . ."

"Aha!" We were startled when Marco joined our speculations. "They wanted to be a couple, but she could not wed in The Church because she was already married!"

We all pondered this for a moment, and I remembered the hints from my Palenque prelate that some scandal surrounded Juanita's history in Tumbala.

"Marco, do you know about a scandal surrounding the Nokom family?" I asked.

"Not that I have heard," replied the young deacon. "Father Ricardo never mentioned that to me, but he does not speak of all he knows. Priests must keep confidences, many spoken during confession."

"Of course," I said. "This was a long time ago."

"Are there records for 1886?" Charlie asked.

Our eyes met in silent communion. We knew my grandmother had the book dated 1886.

"I do not think so. I searched, but the next shelf of books begins in 1890. Some books must have been lost, or destroyed. It is not unusual with such turnover of priests and deacons, and such a damaging climate." Marco shrugged and started returning the books to the cabinet. "Where is that insect spray? I must try and hold back the bichos."

March 31, 2004

Last evening while sharing cigars with Beto outside his cooking palapa, Charlie and I asked about the unusual situation involving Juanita's great-grandmother, the foreign blue-eyed woman. Charlie had brought a flask of brandy along and used it to loosen our host's tongue. After several swigs Beto related the story as told to him, admitting he was not certain of all the facts.

"The village priest did not approve; it was improper," Beto said. "They lived in sin, so it is said. They had some children, most improper. One child, a girl, was called 'La Blanca' because her skin was so pale, almost white. It is said the h'men wanted to send this girl away, said she was cursed. I do not know, it was very long ago . . . yes, yes, the tale told by village gossips was that the pale-skinned girl was the grandmother of Juanita. The mother of Itzel and Xuxa. But from 'La Blanca' on the whole family were bastards—my apologies, Señorita Francesca. So it was said by those who gossip."

"Do you remember the name that 'La Blanca' was given by her family?" I asked.

"Hmmm, hmmm, no I cannot recall." He turned toward the palapa door and called out in Mayan, summoning Isabel who soon stood in the doorway. After a short exchange in Mayan, he wagged his head and made the hand sign for her to go back inside.

"Women! They gossip and they remember everything. It is a hard thing for men; they never forget what they heard. Isabel said the name given this pale-skinned girl was Ximina."

"Ximina," I repeated. "That is an unusual name. Is it Mayan?"

"Maybe, maybe not," said Beto. "Who can know? It was very long ago."

I was ticking off the family tree in my mind: Ele cohabitated with Francesco, one of their daughters was Ximina, and she had two daughters, Itzel and Xuxa. Itzel was the mother of Juanita, but Xuxa raised her . . . and made Juanita strange.

"Ah, my old bones are tired," Beto mumbled. "I go now to sleep. May you pass a good night."

After Beto was inside his sleeping palapa, I leaned close to Charlie and whispered: "Did you understand what he said to his wife?"

"Not everything. He didn't speak in Yukatek Mayan, but some derivation of Cholti'ian, the highland Maya dialect. I've been studying their dialects, you know. There are so many! If I can master three or four, I'll count myself lucky."

"Your linguistic talents will come in handy, I'll bet. Especially if we get a chance to meet with the h'men, Tata Kayum. It's likely he won't speak much Spanish, since he keeps traditional ways."

"Always at your service, My Lady," he replied with a bow. "Well, I think I'll also retire after a tiny wash-up."

Using a flashlight, Charlie went toward the bath stall and I finished a few puffs on my cigar. A narrow rectangle of light emitting from the palapa door gave dim illumination. From the corner of my eye, I caught movement just beyond the lantern's glow. Turning quickly, I made out a dark shadow and softly said: "Quien es? Who is it?"

A voice so breathy that I could barely hear it replied: "Señorita por favor, podemos hablar?"

It was a woman's voice requesting that we speak. I stood and approached her, but she backed away to keep distance. Her Spanish was passable but awkward.

"I come talk you," she said. "I come family woman, tell you things. We meet other place?"

"Are you from the Nokom family compound?" I asked, recalling the young woman who glanced at me as we were leaving.

"Yes, name Luisa," she replied. "Mother no like me talk you. Tomorrow meet?"

"Yes, we can meet tomorrow, where?"

"At the blue flower tree. Ask Doña Isabel, she know where."

"The blue flower tree. I will ask Doña Isabel. When to meet?"

"When sun straight above."

"I will be there when the sun is straight above us."

She disappeared like a mirage, and I stared into darkness deeper than the grave.

As Charlie and I settled into our hammocks, I told him about my brief encounter with Luisa, and her request to meet the next day. He insisted on accompanying me into the jungle and I readily agreed, for at least two reasons: protection and translation. I was concerned that I wouldn't understand Luisa's poor Spanish and he would do better talking with her in Mayan. I also needed his linguistic ability to get directions from Isabel to the blue flower tree. She seemed a bit surprised when he asked, sending me a suspicious glance, but complied with some complex sounding Mayan that Charlie struggled to understand. He nodded and asked a few questions, but seemed satisfied that he knew how to get there. I feared this would amp up village gossip about us, and asked him not to mention Luisa's name.

We set out an hour before noon, following a village road until it narrowed to a footpath leading into the jungle. When the path branched, Charlie took the right fork which soon branched again, this time he went left. After two more forks, the path was partly obscured by dense brush and vines, making us climb over lianas and dodge thorns. We batted at mosquitoes and stinging flies, wishing we'd brought more repellent. I kept checking my watch, worried that we'd be late. Suddenly the path opened onto a round clearing about 20 feet wide. At the far side stood a massive tree with collections of stunning blue orchids tucked into forks of its upper branches. The orchids were opportunists finding a home high above the ground, making the tree appear to be blooming.

Seeming to materialize out of the jungle foliage, Luisa appeared by the side of the tree. She looked startled to see Charlie and I quickly called out in Spanish that it was all right, he was my friend. She hesitated, but held her ground. We approached her and I introduced Charlie, saying he could speak Mayan and understand her better. She nodded and began speaking to him, rapidly and softly. He leaned in to hear more clearly and asked some questions. When she stopped, he turned to me to relay her communication.

"Luisa said that when Xuxa was very old, she told a cousin of Juanita—her own great-grandmother—a secret that was very important. It was something that must be passed down through the women from generation to generation. It was a sacred charge from the ancient ones, from their ancestors. Even if the women did not have the uay mark, they were obligated to pass this secret on. So it was passed down her family to her. When she saw you and learned you were Juanita's granddaughter, and saw you had the uay mark, she understood that the ancient ones wanted you to know. She is fulfilling her duty."

Looking at Luisa in daylight, even though muted by the jungle canopy, I saw that her brown eyes were flecked with hazel. Although she did not have blue eyes of the uay mark, her genetic heritage included light-eyed ancestors. And, she resembled my grandmother more than I had realized. It tugged at my heart while stirring my blood.

"Can you find out what this secret is?" I asked Charlie.

He spoke again in Mayan with Luisa, and she added hand signs that I thought resembled those I'd seen ancient Mayas using on panels that I had restored.

"She says she is sorry, she does not have all the information. Much has been lost over years of oral transmission. What she knows is that there is a place; she thinks it is a cave, deep in the jungle at a location no one remembers. Inside that cave is a treasure, she is not clear what exactly it is. But it is something very precious, very valuable and it came from the far distant Maya ancestors of her family. This legend says a descendant in the future will be able to find the cave, to claim the treasure, and to restore the family to its former greatness. She thinks you are that descendant."

"Oh." A sense of being overwhelmed descended over me. It tied into what Juanita had said, about me remembering who I really was, once I could awaken the lightning in my blood. How would I ever find a hidden cave lost in jungle depths?

Charlie asked more questions, but Luisa could not add anything. She apologized about having so little to offer, and expressed relief that she could pass this obligation on to me. I thanked her profusely in Spanish as Charlie translated. She smiled wistfully and melted into the shadows of the dappled forest floor.

April 1, 2004

This morning Beto came to share breakfast at the cooking palapa and informed me that the h'men Tata Kayum had returned and sent a message to come see him—only me. Charlie bristled but Beto said the terms were set; it was me alone or no visit. Beto said the h'men spoke good Spanish. I was to come to his palapa soon.

Charlie argued with me as I got ready, his blue eyes flashing and golden curls waving with animation. He seemed to care so much, and it endeared him even more. Ever since we'd kissed while doing research in the church archives in Palenque town, I'd been steadily falling in love with him—and it appeared mutual. Perhaps we'll make my parents happy after all. I was able to assuage his concern by telling him he could wait a discreet distance from the h'men's palapa, within shouting range should I need his help.

Beto guided me to the end of a crossroad and down a path not far into the jungle. Charlie waited at the end of the road having been assured voices would carry that far. A cleared area held a sleeping dog, some turkeys, and pigs near the single palapa constructed in cooking style with thin poles and plaster. A striped cloth hung over the doorway and Beto called out, bringing forth a slender middle-aged man with very dark skin. He nodded and Beto left after a brief introduction. Tata Kayum motioned me inside.

The palapa interior was dimly lighted, but I noted an unusual arrangement of things, including dried herbs hanging from strings across the side walls and several crates serving as shelves holding bowls filled with various objects, not all recognizable. Some bowls held herbs, flowers, rocks, brass and copper bells, and seashells. Others contained strange things that could be dried lizard or toad parts. An altar in the center made of large flat stone set on wooden legs held an incense burner and piles of copal incense. Colored fabric and a hammock hung along one wall. There was a three-legged stool near the altar, and Tata Kayum motioned me to sit.

He took a bowl with liquid, water I hoped, and dipped sprigs of fresh basil into it, sprinkling the liquid all over me head to toe while mumbling incantations in Mayan. I recognized this as a purification rite, something any shaman would do before starting his practices. After this, he lit copal incense in a small shell and used an eagle wing fan to blow smoke all around my body. I relished the woody, pungent scent of copal and felt a bit hazy after breathing it in. For some reason I was completely relaxed, and all this seemed familiar.

Tata Kayum placed the shell on the altar, still emitting copal smoke and reached for a large oval-shaped stone. I was aware that all shamans had such stones called a sastun that aided them in divination. It was said that the sastun found the shaman when he or she was ready, appearing suddenly and catching the shaman's attention. This sastun was quartz crystal, a smoky grey color with veins of rose. He held it in both hands, slowly moving it around my head, then near my skin surfaces on both sides. After this scanning, he stood aside and stared into its mysterious depths for some time. Nodding to himself, he set the sastun back on the altar and drew up another stool to sit facing me.

"You have the blood," said Tata Kayum. "The uay mark and the lightning blood." He shook his head and grimaced, black eyes like burning coals sunken behind high cheekbones. His sharp, angular face was dominated by a mountainous nose, skin creased by wrinkles.

"You have abandoned the old ways. You have betrayed your people, lost your heritage, taken the ways of the conquerors. You will not find what you seek. Only the uayob of the ancestors can show the way, and you have lost touch with them."

The harshness of his words shocked me. His animosity was palpable, like a humming sound inside the palapa. Then I realized the humming was within me, a deep vibration that I sensed coursing through my bloodstream. With a jolt I remembered having this sensation before—it was lightning in the blood. It was a communication, recognition of . . . what?

Tata Kayum threw his head back and let out a few guffaws. But he seemed anything but amused, and his penetrating eyes bore into mine.

"Ha! Ha! You have the lightning blood, but you do not know what to do with it."

Swallowing my irritation, I tried to invoke his help.

"Would you help me learn what to do with it?" I asked.

He considered me at length, as if examining something distasteful. The image came to me of rotting fruit.

"Go back. Return to your gringo people. There is nothing for you to learn here."

"I have come a great distance to learn of my heritage." I tried again without much hope.

"Then return back that great distance, and do not trouble us here. Let the past slumber in the ruined cities and jungles. It is no more. Your search is meaningless. Go away."

He rose from the stool and turned away, gesturing toward the door.

"Why did you meet with me, if you now send me away so curtly?" I rose and stood facing his back. Slowly he turned and gave me a look worthy of a Death Lord of Xibalba.

"To see for myself. To see if the rumors might have truth. Yes, there is truth, but you are beyond getting there. You are a foreigner, not of the people. Leave now, before something happens you may regret."

My ears were humming loudly and every fiber of my body was vibrating. A wave of faintness swept over me and I swayed, fearing I might fall. He stepped to the door and drew back the drape. Gathering my strength, I slowly walked into the brightness outside. His implicit threat hung heavily over me.

Charlie came quickly to my side, noticing I was walking unevenly. He held my arm and guided me back to our palapa, offering some juice and making me sit on the floor mats. When my insides settled down, I related what happened with the h'men. Charlie was incensed at my treatment and suggested we give up the quest, saying we'd garnered enough information. I was too disconcerted to make any intelligible reply. He strung up my hammock and made me rest.

Slowly awareness drifted away, and I fell into a fitful nap. Vivid dreams streamed through my mind, images of stone pyramids towering over the forest canopy, cascading waterfalls, broad white plazas gleaming in the hot sun. Hovering on the edge of waking, in this liminal semi-conscious space, I saw myself walking on a jungle path. It was night, but a full moon sent shards of luminous light through foliage, dappling the underbrush. My steps were firm and determined; I was going somewhere special. In the soft illumination, I saw a pale shadow moving ahead on the path. It was a large animal with a long tail, and when it turned its head to look back, I recognized the visage of a jaguar. But this was a white jaguar, and its round eyes were rosy pink. It was leading me to the place where I must go.

The white jaguar was my uay, and it knew what I sought. It would lead me to the hidden cave at the base of a mountain. My lucid dream left me without any doubt I had to meet the jaguar—tonight and alone.

April 2, 2004

That night the moon was full. After dinner I could clearly see Charlie and Beto as they sat outside the palapa having a smoke. My mind was jumping about like a spider monkey, full of conflicting thoughts. It seemed evident that my lucid dream was a summons into the jungle alone, to meet the white jaguar and follow its lead to the hidden cave. I knew Charlie would not let me go without him, so I needed to slip away after he was asleep. The next instant I was fearful, well aware of the dangers in a night jungle. *It's crazy to do this!* repeated in my mind like a mantra.

None the less, I prepared my backpack stealthily by putting in a 6-inch knife, flashlight, matches, compass, water bottle, insect repellant, bandana, and a light long-sleeve shirt. I planned to wear my long pants and a t-shirt to sleep, covered by a light shawl. I set my archeological boots near the door to slip on once outside, thinking how wise it was to have brought them. Around the village we wore sandals. When all was ready, I called through the door telling Charlie that I was very tired and turning in for the night. By the time he finished his smoke, I was in my hammock covered by the shawl, pretending to be asleep.

Of course, I couldn't sleep. Unsure how long this trek would take; I planned to leave by midnight and kept checking my watch. As the fateful hour arrived, Charlie's steady breathing told me he was asleep. I carefully swung feet off the hammock, grabbed the backpack and boots, and tiptoed outside. Donning my shirt and boots near the edge of Beto's clearing, I was plagued by my mind's objections, screaming that I'm crazy and am going to die in the jungle. I nearly lost courage and turned back. Gazing up at the full moon, I murmured prayers to the old Gods and ancestors, the ones whispering in my Maya blood, calling me back to them.

Pure instinct guided me to follow the trail leading to the blue flower tree. Somehow I made the right turns and arrived at the opening, shimmering in pale moonlight. Sounds of the night jungle surrounded me: chirping and clacking insects, croaks of frogs, furtive owl calls, and distant roars of howler monkeys evoking prehistoric dangers. Though the night air was warm, my skin prickled and teeth chattered. I was truly frightened . . . actually, terrified.

Slowly turning in a circle near the tree, I saw a faint trail leading into the dense brush. I pulled out the compass and saw it went south, the direction of the mountains. Bolstering my courage and breathing more prayers to the old Gods, I ventured onto the trail. Once inside the close foliage there was less light, and I took my flashlight in one hand and knife in the other. The trail was little used, and I had to hack through lianas and cut back palmetto fronds. My boot stubbed against a root, and I turned the flashlight down. A tangle of roots strayed across the surface, making me pick my way carefully. My concentration was such that I almost missed seeing one of the thick roots moving.

Moving roots! Snake! My mind screamed a warning. Only inches from my right foot was a thick brown snake, about 3 feet long. As it slithered away, I saw the square-shaped head and blunt snout of the most deadly pit viper in the region, called yellow-jaw or fer-de-lance. Frozen in mid-step with pounding heart, I watched it slip into the underbrush. Only when it disappeared did I break into a cold sweat and count my blessings. The venom of yellow-jaws causes rapid internal bleeding and can kill within hours.

Again I considered turning back. This venture was beyond insane, with very good chance that I wouldn't survive. Yet I continued. A welcome numbness settled over my emotions while my senses were on high alert. Walking noisily and slapping branches, I scanned the trail with the flashlight paying close attention to the roots. Thorny shrubs tore at my shirt as I pushed them aside, and mosquitoes found me probably due to sweating. I swatted and worried about even worse bloodsuckers, taking time to douse exposed skin with repellant. The trail started ascending and became rocky, making footing precarious. Trees were less tall and brush became scrubby, letting additional moonlight onto the path. The climb intensified and I was breathing heavily. Hours had passed, and I needed a rest. I sighted a mahogany tree bordering the trail, checked its base for critters, and sat with a sigh leaning against its smooth bark. After taking a drink from my water bottle, I must have fallen asleep.

In my groggy half-sleeping state, I became aware of something furry rubbing against my face. Then I felt a sharp prick on my nose and swatted automatically. Flapping wings and shrieks around my head jolted me awake. Something was attached to my left earlobe. Shaking my head vigorously and swatting wildly, I leapt to my feet and yelled. A flurry of bats circled around me and my hands were spotted with blood.

Vampire bats! Quickly I took action to fend them off, slicing off a palmetto frond with my knife and swatting furiously at them while screaming: *Get away! Get out of here!*

Shrieking in protest, the small flock took flight and flapped into the distance. I dropped to my knees, shaking all over. Tentatively dabbing my nose and earlobe, my fingers found more blood. I reached into the backpack for the bandana and used it to wipe the blood away. I slumped to the ground and buried my face in the bandana, tears rolling from my eyes. The bitten areas smarted when salty tears washed over them, but I decided that was probably good. I sat for what seemed a long time with the bandana over my face. Now I really wanted to be back in Beto's palapa with Charlie.

Oh, Charlie, will I ever see you again? That thought brought another onslaught of tears. I might have remained blubbering there forever except for my next visitors.

An ear-splitting roar blasted my ears, sounding like it was mere feet away. It was rapidly followed by a cacophony of equally loud roars as a troupe of howler monkeys expressed their displeasure at my invasion of their jungle. Glancing up in the trees, I could barely make out their dark furry bodies leaping through the branches. After a moment of silence, another round of roars shattered the night stillness. As those died away, an echo of distant roars rolled through the canopy. The nearby howlers answered, and then the distant roars repeated.

I couldn't help laughing at myself. What hubris to think the howler monkeys were focused on me! They were simply sounding off to another pack, warning the other monkeys to stay away from their territory. Somehow this gave me some perspective and bolstered my resolve to continue my quest.

As I climbed upward, the jungle closed around me again making the trail narrow. It was difficult going, climbing over rocks and cutting away lianas and brush. I tripped and broke my fall with my left forearm; landing on a rock and making a shallow gash. Muttering curses, I retrieved my tear and blood stained bandana and tied it around my arm, adding more blood. The moon had set and darkness thickened, leaves dripping with dew and splattering my face. I could feel exhaustion creeping upon me. Again I wanted to quit and turn back. The journey seemed endless. Trudging in near despair, a soft grunt caught my ear and threw me into alertness.

It was the grunt of a jaguar. Some think the sound is more like a short cough. Early explorers thought howler monkey roars were made by jaguars, but actually, these nocturnal felines make small grunting or coughing sounds. My heart pounded and a shot of adrenaline jolted through me. But as suddenly as I was terrified, I got an intuitive hit that this jaguar was my uay. Taking deep breaths to calm my heart, I stood still and waited. I deliberately opened myself to the spirit world and felt the humming sensation of lightning in the blood. This time it was soothing and centering. Down the dimly lit trail I caught a glimpse of a large animal, its long tail gently swaying and its coat pure white. Just as in my dream, the jaguar glanced over its shoulder and looked back at me. Our eyes met, and I knew my uay had come to guide me.

Lead the way. With my mind I sent gratitude and respect to the jaguar. I felt it was female, though I could not tell. She proceeded up the path in a stately walk, her tail swishing. I followed her to mountain foothills where the forest thinned until we reached a rocky outcropping with a small clearing. Beyond this the mountainside rose sharply, making it impossible to go farther. The jaguar looked me full face once more, blinked her rosy eyes a few times and grunted, then turned back to the jungle and disappeared. Mentally I offered her thanks and hoped to see her again.

Dawn was approaching, and the sky became lighter. Mists descended from the mountaintops and crept through crevices among the rocks. I looked around at those nearest me, but could not see any sign of a cave. I walked closer, climbing for a better view, but saw nothing that might be a cave opening. Sitting on a level rock, I took out my water bottle and drank, pondering what to do next. The white jaguar must have led me to the right place, but where was the cave?

As I contemplated, a question popped into my mind: what would a Maya do in this situation? The answer was obvious: Mayas would make an offering to the Gods.

The most precious offering that ancient Mayas offered the Gods was their own blood. I knew a great deal about the blood sacrifice made by my ancestors. While they did self-bloodletting, my blood had already been drawn by vampire bats and sharp rocks. I would use my bloody bandana. Quickly I gathered twigs and small branches and set them afire with matches. When the flames were going well, I murmured a prayer of offering and placed my bandana on the fire. Though damp it caught readily and produced thick white smoke, which undulated as it rose and resembled the Vision Serpent I'd seen depicted so many times in Mayan art.

I watched the serpentine stream of smoke rise and blend into mists gently flowing out of rocky crevices nearby. Morphing before my eyes, the smoke and mist seemed to resemble the form of a woman, whose skin and hair were strikingly white. This ghostly wraith glided into one crevice, indistinguishable from the others, and I quickly followed through a tight passage between large rocks, squeezing my body through the final cluster. There, in front of me, was a small cave opening nearly covered by overhanging mosses. Glad that my flashlight was still in my pants pocket, I crawled through the opening into a low-ceiling dry cave chamber, about four by five feet wide. The floor was covered with crumbled pebbles. No animals, bats, insects, or water had entered this chamber, to my amazement. It was a perfect cave for burying artifacts, especially made of wood or paper.

Crouched on my knees, I looked around the cave shining the flashlight all directions. There was nothing obvious. Running my fingers through the pebbles, I searched for an irregularity or crack that might indicate an opening in the cave floor. As though guided by an invisible force, my fingers strayed to the far right corner of the cave. Under the dry debris, I felt a crack and traced its square form. This could not be a natural occurrence. With rising excitement, I brushed the pebbles and debris off and saw faint lines where the rock floor had been cut. Taking my knife from another pocket, I used it to pry the square off. Sweat had coated my face and skin by the time I eased the square rock away. Beneath it was a crypt carved into the cave floor just large enough to hold a small bundle. And inside the crypt, there was a bundle. It was wrapped in cloth that seemed coated with a rubbery substance, now grey and brittle.

My heart pounded, but now from excitement. I knew ancient Mayas used cotton cloth soaked in latex from rubber trees and mixed with preservatives to keep their codices from deterioration. The square shape of this bundle was the right size for a codex. I lifted the bundle carefully and saw several shells and gemstones underneath. These I gathered and placed in my pocket. Making sure nothing else was in the crypt, I backed out of the cave cradling the bundle against my chest. Before working my way through the crevices back to the clearing, I faced the cave and whispered thanks to the ancient Gods, to the white jaguar, and the wispy pale woman.

Sunshine filled the clearing and dazzled my eyes. I sat and emptied my backpack, making room for the bundle. First I took off my shirt and wrapped it around the bundle, and then replaced the compass, repellant, and flashlight. I kept the knife in my pocket and finished drinking the water, putting the empty plastic bottle in a backpack pocket along with the matches. Standing, I surveyed the path I had ascended and wondered if I could retrace my steps back to the village.

At once I sensed Charlie. He was coming to find me. I suddenly knew, with my now-sharpened intuition, that he had recruited a village guide to track me through the jungle. They were following my trail and would reach me soon. With a sigh of relief, I sat down to wait.

April 7, 2004

Rows of symmetrical hieroglyphs and posturing figures spread across six pages of the codex, colors as vibrant and gestures as evocative as when originally painted. The codex that I discovered buried in the dry cave was in pristine condition. The covers were of wood painted with jaguar spots, opening in accordion fashion from left to right. Each page was attached to the next by the longer edge, half as wide as they were long, measuring 4 by 8 inches (10 x 20 cm). Preparation of the pages had been accomplished by an exceptionally deft hand: fig tree bark fibers beaten into thin sheets glued together into proper thickness, then glued edge to edge, fan-folded, and coated on both sides with a calcium carbonate solution to produce a white surface. A smooth-sided stone was used to polish the surface and make it even. In preparation for writing, borders were painted around the edges of each page with red hematite pigment. Grids were formed in diluted red and filled in with glyphs and pictures. Colors used included black made from soot and yellow, green, and blue pigments from insects and plants.

Here we had a priceless and rare Mayan codex in perfect condition. So the epigrapher and codex expert Charlie recruited, Miguel Sosa, told us in hushed tones. He had overseen the removal of its rubbery cloth coating in a climate-controlled lab we scheduled for an evening session at UADY, the university where we worked. We all wore thin white cloth gloves and face masks to reduce exposure to damaging oils and moisture. For some moments we stared, transfixed, as the record of a past society revealed its beauty and mystery.

"Can you read the glyphs?" Charlie asked.

"They appear to be a classic Cholan dialect," Miguel answered, eyes devouring every curl and twist of the complex symbols. "It's written in the cursive style of Palenque scribes. Where exactly did you find it?"

"In a cave at the base of the Sierra Madre mountains near a small village called Tumbala," I replied. "It's not far from ancient Palenque. What would you say, Charlie? Thirty miles?"

"Hmmm, yes, about that distance," said Charlie. "As the parrots fly, that is. Straight across the jungle canopy. It's much farther by roads or trails. Blighter of a trip out there, bouncing around in a dilapidated truck."

I smiled remembering our ride back from Tumbala to Palenque town. We left the same afternoon that Charlie and his guide rescued me. His crushing hug and many kisses rained on my cheeks told me how relieved he was to find me alive and unharmed. He didn't admonish me in so many words, though his subsequent scowl spoke reams. The walk back to the village took several hours, but he was dead set on leaving at once. We thanked Beto and Isabel for their hospitality, gathered our few things and climbed into the bed of the same clunky truck that brought us here. As the truck slowly lurched down the road, I caught a glimpse of Tata Kayum half concealed in the dense brush. For an instant our eyes met, and I shuddered at the smoldering fury flaring from the deep hollows of his sockets. He had ways of knowing that I could barely imagine, and I fervently hoped he would not cast shamanic curses on me.

"Let me get a few reference books," Miguel said, pulling me back to the present. "I think this writing is very similar to that remnant you asked me to decipher earlier. The style is so close . . . give me a moment; I'll be right back."

Miguel returned with his books and writing paper, hunched over the codex, and spent the next hour translating. When done, he read it aloud to us after expressing his amazement at the remarkable story it told.

Translation of the Codex

Here is the story of the women.
Let it be told, let it be said.
By the daughters, the granddaughters, those who know the names,
    descendants through time.

First she came, Lady Cormorant,
Primordial Mother Goddess, Triad Progenitor.
It was a beginning, it was a Creation,
    12 Baktuns, 9 Katuns, 13 Tuns, 4 Uinals, 0 Kins
    8 Ahau 18 Kayab. God 8 is Patron, Lady Uc arrives at 29 days.
It stood up, the Celestial Serpent-K'awiil Deity, in the Great South Sky.

On 1 Ahau, 18 Zotz she is born.
Ix Muwaan Mat, Lady Hawk-Cormorant.
Mother of three sons, Mother of the Triad Gods.
They are known, they are named, they are honored,
    patrons of B'aakal, ancestors of the dynasty.

Many are the sons who ruled, descendants of the Triad Gods,
    Holy B'aakal Lords.
Here their names are not written.
Now are recalled the wives, the daughters, the mothers,
    those whose names are forgotten.

The father does not disappear when enters the road,
    when he reaches the end.
Neither diminished nor destroyed is the face of a king,
    lord, warrior, artist, orator, scribe.
The name of a father, the face of a father, is continued in the son.
But, not so for the mother, whose travail brings forth the child.
Her name, her face is forgotten.
Where is the justice, the honor?

Sad it is, even this scribe, this woman who writes, cannot recall them
  all.
Of those served by memory, by story, even by inscription,
  this scribe now writes, now keeps the word.

She was the first: Lady Yohl Ik'nal, daughter of K'inich Kan Bahlam.
She was eighth in succession, K'uhul B'aakal Ahau, Holy B'aakal Lord,
  so called although a woman.
Named and called as all other Holy B'aakal Lords.
Heart of Wind, She of Visions, Protector of her People.

When danger came, when the Snake Lords plotted attack,
It was envisioned by Yohl Ik'nal, she saw into things.
She saw into their hearts,
    the traitors in her city,
    the cousin who betrayed her,
    the secrets of his plot.
And so it happened, Lakam Ha was prepared and defeated this evil.
And she foresaw that her daughter should marry the son of the enemy
    to pacify the nobles,
    and unite opposing forces within her city.

9 Tuns, 14 Uinals, and 12 Kins after Lady Yohl Ik'nal put on the white
  headband,
    ascended the throne of B'aakal,
She set the stone for the K'altun on 5 Ahau 3 Chen.
Lady Yohl Ik'nal, K'uhul B'aakal Ahau, gave the bundle; she adorned
  her Gods.

Then it came, calamity and suffering, to Lakam Ha.
Her son, her successor, failed to protect his people.
The Snake Lords of Ka'an struck again, chopped down Lakam Ha.
On the back of the ninth Katun, God was lost, Ahau was lost.
The Tun seating was forgotten, the B'aakal Lords entered the road.

The daughter of Yohl Ik'nal was the second: Lady Sak K'uk, Resplendent
  White Quetzal.
She was called forth when her brother, her ruler was lost.
But the Lords of Lakam Ha spoke among themselves,
    "We do not want her," they grumbled.

"Let us find another ruler," they muttered.
"It is nice to do what we want," they said while pillaging the city.

Lady Sak K'uk was worried, her city in turmoil, the shrines desecrated.
But she could not accomplish things on her own.
She went to the cave, the sacred K'ak Lakam Witz mountain.
She descended to Xibalba and met the Death Lords, who meant to eat
    her,
    but the Great Serpent saved her and brought her to Celestial Realms.
Brought her to the Primordial Mother Goddess, Ix Muwaan Mat, Lady
    Cormorant,
    who spoke thus:
    "My daughter, here in the Sky shall I adorn and bundle the Gods,
    "In the Middleworld you shall rule in my stead, until your son
    accedes.
    "Fear not, I shall convince the Lords.
    "Your son Pakal will restore the portal and renew the shrines."

And so it was. Lady Sak K'uk—Goddess Muwaan Mat—ruled for
    three years.
At the end of Katun three, she could not give the Gods' offerings;
    the Goddess thus gave their bundles in the Sky.
Then it was, her son Pakal acceded to the throne two years later.
But he was a youth. Together they ruled for 17 more years.

17 Tuns, 13 Uinals, and 12 Kins after the accession of K'inich Janaab
    Pakal,
    K'uhul B'aakal Ahau, he set the stone for the tenth Katun on 1 Ahau
    8 Kayab.
It was the completion of a half-Baktun.
K'inich Janaab Pakal attributed this Period Ending to his mother, Lady
    Sak K'uk.
This he inscribed, this he honored, on the lid of his sarcophagus.

Then came the wife of Pakal, Lady Tz'aakb'u Ahau, she of Toktan.
Accumulator of Lords, She Who Sets the Progression of Rulers.
Yet that name, that royal designation, did not sit easily upon her.
Her wish was to be called by her own name, Lady Lalak.
Many were her sprouts, but the early ones withered.
Great was her despair, her grief, Pakal's sorrows compounded.

Until she found her strength,
    her power of alchemy, of creating anew,
    until he found his truth, releasing his sorrows.

Here is the continuation of lineage, the progression of rulers.
Four sons were born, four sprouts who grew tall and strong.
The grandmother rejoiced, Lady Sak K'uk relented,
The father acknowledged, Pakal set the progression,
    with all honor, all love to the mother, his wife Lalak.
Here is what happened: two sons followed as rulers:
    K'inich Kan Bahlam and K'inich Kan Joy Chitam.
    Namesakes of their ancestors, keepers of the dynasty.

Yet another task lay before Lalak and Pakal: restoring the Portal to the
    Gods.
When the Great Star appeared in the east,
    when Ix Uc darkened the face of K'in Ahau, the Moon eating the
    Sun,
    then it was Katun 10, Tun 17, Uinal 4, Kin 19 on 6 Kawak 2 Kumk'u.
They danced the Creation, the joining of Itzam Cab Ayin, the Caiman
    Earth Creator,
    Mother and Former of Life,
With K'awiil-Chaak-Yum K'ax, Serpent-Footed Lightning-Scepter,
    Bringer of Life Fluids,
    Young Maize God, Seed of Renewed Life.
From this union the Jeweled Sky Tree was reseeded, the Sacred Portal
    was opened,
    the pathway to the Gods restored.

There were many others.
Many women, wives of Pakal's sons and grandson, their daughters and
    granddaughters.
To list their names, to write these stories, must await another time.
Here shall follow the account of one woman more, daughter-in-law
    of Pakal.
Wife of his youngest son, Tiwol Chan Mat, mother of ruler K'inich
    Ahkal Mo' Nab.

This royal woman Lady K'inuuw Mat, Sun-Possessed Cormorant,
    she of Uxte'kuh, eldest daughter of the ruler.

It is said of her mother's family, they were devoted to Goddess Ix Chel.
Lady K'inuuw Mat was to follow the Goddess at Cuzamil,
   given the gift of prophecy,
   seer of the still water.
But fate called her to Lakam Ha.
It was a fate she did not seek, a fate of difficulty, a fate she met bravely.
Married to Pakal's youngest son, their children not in succession.
Until it came, the difficulty, it was a problem of succession,
   for there were no living male grandsons.

There were granddaughters, but Pakal decreed only a male must
   succeed.
Of this, the complexities of his own succession, inheriting twice in
   maternal lineage,
   created a necessity.
His two older sons, living to succeed him, had no sons.
His youngest son had two daughters. Pakal was growing old.
So a scheme was made, a plot concocted, advised by the priesthood.
K'inuuw Mat and her husband Tiwol were the last hope for a grandson.

But they had produced only daughters. A stronger masculine seed was
   needed,
   a man of power, forceful presence, beloved of the Triad Gods.
That man, though no sprout had come yet from his loins, was Kan
   Bahlam.
So spoke the priests and priestesses:
   "He commands great forces. He is the essence of power."
   "His seed must join his brother's if we want a male child."
   "Let it be so," said Pakal.
And the joint conception was commanded. None would disobey
   Pakal the Great.

Yet there was more difficulty, and here it is:
   Secretly they loved each other, K'inuuw Mat and Kan Bahlam.
   Although in all honor, they kept apart.
Then it happened, the joint conception, and there were two children:
   Twins, one boy and one girl,
   the boy strong and masterful, who became Ba-ch'ok ;
   the girl pale and artistic, who became a scribe.

Lady K'inuuw Mat continued the royal lineage at B'aakal.
Lost in a raid was her husband, then she became wife of Kan Bahlam.
She gave to him ideas, concepts, that preserved the history of B'aakal,
   told its Creation Story and its ruling lineage,
   set in stone structures, in carvings and hieroglyphs,
   the cosmology and sacred wisdom of the Mayas.

Many things she prophesied, K'inuuw Mat.
She saw in the forests, in the mountains,
   stone cities covered with jungle trees and vines,
   deserted and silent, home to lizards and bats,
   the people scattered in small villages.
She saw the lineage into the future,
   that it continued through her own daughters,
   that it merged with pale foreigners,
   that it rediscovered its legacy.
In her seeing, her knowing, the way was shown.

So knowledge was preserved, through her daughter this scribe, creator
   of codices.
The written records of our Maya people.
The spirit of Lady Yohl Ik'nal gave instructions, to hide codices in dry
   caves,
   against dangers and terrors yet unknown,
   against dark times yet to come.

It has been done, it is accomplished.
In the great mountains, in small mountain caves,
   hidden from those who would destroy.
Many scribes, many records in codices, on pottery, in icons and figures.
The great culture of the Mayas is preserved to astonish future generations.

Here is inscribed the story of the women,
By the hand of Sak'uay, daughter of two fathers: Tiwol Chan Mat and
   K'inich Kan Bahlam.
She whose mother was K'inuuw Mat,
   whose brother was K'inich Ahkal Mo' Nab, K'uhul B'aakal Ahau.
She the pale one who continues the B'aakal lineage.

Whose hand set this record on Katun 14, Tun 12, Uinal 2, Kin 19 on 5 Kawak 17 Kank'in.

So it is written. So it is.

Sak'uay

April 10, 2004

We are still reeling in awe of the codex. The three of us put our heads together, placing it into context of what we knew about ancient Palenque history. Contrary to all other surviving Mayan codices, this one was clearly dated to November 15, 726 CE. That placed it during the reign of K'inich Ahkal Mo' Nab III (722 – 736 CE). From what the scribe named Sak'uay said, we knew he was her brother. Four rulers followed, three were his sons and the fourth was probably his grandson. Palenque was abandoned around the time of the grandson's reign, with very little archeological evidence of what happened. This final ruler acceded in 799 CE, the record incised on a blackware vessel found in a burial. The last reference ever made to B'aakal polity was discovered on a clay brick from Comalcalco, dated about 814 CE.

Only 73 years remained in the life of that great Maya city after the codex was completed. Already the unraveling of their complex civilization must have been in process. The collapse of Maya civilization had multiple causes and took place over more than a century, and every region had its unique conditions. In the rainforest surrounding Palenque, with agriculture based on a river floodplain, the most likely conditions included drought and over-exploitation of resources leading to diminished food supply, gradual migration of farmers and commoners, and inability of the elite to maintain their lifestyles. No evidence points to warfare, natural disaster such as volcanic eruption, or epidemics. Apparently, the residents of Palenque left in an organized and orderly way, without violence. It's been suggested that consensus reached by a governing council would lead to this type of abandonment, a peaceable and unified decision.

The particular insights into the Palenque ruling family given by the codex were astonishing. In these six pages we learned more about the women rulers and royal women of B'aakal than in the entire corpus yet discovered. It was both an intimate and a sweeping account. We dubbed it "The Women's Codex."

It confirmed what was known about the reign of Yohl Ik'nal, first woman ruler of Lakam Ha. Yet it added elements of interpersonal conflict and political intrigue previously unsuspected. It shed light on the controversial reign of Sak K'uk; a short three years hotly contested among Mayanists—was this ruler a woman or man, named Sak K'uk or Muwaan Mat, or both? The codex gave a mystical perspective far beyond what archeological digs could provide. The relationship of Pakal and Lalak (Tz'aakb'u Ahau) was revealed in ways never imagined, a rich and profoundly creative love story. The complex situation surrounding Pakal's heirs was revealed in startling detail. We knew the lineage continued through his fourth son, who never ruled, but the heir's connection with Kan Bahlam was a real surprise. Almost nothing was previously known of the wife, K'inuuw Mat. Her role in preserving Maya culture for posterity was quite an eye-opener.

Then came the mystery of Sak'uay, the scribe. Her name translated as "White Spirit Companion" and she claimed to be Pakal's granddaughter through two of his sons. We chuckled at how that feat might have been accomplished! Though we thirsted for more details, those were left to our imaginations. Miguel made a cogent observation.

"In addition to her name, look at the tiny drawing of a scribe's figure near the signature. It was not uncommon for Maya scribes to leave their picture at the end of a codex, especially if they were of royal or noble blood," he said. "Which she was. See, she is bending over her codex, using a feather quill to write. Her chest is bare in common scribal practice, showing her breasts. Her hair is tied in a topknot and hangs down, instead of being wrapped in hairnets as used by male scribes. The glyph under her name identifies her as an *ah tz'ib*, or writer."

"Yes, I see. But look at her coloring—she is painted white, instead of the usual reddish brown of Maya skin," I noted.

"And her name, Sak'uay, we know sak means white," Charlie added.

"Well, there were albinos among the Mayas," said Miguel. "I've seen photos of albino Lacandons, and there are depictions of white-skinned women dressing the Maize God on ceramic vases. I suppose the albino gene must have existed in ancient Maya times."

"Of course!" Charlie exclaimed. "That's why she calls herself 'the pale one.' She must have been an albino."

"Albinos were considered to have special powers," Miguel added. "Although many people feared albinos, they were also thought to be specially blessed by the Gods."

"Well, if that's not The Full Monty!" Charlie exclaimed. When both Miguel and I stared at him blankly, he added: "Uh, going big . . . as in a big discovery."

We could only nod in agreement.

Miguel asked how we planned to reveal this discovery to the professional Mayanist world. Every one of us understood that it would rock that world to its very foundations. The value of this codex was inestimable, and years of research would spin off analysis of the contents. Not only was the document in excellent condition, but it was also "provenanced" meaning that we had an identifiable location for its origins at Lakam Ha. Though not discovered in the city, it clearly had enough ties to be set there. It shed new light on the Palenque dynasty, Maya cosmology and mysticism, and the intentions of leaders to preserve their legacy.

In a word, it was explosive.

"I suppose we should begin by informing our superiors at UADY and my university in Mexico City," I said. "Then of course there's INAH—you can be sure the government agency charged with preserving Mayan cultural heritage will want to be involved from the start. These institutions will send their experts to examine and confirm everything we have, including the objects from the cave, the codex fragment, jade pendant, and old Spanish volume."

"Must we turn over everything to them?" Charlie queried, his brows furrowed.

I knew he was thinking about the family mystery we were trying to solve.

"I'm afraid so," I murmured. "Our careers would be at stake if we held anything back."

"Claro que si!" Miguel exclaimed, looking puzzled. "Everything must be subject to extensive scientific examination; a find this significant needs multi-disciplinary study. Hundreds of research articles and treatises will result, pushing forward our understanding of Mayan civilization. Franci, you will be famous!"

I laughed. Then with a serious expression, I looked each of my companions in the eyes.

"WE will be famous. This isn't just my discovery, you both added expertise that I couldn't have done without. When we inform the university and government officials—which we must do in the next few days—all three of our names will be on the discovery."

Later that evening when Charlie and I were alone, we speculated about how the codex might relate to my family, and my grandmother's secret.

"Let me see if I can recap," Charlie offered. "Your grandmother Juanita, born in Tumbala, was daughter of Itzel but was raised by Xuxa her aunt, who was suspected of knowing secrets that she taught Juanita. This secret knowledge made them 'strange' to the other villagers. Xuxa's mother Ximina was a 'pale one' who also knew the secrets. Ximina must have been albino. The mother of Ximina was the foreigner Ele—who also must have been pale skinned because she was British. I'll bet her name was Eleanor, because 'Elie' is a nickname we Brits use, and the Mayas would spell it phonetically as 'Ele.' We know there were numerous European adventurers in the Chiapas region in the mid-1800s. So there are genes for blue eyes and yellow hair."

"Yes, that's so . . . but what about the Maya side of the family?" I asked. "The Mayan man from Tumbala who married Ele was Francesco Nokom Tzuk. The albinism must have come from his genetics, because their daughter Ximina was more than just light-skinned, and one generation of inter-marriage couldn't produce an albino-appearing child."

"Hmmm." Charlie pondered this point, adding: "Bob's your uncle! Er, you're right. Think about Luisa from the village, a family member not in direct descent from Ele. Remember how her skin was lighter than others and her eyes hazel? Those genes might have come through her Mayan line."

"You're right. Let me think . . . wasn't Luisa's great-grandmother a cousin to Juanita? Francesco had other children before he took Ele as 'wife,' so there's a line descending from them, unrelated to Ele. When they say cousin, we don't know the exact relationship, how many times removed. Frequently 'cousin' simply means a distant relative."

"There's the other part of the mystery," Charlie said. "The Spanish volume I read in Tumbala made clear that the village scandal surrounded the unmarried relationship assumed by Francesco and Ele, making their children illegitimate. They were brave to face village disapproval. I wonder if Francesco ever got excommunicated."

"We'll never know since the Spanish volumes are missing. If he did, that would add fuel to the scandal. Getting back to the albino genes that produced Ximina, and possibly affected Luisa as a mosaic. Let's assume the albinism is on the Maya side," I continued. "Who were the ancestors of Francesco? We know the story of him rescuing the foreigner Ele from a dig at Palenque. We know many villagers living in Tumbala claim roots to Palenque."

We both stared at each other in a moment of shared realization.

"Sak'uay?" we exclaimed simultaneously.

"She would have died in the mid-700s," Charlie reckoned. "Giving an average lifespan of 50 years, that would be about 22 generations from Sak'uay to Francesco. It's a long time, but there's current evidence that the albino gene persists among the Lacandons."

"She says as much at the end of the codex. She writes that 'the pale' one continues the B'aakal lineage."

The implications hit me like a freight train. My heart skipped several beats and tears arose in my eyes. Charlie had to say it, for I was left too stunned to speak.

"Unless I'm off my trolley, your ancestors came from Pakal's lineage," he slowly intoned. "Your grandmother's secrets, and the strange ways of your family, come from the heritage of shaman-kings, of women visionaries and seers, of the divinely ordained B'aakal dynasty."

When I dried my tears and tried to collect myself, I was surprised to see Charlie kneeling before me, both arms crossed over his chest in classic Mayan posture of ultimate homage.

"What are you doing?" I gasped.

"Trying to strike the correct pose for honoring Maya royalty," he replied with a wicked twinkle in his blue eyes. "And also, trying to figure out how an ordinary bloke would propose marriage to a Mayan princess."

June 21, 2012

The summer solstice sun shone brightly over the filigreed roofcombs of the Cross Group at Palenque. Tucked at the foot of steep mountains heavily forested with lush greenery and bordered on one side by a burbling stream, the three temples faced onto a grassy plaza. Centuries of weather had darkened the whiteness of their stucco walls, eons of neglect had permitted platforms and stairs to crumble, relentless grasses and shrubs encroached on foundations. Walls had fallen away leaving arched ceilings exposed; roofcombs had deteriorated into fragments of still-graceful filigrees. But the erosion of time could not conceal the powerful symmetry or the imposing elegance of the heart of Lakam Ha.

Many visitors think the central plaza, the largest open area once paved with gleaming white plaster, now covered by grassy lawns, is the heart of the city. It is the first space visitors see as they enter the ruins, climbing over multiple stepped platforms from the parking lot filled with food and vendor booths. It is natural to assume this, since the central plaza is framed by the Temple of the Inscriptions, Temples XIII and XII in a line on one side, and the impressive Palace with its unique square tower and maze of interior buildings on the other. During Pakal's reign, the central plaza was the core area of the city he had constructed. When his oldest son Kan Bahlam II became ruler, the focus shifted to the Cross Group. Kan Bahlam did this deliberately, creating a stone and plaster earthly replication of the Three-Stone Sky Hearth of Maya Creation mythology, the Belt of Orion suspended from the Milky Way in the Turtle Constellation, the place where the original hearthstones of Maya creation were placed.

The three pyramids of the Triad Cross Group held huge panels on walls of their interior temples telling the unique Palenque creation story. Kan Bahlam is featured on all three panels, both as a youth and an adult, re-enacting the birth and charge of the Palenque Triad Gods. These three Gods, sons of the Primordial Mother Muwaan Mat, gave their special powers and abilities to Lakam Ha rulers, who assumed their personas during rituals. In the Cross Group panels, Kan Bahlam has become each of the Gods in succession, telling their mythology and embedding his personal accomplishments into the narrative. Here he conducted calendar rituals with the population of Lakam Ha gathered in the spacious plaza. A central altar formed a focus for ceremonies and received offerings.

The Cross Group pyramids are situated in alignments to express solar and lunar phenomenon, particularly the solstices and equinoxes. One special alignment happens as the summer solstice sun drops behind the Temple of the Inscriptions. Sunrays stream through the top chamber for a few moments, entering the west window and traveling the long axis of the rectangular structure to exit the east window. From there the rays project across the Otolum River to the Temple of the Cross and highlight the stairway ascending the tallest pyramid of the Cross Group. Once a stela stood upon that exact spot, the only stela ever carved in Palenque. Kan Bahlam II was portrayed on it. Fragments have been found, but the stela is mostly destroyed.

On this summer solstice, 1300 years after the Cross Group was built, its plaza is again filled with people. Men and women dressed in white form circles, chant, and dance to drums and flutes. These are modern pilgrims coming to do ceremony and honor the ancient Mayas. Many groups are led by Mayan elders and priests, who teach the wisdom and rituals of their culture. Faces of pilgrims reflect numerous cultures and countries, skin black or brown or yellow or white, eyes round or almond or slanted. Languages from around the world are heard. The stone cities once lost in the jungle, the deep knowledge and mystical practices of this great ancient culture now newly expressed, draw these people to the Maya lands.

This particular summer solstice is important, and the crowds in Palenque are exceptionally large. It is the year of a period ending, the closure on the 13th Baktun, the completion of a large cycle in the Mayan calendar. Some have speculated the ending of the Mayan calendar on December 21, 2012 signifies a time of catastrophe, an Armageddon, the "end of the world." But, those who understand the Maya ways of time-keeping know one cycle always rolls into the next. If indeed that date marks the closing of Baktun 13—and we Mayanists disagree on correlating the Mayan and Gregorian calendars—then what happens next is the start of a new era. The current Fourth Maya Sun, an era or world age, a period of 5125 solar years or 5200 tuns, eases its burden into the Fifth Maya Sun. And so, the next era begins and the cycles repeat again and again.

I waited patiently as the midsummer sun slowly dropped toward the horizon. The three of us were sitting on an upper step of the Temple of the Cross—Charlie, myself, and our daughter Elena, named after her mysterious ancestor Ele. The crowds of pilgrims began thinning as the park closing at 5:00 pm approached and shadows lengthened across the plazas. We, however, had permission to stay until after the solar phenomenon that would occur in about an hour. Being a famous archeologist has its benefits.

Elena is seven years old, born a year after Charlie and I married. She is an energetic and dauntingly smart child, with clear blue eyes and a head of unruly cocoa ringlets. I'm glad her hair is curly like his instead of straight like mine. In her slender tan face play traces of her Mayan ancestry, with a long straight nose, high cheekbones, and full, sculpted lips. Impossibly thick, dark lashes frame her almond-shaped eyes. She was going to be a knock-out and brilliant as well—look out you machismos!

We wanted Elena to experience her Mayan legacy at this most meaningful time. On several occasions we reviewed the Palenque dynasty with her and traced its continuation through the Nokom family of Tumbala. She easily understood that her ancestors had built this magnificent stone city spread before her eyes, and that all the people in white doing ceremonies were honoring their accomplishments. Earlier we had taken her down the steep interior stairway of the Temple of the Inscriptions to see Pakal's crypt and sarcophagus, and inside Temple XIII to view the empty sarcophagus of the Red Queen. Just a few months ago studies comparing DNA samples from the Red Queen's bones with those of Pakal reported they did not share common DNA. This virtually confirms that his wife, Tz'aakb'u Ahau, was interred in the pyramid adjoining his. We pointed out the panels covered with hieroglyphs in Pakal's and Kan Bahlam's pyramid temples that told her people's history and cosmology.

"Your ancestors did all this," we said. "You have much to be proud of. You are the descendant of the rulers of a great people."

Her eyes followed the sun's descent with anticipation. She had seen drawings of the sunrays streaming from the chamber of Pakal's temple to light up the stairs where we sat. To commemorate the occasion, my friend and colleague Sonia Cardenas was stationed at the entry to the Temple of the Sun with camera in hand. When the moment came, she would take photos of us, illuminated in golden light. Elena would have a memento of standing in the steps of her ancestors.

As the first brilliant rays highlighted the upper roofcomb of Pakal's temple, we moved Elena into position. Moments later sunlight streamed from the chamber onto the stairway, glinting from her widened eyes and wrapping a golden glow around her face. She smiled and held up her hands, palms open to receive K'in Ahau's blessings. After a moment we knelt beside her so Sonia could get photos of the family bathed in sunlight.

When the sun dropped below the trees and dusk quickly settled, Charlie wrapped us both in his arms and kissed our cheeks. Three pairs of lively blue eyes misted and we laughed.

"I guess all our children will have blue eyes," Charlie murmured. "Mendelian genetics, you know." He gently caressed the bulge of my tummy where our second child was just starting to show. Lifting my head, I brushed lips against his.

"Uh-huh. They'll all have the uay mark . . . the legacy lives on."

END

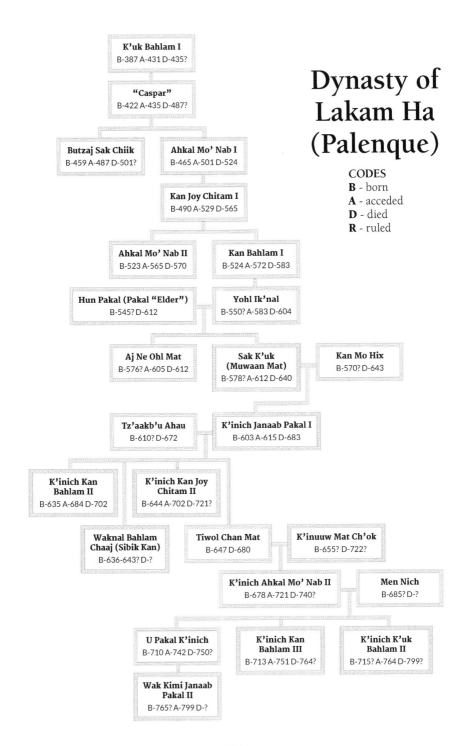

Dynasty of Lakam Ha (Palenque)

CODES
B - born
A - acceded
D - died
R - ruled

K'uk Bahlam I
B-387 A-431 D-435?

"Caspar"
B-422 A-435 D-487?

Butzaj Sak Chiik
B-459 A-487 D-501?

Ahkal Mo' Nab I
B-465 A-501 D-524

Kan Joy Chitam I
B-490 A-529 D-565

Ahkal Mo' Nab II
B-523 A-565 D-570

Kan Bahlam I
B-524 A-572 D-583

Hun Pakal (Pakal "Elder")
B-545? D-612

Yohl Ik'nal
B-550? A-583 D-604

Aj Ne Ohl Mat
B-576? A-605 D-612

Sak K'uk (Muwaan Mat)
B-578? A-612 D-640

Kan Mo Hix
B-570? D-643

Tz'aakb'u Ahau
B-610? D-672

K'inich Janaab Pakal I
B-603 A-615 D-683

K'inich Kan Bahlam II
B-635 A-684 D-702

K'inich Kan Joy Chitam II
B-644 A-702 D-721?

Waknal Bahlam Chaaj (Sibik Kan)
B-636-643? D-?

Tiwol Chan Mat
B-647 D-680

K'inuuw Mat Ch'ok
B-655? D-722?

K'inich Ahkal Mo' Nab II
B-678 A-721 D-740?

Men Nich
B-685? D-?

U Pakal K'inich
B-710 A-742 D-750?

K'inich Kan Bahlam III
B-713 A-751 D-764?

K'inich K'uk Bahlam II
B-715? A-764 D-799?

Wak Kimi Janaab Pakal II
B-765? A-799 D-?

Alliances Among Maya Cities

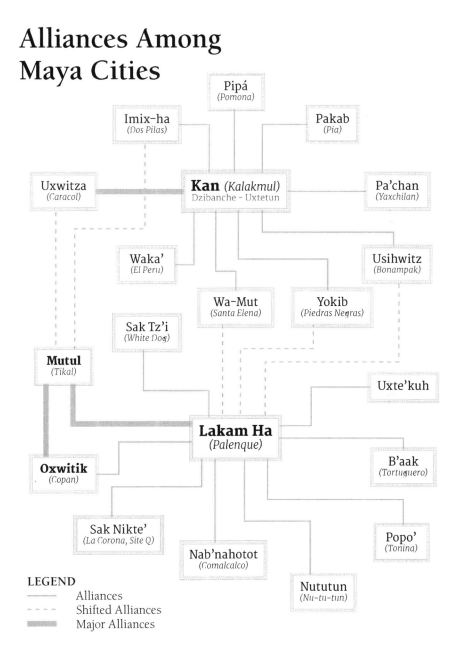

Pipá
(Pomona)

Imix-ha
(Dos Pilas)

Pakab
(Pia)

Uxwitza
(Caracol)

Kan *(Kalakmul)*
Dzibanche – Uxtetun

Pa'chan
(Yaxchilan)

Waka'
(El Peru)

Usihwitz
(Bonampak)

Wa-Mut
(Santa Elena)

Yokib
(Piedras Negras)

Sak Tz'i
(White Dog)

Mutul
(Tikal)

Uxte'kuh

Lakam Ha
(Palenque)

Oxwitik
(Copan)

B'aak
(Tortuguero)

Sak Nikte'
(La Corona, Site Q)

Popo'
(Tonina)

Nab'nahotot
(Comalcalco)

Nututun
(Nu-tu-tun)

LEGEND
- Alliances
- Shifted Alliances
- Major Alliances

Long Count Maya Calendar

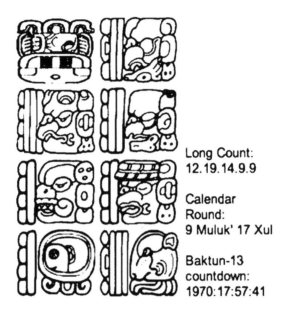

Long Count:
12.19.14.9.9

Calendar
Round:
9 Muluk' 17 Xul

Baktun-13
countdown:
1970:17:57:41

Although considered a vigesimal (20 base) system, the Maya used modifications in two places for calendric and numerological reasons. In Classic times the counts went from 0 to 19 in all but the 2nd position, in which they went from 0 to 19 in all but the 2nd position, in which they went from 0 to 17. Postclassic adaptations changed the counts to begin with 1, making them 1 to 20 and 1 to 18.

Mayan Name	Count	Solar Years	Tun
Baktun	0-19 144000 kin = 20 Katun = 1 Baktun	394.25	400
Katun	0-19 7200 kin = 20 Tun = 1 Katun	19.71	20
Tun	0-19 360 kin = 18 Uinal = 1 Tun	0.985	1
Uinal	0-17 20 kin = 20 Kin = 1 Uinal		
Kin	0-19 1 kin = 1 Kin		

After 19 Kin occur, the Uinal count goes up by 1 on the next day; after 17 Uinal the Tun count goes up by 1 on the next day, after 19 Tun the Katun

count goes up by 1 the next day, and after 19 Katun the Baktun count goes up by 1 the next day.

Thus, we see this progression in the Long Count:
11.19.19.17.19 + 1 kin (day) = 12.0.0.0.0

Increasingly larger units of time beyond the Baktun are: Piktun, Kalabtun, Kinchiltun, and Alautun. These were usually noted by placing 13 in the counts larger than Baktun, indicating 13 to a multiple of the 20th power:

13.13.13.13.13.0.0.0.0

When a 13 Baktun is reached, this signifies the end of a Great Cycle of 1,872,000 kins (days) or 5200 tuns (5125.2567 solar years). But this does not signify the end of the Maya calendar. Larger baktun units occur on stela with numbers above 13, indicating that this count went up to 19 before converting into the next higher unit in the 6th position. When the 5th position (Baktun) reaches 19, on the following day the 6th position (Pictun) becomes 1 and the 5th position becomes 0. This results in a Long Count such as that projected by glyphs at Palenque to a Gregorian date of 4772 AD (GMT correlation), written as 1.0.0.0.0.0.

The Tzolk'in and Haab Calendars

The Tzolk'in (Sacred Calendar)

The Tzolk'in is a ceremonial calendar that orders the times for performing rituals honoring the Maya Deities. It is the oldest known Mesoamerican calendar cycle, dating back to around 600 BCE. The Tzolk'in has a 260-day count, believed to be based on the nine months of human gestation which averages 260 days. The mathematics of the Tzolk'in combines 13 numbers with 20 day names: 13 x 20 = 260. Mayan culture assigns the value 13 to the circle, a sacred number representing spirit and movement. This number also represents the 13 great articulations of the human skeleton, the 13 yearly cycles of the moon, the 13 planets known to the ancient Mayas, and the 13 constellations of the Maya zodiac. Additionally, they subdivided the day into 13 segments each divisible by 13, similar to modern hours, minutes and seconds.

The Maya "month" has 20 days, each with a name. To create the Tzolk'in, each day is combined with a number between 1—13. Since 20 is not evenly divisible by 13, the two sequences do not pair exactly. When the 13th number is reached, the count starts again at 1 while the day names continue from day 14 through day 20. This forms unique combinations until the numbers and names run through a complete 260-day cycle. Then, the Tzolk'in count starts again at day 1 and number 1.

The Haab (Solar Calendar)

The Haab is considered a secular or agricultural calendar, was in use by at least 100 BCE, and has deeply significant numerology. It is composed of 18 "months" of 20 days, creating a mathematical system that resonates through vast cycles and synchronizes with many other calendars through its multiples: 18 x 20 = 360. Each month has a name, combined with a number between 1—20 which is assigned to each day. In ancient Maya counting, the month begins with a "seating" that is recorded as zero, and then the patron deity of the month assumes the throne on day 1 and reigns for the next 19 days. The Haab is used to track solstices, equinoxes and eclipses of moon and sun. Since the Haab count is 360 days, it does not match the solar year of 365.25 days, and the Mayas add a short 5-day "month" to coordinate with the sun's annual cycle. They account for the fractional day by adding one day to the count every four years.

In ancient hieroglyphic texts, the Haab date is recorded next to a Tzolk'in date. This appears as a month name-number combination next to a day name-number combination: 4 Kan 12 Pax, for example. In operation together, the Tzolk'in and Haab create a larger, 52-year cycle called the Tunben K'ak or New Fire Cycle. It is known as the Calendar Round, and is used widely throughout Mesoamerica. The Haab also synchronizes with the Tzek'eb or Great Calendar of the Suns, which tracks cycles of the Pleiades over 26,000 years.

Most Mayan texts that track time combine a Long Count date with a Tzolk'in-Haab date. Using these two separate systems for counting time, the Mayas present amazingly accurate dates.

About the Author

L eonide (Lennie) Martin: Retired California State University professor, former Family Nurse Practitioner, Author and Maya researcher, Research Member Maya Exploration Center.

My books bring ancient Maya culture and civilization to life in stories about both actual historical Mayans and fictional characters. I've studied Maya archeology, anthropology, and history from the scientific and indigenous viewpoints. While living for five years in Mérida, Yucatán, Mexico, I apprenticed with Maya Elder Hunbatz Men, becoming a Solar Initiate and Maya Fire Women in the Itzá Maya tradition. I've studied with other indigenous teachers in Guatemala, including Maya Priestess-Daykeeper Aum Rak Sapper and Maya elder Tata Pedro. The ancient Mayas created the most highly advanced civilization in the Western hemisphere, and my work is dedicated to their wisdom, spirituality, scientific, and cultural accomplishments through compelling historical novels.

My interest in ancient Mayan women led to writing the Mayan Queens' series called *Mists of Palenque*. This 4-book series tells the stories of powerful women who shaped the destinies of their people as rulers themselves, or wives of rulers. These remarkable Mayan women are unknown to most people. Using extensive research and field study, I aspire to depict ancient Palenque authentically and make these amazing Mayan Queens accessible to a wide readership.

My writing has won awards from Writer's Digest for short fiction, and *The Visionary Mayan Queen: Yohl Ik'nal of Palenque (Mists of Palenque Series Book 1)* received the Writer's Digest 2nd Annual Self-Published eBook award in 2015. *The Mayan Red Queen: Tz'aakb'u Ahau of Palenque (Mists of Palenque Series Book 3)* received a Silver Medal in Dan Poynter's Global eBook Awards for 2016.

Presently I live with my husband David Gortner and two white cats in Oregon's Willamette Valley wine country.

For more information about my writing and the Mayas, visit:
Website: **www.mistsofpalenque.com**
Blog: **http://leonidemartinblog.wordpress.com/**
Facebook: **https://www.facebook.com/leonide.martin**

Author Notes

Writing the story of K'inuuw Mat, fourth queen in my *Mists of Palenque* series, required a large dose of imagination. Of the four queens, the least is known about K'inuuw Mat, although a great deal is known about the men who were part of her life. The few recorded historical and archeological facts are quickly summarized: K'inuuw Mat was a royal woman from another city in Palenque polity, possible Uxte'kuh located on the Tabasco plains. She married Pakal's youngest son Tiwol Chan Mat, who died at age 33 and never ascended to the throne, although Pakal did include him when setting succession. After Pakal's death, his oldest son Kan Bahlam II became ruler for 18 years, followed by the second son Kan Joy Chitam II on the throne for 19 years. Neither of these rulers had surviving sons, so succession passed to Pakal's grandson by the youngest son Tiwol and K'inuuw Mat. Pakal had decreed male succession after the "irregularities" of two female rulers in his own descent.

Ahkal Mo' Nab III, son of K'inuuw Mat and grandson of Pakal, became ruler in 721 CE at the age of forty-three. He ruled for 19 years and was succeeded by his oldest son U Pakal K'inich for 8 years and his second son K'ak Bahlam II for 35 years. The last recorded ruler of Palenque, Wak Kimi Janaab Pakal, was possibly a grandson of Ahkal Mo' Nab. He apparently acceded in 799 CE but almost nothing is known about him.

K'inuuw Mat is depicted on a carved tablet from the residential complex Group IV called "The Tablet of the Slaves." She is seated to the left of her son Ahkal Mo' Nab, offering him a K'awiil icon symbolizing royal lineage. Seated at the right is the ruler's father, Tiwol Chan Mat holding up the drum-major hat of rulership. The name glyphs of both parents appear in the inscribed hieroglyphs above their heads. Although certainly the father, and probably the mother were deceased when Ahkal Mo' Nab acceded, they are shown as youthful people in typical Palenque style.

With these few facts, I took considerable artistic license in creating the background and character of K'inuuw Mat. Drawing on themes in Book 3, *The Mayan Red Queen: Tz'aakb'u Ahau of Palenque*, I gave her a family connection with Goddess Ix Chel and the women's island Cuzamil (Cozumel), where she yearned to live and serve. There she learned scrying skills that were tools for her gift of prophecy. But destiny called her to become a royal wife at Palenque (Lakam Ha) and continue the dynasty by marrying Pakal's youngest son. The second theme carried over from Book 3 was the ambition of Kan Bahlam II to rule Palenque, though his elderly father Pakal refused to die, living to 80 years. Considerable data is available about the lives of Kan Bahlam II and his brother Kan Joy Chitam II, so I used this information to help shape events in the story. As with all my stories of Mayan queens, I remained true to events and timelines recorded historically.

K'inich Kan Bahlam II is regarded by Mayanists as a creative genius. He was forty-eight years old when he finally assumed the throne, and eager to leave his imprint on the city. One priority was finishing construction and decoration of his father's funerary structure, the Temple of the Inscriptions. He led his forces in a decisive victory against Tonina (Popo'), killing the ruler and spreading Palenque's power eastward. His major accomplishment was building the Cross Group, a triadic temple arrangement reflecting the three cosmic hearthstones of Maya creation and re-telling his city's origin mythology in lengthy hieroglyphs. Rich in symbolism and history, these are considered "the most revealing temples in the entire ancient Maya world" by noted archeologists David and George Stuart. Kan Bahlam also developed an astronumerological language called Zuyua and created the 819-day calendar count to interweave celestial patterns with worldly events in his own history and Palenque mythology. He cultivated a group of intellectual collaborators, members of the royal court and eventually nobles from other cities, who maintained power through Zuyua coded language and astronomical symbolism. His Cross Group constructions, language codes, and astronumerology were intended to maintain Lakam Ha's prominent place for generations to come.

There is no historic evidence for a relationship between K'inuuw Mat and Kan Bahlam. Their immediate, magnetic attraction, and how this played out in their lives, is entirely my creation. No details about family relations during the reigns of Kan Bahlam and Kan Joy Chitam have survived, but we do know the latter was defeated and possibly held captive by Tonina for around 10 years. Succession was no doubt a sensitive matter. Since these two sons of Pakal had no male heirs, it became crucial that K'inuuw Mat and Tiwol Chan Mat have a son. This gave an opening to insert drama in the family story. Though K'inuuw Mat resisted the attraction to Kan Bahlam, he found opportunity in this need for producing a son to contrive the "joint conception" of my story. His motives were mixed and so were hers; this seems a human propensity. It added spice and gave cause for interpersonal conflict, all necessary for an engaging story arc. It also gave a believable reason for Ahkal Mo' Nab, nephew of the prior two rulers, to succeed—since in my story Kan Bahlam considers him to be his own son.

Nothing is known about Kan Bahlam's wife, though certainly he would have married and tried to produce an heir. Kan Bahlam's purported sterility due to jungle fever is my creation. Tiwol Chan Mat's early death is recorded, but not how he died. The widowed K'inuuw Mat's marriage to Kan Bahlam (whose wife committed suicide for her traitorous deeds in my story) is another completely invented situation. It gave a poetic completeness to their passionate relationship. Her role as muse for his creative efforts, and her prophetic mandate to preserve Mayan culture for future generations, are also fictional.

There is no record that K'inuuw Mat and Tiwol Chan Mat had any other children than Ahkal Mo' Nab II. However, women would not have been recorded unless they became wives of rulers or ruled themselves. So, the daughters are all fictional characters. Thanks to suggestions of a beta reader, I constructed the twin birth that nearly killed K'inuuw Mat and gave Kan Bahlam a heroic role during delivery. The albino daughter Sak'uay grew into a strong character completely unforeseen in initial planning of the story. She became the link to future generations, both through her scribal skills and by hiding caches in caves, and through her family descendents who eventually led to modern archeologist Francesca Nokom Gutierrez.

The archeological Field Journal written by Francesca brings everything together in this final installation. It was no small challenge to tie all the strands in believable ways, and I hope that I've achieved that. As Francesca explores her Mayan roots and develops her intuitive skills by reading the "lightning in the blood," she realizes her personal link to Lakam Ha and the Bahlam dynasty. The long saga involving the foreign woman Elie and her mystical relationship with first Mayan queen Yohl Ik'nal draws to a conclusion. The attainments of the Mayan queens including Yohl Ik'nal, Sak K'uk, Tz'aakb'u Ahau (Lalak), and K'inuuw Mat are recorded in a women's codex by Sak'uay to be discovered by distant descendent Francesca, aided by her colleague and later husband Charlie Courtney, British linguist. Francesca and Charlie bring their first daughter to Palenque for 2012 summer solstice, where the girl experiences the greatness of her Maya ancestors.

Pilgrims from around the world perform ceremonies in the plaza of the Cross Group. The world recognizes the magnificent accomplishments of Mayan civilization. The ancestors are honored. The cycle is complete.

Notes on Orthography
(Pronunciation)

Orthography involves how to spell and pronounce Mayan words in another language such as English or Spanish. The initial approach used English-based alphabets with a romance language sound for vowels:

Hun – Hoon	Ne – Nay	Xoc – Shoke	Ix – Eesh
Ik – Eek	Yohl – Yole	Mat – Maat	May – Maie
Sak – Sahk	Ahau – Ah-how	Yum – Yoom	Ek – Ehk

Consonants of note are:

H – Him	J – Jar	X – "sh"
T – Tz or Dz	Ch – Child	

Mayan glottalized sounds are indicated by an apostrophe, and pronounced with a break in sound made in the back of the throat:

B'aakal	K'uk	Ik'nal	Ka'an	Tz'ak

Later the Spanish pronunciations took precedence. The orthography standardized by the Academia de Lenguas Mayas de Guatemala is used by most current Mayanists. The major difference is how H and J sound:

H – practically silent, only a soft aspiration as in hombre (ombray)
J – soft "h" as in house or Jose (Hosay)

There is some thought among linguists that the ancient Maya had different sounds for "h" and "j," leading to more dilemma. Many places, roads, people's names and other vocabulary have been pronounced for years in the old system. The Guatemala approach is less used in Mexico, and many words in my book are taken from Yucatek Mayan. So, I've decided to keep the Hun spelling rather than Jun for the soft "h." But for Pakal, I've resorted to Janaab rather than Hanab, the older spelling. I have an intuition that his name was meant by the ancient Mayas to have the harder "j" of English; this gives a more powerful sound.

For the Mayan word Lord—Ahau—I use the older spelling. You will see it written Ahaw and Ajaw in different publications. For English speakers, Ahau leads to natural pronunciation of the soft "h" and encourages a longer ending sound with the "u" rather than "w."

Scholarly tradition uses the word Maya to modify most nouns, such as Maya people and Maya sites, except when referring to language and writing, when Mayan is used instead. Ordinary usage is flexible, however, with Mayan used more broadly as in Mayan civilization or Mayan astronomy. I follow this latter approach in my writing.

Names of ancient Maya cities posed challenges. Spanish explorers or international archeologists assigned most of the commonly used names. Many original city names have been deciphered, however, and I use these whenever they exist. Some cities have conflicting names, so I chose the one that made sense to me. The rivers were even more problematic. Many river names are my own creation, using Mayan words that best describe their characteristics. I provide a list of contemporary names for cities and rivers along with the Mayan names used in the story.

Acknowledgements

It takes a village to raise a child, and it takes a worldwide network of experts to research a civilization. Over two-and-a-half centuries of Maya exploration and research underlie these stories of Mayan queens. Ranging from 17th Century adventurers venturing by foot to find fabled cities of stone in deep jungles to 21st Century Lidar technologists in aircraft mapping footprints of cities buried under centuries of foliage, a long line deserves acknowledgement. Experts from many disciplines have contributed, including archeology, anthropology, history, epigraphy, linguistics, ethnology, art history, and iconography who have added to our understanding of the rich and complex Mayan culture. My profound gratitude to all the experts in these fields whose work has given me a foundation for creating characters, settings, and events.

Several writers' and researchers' work has especially helped shape my creation of setting, characters, and plot of **The Prophetic Mayan Queen: K'inuuw Mat of Palenque**.

Rosita Arvigo left the U.S. to study traditional healing in Mesoamerica, apprenticing with a Mayan master of plant medicine in Belize, Don Elijio Panti. In her books *Sastun: My Apprenticeship with a Maya Healer* (Harper San Francisco, 1994) and *Rainforest Remedies: One Hundred Healing Herbs of Belize* (Lotus Press, 1998) she describes her studies and spiritual journey to inherit his work. These books provided essential information for healing and divinatory aspects of Maya culture. In her novel *The Oracle of Ix Chel* (Story Bridge Books, 2015) I learned a great deal about the women's island of Cuzamil (Cozumel) and the elaborate processes of oracular prophecy. I feel deeply indebted to Dr. Arvigo and heartened to find another author writing fiction about ancient Mayan women.

The works of several women scholars provided background about roles of ancient Mayan women: Traci Ardren, Inga Clendinnen, and Andrea Stone. For information about how ancient Maya royal courts were populated and functioned, I am indebted to Takeshi Inomata and Stephen D. Houston, editors of **Royal Courts of the Ancient Maya** (Westview Press, 2001) and Sarah Jackson who authored **Politics of the Maya Court** (University of Oklahoma Press, 2013).

I returned over and over to the foundational work of David Stuart and his father George Stuart (Stuart & Stuart: *Palenque, Eternal City of the Maya*, 2008). The Stuart's detailed work on Palenque's history was invaluable, helping me see the city and its rulers in a broad context. Especially helpful were descriptions of the Cross Group temples and inscriptions. David Stuart's exquisite renditions of carvings and inscriptions from Temple XIX tablets informed my understanding of later rulers, especially Ahkal Mo' Nab and his sons. (Stuart, D: *The Inscriptions from Temple XIX at Palenque*, 2005). His translations of the glyphic texts from the temples of the Cross Group were invaluable in creating my rendition of Kan Bahlam's re-telling the Palenque Creation Mythology (Stuart, D: *The Palenque Mythology: Inscriptions from the Cross Group at Palenque*, University of Texas at Austin, Sourcebook for The 2006 Maya Meetings).

Gerardo Aldana's brilliant doctoral research, published in book form (Aldana: *The Apotheosis of Janaab' Pakal*, 2007) provided an exceptional basis for the astronomical and numerology achievements of Kan Bahlam II. Aldana described these amazing calendric accomplishments exemplified in the 819-day count, what he termed "K'awiilian astronomy," and the Zuyua coded language used to maintain elite power.

Edwin Barnhart generously gave me permission to use and adapt his maps to provide visual images of Palenque as it spread across a narrow ridge of the Sierra Madre de Chiapas Mountains. The many rivers and cascades crossing the ridge gave the ancient name Lakam Ha, "Place of Big Waters." Dr. Barnhart directed the Palenque Mapping Project, uncovering numerous hidden structures in the old section and demonstrating that Palenque was a very large city. His detailed maps guided me time and again in spatial locations within the city so I could envision the layout of plazas, palace complexes, residences, and temple-pyramids.

Alonso Mendez, Edwin Barnhart, Christopher Powell, and Carol Karasik compiled descriptions of solar and lunar phenomena that involve the Cross Group, especially the Temple of the Sun and Temple of the Cross. (*Astronomical Observations from the Temple of the Sun*, Maya Exploration Center, 2008). The Mayas purposefully linked natural phenomena, human society, and the divine through astronomical alignments during the solstices, equinoxes, zenith and nadir passages of the sun; as well as lunar stations. Kan Bahlam II particularly employed this symbolism to proclaim his royal power and his embodiments of stellar deities and ancestors. This work was essential to my understanding of these alignments.

Dennis Tedlock has gifted anyone interested in the Mayas by providing lyrical translations of several ancient and colonial Maya documents (Tedlock:

2000 Years of Mayan Literature, University of California Press, 2010). He gives both phonetic Classic Cholan and English translations of the words written by actual Maya scribes over 1500 years ago. Tedlock is best known for his poetic rendition of the *Popol Vuh*, story of Maya creation mythology. From these examples I created a style for ceremonial language that followed the sentence structure and cadence used by ancient scribes. Mayan language follows a verb-object-subject (VSO) sequence while English follows the subject-verb-object (SVO) word order. Many Mesoamerican languages use VSO. I used VSO for dialogue in many instances, to maintain the feel of a different culture and reflect Mayan speech patterns: VSO—"Loves she him." SVO—"She loves him." Words were sacred to the Mayas and filled with life essence, *itz*.

Theories about the "Maya collapse" that occurred around 900 CE emerge in this final book in the *Mists of Palenque* series. New research appears frequently examining the many factors involved: overpopulation, warfare, competition for resources, ideological decline and failure of the kingship system, drought and environmental degradation; all leading to malnutrition, disease, lowered birthrate, social disintegration. The most thorough book on Maya collapse is by David Webster, using Copan as a case example (*The Fall of the Ancient Maya: Solving the Mystery of the Maya Collapse*, Thames & Hudson, 2002).

For Palenque, overpopulation and outstripping agricultural capacity seem prominent. No ultimate disaster struck; rather, common people just began leaving and the elite could no longer sustain their lifestyle. There is no sign of battle destruction or burning. I used the ideas put forth by Edwin Barnhart that the abandonment of Palenque seemed a unified and peaceable decision made by the consensus of a council (*Palenque's Settlement Pattern and Social Organization*, Maya Exploration.org, 2005).

To my beta readers and Maya Visions Facebook Team, my warmest thanks for all your support. Your early ideas and feedback shaped how the story evolved, and guided me in editing out overly technical sections.

To my publishing and editing team at Made For Success, this venture would have been impossible without your know-how and encouragement. You're the greatest!

Other Works By Author

The Visionary Mayan Queen:
Yohl Ik'nal of Palenque
Mists of Palenque: Series Book 1

Amazon Kindle Top 100 Books, Amazon #1 in Historical Fiction and Historical Fiction Romance – Ancient Worlds

 Writer's Digest Self-Published eBook Award in Mainstream/ Literary Fiction for 2015

In misty tropical jungles 1500 years ago, a royal Mayan girl with visionary powers—Yohl Ik'nal—was destined to become the first Mayan woman ruler. Last of her royal lineage, her accession would fulfill her father's ambitions. Yohl Ik'nal put aside personal desires and the comfortable world of palace women to prepare as royal heir. Love for her father steeled her will and sharpened her skills. As she underwent intensive training for rulership, powerful forces allied to overthrow the dynasty and plotted with enemy cities to attack.

As the first Queen of Palenque, she built temples to honor her father and her Gods, protected her city and brought prosperity to the people. Her visionary powers foresaw enemy attack and prevented defeat. In the midst of betrayal and revenge, through court intrigues and power struggles, she guided her people wisely and found a love that sustained her. As a seer, she knew times of turmoil were coming and succession to the throne was far from certain. Could she prepare her headstrong daughter for rulership or help her weak son become a charismatic leader? Her actions could lead to ruin or bring her city to greatness.

Centuries later Francesca, part-Mayan archeologist, helps her team at Palenque excavate the royal burial of a crimson skeleton, possibly the first Mayan queen's tomb ever discovered. She never anticipated how it would impact her life and unravel a web of ancient bonds.

Praise from Reviewers and Readers:

"A story that is fully imagined yet as real as the ancient past that it gives voice to once again . . . The characters here are fully realized, vivid and alive, and often do surprising things . . . The reader is able to understand the truth of these people's lives and struggles while also welcomed in to a conception of the world that is bigger than anything they might have expected or experienced before."

~ Writer's Digest 2nd Annual Self-Published eBook Awards (2015)

". . . storytelling that leaves you breathless and amazed at the life Yohl Ik'nal leads as she uses her visionary ability . . . in an era of uncertainty. It's about royalty and leadership, about family and strength, determination and faith."

~ The Bookreader Review

"Spellbinding, exciting and beautifully paints a picture (of) the world of the ancient royal Mayan Queens."

~ S. Malbeouf

"A page turner . . . draws the reader in with the drama of the era . . . One can smell the incense, feel the tension, share the spirituality, experience the battles, and live the lives of the characters."

~ H. and N. Rath

". . . vibrant storytelling, strong dialogue and authentic characters . . . that ring true to the Mayan culture . . . stunning job of keeping this story fast-paced, compelling, emotional and engaging to the very end."

~ S. Gallardo

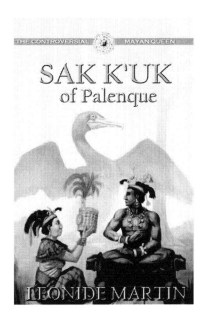

The Controversial Mayan Queen:
Sak K'uk of Palenque
Mists of Palenque: Series Book 2

Amazon Kindle Top 100 Books, Amazon #1 in Historical Fiction and Historical Fiction Romance – Ancient Worlds

Strong-willed Sak K'uk, daughter of Yohl Ik'nal, assumes rulership of Lakam Ha after her brother is killed in the devastating attack by arch-enemy Kan, which leaves her people in chaos. She faces dissident nobles and spiritual crisis caused by destruction of the sacred portal to the Gods. Undertaking a perilous Underworld journey, she invokes the power of Primordial Goddess Muwaan Mat to help her accede to the throne and hold it for her son, Janaab Pakal, until he is old enough to become ruler. His destiny is to restore the portal and bring Lakiam Ha to greatness. Their intense trials together forge a special bond that proves both a blessing and a curse.

In modern times archeologist Francesca continues her quest to uncover the identity of the crimson skeleton found by her team in a rich burial at Palenque. Further examination of the bones confirms that the skeleton was a royal and important woman, dubbed The Red Queen. Francesca is also perplexed by her grandmother's cryptic message to discover her true self by listening to the lightning in her blood.

Praise from Reviewers and Readers:

"Martin's writing and characterization are both excellent . . . she writes with loving detail about . . . Mayan life . . . The story is a seamless blend of history and mythology . . . Sak K'uk believes that Pakal is meant to be the next ruler . . . (but) Ek Chuuah, who was injured and exiled . . . will stop at nothing to harm the royal family, even to the point of devising a plan to desecrate one of their holiest shrines . . . can't wait to read the third book in the series."

~ Jo Niederhoff, The Seattle Book Review (2017)

"The Controversial Mayan Queen... is well-done, entertaining, and revealing... profile of a Mayan leader simultaneously struggling with family life and the future of her people... the emotionally charged and complex relationship between Sak K'uk and her son... lends it an extra dimension that is unexpectedly and compellingly engrossing."

~ Diane Donovan, Editor and Senior Reviewer,
The Midwest Book Review

"The author has great skills at world building and crafting a story that will keep the reader engaged and entertained from cover to cover. Great author voice and writing style . . . an entertaining mix."

~ Writer's Digest (2016)

"Beautifully written account of the Mayans, their culture, and how one woman held them together! This book gives the reader an inside view of this ancient culture and the reader just can't help but learn something from it! I guarantee if you like ancient history told in story form as I do, you won't be able to put this book down!

~ D (Amazon reviewer)

". . . this second book in the Mists of Palenque series . . . weaves a fascinating tale of the transition in the leadership of Lakam Ha after the reign of Yohl Ik'nal . . . reveals the interplay of events that allow the prophecies to be realized . . . The tale is a superb one and I highly recommend it for other readers.

~ *Peter H. Berasi*

"I have visited Palenque and other Mayan ruins, and Leonide Martin makes these cities come vividly alive for me . . . incredibly engaging scenes, her description is masterful . . . research is thorough . . . made me feel like I was walking through the world of the ancient Maya . . . I'm especially thrilled that the royal women of the Mayan culture are the focus of the series . . . fantastic supplemental reading in any class on ancient Mexico or Guatemala."

~ *M.M. Drew*

"If you are a history buff – or if you are not – you will enjoy this well researched and well written book . . . will open a window into pre-Columbian Central America and allow you to understand the habits, the beliefs, the culture and the values of the Maya . . . "wrapped" in a story that is interesting and intriguing. This book is going into my "read again" list . . . You won't go wrong buying this book. Settle down and enjoy it."

~ *A. Pabon*

The Mayan Red Queen:
Tz'aakb'u Ahau of Palenque
Mists of Palenque: Series Book 3

Silver Medal Winner – Dan Poynter's Global eBook Awards 2016

The ancient Maya city of Lakam Ha has a new, young ruler, K'inich Janaab Pakal. His mother and prior ruler, Sak K'uk, has selected his wife, later known as The Red Queen. Lalak is a shy and homely young woman from a nearby city who relates better to animals than people. She is chosen as Pakal's wife because of her pristine lineage to B'aakal dynasty founders—but also because she is no beauty. She is overwhelmed by the sophisticated and complex society at the polity's dominant city, and the expectations of the royal court. Her mother-in-law Sak K'uk chose Lalak for selfish motives, determined to find a wife who would not displace her in Pakal's affections. She viewed Lalak as a breeder of future rulers and selected her royal name to reflect this: Tz'aakb'u Ahau, the Accumulator of Lords who sets the royal succession.

Lalak struggles to learn her new role and prove her worth, puzzled by her mother-in-law's hostility and her husband's aloofness. She learns he is enamored of a beautiful woman banished from Lakam Ha by his mother. Pakal's esthetic tastes obscure his view of his homely wife. Lalak, however, is fated to play a pivotal role in Pakal's mission to restore the spiritual portal to the Triad Gods that was destroyed in a devastating attack by archenemy Kan. Trough learning sexual alchemy, Lalak brings the immense creative force of sacred union to rebuild the portal. But first Pakal must come to view his wife in a new light.

The naive, homely girl flowers into a woman of poise and power, establishes her place in court, and after several miscarriages that bring her marriage to crisis, she has four sons with Pakal to assure dynastic succession. Her dedication supports him in a renaissance of construction, art, and science that transforms Lakam Ha into the most widely sought creative center in the Classic Maya world.

Praise from Reviewers and Readers:

"The Mayan world and its underlying influences come alive, making for a thriller highly recommended for readers who also enjoy stories of archaeological wonders . . . Oracles and divine visions, priests and priestesses, goddesses and . . . malevolent forces: all these are drawn together in a clear portrait of ancient Mexico and the lush jungles surrounding Palenque."

~ Diane Donovan, Editor and Senior Reviewer,
The Midwest Book Review

"The quality of this novel is top notch . . . Lalak is lovely and beautifully written...crafting believable yet mythical characters that carry the story almost effortlessly. The plot was interesting and very unique . . . not predictable like so many books on the market these days . . . fans of complex world building will be absorbed by this one—with pleasure!

~ Writer's Digest 3rd Annual Self-Published e-Book Awards (2016)

". . . a fascinating journey into the life of the Mayan Red Queen . . . the story of Lalak, a kind, perceptive—and homely young woman who is whisked away from everything she knows to an arranged royal marriage. Mayan cities, Mayan art, music, and clothing is exemplified throughout . . .

pulses with ritual and sex magic . . . tastefully written with a beautiful weave of historical fact."

~ *East County Magazine (January 2015)*

"I absolutely loved this book! . . . a story of courage, patience and love . . . Historical fact, Mayan mysticism and the delightful imagination of this incredible author . . . makes me feel as if I had been there. So picturesque and beautiful. It was such a creative and inspiring story and I would encourage anyone to dive into this lovely world!

~ *Carol Clancy*

"*The Mayan Red Queen* is my favorite of this series so far! An outstanding read, and kept me so engaged that I hardly put it down . . . characters are thoroughly and carefully developed. Their issues are those with which we humans have grappled since the beginning of time . . . love, commitment, jealousy, revenge, duty, responsibility, and conflict resolution . . . Beautifully and affirmatively . . . illustrates the age old process of men and women searching for meaning in their lives. . ."

~ *Cheryl Randall*

Dreaming the Maya Fifth Sun: A Novel of Maya Wisdom and the 2012 Shift in Consciousness

The lives of two women, one modern and one an ancient Maya priestess, weave together as the end of the Mayan calendar approaches in 2012. ER nurse Jana Sinclair's recurring dream compels her journey to jungle-shrouded Mayan ruins where she discovers links with ancient priestess Yalucha, who was mandated to hide her people's esoteric wisdom from the Spaniards. Jana's reluctant husband is swept into strange experiences and opposes Jana's quest. Risking everything, Jana follows her inner guidance and returns to Mexico to unravel her dream. In the Maya lands, dark shamanic forces attempt to deter her and threaten her life.

Ten centuries earlier, Yalucha's life unfolds as a healer at Tikal where she faces heartbreak when her beloved, from an enemy city, is captured. Later in another incarnation at Uxmal, she again encounters him but circumstances thwart their relationship. She journeys to Chichén Itzá to join other priests and priestesses in a ritual profoundly important to future times.

As the calendar counts down to December 21, 2012, Jana answers the call across centuries to re-enact the mystical ritual that will birth the new era, confronting shamanic powers and her husband's ultimatum—and activates forces for healing that reach into the past as well as the future.

Fans of historical fiction with adventure and romance will love this story of an ancient Maya Priestess and contemporary woman who unravel secret bonds to fulfill the Maya prophecy that can make the difference for the planet's future.

Praise from Reviewers and Readers:

"Travel through time and space to ancient Maya realms . . . details are accurate, giving insight into Maya magic and mysticism and bringing their message of the new era to come."

~ Aum-Rak Sapper, Maya Priestess and Daykeeper

"Few people have listened to this call and made pilgrimage to ancient Maya centers, but many will follow . . . to serve the planet in the Fifth Solar Cycle."

~ Hunbatz Men, Itza Maya Elder, Daykeeper and Shaman

". . . power-house historical novel . . . unlocks (Mayan) civilization . . . This well documented book is spellbinding, romantic, thought provoking and gives an insightful look into the spiritual side of ancient Mayas...a must read!"

~ J. Grimsrud, Maya travel guide